1516

D1040981

DATE DUE			
APR 06 2015			

Jacobs

Jacobs, Linda,

Summer Of Fire(#1) : Book One

Yellowstone Series (Yellowstone Park Fire)

F
Jacob

Dedication:

*This book is dedicated to the men and women
of emergency services everywhere.*

And always, to Richard.

Published 2005 by Medallion Press, Inc.
225 Seabreeze Ave.
Palm Beach, FL 33480

The MEDALLION PRESS LOGO
is a registered tradmark of Medallion Press, Inc.

Copyright © 2005 by Linda Jacobs
Cover Illustration by Adam Mock

Printed in the United States of America

Library of Congress Cataloging-in-Publication Data

Jacobs, Linda.
  Summer of fire / Linda Jacobs.
    p. cm.
  ISBN 1-932815-29-5
  1. Yellowstone National Park--Fiction. 2. Forest fire fighters--Fiction.
  3. Women fire fighters--Fiction. 4. Fire fighters--Fiction. 5. Forest fires--
  Fiction. 6. Montana--Fiction. I. Title.
  PS3610.A35645S86 2005
  813'.6--dc22
                                    2005008883

6.3.13
6.99
BN

Foreword:

My love affair with Yellowstone Park began in 1973, when I spent the first of three summers studying the field geology of Wyoming for my master's thesis. I have since returned to the park in every season, accessing the archives for the rich history of both the land, and man's brief tenure there.

While researching a historical novel set in Yellowstone, I was continually distracted by references to the fires of '88. Like much of the nation, I had tuned in, spellbound, to the nightly reports of America's first National Park in flames. Like many of Yellowstone's three million annual visitors, I held my breath, dreading the destruction being depicted, yet seduced by the beauty of wildfire.

Over lunch in the Houston Public Library, I examined Ross Simpson's The Fires of '88, published by American Geographic and Montana Magazine. After an hour's perusal of choppers ferrying water, tankers spraying retardant, and the faces of the men and women on the lines, I came to a conclusion.

There was a story here . . . one that over thirty-two thousand firefighters had shared. There was a vivid setting of beauty and peace, where a forest must go through the crucible of fire to achieve rebirth. To this place came my fictional characters.

A female firefighter troubled by the loss of a comrade-in-arms, a park biologist scarred by grief over his wife and baby daughter, and a Vietnam veteran helicopter pilot who seeks the adrenaline high . . . each find that in a world turned upside down, they cannot escape their greatest fears. Only through their private trials can they emerge reborn from their summer of fire.

With the help of a number of people and references, I have attempted to create as authentic a reconstruction as possible of Yellowstone's 1988 fires. Clare, Steve, and Deering do not exist, but the backdrop against which their story is told most definitely did. Some public figures such as the Secretary of the Interior, Park Superintendent, and the fire's Incident Commanders have been fictionalized; their characters are intended to bear no resemblance in word or deed to real persons. Any errors or omissions are my own.

My husband, Richard Jacobs, a founder of a Fort Bend County, Texas, volunteer fire department in 1975, served as consultant on structural firefighting, and assisted in preparing the fire maps. These are the authentic reports released daily by the Greater Yellowstone Unified Area Command of the Forest Service and National Park Service to the three thousand journalists who covered the fires' story.

My visit to the Texas A & M Brayton Firefighter Training Field was an eye-opener. Beneath the blazing July sun, fighting fire in full turnouts, I found the men and women to whom society owes a debt.

Dr. Catharine Raven, who is both biologist and wildfire fighter, gave valuable insights into many themes of the book. She fought the fires of '88, a life-altering experience that set her on the path to becoming a scientist. Eleven years later, she was still fighting the summer battles of the west. In addition to helping me get in touch with major characters, she also has ties to the Native American community, as the character of Clare does. The magic is that the book was largely complete when we met.

I thank Dr. Lee Whittlesley, of the Yellowstone archives,

for showing me around on my several visits there. In 1996, Ken Davis, who was manager of the town of West Yellowstone, revealed the fascinating story of a community under siege, and opened my eyes to the lives of the summer migrant workers of the West. Gayle Mansfield of the West Yellowstone News and Ronald Diener of the Jackson Hole Historical Society helped me through their stores of information. Workers at the Jackson Hole News were also courteous and helpful in letting me review back issues of the paper. The jumpers at West Yellowstone Smokejumper's Base gave me an extensive tour and told tales of leaping out of their Beech at one hundred ten miles per hour.

Several nonfiction books were of great use in my research, including Michael Thoele's Fire Line: Summer Battles of the West, and former Chief Ranger Dan Sholly's Guardians of the Land. In addition, I was fascinated by the photojournalist's eye view of the fires in Yellowstone's Red Summer by Alan and Sandy Carey, Yellowstone on Fire by the staff of the Billings Gazette, and Ross Simpson's previously mentioned work.

My primary consultant on helicopter warfare in Vietnam was Michael Harvey, an oil industry entrepreneur, who served two tours as a front line Huey pilot. In addition, Robert (Dick) Vaughan, noted author and another chopper veteran, provided insight as to aircraft terminology. Any errors are mine.

For commentary and editorial assistance on various drafts, I thank Charlotte Sheedy, Greg Tobin, Robert Vaughan, Elizabeth Engstrom, Sarah Lazin, Ann Close, John Byrne Cook, Caroline Lampman, and Deborah Bedford. Rita Gallagher helped me to understand the structure of a novel and Sam Havens how to present the story.

Lastly, there is the late Venkatesh Srinivas Kulkarni, consummate writer and teacher, beloved friend, and citizen of the world. I also acknowledge the steadfast support of my Rice University critique group, Marjorie Arsht, Kathryn Brown, Judith Finkel, Bob Hargrove, Elizabeth Hueben, Karen Meinardus, Joan Romans, Angela Shepherd, Jeff Theall, and Diana Wade.

LINDA JACOBS
SUMMER OF FIRE

Gold Imprint
Medallion Press, Inc.
Florida, USA

PROLOGUE

Black smoke billowed from the roof vents. At any second, the flames would burst through, adding their heat to the already shimmering summer sky. Wood shingle, Clare Chance thought in disgust, a four-story Houston firetrap. She drew a breath of thick humidity and prepared for that walk on the edge . . . where fire enticed with unearthly beauty, even as it destroyed.

Fellow firefighter Frank Wallace, over forty, but fighting trim, gripped her shoulder. "Back me up on the hose." Although he squinted against the midday glare, his mustachioed grin showed his irrepressible enthusiasm.

"Right behind you," Clare agreed. In full turnouts and an air pack, she ignored the sultry heat and the wail of sirens as more alarms were called. Helping Frank drag the hose between gawking by-standers and shocked apartment residents, she reflected that the toughest part of the job was watching lives inexorably changed.

A commotion broke out as a young Asian woman, reed thin in torn jeans, made a break from the two civilians holding her. She dashed toward the nearest building entry crying, "My baby!"

Frank dropped the hose, surged forward and grabbed the woman. "Javier," he grunted. "Take over."

Javier Fuentes, lanky, mid-twenties, took the handoff and restrained the woman from rushing into the burning building. Her dark eyes went wide as she screamed and struggled. Her short legs kicked at Javier's shins.

Adrenaline surging, Clare demanded. "What floor?"

"4-G . . ." the woman managed. "He's only two. "

"Let's go," Clare told Frank without bothering to ask why the child had been left alone. As she bent for the hose, her sense of purpose seemed to lighten the weight of her equipment.

They headed in.

The building's peeling doorframe had been defaced by purple graffiti and the interior stairwell smelled faintly of mold and urine. New and sparkling in the seventies when oil jobs had enticed northern immigrants to Houston, the housing had fallen into disrepair.

At the second floor landing, Clare and Frank met smoke. She tipped up her helmet, covered her face with the mask, and cranked the tank valve. Beside her, Frank wordlessly did the same.

As they moved up, Clare made sure the hose didn't snag around corners while Javier and others fed slack. Business as usual, so far, and they would find that young mother's child.

At the third floor and starting blindly toward four, Clare

felt the smoke grow hotter. She crouched below the deadly heat and told herself that she could breathe. Positive pressure prevented fumes from leaking into her mask, and the dehydrated air cooled as it decompressed.

In, out, slow . . .

Isolation pressed in with the superheated atmosphere. She couldn't shake the feeling that Frank had left her, belied by his tugging on the hose. At times like these, she had to keep her head on straight. No giving in to claustrophobia and no thought of turning back.

If you misguessed the dragon in the darkness, you would pay with your life.

Fourth floor hall, and Clare went onto hands and knees. Darkness and disorientation complete, she concentrated on keeping the hose in line and her breathing steady. The worst humiliation was if she sucked her tank dry and had to make an ignominious exit.

Ahead, Frank cracked the nozzle for a bare second. Heat slammed down as the spray upset the thermocline. He hit the valve again. A glimpse of not quite midnight winked from the shadows, now there and then gone. Clare ground her teeth and her chest tightened as they approached 4-G.

The door stood ajar. A good omen, she hoped, as she and Frank accepted its invitation and crawled inside.

Drapes and couches blazed, giving off toxic gases that made her glad for filtered air. The ceiling sheetrock was burned away, revealing the space beneath the roof where storage boxes blazed. Did they contain old clothes and junk, or precious family heirlooms from Southeast Asia, belonging to the young woman who waited below?

A thousand degrees from above drove Clare and Frank onto their stomachs. While hot water rained onto shag carpet, she inched along, one gloved hand feeling the way and the other on the hose. If you let go of your lifeline, you could lose orientation, the sure first step to a mayday situation.

Through the drop-spattered mask, there was no sign of life in the living room and nothing that looked like a crib or playpen. Clare looked toward a door that must lead to a bedroom, but flames licked at the frame and walls. No haven there. Sick with the possibility of failure, she dragged herself toward Frank. She had not yet told a mother that her child had died in a fire.

If hell existed, this must be its antechamber. Frank lay ahead of her, directing the hose. By the tugs, she felt him move forward, risking the dragon backing around and coming down with searing breath. Clare found herself staring at the constantly changing colors of combustion, unable to resist the inferno's splendor. Her love-hate relationship with fire hurt most at times like these.

An ominous rumble began, the vibration resonating in her chest as though the dragon cleared its throat. Cold horror cut the heat.

Through the steam cloud from the power cone, she caught a shifting in the rafters, a barely perceptible sideways slide. She couldn't grab Frank's collar to warn him, couldn't do a thing except scream his name into the maelstrom.

One moment, Clare was crawling toward him. The next, he disappeared in a shower of light.

CHAPTER ONE
Yellowstone National Park
July 25, 1988

Extreme Fire Danger.

Clare Chance gave a bitter smile at the warning sign on the Grant Village Laundromat. The lodgepole pines behind the building burned like merry hell. With the drought that had parched Yellowstone since May, moisture in the forest fuels had ebbed, making the park a two million acre tinderbox. The wind that came with the dry fronts completed the equation for disaster.

Clare hooked a hose to a hydrant and dragged the other end across the parking lot to water down the Laundromat roof. Beneath the heavy coat of the Houston Fire Department, sweat ran between her breasts and down her sides. At least it wasn't as hot as it had been in Houston on that ill-fated July afternoon, over three weeks ago.

Quick agony swelled her chest until she felt it would burst. The flaming forest became a wavering vermilion blur as she blinked hard and hoped Javier Fuentes and the other men of

HFD didn't notice her tears.

Coming to the West to fight wildfire had seemed a convenient escape after she'd witnessed Frank Wallace's death. If it could happen to him, it could happen to anybody. He was . . . had been . . . one of the good guys, an older veteran who'd acted blind to the fact that she wasn't one of the boys.

Since becoming a firefighter, Clare had learned she didn't qualify as a bona fide adrenaline junkie, but she'd tried to match anybody's bravado. People who hadn't seen her coach basketball or yell at her trainees at the Texas A & M fire school were surprised to learn what a thirty-seven-year-old woman did for a living.

Today, at Grant Village, she watched the younger men from Houston with a warning on the tip of her tongue. The wind shifted continuously, first a puff on the back of her neck and then relief for her heated forehead.

Watering down the buildings was a last ditch effort before they would have to fight the approaching flames face-to-face. Clare didn't know what she'd been thinking when she'd assumed wildfire was somehow tamer than structural fire. Less collateral damage, maybe. In the forest, the odds were against her having to face another distraught mother.

A single look at Clare's face when she emerged from the burning apartment house told Tammy Nguyen that her small son Pham was gone. Strangers, yet kindred in loss, the two women had gone into each other's arms and sobbed. Channel Two News had carried it at six and ten.

Clare had forced herself to face Frank's wife, Jane, too, beside the closed casket. Within the older woman's kindly embrace, she had thought her heart would break.

On this, another sizzling afternoon, her hand on the rough-textured hose felt familiar, yet somehow distant. She was still getting used to the pungent incense of burning evergreen, so different from the grassy aromas of the Texas coast.

The two-way Motorola radio at her belt gave a crackling sound. She passed off to Javier Fuentes, who'd been first to sign on with her to fight wildfire. "Chance here."

"We've got to get those civilians out of Grant Village." Garrett Anderson's deep Atlanta drawl came over the airwaves. She imagined him behind a desk in West Yellowstone, his ample stomach hanging over his belt while he chomped on Fig Newtons and drank mugs of creamed coffee. One of the seasonal bosses of big fire, he'd been the first black to make fire general at the training center in Marana, Arizona. He was also the man who'd arranged through Clare's boss at A & M for her and the men from Houston to be here.

She put her foot onto the running board of the fire truck and pulled off her hard hat. God, her sweat-soaked head itched. The side mirror revealed heat-reddened cheeks beneath bloodshot amber eyes. "I thought the evacuation was proceeding as planned, Garrett."

There's a bottleneck on the road out. Harry Gaines's crew set a backfire that got away."

"You mean that's not the Shoshone trying to burn down the Laundromat?" She considered the wildfire fighters' eccentric habit of tagging fires with a name. It was as though naming their adversary made the fight a more personal one.

"When you see the Shoshone, you'll know." Garrett

sounded grimly certain. "The backfire's jumped the road and nobody will drive into the smoke. I'm trying to raise a chopper to drop water, but I need you to get those cars moving before the Shoshone gets there."

Clare glanced back at the battle beside the Laundromat. "We'll go as soon as we can."

"Go *now*. The Shoshone has crowned."

When wildfire leaped into the treetops, Garrett had told her it released the energy of an atomic bomb. It sounded improbable, but when she cocked an ear, she heard a distant dull rumble like an approaching train. Her nostrils flared at a fresh and stronger mix of tart resin and char. Her heartbeat accelerated.

With a tap on Javier Fuentes's shoulder, she cupped her hands and shouted to the others from Houston, "We've gotta leave you. If it blows up, head to the lake and get in the water."

Javier leaped to the driver's seat of the fire truck. As she climbed in the passenger side, she said a silent prayer for the safety of the men they left behind. She hadn't gone an hour in the past weeks without asking what she could have done to prevent Frank's death. "These things happen, Clare," her friends at the station had drilled her.

They were right. Before she'd joined the ranks, she'd seen on the news that every few months some firefighter paid the ultimate price.

"You have to pick up and go on," they'd said.

She had, but in a different direction. Her flight to Yellowstone, and that's what she now knew it to be, had been a headlong rush toward peaceful woodland and natural beauty.

She'd believed she wouldn't have to face another monstrous specter of dancing heat and light.

Javier steered along the deserted inbound lane to Grant Village, past the stopped column of sedans, pickups with camper shells, and trailers. Despite the emergency, he drove slowly, bronzed hands light on the wheel.

The approaching fire had been started by a lightning strike at Shoshone Lake, six miles southwest. After smouldering and creeping along for a month, high winds had fanned it into fury.

They came to the head of the line, a stopped behemoth of an RV. Ahead, perhaps a hundred yards, tightly spaced pines burned on both sides of the road.

Clare clicked the Motorola's button. "Come in, Garrett." She slid out of the truck to scan the sky. The sun was reduced to an intermittent copper disk. "Come in."

On the RV driver's side, she hailed an elderly man with wild white hair and wire-framed glasses. "I'm Clare Chance with the firefighters," she told him in what she hoped was a reassuring tone. She'd always had a raspy low voice that people mistook for a man's on the telephone.

"What shall we do?" The ginger-haired woman passenger leaned across.

"A helicopter is going to dump water ahead," Clare told them. "As soon as the fire dies down I want you to drive as fast as you can."

The runaway backfire wasn't going to kill anyone, but the Shoshone's rumbling underpinned all other sound. If it arrived before they could escape . . .

She prayed the chopper came soon.

❦❦❦

Steve Haywood looked out the helicopter window into hell.

Great tongues of orange flame leaped through the crowns of lodgepole pines, then reached another two hundred feet into the white-hot sky.

"Swing over Grant Village," he ordered pilot Chris Deering through their headphones, wishing he were anywhere but in the air. Although this recon flight over Yellowstone's raging forest fires was important, Steve had already decided that for him it was a terrible idea. He wiped the sweat at his temples, right where the gray had started last year.

Steve watched Deering peer out at the boiling smoke through his Ray Ban Aviators, noting the sunburst of lines around the pilot's coffee-brown eyes. As he gauged the faint smile playing at the corners of the taut mouth, Steve realized that Deering was actually enjoying this.

He knew the type. All over the mountain west, wherever choppers were flown, there were guys in military-style flight suits with winged patches on their shoulders that proclaimed *Vietnam Helicopter Pilots Association.*

He'd come to Yellowstone for the peace it afforded, not to wind up in a war zone.

Deering fiddled with the radio and was unable to raise West Yellowstone Airport, as had been the case for about five minutes. He banked the Bell 206 into a steep turn and Steve looked straight down into leaping flames.

SUMMER OF FIRE

It wasn't the fire that had him on edge, but the flying. His decision to do recon had been one of those grand defiant gestures; he hadn't wanted to tell his boss Shad Dugan that he was unwilling to get back on the horse that had thrown him.

Turbulence seized the chopper. Steve's stomach clenched as they plunged earthward and then rebounded. Reaching for a handhold, he saw that his palm left a damp print on his green fire-retardant trousers. In the three years he'd been a park biologist he'd successfully stayed out of aircraft, preferring to visit the backcountry via the serenity of horseback. If only he were on a remote trail right now, breathing clean air instead of eating smoke from thousands of torching trees.

Deering took them lower into even rougher air.

Looking out through the bubble of glass, Steve tried to ignore vertigo and focus on the solid earth. Below, in Grant Village, at least twenty fire trucks lined the south shore of Yellowstone Lake. Near the boat ramp, pumpers equipped to fight wildfires suctioned water from the lake. With hoses connected to hydrants, firefighters sprayed the roofs of the visitor center and lodge.

Deering dipped the chopper left and Steve looked where he pointed. The road out of the village was a narrow corridor between two walls of flame. Down this slender needle, a dozen cars and several fire trucks were threaded. The knot inside Steve twisted tighter as he realized that they were stopped.

Black smoke billowed around the Bell's windshield and the visibility went to zero.

"Fuck shit!" Deering pushed right pedal.

"Easy," Steve blurted. The hard look Deering shot made

him wish he'd kept his mouth shut. The pilot obviously didn't think a ranger should be telling him how to fly his chopper. His pride of ownership had been clear at the airport. Steve had stood on the ramp with reluctance while he showed off the custom paint, ultramarine edged in gold.

Deering moved the collective between the seats and put the Bell into a climb. The veins on the back of his hand stood out where he gripped the cyclic stick in front of him.

Steve tried to look through the window, but merely saw his reflection against the roiling blackness. Silver-gray eyes rimmed with red gave testimony to the irritating smoke. His thinning blond hair revealed a sunburned forehead between the insulated headphones.

The sky lightened, and as the chopper broke back into clear air, Steve realized he'd been holding his breath.

He exhaled and found it didn't help him relax. He kept a wary eye on the way Deering's feet feathered the pedals while adjusting the pitch of the rotors. They made another pass over the stalled line of cars and trucks. This time Deering avoided the smoke.

"Okay, *Doctor* Haywood, look behind you." The pilot's patient tone said he regarded Steve as learning-impaired.

On the rear deck, coarse canvas made a crumpled pile, a bucket attached to a cable hooked beneath the chopper.

"I want you to climb in back," Deering continued, "open the door, and shove that out."

Steve bristled. He'd fought the summer fires of the West for three seasons during college and several times since coming to the park. "Wouldn't it be smarter if we landed to deploy the bucket?"

"Just do it!" Deering snapped.

Steve thought about the people trapped in their cars, choking on smoke. He'd felt that same heat on his own back as he bent to dig a fire line. Experience had taught him that each wildfire had its own personality, from how it devoured the forest to the play of colors in its flames. What they shared was that they could all turn deadly . . . as could the process of fighting them.

Steve hurried to remove his shoulder harness and squeeze between the seats. The collapsed bucket made an unwieldy orange heap on the metal deck, with the cable snaking through a notch in the doorframe.

"Be sure," Deering's distorted voice came to him through the headphones, "to pitch the bucket clear of the skids."

Steve slid open the door. After looking through tinted windows, brilliant light shocked him. The blast of wind and high-pitched whine of the helicopter was much louder. Turning to his task, he tugged at the bucket, but failed to budge it.

Five years ago, he could have tossed it out. Now, at thirty-eight, multiple surgeries had left him with knees he could no longer rely on. Ignoring a stab of pain, he bent and put his shoulder behind the work.

As the amorphous shape inched toward the bright day, he prepared to give the bucket an extra shove. Just then, the helicopter hit a pocket of rough air and dipped, nearly pitching him out. He clung to the doorframe, watching the bucket dangle perilously close to the left skid.

Deering flipped a switch and the cable paid out. The chopper banked and lost altitude until it hung so low over the lake that Steve had a clear view of white-capped waves. He wondered if he should return to his seat, but as long as he stayed back from the wind torrent, the fresh air cleared his head. Through the open door was West Thumb, a smaller arm of the cobalt expanse of Yellowstone Lake. Onshore, the hot springs of West Thumb Geyser Basin shone in a hundred colors.

"Let me know when the bucket's full," Deering directed.

Steve forced himself to approach the door. Downwash from the rotors beat the lake in a wide circle as the bucket touched the water. The canvas grew dark and slowly sank.

It seemed to take a long time to gather a hundred forty-four-gallons, while Steve held onto the chicken bar above the door. Deering manipulated the controls with barely perceptible adjustments that kept the craft in a hover. When the bucket was finally full, Steve said, "Ready."

"We're heavy on fuel," Deering replied. It had been less than twenty minutes since they'd taken off from West Yellowstone Airport. "Fighting this wind with a full load is going to be a bitch." He powered up to climb.

Blown sideways, the craft turned up on its side and the bucket's sunken weight skewed out from under it.

Steve fell away from the open door to land hard on the small of his back. Cleats designed to hold a rear seat in place bruised him and his headphones slid across the metal deck. He retrieved them in time to hear Deering breathe, "Sum bitch."

The Bell's engines whined in crescendo and, for a long moment, it seemed to hang motionless. Steve's toes curled inside his boots. Although it had been years since he'd seen the inside of a church, he found himself sending up a prayer.

When the bottom of the bucket pulled free, the chopper picked up speed and careened toward the burning shore. Flames leaped from the tops of the pines right down to the narrow rocky beach.

Too fast, Steve thought, crouching on the deck. At the same time, he realized that they hadn't gained enough elevation to clear the trees. They were unbalanced, skewing sideways.

"Release the bucket," Steve shouted into the roaring wind.

"Can't. Cable's hung on the skid, thanks to you." They headed fast for the inferno. Deering muttered a string of obscenities, the kind of language usually heard at the end of black box flight recordings.

Steve clambered to his feet and clamped his teeth hard. With a wary look at the blur of rotors, he figured it was at least a hundred feet to the water since the bucket wasn't quite dragging. He should have known better than to fly, to once more leave the solid earth and put his fate at the mercy of wind, machine, and human fallibility.

All the fight seemed to have gone out of Deering while Steve watched his silent battle to keep the chopper aloft. His gaunt face was set in resignation, as if he were already contemplating the loss of the craft he'd shown off so proudly at the airport.

By God, this time Steve would not go down with the ship.

With as good a running start as three steps could give him, he leaped out of the helicopter.

Spreading one hand to protect his crotch, he placed the other across his chest and assumed a cross-legged position. His stomach felt as though he left it ten feet above as he plummeted.

Hurtling toward the water, Steve remembered his life vest beneath the front seat. He'd followed the pilot's lead in not wearing the bulky, bright-orange device. Hot shot Deering must have thought a quick turn over the lake didn't count as flying over water.

Coming up fast was all the deep blue one needed to drown in on a perfectly beautiful day.

Steve hit feet first with a mighty impact and drove deep. The cold shocked him, once, and then again, as he plunged into a more frigid layer. Spreading his arms, he pulled down until he felt his rate of sinking begin to slow.

Finally, he poised motionless in the dark.

It could have been peaceful, realizing that he'd safely separated himself from the flying machine, but it took him back, painfully, to that potent instant when the screaming metal of the Triworld Air 737 had fallen silent.

Just before he turned toward his family.

As if they remembered, too, Steve's debilitated knees throbbed in the cold water.

He began to swim up. His heavy boots and clothes acted as sea anchors, trying to take him back to the depths. It was a good thing he'd once been a strong swimmer, but how would he fare now?

As he pulled toward the light, it began to brighten from cerulean to the shade of an October sky. He kicked the last few feet into slightly warmer water and his head and shoulders broke the surface. Chest heaving to suck in air, he found that panic's icy fingers gripped his lungs.

A loud whining surrounded him. He swiveled his head and found the chopper still in the air. For a paralyzing moment, he watched it skate straight for him. Through the windshield, a flash of light caught Deering's sunglasses.

With a desperate gasp, Steve dove back into the lake's cold embrace. The frigid water compressed his chest as he kicked and pulled through the first thermocline. The Bell's impact pushed him deeper. Water churned as the tail and main rotors of the helicopter thrashed up a wake. He kept stroking, expecting any second to be chopped to pieces.

Whispering tendrils of black began at the edge of Steve's consciousness.

"Mayday, Mayday." Deering spoke tersely into his headset. "I have ditched off West Thumb." Water rose over the windshield.

He'd done a helluva job leveling out and pulling off power, if he did say so himself. Despite the rough setdown, he'd hit the water without the transmission coming through the cabin and taking out the pilot's seat. Back in Vietnam, Deering had lost his friends Joe Silva and Skip Harlan to just that accident. One night they drank tequila shots together, knowing they would still be lit when it came time for the predawn climb into the cockpit.

The next evening Deering drank alone.

Despite the shaking up, he'd climbed into the next available Huey and taken the controls. Flying was his life, all he'd wanted to do from the time he was six and his father had taken him to the Pocatello airport to gaze wide-eyed at the planes.

"Will have to abandon." He stripped off his headphones and reached into the cold calf-deep water for the personal flotation device he cursed himself for not wearing.

The omens had all been bad this summer.

It had been years since Deering had seen a firestorm like the one sweeping toward the campground at Grant Village with those poor S.O.B.s trapped and waiting for it. He should be helping instead of sitting on his ass in a brace position while his helicopter filled with water.

Where in hell was Haywood?

Dr. Steve Haywood had rubbed Deering the wrong way from the moment they met on the tarmac at West Yellowstone. Blond and balding, a few inches shorter than Deering, Haywood had greeted him amiably enough, but Deering had divined with a pilot's sixth sense that his passenger hid a fear of flying. With a roiling animosity Deering had figured for a cover, Steve had hefted his sturdy body stiffly into the Bell, slammed the passenger door, and planted his booted feet on the deck.

The chopper capsized, rolling over onto the open rear door. The numbing rush climbed past Deering's waist.

During his offshore safety training, the clear warmth of a swimming pool had made it easy to do the drill. As the training cage submerged, you reached your right hand for an orientation point on the door handle and placed your left on the seat belt beside the buckle. Not easy to do while they flipped you upside down, so they made you do it until you got it right, or the instructor gave you a break.

Today he couldn't buy one.

Deering looked down at his left hand in the rising water, at the bandage where he'd had a skin cancer removed three weeks ago. He'd spent a little time thinking about mortality, and had somehow omitted telling his wife, Georgia, about the diagnosis.

Better he should have waited for today if he wanted to think about dying.

His aircraft rolled upside down and he tried to keep track of his life jacket.

Wait . . . wait . . .

All those years, Georgia had waited and worried, first during Nam when a shitload of guys got *Dear Johns*, then later when he'd flown timber charters and forest fires all over the West. Petite Georgia's coppery hair shone like the sun, even at night. Today she was probably at their home in Lava Hot Springs, Idaho tending her summer garden beside the Portneuf River.

Cold water covered Deering's mouth and nose.

Count it out. One cucumber, two cucumber.

At least to eight while the craft's inverted.

Deering pushed on the door handle. The force of water pressed back.

Hell, he hadn't done anything by the book today. Why not swim out through the rear door?

Halfway through the space between the front seats, he found out why not as his flight suit snagged on the collective.

He told himself he had plenty of air, that it had only been around twenty seconds since the water had flooded his face. The lake was clear, but he couldn't see anything through the rush of bubbles.

Pressure and darkness came down and desperation swelled. The chopper dropped steadily while he tried to ease the pain in his ears by clearing them. As the water grew colder, he kicked harder, smacking his head smartly on his way out through the rear door.

Free of the cabin, Deering fought toward the surface, still carrying the life jacket. He secured the strap around his wrist and pulled down hard on the toggles that inflated it. The extra lift nearly tore it away, but he managed to hold on as he accelerated through the brightening water.

His head broke the surface and he inhaled deeply, enjoying the draught better than the first sip of any beer he'd ever cracked. Before he could celebrate, he had more trouble. He struggled to lay the unwieldy vest open on the water and get his right hand through it. His arm, already growing heavy and numb, would not slide into the hole. Hugging the vest to his chest, he floated on his back.

Smoke billowed into the sky; an ironic parody of the towering cumulus that everyone prayed might bring rain.

Deering raised his head to see how far it was to the timbered shore. It looked like a long goddamn swim. The old adage about staying with the aircraft didn't apply when it was probably still drifting down through the almost three hundred feet of water his map had indicated was in West Thumb.

Georgia would be crazy. The Bell was a long way from

paid for and the insurance company was going to be all over his ass.

He stirred his arms and legs, treading water in a three-sixty looking for Steve Haywood. His spirits sank further as he remembered that his passenger's life vest rested beneath the left front seat of the Bell, on its way to the bottom.

CHAPTER TWO
July 25

What about the road up there?" the RV's driver asked in a querulous voice.

Behind him, Clare watched a reddish glow advance beneath a smoke veil. Although the backfire seemed powerful, it could not compare with a conflagration that had been a month in the making. The Shoshone's rumble became a roar, a hollow warning that presaged firestorm.

Clare's heart pounded. If they couldn't get these people out of here, the main body of the fire was going to sweep over them. She strained her ears, but there was no familiar whop of rotors bringing relief.

"Clare," Javier Fuentes said from behind her shoulder.

She turned. Instead of speaking, he jerked his head away from the RV. They trudged along together, her head barely coming up past his shoulder. Once out of earshot, she paused.

Javier's face looked white beneath his tan. "The chopper crashed," he blurted. "Down in the lake off West Thumb."

Clare pressed her lips together. In the five days she'd been at Yellowstone, she'd supervised several teams in stopping the advance of fire onto utility lines. Save the property was the rule, but not at the risk of safety.

Today was the first time she'd seen lives threatened.

She'd been counting on the effect of the water drop to beat back the heat beside the road. Without it, it was probably still possible to drive through, but only if none of the drivers panicked and stopped.

Javier waited for instruction with alert dark eyes. As his superior, she was to command the next action. A look at what was becoming a tunnel of flame gave no encouragement. The Shoshone rose to a banshee wail.

In the moment she continued to hesitate, Javier suggested, "How about we get these folks moving?"

"Okay." She forced an even tone. "Get the man in that RV driving, no matter what it takes."

"Yes, ma'am." Javier turned away.

Although it had been a break of mere seconds, a flick of his eyes said he'd noticed. Javier had been the one who reached her first, while she kicked at the fallen roof covering Frank and bent to put her gloved hands into the fire. Now, she had to admit that she'd been out of her head, trying a desperate rescue where none was possible. Javier had pulled her out of the building, refusing to let her sacrifice her life.

"Let's go!" Clare shouted. People who had their car windows up against the smoke began to lower them. "There's just a short stretch and then you'll be in the clear." She tried to keep her voice from going shrill.

Determination dawned on the faces of drivers who'd been looking helpless. The RV started. Clare went to the next vehicle, a white Caprice. Slapping the hood with the flat of her palm, she shouted, "Move it!"

It seemed to take forever for the line of traffic to pass. Each time someone slowed at the sight of leaping flames ahead, she rushed their vehicle and shouted through her raw throat for them to keep going. Gradually, the bottleneck cleared.

Clare waved at Javier. "We've got to check that crash site." As wildfire fighters, it wasn't in their job description, but city EMT training had her ready to move.

Javier drove as steadily as he had before. He was a good man, strong and solid. If she had to go into a closed warehouse where fire awaited the fuel of fresh air, she would want him with her.

Heat blasted through the open window along with the sharp snap of fire's voracious feeding. The bare skin of her arm felt as though she held it too close to a broiler. "Javier . . . "

He obliged by picking it up perhaps ten miles per hour.

Through pursed lips, he began to whistle "Singin' in the Rain." She'd heard him do that before, when they were in a smoky hotel corridor and visibility was nil. They'd crept forward, waiting for the dragon to reveal itself.

It had been that way for her and Frank in the fourth floor hall. A dark tunnel that lead to their quarry, born of fuel, oxygen, and heat. What unbelievable fortune, the flying fickle finger of fate, or just plain damned being in the wrong or right place--Frank had ended up in the morgue while the blistering heat drove her back from the light.

SUMMER OF FIRE

About a quarter mile out on the Grant Village road, the monster bared its teeth. Seeing trees on both sides fully involved, Clare rolled up the window. Her instructor boss Buddy Simpson at A & M had warned her about wildfire. "Every one is different," the Texas good old boy had hammered. "If the fuel is dry enough you'll get a fire, but after that it's anybody's guess."

Clare imagined times past, when Native Americans or settlers from the East had faced a fire such as the Shoshone. They'd had no truck to escape in, nor any pumpers or hoses to save their houses. Men and women had passed buckets until the verdict was a changed land and a new village to be built.

Now the Shoshone caught up with the backfire. The roiling glow had an eerie life, crimson, then flaring orange and wavering purple. As much as the sight exhilarated her, Clare also hated to see the forest burn. How many years must pass before it would be restored?

The heat grew more intense. Javier gunned the engine, his hands now white-knuckled. He, like Clare, wore Nomex fire retardant clothing, tested at DuPont to withstand the heat of a blowtorch. She hoped they didn't get a chance to find out.

Just ahead, a tree uprooted and cartwheeled across the road. Javier hit the brakes. The truck slewed sideways.

Clare nearly shrieked, but caught herself in time to keep from scaring the bejesus out of the driver. She ducked and braced against the dash. As Javier fought for control, two wheels dropped off the pavement. Gravel thrown up by the tires hailed against the undercarriage.

Her stomach clenched, for if they ended up on foot there

25

was no telling what would happen.

After driving half in the ditch for thirty yards, Javier managed to pull back onto the highway. Clare felt as though the truck's heater ran full blast as they sped through the screaming gale.

When they broke out, it happened suddenly. One moment they were driving through burning forest and the next, they were in the clear on the main highway. The wide thoroughfare with broad shoulders formed an efficient firebreak.

Clare rolled the window down and savored the breeze on her hot cheeks.

They left the flames behind and took the turnoff for West Thumb Geyser Basin, a mile from Grant Village. Javier parked and she ran down the boardwalk that bridged the thin crust. On either side were algae-coated spring deposits in hues of mustard, lime, and rust. Steam rose from clear turquoise pools and was whisked away. A hundred yards downslope, the boardwalk curved and ran along Yellowstone Lake.

"I don't see anything." Javier caught up with her in a loping stride. The wind that had fed the fires since June blew his dark hair and whipped the lake into whitecaps.

Clare fiddled with the Motorola and tried again to call West Yellowstone.

"Go back to the pay phone by the restrooms and see if you can talk to Garrett," she told Javier. "Let me know if they've rescued anyone."

Left alone, she looked up and down the beach. West Thumb seemed an oasis next to the Shoshone raging to the south. The pale smooth rock of the Fishing Cone broke the water's surface a few feet offshore, while the shadows of trout hung nearby. Swirling eddies indicated more springs flowing into the lake.

Despite, or perhaps because of, the fire's sideshow, a number of tourists strolled the geyser basin. A man with a video camera gestured for his slender blond companion to stand farther left so the plume of smoke would be in the background.

Clare headed for them. "Did you see a helicopter go down in the lake?"

The woman gasped and shook her head. The man pointed toward the fire. "Heard an engine over that way a while ago."

Another scan of the lake turned up no sign of a floating wreck.

Clare watched the Shoshone leap through the treetops and wondered if tourists should be this close. At the flame front, pines exploded as their moisture flashed to steam. She'd always been mesmerized by fire, but until her husband, Jay, had left her, she'd never considered the challenge of fighting it for a living. Jay and her daughter, Devon, didn't understand why she'd rushed to finish the academy nine months shy of the thirty-fifth birthday cutoff.

When she looked back, it became clear. Needing a life to replace the one that had been focused on family, she had discovered the brotherhood of fire.

Thousands had attended Frank's memorial in Houston's Rice University Stadium. Members of the Houston Fire and Police Departments had taken off work, along with representatives of departments all over Texas. The procession had stretched for miles while traffic cops struggled to deal with parking. Family and friends were overwhelmed by the presence of the city mayor and other dignitaries, as well as the ceremony of pipers and buglers. Frank's coffin had been flag-draped, for he was a Navy veteran.

Clare had nearly stayed home. She'd wondered how many might whisper that she could have done more to save Frank. Who of them thought that if Frank had taken Javier, or any other man into that apartment house, he'd have walked out with little Pham Nguyen cradled in his arms.

They'd called Frank a hero, and her as well, but she had not been able to trust embraces and smiles. The department psychologist had warned about survivor's guilt and post-traumatic stress, but putting labels on feelings you couldn't control didn't solve anything.

The only thing she figured might help was carrying on. Right now, that meant helping the people on board the chopper lost in Yellowstone Lake.

❀❀❀

Deering floated with one arm tangled in his life vest, his teeth chattering. He wondered how much longer he could hold on.

He'd covered a fraction of the distance to shore. It looked like maybe a hundred yards to the line of trees, but it might as well be miles. He watched the Shoshone leap to the sky and eat its way toward where he would come ashore . . . if he made it.

Numbness stole over him and his shaking stopped as

though the water had become warmer. He imagined he was home, lying beside Georgia in their bedroom with sun on the corner. He could take a little nap.

Deering closed his eyes. Cold water slapped at his face and into his ears, but the sensation seemed far away.

Through a growing lethargy, he heard a faint familiar rhythm. It reminded him of early morning in Nam when the first chopper in the air made a solitary song.

Opening his heavy lids, he identified the boxy silhouette of a Chinook, with rotors fore and aft. The big machine could carry thirty firefighters and their field gear or airlift a thousand gallons of water in a sling. Deering waved, shocked at how heavy his arm felt. He wished he had a purple smoke to signal with.

Without showing any sign of seeing him, the pilot guided the Chinook north past the whitened ground of West Thumb Geyser Basin.

Deering studied shore and struck out with rubbery arms and legs, failing to make headway in the wind-driven chop. It wasn't fair that it should end like this, that he should fail with land in sight, all Georgia's fears realized.

Behind him, the sound of rotors once more grew louder. His heart surged and adrenaline came to his rescue.

The Chinook came in low and hovered about a hundred feet off the water. The chopper door slid open and someone reached to a cable on a pulley.

The horse-collar landed three feet from Deering. In the chop, it looked like thirty. He reached to stroke and his hand splashed into the lake. The man above shouted, but the whipping wind and whine of rotors turned it to gibberish.

The Chinook moved forward, sweeping the horse-collar through the water. Deering saw it coming and let go of the vest he'd only partially donned. For a panicky moment, he was afraid he'd made a mistake, but the collar came into his hands. Although he was tempted to drape himself over it, he risked falling out when they lifted him. Another minute ticked past in the frigid water while he struggled to get the sling around his back and under his arms.

Aloft, the winch started and Deering lifted clear, dangling like a doll. He rode the twisting cable up through bright sun that failed to warm. Stiff wind whipped his flight suit, snapping the sopping cloth.

All the way up, he felt the remembered disgrace, the deep sense of leftover shame from his war years. A pilot who lost his ship was lower than whale shit, and he'd been there before--with a shot-up rotor, surrounded by VC, praying for rescue, yet reluctant to face the fellow soldiers put at risk to save him.

When most of the cable had rolled up, Deering's rescuer reached for him. The big man was alone in the rear compartment. "We were heading back from dropping groundpounders out east and heard your Mayday."

Deering was dragged through the doorway. The horse collar stripped over his head. When he fell forward to land with his cheek on the deck, he appreciated the heat of the metal.

SUMMER OF FIRE

Clare watched the Chinook bank away from West Thumb. Thank God, someone had been rescued, perhaps the pilot judging by what looked like a flight suit. Had there been more than one person aboard?

The wind gusted, she guessed at over forty miles per hour. Her pants and shirtsleeves popped like sails and she wished she hadn't left her turnout coat in the truck.

She cast another look at the crown fire eating its voracious way up the lake shore and noticed something out of place in the world of gray pumice, pink rhyolite and pine. A hundred yards down the beach something lay half in the water. With a squint, she recognized the beacon of a yellow Nomex fire shirt.

As she leaped from the end of the boardwalk, she slipped on a white crust of pea-sized rocks. For an instant, she teetered on the rim of a hot pool, remembering stories of people and animals parboiled in Yellowstone. When she regained her balance and ran down the beach, it was tough going. Trees that had been battered down by winter storm waves tripped her.

The smell of fire grew stronger as she struggled. Hung up in ragged limbs, she twisted to the side, trying to ease herself out without tearing her trousers. A look ahead showed the potentially drowned person, lying between the approaching flames and the lake.

To hell with it.

She ripped her pants and splashed the rest of the way through shallow water.

A broad-shouldered man in fire-retardant olive trousers

and the yellow shirt lay on the rocks, his clothing and dark blond hair streaming. He might be thirty or fifty years old, face down with one arm flung over his head.

The wind shifted to blow onshore as the convection cell sucked oxygen to feed the flames.

Clare crouched and called, "Are you all right?" She felt the déjà vu of the opening steps of CPR. The last time was in Houston on a heart attack victim and the man had died anyway.

She pushed away the vision of performing ventilations in waist deep water, for without a solid surface she would not be able to do effective chest compressions.

"Can you hear me?"

She checked for a pulse in the carotid artery at the side of his neck. Feeling a flutter beneath her fingers, she exhaled a sigh.

Not a hundred yards away, the Shoshone reared like a cobra.

Clare rolled the victim over and discovered a Park Service badge and nameplate. "Damn you, Steve Haywood," she raged. "Talk to me!" That one wasn't in the rescue manual.

He stirred and opened his eyes, silver gray like the sheen of light on a lake before a storm. The look on his face was one of confusion.

Flames spotted not thirty yards away. A two-foot thick pine blasted apart with a crack like a howitzer. "I hate to tell you this." Clare forced a note of cheer. "You're about to go swimming again."

Steve was fresh out of adrenaline, but he knew he had to move. He felt the woman's hand beneath his shoulder and, with her help, he managed to get to his knees. Although his legs threatened to collapse, he crawled back into the freezing lake.

She stayed with him, shedding her rubber boots. Dazed, he looked at her turnout pants and Houston Fire Department shirt. "What are you doing here?"

"I hope to God I'm saving your ass."

He hoped so, too. Not because he looked forward to spending more time on this planet, but because he needed to survive in case Deering managed to dodge the bullet. If Steve had his way, he'd see to it that Deering never flew again. The Triworld Airlines pilot had paid the ultimate price, but late at night Steve still woke up sweating, wanting to kill Captain Todd Neville with his bare hands. After four years, the shock of Susan's screams and Christa's pitiful wail as the jet plunged was still as vivid as the night it happened.

"Deering?" Steve asked the woman helping him into the lake.

"The pilot?"

He nodded.

"I saw someone picked up by chopper."

Steve's anger warmed him as he waded after her, twenty-five, then fifty feet from shore.

The Shoshone burned hotly, crackling and roaring toward West Thumb's boardwalks. He looked back at it . . . once.

This summer's fires were like nothing he'd even seen, not

in the early seventies when he'd dug line a few feet from the creeping edge of flame or during his past three years in Yellowstone. The park's recent wildfires had barely blackened the bark.

The inferno came closer, right down to the water. Steve felt the heat on the back of his head, almost blistering despite his wet hair, and knew he would be burned even at this distance.

"Survival floating," the woman directed. Her short blond hair was wet, too, revealing dark roots. "You know it?"

He answered by pushing off into a dead man's float, then curled until only his back broke the surface. They would conserve their energy until they needed to take a breath, then draw their arms and legs together just enough to raise their faces for air. People could supposedly do this for hours, but that assumed the water was a lot warmer.

It had been freezing that night in Alaska, too, when the 737 plowed into a snowbank and slid a thousand feet to crash into a cliff. Steve had thought he was dead until the cold rushing through the broken fuselage and the pain in his shattered knees had brought him around. Frantically, he had looked for Susan and Christa.

The scientist in him knew the facts, but looking back on that night Steve always thought the cold had come from the frozen hollow heart of a man who had lost everything.

The firefighter's fingers encircled Steve's wrist and held on.

CHAPTER THREE
July 25

Clare's strained face, streaked with soot, stared back from a mirror at the Lake Hospital. More of a clinic, the small complex beside the Lake Hotel was the best care available in the center of Yellowstone. They'd given her a room to take a hot shower and some green scrubs to put on in place of her sodden Nomex. Down the hall, the helicopter pilot and the ranger she'd rescued were being treated.

Deep shadows marked the skin beneath her eyes. For years, she'd prided herself on being able to sleep through the station alarm when she wasn't up on the roster, but since Frank had died, sleep was a nightmare landscape.

Clare brushed sweaty bangs from her forehead, and checked for the gray she blamed on Jay's leaving her. Although she frosted her coal dark hair to mask the evidence, the blonde in the mirror sometimes still surprised her. Stripping off her filthy fire clothes, she unhooked the damp bra that stuck to her and wanted to throw it as far as she could. With a silent entreaty, she turned the faucets.

Steam rose. There was nothing like the sluice of hot water when you'd been shaking with cold. She and Steve Haywood had been in the lake for long minutes, until the Shoshone's fury passed. Then they'd worked their way along the shore to West Thumb, where Javier had carried the ranger to the truck.

Beneath the spray, Clare lathered luxuriously and lingered to soak in the heat with bent head.

When she climbed out of the shower, the pale green of fluorescent lights washed out her naturally healthy color. For reassurance, she assessed her body. Not that there was or might be any man to appreciate the results of weightlifting during slow times at the fire station. Her upper arms and smallish breasts were firm. Dark aureoles reminded her that her great-grandfather had been a quarter Nez Perce.

She'd asked her mother about her family and been told her great-grandparents William Cordon Sutton and his wife Laura had ranched in Wyoming through the nineteen twenties, along with their sons Cordon, Jr., and Bryce. "Why did my Granddad come to Texas?" Clare had been around ten, stirring a soggy bowl of Cheerios and hoping she didn't have to finish breakfast.

Her mother shrugged. "Your Grandfather Cordon was a man of few words. He once said his mother Laura was the writer in the family, but I've never seen any of the journals she was supposed to have kept."

Young and inspired, Clare had started a journal of her own that very afternoon, proudly opening a blank, lined notebook and inscribing her name in purple ink on the flyleaf. That was as far as her efforts had gone.

Over the years, she'd often wondered about her great-grandmother's life on the frontier. Now that she was in the West, she hoped to dig up some family roots.

Dressed and in the hospital hall, Clare looked for a telephone. Although her wallet was damp, she extracted her long distance calling card and dialed Houston.

Devon should be home from her job guarding at the Springwood Community Pool. Taller than Clare, she'd turned out big and muscled like her father. Her blue eyes still resembled the ones Clare had smiled into during diaper changes, but in recent years, those eyes had turned defiant. One semester her grades were As and Bs, the next incompletes, with screaming matches and door slamming. Clare wondered how she'd managed to make it through until Devon had achieved a spring graduation from Houston's Stratford High.

If Jay hadn't left, things would be different. It had been damned sure her pittance from teaching P.E. and coaching girls' basketball wasn't going to cover the house payment, even with child support. The Houston Fire Department didn't pay much more, but it was the most rewarding job she'd ever had. Each wreck she ran, every fire put out, made a difference in someone's life. So far, she'd pulled in enough to keep her and Devon in their pleasant house on the west side of Houston, but that was going to change.

In October, when Devon turned eighteen, the monthly money from Jay was going to cut off like a pinched hose. Clare had not had the heart to tell her daughter she'd already talked to a Realtor.

The answering machine came on and Clare imagined her voice echoing in the empty house. She pictured the place in the fall, vacant, with silverfish in the sinks and a lockbox on the door. Even worse, with a new family's indentions in the Karastan Clare and Jay had selected together.

❦❦❦

Two hours after being brought to Lake Hospital, Chris Deering took a bite of mushy meatloaf and wished for the veal cordon bleu being served in the Lake Hotel, not two hundred feet from his bed. He swallowed and thought that with the Park Service paying him a thousand an hour he rated better chow.

Of course, the lion's share of the money was for his pride and joy--the 206B Jetranger he'd bought new in 1981. Dark blue with gold stripes and her name, *Georgia*, painted on the fuselage. Of course, she wasn't a thing like the real Georgia, who hated flying, so he secretly thought of her as *Georgie*. When he climbed into her cockpit and strapped on the pilot's seat, everything was in its proper place. He'd always believed, like so many instinctive pilots, that it was he who truly flew, the machine an extension of him.

Now it had gone to hell.

He forced his fingers to release their clench on the hospital's dull knife, and with an effort, decided not to play Monday morning quarterback. When a pilot flew that route, he wound up losing his nerve.

As soon as a warm bath had brought his body temperature

to normal, Deering had called his insurance company. First Annoyance, as he called them, had said that someone would get back to him.

His fork clattered to the plate. He hadn't given them this number so they would call his home. Shifting to find a more comfortable position for his tall frame, he set aside his dinner tray and pulled the phone to him.

He winced when the receiver contacted the cheek he had bruised landing on the Chinook's deck. At home, Georgia would brighten at the sound of the phone and hope it was he, never dreaming he'd ditched and drowned his helicopter. When she answered, he wasn't ready.

"Georgia?"

"Who else?" He saw her slightly gap-toothed smile as if she were standing beside his bed.

When he didn't speak for a long moment, she said, "Where are you?" He envisioned the frown that spread across her freckled face, draining the joy from her eyes. His hand slicked with sweat on the receiver.

"In the hospital at Yellowstone. I'm okay."

"Okay? What are you doing in the hospital?" Her voice went shrill, and Deering thought that she—five-feet-two inches of solid intuition with knowing green eyes—could always read him.

He drew a ragged breath and felt the cold that had taken hours to shake creep back. "I had to ditch the Bell." He drew the blankets he'd shoved down back toward him.

"When will it be enough?"

"It's never enough!" All the years they'd been together and

she still didn't get that flying was his life.

"Do you know anything about sitting here alone, knowing you could get killed any time?'

The fight drained out of Deering, and he listened to the static whine of the connection.

Finally, Georgia spoke, small and teary. "Are you hurt bad?"

By instinct Deering reached for the Marlboros he always kept in his breast pocket and encountered the folds of his hospital gown. Damned thing let the breeze up his ass. "I told you I'm okay," he grated. "I ditched in the fucking freezing lake and they warmed me up."

"Lake?"

"The chopper's in West Thumb. Map says it's three hundred feet deep."

"I'm glad." Her voice turned venomous. "I hope they never bring it up."

Before he knew he was thinking about it, Deering stabbed his finger and disconnected the call. The dial tone hummed harshly while a hot sting flushed his arms and burned his fingertips. Whenever Georgia pushed that particular button, the one that said she would never understand his flying, it shot him up with quick rage. Today, with their livelihood on the bottom of Yellowstone Lake, it damn near blinded him.

"Excuse me." The voice was low and husky, but the small person in hospital greens was clearly female. "I thought this was Steve Haywood's room."

Deering had asked and found out Steve was recuperating in a room down the hall. At least he wouldn't sue for big medical expenses.

"Not here." Deering still seethed at his wife as the diminutive woman paused on the threshold. A closer inspection revealed a heart-shaped face accentuated by streaked blond hair. Big eyes of a rich bronze hue seemed suffused with sadness.

"If you like," a slow smile spread over his face, "you can check under the bed."

She grinned. It lighted her eyes, and Deering wondered if he had imagined her sorrow.

He considered the storm that roiled in Georgia's eyes this minute. His wife had been trying to get him to stop flying for years, imagining somehow that renovating the Victorian house she'd inherited into a bed-and-breakfast could give him the kind of rush he was addicted to.

"I'm sorry to disturb you." The woman in his doorway turned to leave.

All at once, Deering couldn't stand that Haywood had all the luck this afternoon. "Chris Deering," he offered. "Everybody calls me just plain Deering. My chopper went down in the lake."

"Clare Chance." Her arms crossed over small but well formed breasts that the hospital uniform did not conceal. "With the Houston Fire Department."

"Say what?"

"The hospital gave me dry clothes. I was out at West Thumb looking for survivors and found Mr. Haywood on the shore."

"Doctor."

"Beg pardon?"

"It's *Doctor* Steve Haywood, park biologist," he finished, trying to sound neutral.

❦❦❦

Steve Haywood shivered beneath the Lake Hospital's blankets and wished he weren't alone. It had been a long time since he'd desired the company of another person.

That made it tough to admit he wished his rescuer hadn't disappeared when the ambulance unloaded him. He had caught her name when she'd given it to the driver—Clare Chance. With her fingers coiled around his wrist, she'd almost kept him from minding the cold water.

He could still see the concern on her face as she'd helped him out of the lake. She didn't look a thing like his Susan, but in his mind, some essential nerve bound the two women.

Steve sipped lukewarm hot chocolate that needed a shot of brandy. That sickening plunge before he'd hit the water . . . he'd been falling, falling like the other time. The last moments of Triworld Air's Flight 2072 had been the longest of his life, the screaming speed and wild gyrations in contrast with freeze-frame shots of his life.

Strange how nearly dying again this afternoon made him remember the things that were most important, like the day he met Susan.

He had been in his usual hurry that April morning in 1976, eager to check on the bacteria cultures he'd left at eleven-thirty the night before in his graduate laboratory. As was his habit, he pulled open the side door of Duke University

Cathedral to take the short cut through the nave. He had crossed halfway, walking briskly in front of the ornate altar rail when a theme of what sounded like pure joy burst from the organ's tall pipes.

He stopped.

Music poured over and around him, reverberating richly in the stone arches, enhancing the stained glass jewels of morning light. He'd heard the organ before, students practicing their scales and the staircase progressions of simple Bach. He'd paused to listen to the notes of Sunday's hymn, the majesty of "Oh, God Our Help in Ages Past."

Of all the music he'd heard swell to the rafters, Steve had never experienced anything like this score that began in climax yet climbed higher, striving toward the pinnacle a soul could reach.

Opening the gate that led onto the altar, he passed the lectern with no doubt that a visiting concert organist was reviewing his program. He planned to ask for the date and time of the performance as well as whether his works had been recorded. He hoped so, for this music could enliven his lonely rented room late at night while he pored over the results of genetic experiments on *Drosophila,* the common fruit fly.

Steve poked his head over the rail and looked into the organ box. Although the spilling progression of notes was stemmed, the nave reverberated with those already on the air.

"You startled me." Sleek hair of gold spilled over delicate shoulders.

"I'm sorry, but could you tell me who composed that music?"

"Susan Sandlin."

Steve nodded sagely. He had never heard of a composer by that name.

The organist smiled, her clear blue eyes on his. She put out a hand and he felt strength in her slender fingers. "I'm Susan. I wrote it."

In his room at the Lake Hospital, Steve slammed his fist into his open palm and swore at whatever excuse for a deity ran this shithouse of a world. Christ, he needed a drink.

He swung his legs over the side of the bed. His right knee, the one he sometimes favored by limping or even bringing out his cane, protested his weight. Every time it pained him, he set his teeth against the associated overwhelming sense of loss.

He'd call Moru Mzima, the naturalist he'd been working with for the past year, and ask to be picked up in the sunroom at the Lake Hotel. The historic nineteenth-century inn, three stories clad in yellow clapboards, stretched for a hundred yards on a bluff overlooking Yellowstone Lake. The sunroom was one of Steve's favorite places if he had to be inside rather than beneath the soaring dome of sky. One could look upon smooth cobalt water that could turn raging gray in minutes. On the far side of the lake, the Absaroka Mountains lifted their green heads.

Steve had often sat in the sunroom and thought about the days when the Grand Loop Road ran between the hotel and the lake, the Yellowstone and Monida Company bringing guests in stagecoaches. Although science was his livelihood, since coming to the park he'd immersed himself in stories of the fellow human travelers who'd passed this way.

A connection with those long dead brought hope that Susan and Christa were not so far away.

Today, his focus on the sunroom was not about history, but the fact that cocktails were served in the lovely glass-walled lounge, beginning at noon.

🔥🔥🔥

In the hallway outside Deering's room, Clare spotted a coffee machine and went for the dual jolt of caffeine and sugar. Sidetracked from her mission to check on Steve Haywood, she slumped into a plastic waiting room chair and cupped her hands around the warm cup.

The pilot . . . Deering was cocky. Especially for a guy who'd just crashed and, well . . . he hadn't burned. Not in a lake kept cold year round by eight thousand feet of elevation.

Something about him reminded her of her ex. Jay was a hard driving, in-your-face kind of guy. It was what had originally attracted her and, ultimately, had been their downfall.

She'd known something was wrong with her marriage, but hadn't wanted to face it.

First, the family suppers she and Jay had prepared together and called culinary delights gave way to his business dinners. A moderately successful homebuilder, Jay had told her, "You have to schmooze the clients."

There was never a satisfactory explanation for why she could not join him. It was always "You'd be bored," or "Devon needs somebody home." After a while, she stopped asking and devoted herself to her job, with its evening basketball practices and games.

Then the scent of perfume, that Jay supposedly hated, came wafting from his size eighteen collar or maybe from his newly styled pale brown hair. "Oh, that damned Karen Eisner at the office," he'd bitch. "She must bathe in the damned stuff." Clare went along because Jay was so emphatic in his distaste when she wore fragrance.

The phone calls with nobody there were amusing at first. "If a woman answers," Clare had teased. Soon nobody was laughing.

Finally, there had been the woman friend who was no longer a friend. Over chicken salad and white wine on the patio of a French-style café, at a table overhung by fuchsia bougainvillea, "I just think you ought to know, Clare, that everybody's laughing at you." The news came with a name, Elyssa Hendron, unmarried twenty-something with doe eyes and a developer daddy with a fortune.

Clare had asked herself the question Dear Abby, or was it Ann Landers, always posed. Would she be better off with Jay or without him? After studying how just-turned-thirteen Devon adored her father, Clare determined to stick it out.

Looking the other way and stomaching the nausea lasted a bare month.

Jay had breezed in at one-thirty a.m., smelling of Obsession and musk. That he lacked the garden variety respect to shower before coming home turned a key in the box she'd locked her feelings in.

"You want to go to her, then go!" Clare shouted.

Without hesitation, Jay roared, "If that's what you want,

you've got it."

They stared at each other. Her pulse leaped at her temples while a vein in his forehead throbbed. She waited for his expression to soften, for him to take it back.

His footsteps sounded loud on the hardwood floors as he went back and forth to the garage. Devon crept down the stairs, her cotton nightdress flowing like Cinderella's gown, golden hair the color Clare had seen in Jay's childhood pictures, spread wild over her shoulders.

When Jay came out of the bedroom with a load of shirts on hangers, Devon clasped his arm with both hands. "No, Daddy!"

Jay shoved his daughter away. "Someday you'll understand."

All Clare understood after nearly five years was that she was alone, trying to raise her daughter as best she could, while Jay built his second wife a million dollar house. The contacts he'd made through Elyssa's developer father had made him wealthy. Since it happened after the divorce, the judge had not seen fit to raise the child support.

Clare pushed to her feet in the waiting room and dumped her coffee in the trash. Once more, she searched for Steve Haywood, finding the room with the correct number vacant. Upon learning that he'd checked out without permission, she felt a stab of concern. She tried to comfort herself with how many times she'd transported someone and never learned his or her fate.

That was the norm. You used the Jaws of Life to open a car roof like a can of tuna, stabilized and packaged a young woman. On the jerky ride through Houston streets, you started an IV, noting the wide gold wedding band on her left hand. When she had trouble breathing, you started bag ventilating. At the ER, you stood by until the gurney smacked open the swinging doors and they took her into a treatment room. You stood hugging yourself and sent a little prayer down that hallway. And one for the husband whose phone would ring as soon as her wallet was searched for ID.

Then you walked away.

Today, Clare couldn't shake the memory of Steve Haywood's troubled gray eyes.

CHAPTER FOUR
July 26

Garrett Anderson towered over Clare as the heavyset fire general's hand engulfed hers. She'd arrived a few minutes early for their meeting in West Yellowstone and seen him on the lawn as she parked her rental car on the street.

"Hear you had a bit of excitement yesterday," he offered.

"You might say that." She forced a smile, along with the signature casual tone of the fire fraternity.

"Are our mountain lakes a bit more refreshing than your blood warm Gulf of Mexico?" The tinge of Atlanta in his voice was even more pronounced in person than on the Motorola.

Her smile turned genuine. "You're no more used to forty-five degree water than I am."

"Don't bet on it," he chuckled. "I've been in Boise seven years."

Clare was still getting acquainted with Garrett, having seen him only twice before. Buddy Simpson at A & M had warned her that beneath the deceptively soft-looking physique and laid-back manner was a man of steel.

Together, they approached the headquarters of the newly created Greater Yellowstone Unified Area Command, set up in what had once been the Union Pacific Railroad's dining hall. At the end of the rail line to the park, late nineteenth-century tourists had been served on Limoges china while waiting to catch stagecoaches into Yellowstone.

Thirty-foot rock chimneys flanked both ends of the hundred-foot long construction of stone and weathered wood. Great walls of windows lined the sides. Behind, ravens strutted in an area that appeared to have been the railroad right-of-way, now devoid of tracks.

Garrett got to business. "Welcome to another level of fire management bureaucracy. You know I'm Forest Service, out of the Boise Interagency Fire Center. Our partner agencies include National Parks, Office of Aircraft Services, Bureau of Indian Affairs, Fish and Wildlife, and the National Weather Service." Buddy had told Clare that Garrett was one of less than twenty Incident Commanders in the country, calling the plays in a military style organization.

"So where does this Unified Area Command fit in?" She paused on the stairs flanked by elegant rock walls leading up to incongruous modern wire mesh doors.

"Starting today, the National Park Service and Forest Service are to coordinate over the park and surrounding areas. They've put me in charge." Garrett rolled his expressive eyes. "But I expect I'll be acting more as referee with those two groups."

Clare had not realized how influential Buddy's friend in wildfire was.

50

Garrett reached for the door and held it open for her. "I'll show you the latest fire extents map."

Something dark in his tone made her say, "I have a feeling I'm not going to like it."

In the doorway, they stepped aside to make way for two young men carrying a metal desk.

Inside, an empty vaulted room with pine beams ran the width of the building. Their footsteps echoed on the scuffed pine floor that bore the dusty prints of the movers. Garrett led the way through a pair of metal swinging doors that looked out of place in the otherwise rustic room.

A dramatic staircase led down into a larger space that had once been the main dining room for travelers at Yellowstone's western gateway. Looking at the soaring space, however, gave Clare the impression of a symphony played by a tone-deaf orchestra. The fireplace had been boarded up, cheap fluorescent fixtures hung from the ceiling, and squares of speckled tan linoleum covered the floor.

More movers shuffled in with furniture. A woman from the phone company clasped cables together with ties.

Garrett rubbed his bald head that bore the sheen of old mahogany and led Clare to a large mounted mosaic of topographic quadrangle maps. Clear plastic overlaid Yellowstone and the area surrounding it, with the extent of the burned areas outlined in black marker.

"The Yellowstone fires have increased tenfold, from eighty-six hundred acres to eighty-seven thousand in the past week." Garrett's thick finger pointed out the largest burn of nearly fifty thousand acres in the unpopulated eastern highlands of the Absaroka Mountains. "The Mist and Clover fires started July ninth and eleventh and burned together on the twenty-second." He moved his hand west. "Our problem now is the North Fork. It's heading for Old Faithful."

She studied the oblong streak that began about ten miles due south of West Yellowstone and stretched in a north-easterly curve.

"Started four days ago," Garrett went on. "Some loggers took a cigarette break in the Targhee National Forest, not three hundred yards from the park boundary. With Old Faithful and Madison in its path, we'll have one helluva battle."

"And no rain in sight," she added.

He nodded. "That's the worst news." With a gesture toward the map, he said, "I wanted you to see this. With your background training firefighters, I'll need you to teach the military that will be brought in."

She'd suspected when she left Texas that her instructor experience might be brought into play. Now that she'd seen the Shoshone rear like a cobra, she wondered what she could bring to the picture. "What makes you think soldiers will be needed? The policy is to not to fight the fires inside the park."

"The Yellowstone Superintendent has suspended the natural burn policy. We're to put 'em all out." His tone rang with finality.

She looked at the command center, imagining it full of workers relaying information on weather, manpower, and terrain, deploying everything from helicopters to toilet paper.

Garrett's eyes moved from the fire map to meet hers. Broken blood vessels marred the whites of his, suggesting that the fire season was already taking its toll on his sleep. "When we bring in green troops, it'll be your job to see that nobody gets killed."

Clare's chest tightened. She thought of a child burned to death, or if perverse fortune had smiled, overcome by smoke before flames reached him. Little Pham Nguyen had not yet turned three. And Frank . . . better to think of his Jane receiving the folded flag and the bugler sounding "Taps" than to keep replaying the events of July 1. When she was awake she had some choice, but at night . . .

Garrett ignored a ringing phone and awaited her answer.

If he knew she'd seen a firefighter down so recently, maybe he'd think twice about trusting her. But Buddy Simpson at A & M had relied on her to supervise training the week after Frank was buried. A good friend and mentor, Buddy had stuck his neck out recommending her to Garrett, one of the top Incident Commanders in the nation.

She straightened her back. "You can count on me."

Outside Fire Command, Clare was surprised to find pilot Chris Deering lounging on the rock stair railing. Jeans and a T-shirt advertising Lava Hot Springs, Idaho, accentuated his slim frame. "I thought I saw you go in here."

"If it isn't the downed aviator." She brushed back her hair from where it had fallen over her forehead. "Are you all right?"

The white look beneath his tan had disappeared since she had seen him at the hospital yesterday, but the bruise on his cheek was livid. Although the sun shone full on his face, he reached to take off his mirrored sunglasses. "My pride is in tatters. I'm fine as ever." Dark eyes flicked over her. A speculative glance at the front placket of her yellow Nomex shirt, a swift perusal of her cinched up olive fire pants, and his attention returned to her face.

She leaned back beside him against the rail. He was tall for a pilot, having nearly a foot on her five-three. Across the dry-looking lawn and a potholed parking lot, another rustic stone structure, the old Union Pacific Railway Station, was not nearly as interesting as she pretended.

Since Jay had gone, she'd hated the cheap feeling of being on the market. Once, she'd gone to one of those Houston singles bars on lower Westheimer. The guy who'd hit on her expected she wanted the same thing as he, a quickie at a chain motel. Even if she'd been into sex with somebody she'd barely met, she would have discounted that loser as married. Further forays in the dating world had confirmed that if a guy was halfway interesting, she could bet her back teeth there was a wife or long-term gal in the picture.

Deering continued to lounge, but she detected an awareness in him as he tossed off, "Where you staying?"

"I've got an employee cabin at Old Faithful."

"That's a forty mile drive," Deering observed. "You ought to stay here in town like I do."

"Old Faithful is central to my work." She avoided his eyes by glancing toward the motels, restaurants and souvenir shops on the opposite side of the wide street. False fronts gave the impression of a Wild West town.

Following her gaze, Deering said, "Did you know that the streets were built this wide so a horse and stagecoach could turn around in them?"

"Hadn't heard that."

"Have you been in the Bear Pit Bar at Old Faithful?" His hand traced the arc of the metal rail.

"Haven't had time." Enjoying the game despite her instinctive reticence, she finally gave him a level look. His lazy smile intrigued.

"If you're at Old Faithful this evening," Deering was direct, "I'll drive over and buy us a drink."

Decision time. He'd conveyed his interest but not the slack-jawed lust of a man on the make. Old Faithful was her turf; he'd never find her cabin . . . unless she showed him the way.

"Seven-thirty," she agreed.

In the Old Faithful Inn lobby, Clare checked the intricate metal clock on the towering fireplace of massive pink stones. Guests rested in rockers on an Indian print rug, an island in the polished golden floor. The appointed hour was near, and although the Bear Pit's open door invited, she headed for the nearest pay phone and dialed.

If there was one thing she hated more than dealing with her ex, it was having his wife answer. "Elyssa," she said flatly, twisting the phone cable. "Is Devon there?"

"Can't heah you . . ."

"I said, is Devon there?" Clare raised her voice over the din in the lobby and felt like a fishwife. Elyssa knew who she was.

Thinking of dusty boots left in her cabin, she imagined Jay's wife in her flowered chintz drawing room, her feet shod in soft Italian kid--Texas music in her voice when she wanted something like making the visitation more convenient for her.

"Ah imagine Devon's heah somewhere."

Yes, Clare knew how palatial the house Jay had built Elyssa was and how loosely she monitored the girl who was not her daughter.

Clare waited, imagining annoyance twisting Elyssa's penciled lips like she'd bitten an unripe persimmon. By the long metal hands of the fireplace clock, it took four minutes of long distance until Devon came on. Muted background sounds were probably the twenty-four inch color television Jay had given her for her designer bedroom. Clare couldn't afford a luxury like that for a teenager.

"Where are you, Mom?"

"I'm in the lobby at Old Faithful. Lots of folks coming in for the night."

Through the open doors, she could see the loading zone with buses discharging passengers and pungent diesel smells. After what had happened at Grant Village, she wondered if they should think about an evacuation here.

Almost everyone who came through the red, wrought-iron-trimmed double doors stopped and looked up. The soaring atrium lobby, crafted entirely of local wood, had been conceived by architect Robert Reamer in 1902, long before

Hyatt considered the concept. On the underside of the dark, shingled roof, Clare noted a network of pipes and sprinkler heads. She didn't plan on telling her daughter that if the wind did not shift or lie down, she, along with a thousand other firefighters, was going to defend Old Faithful.

A pregnant woman entered, bending to hold the hand of a chubby toddler. Devon had been like that once. The child looked with wide eyes at the soaring balconies trimmed in knotty pine.

"Are you staying at the hotel?" Her daughter's voice was bright and Clare's heart gave a little mother's lift. Maybe Devon actually missed her.

"I've got a cabin." A smacking sound came through the line. "Are you eating?"

"Pizza. Jay and Elyssa are going out."

Clare considered how poorly Devon received her balanced diet lecture, and really, it was Elyssa's fault for letting her eat like that. She tried another tack. "Did you work at the pool today?"

"Yeah." Devon sighed and Clare imagined her flipping back her blond hair with a desultory hand. The turned up nose would be down and the china doll eyes vacant.

"If work is so boring why don't you reconsider applying to A & M?" It was a long shot with Devon's grades, but both Jay's dad and Elyssa's influential father were alumni.

"Don't start. I'm not going to school anymore."

Clare's face warmed. "Try and find a real job with your high school diploma." It was no use, but she couldn't stop. "Flipping burgers for minimum wage is all that's out there."

"I'll look for something in the fall since I'll need a place of my own."

Clare closed her eyes. "This is the first I've heard of you wanting to move." She'd married Jay when she was too young, to get out from under her mother, and was dead set against Devon making the same mistake.

"I know you're selling the house." Devon laid down her winning hand. "That Realtor left a message on our answering machine."

"Oh, dear."

"Is that all you can say? You're selling our house and didn't bother to tell me."

The tight feeling that she'd seldom been without since Frank died intensified. "Darling, I thought it would upset you."

"You thought I wouldn't find out? I'm old enough to know what's going on." Devon's voice went squeaky. "Are you moving to Yellowstone?"

"Of course not. When you turn eighteen, the support from your father cuts off." Always now, Jay was Devon's 'father,' a way of pretending she'd never known the man. "I can't afford the house on what I make."

Saying it stung more than she'd imagined.

Devon chomped pizza and swallowed loudly. "Speaking of our house, I'm going home. I don't want to stay here with Elyssa."

Might as well waste her breath. "No."

"I stay alone when you're at the fire station."

"That's three minutes away." Clare felt her control over Devon slip further. "You usually go to your father's."

"In October when I'm eighteen . . ." An echo of Clare's own youthful voice telling her mother that. "I can go anywhere and do anything I like."

"You aren't there yet."

She didn't know if Devon heard her last or not, for the dial tone sounded loud in her ear. She leaned against the log wall while guilt warred with her resolve not to rush back to Houston.

She'd come to Yellowstone to break the cycle of feeling she couldn't go on. She owed it to herself and the department to come back stronger. Today, she'd made a commitment and Garrett Anderson was counting on her.

As she replaced the receiver, she caught a whiff of the woodsy scent she'd put on. It wasn't something she'd wear to the fire station, but this evening she'd pulled out a frosted bottle of Wind Song and splashed it over her, relishing the cold tightening of her skin. The summer ritual was an old habit she had only recently reacquainted herself with.

Clare had grown up in the well-ordered suburbs of Bellaire, Texas, back when Houston's great anastomosing arms had not yet embraced the satellite town. Her friend, Annie McGrath on Elm Street, had shown off the assortment of perfume her mother Jewel kept on a mirrored tray in their turquoise tiled bath. One day Jewel had caught Clare and Annie sampling and joined them, sitting on the edge of the tub and reaching for a cobalt bottle of Evening in Paris.

"Your father used to buy this for me during the war." Jewel smoothed back her daughter's curling red hair and touched the stopper to the fair skin beneath Annie's dainty ears.

When she was thirteen, Clare's first perfume had been crisp Chanel No. 5, a birthday gift from her mother who hoped she'd grow up to be lady. Constance, who wrapped teapots with cozies and arranged flowers Japanese style, had never gotten over her daughter becoming a P.E. coach . . . or a firefighter.

At Clare's senior prom, floral White Shoulders had been wasted on pimply, damp-palmed Billy Meyer. The football player she longed for dated a cheerleader, rather than a fellow athlete like Clare.

Jay hadn't exactly told Clare she couldn't wear perfume during their fifteen-year marriage. He'd just screwed his handsome face into a scowl and fanned away the smell, making the stale leftovers of Elyssa's Obsession all the more hurtful. Before the ink was dry on the decree, Clare had launched an assault on the Houston Galleria's perfume counters. A mirrored tray identical to Jewel McGrath's occupied a place of honor on her sinktop at home.

This evening, in addition to wearing cologne, Clare had selected the one dress she'd brought with her. The slight slip of sundress in a deep violet was more suited for a humid Texas night, but it made her feel daring.

With the easy appreciation that liquor bestowed, Steve Haywood leaned against the dark wood bar in the Bear Pit. He'd walked out of the Lake Hospital yesterday and not been sober since.

SUMMER OF FIRE

Sea green light shone onto the glass screen dividing the bar from Old Faithful's cavernous dining room. Etched into thick panels was a group of bears in nineteenth-century clothing, playing cards, dancing, and shooting one another with seltzer bottles. Party animals--and no matter how much Steve had drunk in the past four years, he'd never found that carefree plane of non-existence.

Maybe he'd find it tonight, with enough Jack Daniels.

He sipped and surveyed the summer crowd occupying heavy wooden tables and chairs in the half-round bar. Here was an eclectic mix of tourists and folks working the park. Bartender Annabel Eaton stood behind the long western-style counter and wiped a glass with a rag. They were old friends by now, and Steve could tell Annabel thought he'd had enough to drink. He'd need to slow down so the heavy-set, earnest, kindergarten teacher from Des Moines would continue to serve him.

Over there was off-duty waitress Pamela Weber, with velvet, Italian-movie-star eyes that could have graced the pages of a men's magazine. Tanned legs stretched a mile below tight white shorts. Steve hadn't been to bed with her; in fact, he hadn't slept with a woman in the four years since Susan, but, with Pamela, he'd come close. Back in June, she had attracted his attention while he was walking around the geyser basin. She'd invited him to go hot potting, the summer employees' name for swimming in the thermal springs. He'd had too much to drink and the warm water had relaxed him so much he'd been unable to rise to the occasion.

Pamela spotted him, gave an airy wave, and turned her

attention to the man buying her drinks this evening. Steve sighed and took another long and joyless swallow of whiskey.

Twenty feet away, Clare Chance paused in the doorway. Everything seemed suddenly sharp to Steve as she swept the room with that deliberately blind stare women bestow on a roomful of strangers. Those eyes, almost haunted—or maybe she just suffered from the lack of sleep of many on the fire lines.

In a bright dress that left her golden shoulders bare, with streaked tawny hair over her rounded forehead, she strode purposefully to the bar. Steve watched her stand on tiptoe in flat-heeled leather sandals, accentuating the corded muscles of her calves. Her extraordinary presence had caused him to forget that she was barely taller than five feet, and made it difficult to believe she had manhandled him into the lake.

With the champagne she'd ordered, Clare drifted toward the curved outer wall of windows. Steve cursed himself for not having noticed Deering before. The pilot looked as cocky as ever, lifting his beer mug and toasting Clare's approach. A small sideways flick of eyes said he'd seen Steve. "You should have let me get your drink." Deering's proprietary note carried.

Steve decided he needed fresh air. His exit was marred by a stumble at the slight step up into the lobby. From the front desk, he heard an elderly woman shrill, "The bath is down the hall?"

"I'm sorry, ma'am," the clerk said. "The old wing does not have private baths."

Steve turned right and opened the outside door. The

combination of a difficult climate and the drought created earth covered with sparse brown grass and volcanic gravel. Moving away from the building, he inhaled the tang of smoke on the breeze.

In the past twenty-four hours, the North Fork fire had tripled from twenty-five hundred acres to over eight thousand. Although no evacuation had been called, some of the tourists feared getting caught by the fire that was still six miles from the inn.

He guessed people were frightened of things that spoke to them at a visceral level. Some kid who'd accidentally gotten locked in a lightless closet would spend his life sleeping with a nightlight. The very idea of flying turned Steve witless, and ditching in the lake had necessitated the liberal application of alcohol for its anesthetic properties.

Yesterday afternoon, Clare Chance had not been afraid. She'd faced the exposed fangs of the Shoshone . . . and saved his worthless life.

"What's the word out of Fire Command?" Deering asked.

Clare looked across the Bear Pit table at the sharp-nosed pilot wearing slim fit Wrangler jeans, an open-necked shirt that revealed dark chest hair, and well-worn cowboy boots.

"Not good." She shook her head and saw his eyes go to the gold hoops at her ears. "We're in for a long haul."

She traced a wet spot on the table and checked his sinewy left hand. A flesh-toned bandage there, but no sign of a wedding ring, or even the telltale band of shrunken flesh that said it was in his pocket.

A sip of champagne refreshed her throat that was dry from the high thin air. "Rumor has it we're about to throw everything we've got at the fires."

A deeper line etched between Deering's brows. "You don't sound like that's a good thing. Most of the firefighters I know like saving the burning forests."

Clare looked out the window, but rather than the dark shingled side of the inn's opposite wing, she saw a wall of flame. "Yesterday, I got a close-up of the Shoshone at Grant Village." She turned her gaze on Deering's gaunt face, marked by the purpling bruise. "And you lost your helicopter. Before this is over, somebody is going to get killed."

"Damned right. Haywood and I lucked out when we ditched, but somebody dies every season." His prominent Adam's apple bobbed as he swallowed beer.

Clare paid attention to her stemmed glass to avoid the intensity in Deering that she wasn't ready for. "I'm going out on the lines west of here in the morning to try to keep the North Fork from burning this place down."

"That would be a shame. One thing for sure, if it burned, they'd never be able to replace it." Deering studied his own glass for a moment and then tapped it with a long finger. "If I were going up in the morning, this would be Coke."

That was good, for she'd caught a glimpse of Steve Haywood looking soused—he'd even tripped going through the door. He was out there now, leaning against the wall of the breezeway between the old and newer wing of the inn. When she looked directly at him, he turned his head away as though she'd caught him staring.

She checked out Deering, comparing the sturdy blond scientist and the tall rugged pilot.

Deering met her eyes in a questioning, no, maybe a questing, way. "I need to get back in the air," he said with an air of confiding.

Why did it not surprise her that this man was ready to fly again? "I can imagine you'd get antsy being grounded," she sympathized. "Were you in Vietnam?"

"How'd you know?"

"Lucky guess. The right age . . . You have family?"

He cleared his throat. After a little pause, he said, "Wildfire's tough on commitment."

In her peripheral vision, Clare saw Steve reenter the Bear Pit, a man on a mission. "Annabel, I need a Jack," he barked. "Make it a double." When he leaned on the bar, his elbow slipped in a puddle.

"Excuse me," Clare murmured to Deering.

She approached Steve from behind. Maybe because she'd rescued him, it disappointed her to see him like this. Before she knew what she was going to say, the words came out. "Don't you think you've had enough?"

Steve turned with the slow care of a man who'd had too much to drink. Her head barely clearing his shoulder, she looked up at him steadily.

"You again." It sounded as though he was accusing her of something.

A flush rose from her chest and spread across her cheeks.

"Why are you doing this to yourself?"

His silver-gray eyes went wide. "Whaddaya mean? I'm just having a few to celebrate . . ." He steadied himself on the bar. " . . . tomorra's visit of the honorable Secretary of the Interior and his muckey-mucks." He made a bowing gesture that indicated obeisance, then met her eyes. She recognized the look of sadness and defeat she'd seen lately in her mirror.

Maybe she conveyed something, for the bluster went out of him. "I'm sorry. I shoulda thanked you . . . saving my life."

She started to soften, but he caught his boot toe in the bar's brass foot rail and lost his balance. Blind anger that she knew was irrational turned her back toward Deering with a tart, "Someday when you're sober you can thank me properly."

CHAPTER FIVE
July 27

The next morning Clare found it hard to believe there could be any threat to this pristine forest. She rode in a troop carrier with ten other firefighters on their way to divert the North Fork from Old Faithful. Almost everyone had his or her head down trying to catch a last few minutes of sleep despite the hard bench.

Although the rising sun angled through the trees on the small forest track, its warmth did not reach beneath the truck's canvas tarp. In Houston, the July temperature and humidity had both hovered near one hundred.

Before leaving, she'd visited her mother. They had sat in Constance's back yard in suburban Bellaire, ignoring the glass-walled office building that towered over the squat, one-story bungalow. The roar of traffic on Loop 610 formed a constant stream of white noise.

Pouring lemonade from a sweating pitcher, Constance said, "Are you sure about this Wyoming, dear? You're still suffering over your . . . friend." Her arch pause suggested Frank might have been more than a co-worker.

That was ridiculous. Frank had treated Clare like the big brother she'd never had, being an only child. Without bothering to correct her mother, she said, "That's precisely the point. I need a change and my job will be waiting when I come back."

She didn't say that one more night in Houston, where nightmares wakened her with almost hourly regularity, was more than she could stand.

"But, dear, Devon is at a delicate age." A stranger might believe that Constance, with her wide dark eyes and innocent delivery, was being sweet. Clare knew better. "Mother," she warned, "one of the A & M trainers called a friend in fire command at Yellowstone. Garrett Anderson is expecting me."

"Of course, dear, but Devon . . ." Constance pushed back her silver hair where it had fallen over her forehead.

Clare sipped her mother's perfect lemonade deliberately. "Taking care of Devon is just an excuse. She could stay with you, but you haven't been willing to have her overnight since she set her mattress on fire."

"Can't you teach her safety? And you a firefighter." Constance's tone said she regarded her daughter's profession as no better than ditch digger.

Clare busied herself selecting a fat oatmeal cookie from the symmetrical arrangement on a platter.

"She still smokes, you know." Constance lowered her voice as though Devon could overhear. "I smell it on her."

"A lot of the other kids smoke. She gets it on her clothes from being around them." Clare defended Devon even though she knew her daughter probably did smoke, and lied about it.

"I hope you're right about her being okay at Jay's while you're gone. Her visits there are usually shorter, and you know that fish and family . . ."

"Stink after three days." She didn't need to check her watch to know that she and Constance had exceeded the three hours they usually required. "Devon needs a relationship with her father," she parroted, from years of repeating the mantra.

Her mother's mouth made a line. "You ask me, you should have sole custody, after he . . ."

Clare had emphatically not asked, but every time Devon left for visitation, she stifled the same thought. "You know that in family law court, you get all the justice you can afford."

Beaten back on the new front, Constance returned to the West. "This Wyoming . . ." She gave another of her signature pauses and smoothed the skirt of her yellow-flowered house-dress. "You know they have bears up there."

"Yes, Mother."

"I'm serious." Constance's hands fluttered, a sure sign that she had found something to worry about. Her vigilance was steadfast, such that she fretted over everything from refusing to get onto an airplane to shredding magazine covers marked with her name before putting them in the garbage.

Clare had learned to live with it, but the familiar charade rankled. It had gotten worse in the seven years since her parents divorced. Her father kept busy with his new wife and twin baby sons, reminding her too painfully of losing Jay to ten-years-younger Elyssa Hendron.

Looking at a mass of greenery topped by spiky red flowers, Clare tried, "Your cannas are doing well this year."

"Don't change the subject," Constance persisted. "You were too young to know your Grandfather Cordon before he died, but he told me they broke ice in the water buckets in June. The homestead was in Jackson Hole, just by the Snake River."

"With the drought and the fires, I hardly think I'll get cold."

In the back of the truck, Clare had time to regret her smug assurance, pulling on rough gloves and flexing stiff fingers to soften the leather. The cotton bandanna issued with the fire uniform did not keep her ears or neck warm beneath her hard hat.

The truck jerked and swayed on the rutted track. It was strange to be on the way to a fire at such a slow speed, without the strident sirens and the klaxon of the air horn parting traffic.

Clare clamped her teeth against the opening of the instant replay of Frank's death. Reliving the experience did no earthly good. Both the psychologist and the guys at the station had made that clear. She focused instead on what she'd seen the day before yesterday at Grant Village. For sheer force and power, no fire she'd ever seen compared to the Shoshone.

As her chest stayed tight, Clare reminded herself that despite Garrett Anderson's pessimism, this unusual fire behavior and weather weren't likely to last. According to historic data, it usually rained more in late July and August.

The truck rounded a bend and braked.

"Deer," someone said. A dozen soft-eyed does stared at the

intruders from the dappled shade. One leapt high, and like the quick communal reaction of a school of fish, the others exploded and shot across the track in pursuit. Clare thought of *Bambi,* how at five she'd cried in the theatre when the forest fire sent the animals fleeing.

The truck moved on, rocking, as the track grew fainter.

A young man who appeared no older than Devon studied Clare. Probably a college linebacker, his broad shoulders pressed against the boards. Like many of the fire crew who eschewed shaving during the season, he sported a shaggy brown beard. A faint smile played at Clare's lips. Back in Houston, her routine was set in a way that did not include meeting new men. Here the faces were as fresh and different as the land.

Last night she had enjoyed talking with Deering. He seemed friendly and open, although she'd detected complexity below the surface. He had promised to leave a message for her at Fire Command, so they could have dinner when she had the chance to be in West Yellowstone.

As the truck negotiated the broad expanse of Little Firehole Meadow, Clare started to feel warmer. Dry golden grasses stirred in the vehicle's wake. Ahead, a gray shroud hugged the ground, and in another minute, she had a view of the fire front, six-inch flames licking their way through the undergrowth.

The sight of their adversary reminded her of the night she'd made her decision to fight the summer battles of the West.

It was at Frank's wake in a popular Irish bar, and she'd been pretty well into the Guinness Stout. Raucous male laughter surrounded her as the acne-scarred young man tending bar turned on the television. Male swimmers backstroked, competing with honed bodies for spots in the October Seoul Olympics. Clare paid attention, for she had swum competitively in college and kept up with the new generation of men and women in the sport.

The bartender changed channels, flipping past local news and the MacNeil-Lehrer Report. Behind Lehrer's shoulder, a forest fire raged.

"Hold it there," Clare ordered.

Lehrer read his copy. "Wildfires have burned over fifty thousand acres in five western states. In this driest summer in park history, several fires are burning out of control in Yellowstone under the Park Service's *let burn* policy. This allows fires started by lightning to run unless they threaten life or private property."

"I heard they're gonna be bringing in help from all over the country." Javier Fuentes set his brew on the table littered with dead soldiers.

The TV showed a line of firefighters walking up a forest road. Dressed in olive trousers and yellow shirts, they wore hard hats with bandannas tied around their foreheads as sweatbands. Clare recognized their heavy tools as Pulaskis, a combination axe and hoe, heavier than her crash axe at the station. Smoke swirled around them.

She drew a deep breath. Fire was sweeping across the land of her ancestors. She felt as though she could smell the smoky tang of pine forest and feel the comfortable heft of the fire tool. The decision that her job with HFD could go on hold hit her with the swiftness of a blow. Devon could stay with her father for a while.

"I'm going out there," she told Javier.

"Count me in," he had agreed. The miraculous thing was that after they had slept on it, neither they nor the other guys who'd sworn aboard had changed their minds. After her mandatory consultation with the department psychologist, the station chief had agreed to let her go. She and the Houston crew had worked the line together only a few days before she was called to be a trainer.

Clare snapped out of her reverie when the truck driver cut the engine. The only sounds were that of a crow's caw and the brisk crackling of the North Fork. Then the firefighters moved, piling off the tailgate, their boots making hollow sounds on the metal. Voices rose and they passed tools.

Clare felt the odd person out, having come to observe so she could direct others later.

The hotshots' assignment for the day was to cut a three-mile line along the southeast flank of the North Fork, while aerial bombardment with retardant liquid was used on the most active front. Before they got to the place where they were to work, Clare felt the first trickle of sweat between her shoulder blades.

To build a fire line, the sawyers started, revving up their chainsaws and felling trees over a fifteen-foot wide corridor. Afterward, the hotshots with Pulaskis cleared a two-foot wide swath, careful to hack out every vestige of roots that could keep a fire smouldering.

Clare had thought she was in shape, but the crew had been digging line since mid-June. As the morning wore on, she found that she was only able do about fifty feet an hour, while the others managed to clear at least a full chain, or sixty-six feet.

Toward noon, she fell farther behind. Her back and arms ached from bending and wielding the heavy Pulaski. She stopped frequently for water breaks, figuring that if she got dehydrated, she would be worse than useless. When lunch was finally called, she was torn between whether to sit and risk stiffening or to stand and eat. The sight of the crew lolling on the ground decided her.

With a care for her aching back, she sat and took off her hard hat. Dampening her sweat soaked bandanna in fresh water from her canteen, she attempted to wipe some of the salty grime from her face and hands before eating.

The day wasn't half over.

After choking back a pair of dry bologna sandwiches, she leaned against a tree trunk and closed her eyes. Against the shifting sparks that decorated the backs of her eyelids, she saw Deering again, smiling at her with teeth that shone white against his skin.

But thinking of last night opened a darker dimension. When she had first seen Steve Haywood, she'd had a distinctly different impression of the park biologist. Going back into the lake after he'd fetched up on shore, he'd seemed a real trouper, not at all like the sodden wretch who had nearly fallen on the floor at the Bear Pit. Shortly after she'd been rude to him, she'd turned from her conversation with Deering to find him gone. Too late, she wished she'd done something to keep him from driving drunk.

Sitting against the tree, she found that even thinking used

too much energy. It was just on the borderline between warm and hot, and rest felt so bonelessly wonderful. The sharpness of fresh-cut pine overpowered the undercurrent of smoke while insects droned around her head. Gradually, the voices of the crew muted, then fell silent . . .

She was inside an apartment complex that was burning faster than the Houston Fire Department could put it out. The wood shingle roofs were igniting from flying sparks so that the flames leaped from building to building. Sirens shrilled as more and more alarms were called.

Inside the smoky apartment hallway, Clare and Frank approached a closed door that poured smoke from around the edges. No other firefighters came from the opposite end of the building, leaving them alone to assault this cell of the larger conflagration.

"All for us," Frank said through the mask on his air pack. She imagined the usual twinkle in his deep brown eyes.

Facing away from the door, Clare raised her leg and brought it back into a mule kick. The panel swung wide, back against the interior wall with a bang.

Light suffused the hall. Heat struck out and pounded. She crouched and turned to face the inferno. She'd been in worse situations, but couldn't shake a bad feeling. Her rapid breathing hissed in her mask and she told herself she could stay the course.

Frank cracked the valve and sent up a power cone. Steam rose and hot water began to fall like rain, running down her helmet and into the neck of her coat. Over the fire's roar was an overprint of snaps and pops that didn't sound right.

She took a hand off the hose. Immediately, over a hundred pounds of pressure threatened to tear it from her remaining hand and Frank's. Nevertheless, she clutched his arm, with the strength born of premonition. "Don't go any farther!"

"Son of a bitch! Will you look at that?"

Clare jerked and her heart took off like a greyhound after the mechanical rabbit. She stared through open eyes at the after-image of the flaming apartment. Gradually, she realized that she sat beneath a tree with the midday sun slanting through the branches, hoping she'd not called attention to herself.

"No shit, man," someone replied to the request to 'look at that.'

Clare swiveled toward the unmistakable crackling and saw what had happened. Not a hundred yards back, the North Fork had jumped the line, rendering the morning's work useless.

CHAPTER SIX
July 27

R andolph Mason." The Secretary of the Interior greeted Steve Haywood. Mason's entourage had stopped this afternoon on the road from Norris Geyser Basin to Mammoth Hot Springs.

The Secretary's handshake was firm, his presence more commanding in person than through the filter of television. He carried his tall frame elegantly, his coal black hair lending a distinguished air to his jeans and chambray shirt.

"Pleased to meet you," Steve replied, hoping Mason didn't catch the tremor in his hand. He had slept in his truck last night at Old Faithful, too drunk to drive.

He looked past the Secretary at fire general Garrett Anderson, moving with startling agility down the steps of the TW Services bus. The big man wore a ball cap decorated with a flaming tree and the words *Rocky Mountain Incident Mgt. Team.* Last night after Clare had walked away, a firefighter had told Steve she was a friend of a friend of Garrett, who'd pulled strings to get her an employee cabin at Old Faithful.

Steve looked up from the roadside parking lot at Roaring Mountain, a bare, bleached slope that smoked from hundreds of steam vents. It always came as a surprise, after driving for miles through the unrelenting corridor of pine, to come upon the scar that looked as though it had been quarried.

A cluster of press piled off the advance bus. The Washington contingent looked as though they'd bought their stylish outdoor clothing at Abercrombie and Fitch just before boarding the plane. The press corps, mostly westerners, wore rugged jeans and scarred footwear that was suitable for rough terrain.

Secretary Mason smiled at the reporters.

A lanky cameraman with an untidy coffee-colored ponytail stepped in closer. The stocky young woman with him thrust her mike at the Secretary's face. "Carol Leeds, Billings Live Eye." Her mane of red hair spilled over the shoulders of her denim jacket. "Is it true the Park Service made a serious error in judgment when they let the fires burn out of control in the park?"

Garrett Anderson murmured to Steve, "Cutting right to the chase."

Mason studied Carol Leeds with sharp blue eyes for so long that the group of reporters broke ranks.

"Mr. Secretary . . . "

"Secretary Mason . . . "

"Do you support the Park Service . . .?"

Mason raised his hand and waited for quiet. "Certainly, I support the men and women in whose hands lies the stewardship of Yellowstone, our national's crown jewel."

Steve thought that he could never be a politician. He would have told them wildfire was natural, that in Yellowstone man had been just standing in the way of the inevitable since before the turn of the twentieth century.

For when Native Americans dominated the land, the Smoky Bear phenomenon hadn't existed. They used fire to clear fields and forest undergrowth and early settlers followed their lead. How ironic during this season's blowup that Yellowstone had been the first place in the nation with fire patrols, set up by the U.S. Army in 1886. Fire suppression for a hundred years had let the forests grow until the level of fuels was at an historic high.

"What's going to happen at Old Faithful?" blurted the freckle-faced journalist Mason chose next.

Garrett Anderson interceded. "Mr. Secretary, if I may?"

Mason nodded.

"We've got a thousand firefighters digging line and setting backfires west of Old Faithful," Garrett told the press. "For the time being, I feel safe to say the danger to the complex has been averted."

Impatient to get his part of the program over, Steve took the lead onto a foot trail that wound along the base of Roaring Mountain. Park Superintendent Tom King, a beanpole of a man, fell into step, his neatly pressed uniform of gray jacket and darker pants made a sharp contrast to the Secretary's vacation wear. The press followed like a pack of hounds.

As the hill steepened, Steve felt the incline. His heart started to pound and his dry mouth made him aware of his hangover. Garrett Anderson caught up with him. The thick-waisted fire general put it on Steve as they continued to climb. "You met Clare Chance," Garrett said in the soft accent of a fellow southerner.

"Things were happening a bit fast for us to be properly introduced the day that chopper crashed." He failed to mention how he'd distinguished himself last night at the Bear Pit.

"Clare's quite a gal."

"I thought so." Steve tried not to sound out of breath.

Garrett smiled. "Friend of mine at the Texas A & M fire school recommended she train the troops to fight fire."

Clare went up another notch in Steve's estimation. Last night he'd been looking at her bare shoulders and legs and thinking she looked all woman. Now, he was reminded how she'd saved him from the Shoshone and realized if she were going to train the military, she must be one tough woman.

"*If* we have to bring in soldiers," Steve tempered.

"When."

He figured Garrett had the experience to be a reasonable judge.

"Next week we're bringing in the experts at predicting fire behavior." Garrett removed his cap and mopped his head with a bandanna. "But you mark my words." He swept his arm to encompass the pine-studded plateau. "If we don't get rain soon, all this will look like that."

He pointed to the smoking ruin of Roaring Mountain.

Steve chewed on that while he made it to the place he'd planned to show the visitors.

"Are you ready for your fifteen minutes of fame?" Superintendent King asked with a flash of smile.

Through his now-throbbing headache, Steve grinned back. Park HQ at Mammoth was a small town and he knew Tom King well.

Stepping into the middle of a clearing on the backside of Roaring Mountain, Steve waited while the press fanned out. Secretary Mason wore an attentive look on his hawklike face.

Raising his voice for the crowd, Steve began, "Nine years ago, a lightning strike started a fire here." Long trunks of the fallen lay scattered, and a few silver ghosts still stood, having weathered the weight of snows and the ravage of high winds.

"It looks like hell to me." The heckler seemed to be part of the press.

"We call these doghair thickets." Steve pointed to patches of seedlings that grew cheek by jowl. "It takes a fire to open the cones of the lodgepole and release the seeds. When it happens, every hundred to four hundred years, many thousands of small trees grow back right away."

"Who'd want to vacation here, though?"

Steve saw him this time, the ponytailed cameraman from Billings.

"Many burned areas don't look this bad," Steve tried. "Often the debris on the forest floor smoulders slowly, leaving the mature trees with damage only to the lower branches, like over here."

There was no response from either the press or the visiting entourage. So, how many laymen were interested in listening to a biologist blather?

Steve faced the crowd squarely. "What's at stake in Yellowstone this summer is a basic question of how to manage wildfire. In the northern Rockies, the climate is too dry and cold for decomposition, so the fuels continue to build until there's a fire. After nearly a century of suppression, in 1972 the park decided to manage its resources differently. That meant no putting out natural fires, those started by lightning."

"So what happened?" Carol Leeds from Billings asked.

"Very little." He gestured toward the burn he'd been showing them. "Between 1972 and 1987 around thirty-four thousand acres, or less than three percent of the park was renewed. Until this summer."

"I believe that this morning's report tallied over eighty-eight thousand acres," Garrett Anderson spoke up.

As Steve started to lead the way to another section, he noticed that the Secretary of the Interior seemed most impressed with this last statistic.

🐾🐾🐾

Three hours later in Mammoth, Steve opened the basement door into the Yellowstone Park archives. Upstairs, in the stone headquarters building that had once been Fort Yellowstone's bachelor officers' quarters, tourists studied exhibits of old uniforms and weapons.

"Everybody buy your story about fire being natural, like granola and alfalfa sprouts?" Walt Leighton asked from inside his office.

"What do you think?" Steve shut the door harder than he'd intended.

Walt, the park historian, uncoiled his long frame. He came

out of his closet-sized office into the main room lined with filing cabinets. "I'd say the important thing is whether Randolph Mason bought it." His bushy brows knit above his narrow nose.

Steve leaned against a table topped by a microfiche reader and looked up at Walt, who was easily six-four against his own five-ten. "What can Mason do? Superintendent King decided days ago that this season's fires would not be allowed to burn free."

"The Secretary of the Interior can change policy for the long term." Steve recognized Harriet Friendswood's voice and turned.

She came out of the back room where historic documents were stored. Meticulously, she stripped off white cotton gloves that kept skin oils from antique papers and looked at her purple plastic Timex. "Quittin' time."

Steve smiled and her soft brown eyes lighted. Harriet wasn't bad, early thirties, medium build, and shoulder length chestnut hair. Although she had been pursuing Steve in earnest for the entire six months she'd been here, he figured that if there were a spark he would have known right away.

"I've got a roast in the oven." She gave a come-hither look. "Plenty for two."

He'd tried one of her dinners and come home with the conclusion that he was the better cook. "Oh, no thanks. I'm just gonna go through some documents here."

"Your loss." Harriet secured her purse, told Walt good evening and walked out with her shoulders square beneath her flowered print dress.

Steve watched her go and found the historian's sharp eyes on him. For years, Walt had been trying to get him to come out of his shell as far as women were concerned. Now he said nothing as he prepared to leave for the day. Although the archives were officially closed, Walt seemed to understand that Steve's fascination with history kept his mind off his lost wife and child.

He wondered what Walt would think of him comparing Clare Chance with Harriet. If Clare had invited him to dinner, he might have gone.

With careful hands, he opened a filing cabinet. The familiar and ordinary folders inside held treasure that could never be measured in dollars and cents. His cotton-gloved fingers skipped across the tabs that revealed the vintage of the ancient documents, primary sources of historic information. Here were the records of the military commandant of the park in the year 1892, handwritten notes that mentioned the grand opening of the new Lake Hotel, with a lavish party thrown by its owners, the Northern Pacific Railroad.

By 1900, park headquarters had acquired a typewriter and carbons. Tissue thin papers revealed a long correspondence with an eastern procurement officer, an effort to put the soldiers who patrolled the park into Norwegian cross-country skis. The letters began politely enough in January, but by April a single terse sentence appeared beneath the salutation --Send skis now.

With a grin, Steve opened the next file of letters. He turned a nearly translucent page and noticed a fresh wave of the familiar, faintly musty smell of the basement archives.

Beyond the windows, golden afternoon beckoned, so he took the folder to a picnic table beneath a spreading cedar. There, he immersed himself in the life of the old fort, where horses and Army wagons had used the very path he sat beside.

Half an hour later, a shadow fell across his notes. He heard a pressurized pop and release and looked into the label of an Olympia can. Walt, wearing jeans instead of his ranger uniform, slid a hip onto the table and climbed up, propping his booted feet on the seat. "Beer?" He set down a paper bag that looked to contain the rest of a six-pack.

Steve had never heard of Oly when he was growing up in North Carolina, but he'd learned to appreciate the finer things of the West. He could just about taste the clean effervescence as he reached.

"Why are you doing this to yourself?" Clare Chance had surveyed him coolly, with eyes that reminded him of the finest amber liquor. She was something else, as he'd realized last night lying in the bed of his truck, and again when Garrett Anderson had praised her on the trail up Roaring Mountain.

With his fingers almost touching the sweating can, Steve stopped.

A puzzled expression gathered on Walt's sharp features.

With an effort, Steve lowered his hand to the weathered boards. "No," he said roughly, "thanks."

"Haywood turns down a brew?" Walt's brows lifted.

Both men went silent as a pair of young male tourists, identified by their name brand sportswear and the fact that they were strangers, passed the picnic table. They started across the street toward the open field that had once been the parade ground for Fort Yellowstone. With the ancient letters still on his mind, Steve envisioned the afternoon review of cavalry and infantry while wives, camp followers, and guests of the huge wood frame National Hotel looked on. How different the Mammoth of today was, with its eclectic mix of ancient and modern architecture.

When the tourists had gone, Walt sipped from the beer he'd offered Steve. "When I went home, I happened to catch the national news."

Steve tensed. "The fires are a regular six o'clock circus."

Walt nodded. "Secretary Mason took a chopper ride with Ranger Shad Dugan and saw that the Clover-Mist really exploded today. When Dugan mentioned we've suspended letting natural fires burn, Mason said that after all this settles down, the entire park policy on fire would require review."

"Damned bureaucrats. Thinking they know what's right for the forest because they were elected or appointed." The bag ripped as Steve pulled out a beer.

CHAPTER SEVEN

The terrain south of West Yellowstone was relatively flat, making it a good place to acclimate the soldiers to the forest. Clare was pleased that her first group of forty troops from Fort Lewis, Washington, seemed to be in reasonable shape. They'd hiked several brisk miles with full packs, a gallon of water, and heavy Pulaskis.

In an area that had been clear-cut for timber, Clare stopped the column. As typical young people, the soldiers broke ranks and milled about in the midafternoon sun.

Time to talk safety, and these kids had no idea how dear that subject was to her heart. Rather than tell her own and Frank's story of how quickly dreams could become disaster, she began, "Edward Pulaski, the inventor of your fire tool, was a Forest Service ranger in Idaho back in 1910. One day, he and forty-five men got caught, surrounded by fire."

Some restlessness and murmuring continued. Sergeant Ron Travis, the troops' bantam leader, stood at parade rest, making Clare suspect he was permitting the lax behavior as a insult to her. All day he had been disdainful, walking a fine line between accepting her authority and laughing when she'd only halfway turned her back.

She determined to plow on. "Pulaski led his men to an abandoned mine, the War Eagle. They wet themselves down with water from a seep and hung dampened horse blankets across the tunnel mouth."

The troops showed the same reluctance to listen as the high school students Clare used to have in P.E. Today, she wasn't going to blow a whistle, but tell a story that might reach them.

"The firestorm of 1910 was the worst in the history of the West. Three million acres of western Montana and Idaho burned in two sweltering August days. The fire generated hurricane force winds that rushed up the hill and filled the mine with smoke."

Some of the soldiers fingered the bandannas she'd told them were to go over their noses and mouths under smoky conditions.

"Those men wept, and not because their eyes stung. The air grew fouler, until p rew an audible breath.

"Everyone passed out. The next morning, they awakened one by one . . . The last five did not. Pulaski lay by the entrance and they thought he was dead, too. Then he spoke to them."

Clare had the troops' attention. "When we go out to the fires, you're going to see small flames creeping along the ground, but don't ever forget you're here because over one hundred-fifty thousand acres, almost ten percent of Yellowstone has burned." Her mind spiraled down a vortex into a raging inferno, a blazing apartment superimposed over the awesome might of the Shoshone firestorm. "Never lose sight of how quickly disaster can strike."

She let a moment of silence pass. In her mind, it was a memorial to both the fallen men of Pulaski's group and to Frank Wallace.

Sergeant Travis looked bored. If she had wanted to slap him earlier, now her palm fairly itched. Instead, with the efficiency she used to set basketball players running laps, she called, "Now you're going to show me how fast you can make a fire line."

She bent to demonstrate how the Pulaski was used. "Everybody works in a row. You 'strike', turn the sod, and keep moving. I'll be checking to make sure you clear down to a mineral soil that won't burn."

The team lined up, spread out, and began to emulate her motions.

"I want it two feet wide, from here down to that dead tree." She pointed. "And I want it in ten minutes." A good hotshot team could do the deed in five.

As the troops worked, Clare paced their ranks. "You want to watch out for wind shifts that can send fire speeding in your direction. If flames catch up to your line, you see if it holds. If not, fall back to another position." She stopped and cautioned a young man, "Hold your Pulaski tighter. You're going to get a blister."

She raised her voice. "When you're on a fire, you may find yourself working up to fifty hours straight without a trip back to a camp. You'll sleep where you drop, leaned against a tree or stretched out in the dirt of a fire line."

That was something Clare had yet to experience, but the troops didn't need to know. It gave her a sense of satisfaction to see Sergeant Travis look unhappy. She hoped the next group would come with a more enlightened commander.

"Snags are standing burned trees," she went on. "You'd be surprised how slight a breeze can bring one down without a sound. When you're digging, keep up your awareness of everything around you. Somebody is killed by a snag every season."

She moved down the line without speaking. A soldier with his head bent over his work formed an attractive target. "Gotcha." She tapped his shoulder.

He jumped. A chorus of laughter spread.

"Not funny!" she shouted. "He's a dead man."

It got quiet fast.

Clare studied the soldiers' fresh faces. As part of the volunteer Army, they had asked to serve, but in the late eighties, she imagined most thought they'd never see danger.

It took fifteen minutes for them to reach the tree she had set as a goal. She berated them severely although she thought they'd done a credible job for rookies. Gathering the group, she said, "You've probably been wondering what was in those pouches I gave you to hang on your belts."

A number of the young men and women nodded.

Clare unsnapped the flap top of her own pouch and drew out a folded mass of material that looked like silver foil. "This is your last resort in case you are overtaken by flames."

Their incredulous looks mirrored the disbelief Clare had felt when she was first acquainted with the tissue-thin Mylar shields. She shook it out and the wind caught it, making it billow like a sheet on a clothesline.

"Insert your hands through the corner straps," she instructed, spreading her arms wide. "Put your boot toes through the bottom corners." The blanket fluttered behind her like a cape. "If you have time, you'll clear a patch of bare earth to lie in. If not . . .

Clare heard Sergeant Travis mutter, "Then kiss your ass good-bye."

She went down onto the ground. For a long moment, she lay still beneath the silver tarpaulin, imagining that choking smoke and superheated air seeped beneath the edges. Without an air pack, she did not believe these things could possibly save lives.

It was quiet in the sunny glade. Insects droned and the wind soughed through pine boughs. Clare imagined the roar of the Shoshone, trees exploding, without the convenience of Yellowstone Lake at her feet.

When she got up, she threw the shelter at Sergeant Travis. He took it, but instead of folding it, he crumpled the foil over his arm. "It's your turn," she told the troops. "Break 'em out and cover up."

As she watched their awkward rehearsal, a flying tanker headed in from the fires, on a line toward West Yellowstone.

Over a week after ditching, Deering was still grounded. On the tarmac at West Yellowstone Airport, he held tight to the nozzle as he filled a DC-7 tanker with fire retardant.

None of the charter companies he'd hit up wanted help. Every turndown had cut like a blade and he imagined that his wife wielded them all. Not only did Georgia hope his Bell was lost, she'd be dancing if she knew he was a grunt on the ground crew.

As soon as the belly tank was full, the plane taxied toward another bombing run.

Deering removed his goggles and lugged the hose back to the battery of cylindrical tanks. Gary Cullen, a dough-faced youth whose father owned the local Red Wolf Motel, was already mixing bags of fertilizer and red dye for a fresh batch of retardant. Since Deering had joined the ground team, Gary had treated him with the suspicion small town residents often extended to outsiders.

"Just gonna smoke." Deering walked off the ramp away from the planes and fuel trucks, patting his retardant-soaked coveralls for his Marlboros. After several tries, he managed to light a limp cigarette. Georgia was always on him to quit.

That little gal Clare, he didn't think she smoked. Quick guilt slashed, for he hadn't worn a wedding ring in years, and he had failed to mention Georgia. He told himself that his reply to Clare's question about family hadn't been a lie. Summers in fire *were* tough on commitment.

Not exactly a lie.

Thankfully, common sense had prevailed and he hadn't left a message for her at Fire Command. On the other hand, he hadn't phoned home either, still too angry with Georgia. Last week at Old Faithful when he'd told Clare he needed to be flying, he'd been as shocked as if the words had appeared in a cartoon balloon. If he'd said that to Georgia, she would have shrieked. Saying it to another woman who understood his sense of loss made it feel doubly like betrayal.

The DC-7 he'd filled revved up in a low-pitched drone. The plane swept down the runway, gathering speed with each passing second. With the need to get back in the air an almost physical ache, Deering pictured himself in the cockpit with the patched concrete rushing past at over a hundred miles per hour.

The tanker's speed increased until it seemed it would be out of runway. The weight of two fifteen-hundred-gallon tanks riveted onto the aircraft's belly made it necessary for the rest of the plane to fly empty. The engines rose to a scream and finally, the pilot let the DC-7 have its nose. It swooped up and over the spiky mat of hundred-foot trees, that appeared as matchsticks from the air.

His chest ached and his anger at his wife renewed. Deering yearned for his *Georgie,* still in Yellowstone Lake. Not until next week did the insurance company plan to salvage it. As his claim had not been settled, the salvage outfit was gambling between two possible outcomes--payment from First Assurance or taking title to Deering's helicopter.

He refused to consider that, focusing instead on the moment when he would see his prize emerge from the lake. A complete overhaul would put off flying it until next year's season, something that should make Georgia the happiest woman in Idaho.

He couldn't help but think again of Clare. If he got a flying gig, she'd help him celebrate.

Another tanker landed and he recognized by its blue-on-white paint job that he knew the pilot. Adam Parker was a fellow veteran of Vietnam from the fixed-wing side. Adam and his copilot moved off the ramp for a smoke while Gary Cullen helped Deering drag the heavy hose. After coupling, it took under five minutes to load several thousand gallons of retardant, then quick-release.

When the crew came back to board, Deering said, "Hey there, Parker." He removed his goggles and bandanna so Adam could recognize him.

"Deering!" Adam's broad face, splotchy from the heat, broke into an astonished look.

"The hell you doin'?" He gestured at Deering's soaked coveralls and tapped his younger copilot on the shoulder. "Last time I saw this guy, he was flying his own helicopter."

Deering's face warmed. He hoped the other pilots would chalk it up to the scorching afternoon. "I had to ditch in Yellowstone Lake when the Shoshone came through Grant." He tried to sound casual, but he was sick of explaining the accident.

"Why aren't you flying for one of the other charters?" Adam asked.

"I talked to most of them and the word was they had help."

"Hell, talk to them again. Folks are gonna need relief."

"Yeah." Deering looked at the DC-7. "Even this lumbering giant is starting to look good."

Helicoptering could be a risky business, but flying tankers was even more dangerous. Taking their large size and heavy payloads so close to the ground, not one season had passed since they started in 1956 without the loss of one of the fifty or so tankers. Everybody in the close-knit community had lost at least one person they knew.

"It's a bitch out there," Adam declared. "Like clockwork, every day at noon the temperature inversion breaks and all hell with it."

"Tell me about it," Deering chimed in as though he were still flying.

"See that fellow there?" Adam pointed.

Deering recognized Demetrios Karrabotsos. The stately, silver-haired owner of Island Park Helicopters seemed to lead with his chin as he strode toward a mess tent. Deering had heard that he was a veteran of both Korea and Vietnam. Although he'd seen the older pilot from a distance, they had never met.

"I heard that Island Park is understaffed," Adam went on.

"I've tried to see him, but he's always out."

The tanker pilots climbed back aboard and Deering watched as before, until the blue and white fuselage became a silver spark against the sky. When he blinked and could no longer find it, he ignored a dark look from Gary Cullen, and dogged Karrabotsos toward the concession area.

Despite the warming day, he bought a Styrofoam cup of steaming coffee, sipped and found it bitter. Sighting his quarry straddling a flimsy folding chair, he approached. "Demetrios Karrabotsos?"

"Yeah?"

"Chris Deering, of Deering Charters over in Idaho." He tried to keep his outstretched hand steady and not to stare.

Although the older pilot must have once been a handsome man, his face and neck were deeply incised by shiny scars that had to be burns. In his bulky flight suit, he looked formidable.

"Heard of you." The voice was gravelly, as though flames had seared his vocal cords as well. Black eyes studied Deering until he felt like a target in a gunner's sights. "I go by Karrabotsos," he finally offered, belatedly shaking the hand Deering had in the air.

Pulling out a chair, Deering sat and held his cigarette by his side. "Pretty wild fire season."

"Worst since the blowup of 1910," Karrabotsos agreed.

"This drought and wind keep up . . . " Deering sipped his coffee nervously. More small talk might be in order, but, fingers crossed, he started his pitch. "I'm a one aircraft service and I've been grounded since I ditched my Bell."

"Heard that." Karrabotsos did not sound quite as neutral as before.

Deering took a deep drag on his Marlboro. "I wonder if you might need a pilot."

"Nope."

He exhaled smoke. "This is going to get worse before it gets better. Your craft . . . You have four of them, don't you, will be busy day and night. Even if you have a full staff . . . " He paused to allow Karrabotsos to admit he did not.

The two men stared at each other. It went on so long that Deering concluded either Adam was mistaken about Island Park being understaffed, or Karrabotsos did not want to admit it.

"Your men will still need relief," Deering said.

Karrabotsos studied him again with eyes shiny as ripe olives. "How'd you wind up in the drink?"

Sweat broke out in Deering's armpits. "Bad luck. We've all been there, especially us vets." He forced a smile to include Karrabotsos. If those burns had come from combat or a crash . . .

The other man's face stayed stony. "Word has it you had a park ranger on board. Seems this fellow told a bartender friend of his, who told a member of a tanker crew, who told one of my pilots . . ."

"What is this, some goddamn game of kids' gossip?" Deering's face warmed.

"He said you're reckless."

Georgia would have cheered.

"A dangerous hot shot," Karrabotsos went on, "who didn't need to trash a million dollars' worth of helicopter."

"Haywood's a fucking liar!"

"That may be." Karrabotsos shrugged. "I'm not willing to take a chance."

CHAPTER EIGHT
August 3

Clare woke in her cabin at Old Faithful. She checked her watch that she slept in from force of habit at the fire station. Ten minutes to her four-thirty alarm, not enough time to get back to sleep.

Disjointed snippets of dream played on her mind's dark canvas. While she slept, she'd visited a world that had existed before July 1. In the firehouse kitchen, she'd been helping Frank test drive a chili recipe for a charity cook-off.

Clare had looked up from slicing onions, her eyes watery.

Frank pointed with the knife he was using to cut sirloin. The laugh lines around his eyes crinkled. "Don't let the boys catch you being a crybaby."

Sage advice, even from a dream, and now upon waking, she planned to follow it. Especially with Sergeant Ron Travis, whose cocky manner said he was always alert for weakness.

In another midnight excursion, she and Frank had been showing a group of Special Olympian kids around the firehouse. As usual, one of the tour heights was sliding down the pole.

Frank waited at the bottom, ready to catch a slip of a girl around eight. Clare demonstrated wrapping legs and arms around the pole and supervised getting the girl in position. "Ready?"

A tight and wordless little nod stirred the child's strawberry blond bangs.

"Set . . . go." Clare let her slide.

A joyful trill echoed in the cavernous garage.

When Frank caught the girl, she metamorphosed into a boy of around two with hair like black silk. "He's with me now," Frank called, suddenly wearing full turnouts, air pack and mask. The apparatus bay began to fill with drifting smoke.

Every instinct said to slide and rescue Frank and the little boy. From somewhere in the haze, a woman's voice cried, "My baby! Please help my baby."

Clare hesitated. In that bare second, smoke blotted out everything. From below, Frank sounded far away. "Once you start down you can't come back."

In her bed at Old Faithful, gooseflesh pricked Clare's arms. With an exclamation of disgust, she threw back the covers and put her feet to the chilly boards. Morning could be frigid, especially with this coldness inside her.

She tried to conjure up Frank's face. There was his sturdy frame, his tough hands with thick fingers. His head, set atop shoulders strong from weightlifting, was a blur.

It was too soon to lose her picture of him. Her Timex's date indicated August already, just over a month, and if she couldn't see him now . . .

With pounding heart and a dry mouth, she tried to call up bits and pieces. Frank's ruddy cheeks bore spider veins from years of subjecting his fair complexion to the outdoors. There was the scar above his left brow, where he'd scoped himself with his Winchester while whitetail hunting with his Dad. All of sixteen, he'd refused to leave the field to get stitches.

No matter how she tried, Clare couldn't see Frank's eyes. In her nightmares, they bore the opaque sheen of death.

She'd talked to people whose dreams of the deceased comforted. Her mother Constance had told of awakening in bed with the palpable sensation of her father's arms around her. Frank had watched cancer waste a friend to emaciation, yet in his sleep, his friend came and shook his hand, restored to former health and vigor.

How much Clare would give for a sign from Frank, that he did not blame her.

Since the night she'd seen Steve Haywood drunk, she'd thought a bit about how people handled things they didn't want to face. Too bad he thought a bottle could solve his problems, whatever they were.

Steve woke to a pounding that matched the throbbing in his head.

He'd done it again.

Some folks stopped drinking by taking it one day at a time, but he simply kept on, one day and one drink at a time. Today brought yet another defeat.

The pounding continued.

Someone at the door, he realized through a fog. Whoever it was seemed damned determined.

The small, dark bedroom of his house in Mammoth Hot Springs spun. The bottom of this hangover was out there, waiting to give him the shakes and the sickness. It would seize him maybe twelve hours after he'd found himself playing inarticulate, discordant chords at Susan's piano, with tears pouring down his stubbled face.

How could he have let himself come to this? After Susan and Christa died, he'd thrown himself into his work back in Washington. A few months later, he'd discovered that only when he drank could he imagine what life would be like if they hadn't died.

Getting unsteadily to his feet, he pulled on a pair of shorts and a dirty T-shirt from the floor. The clock beside his picture of Susan said eleven-thirty. Ancient venetian blinds leaked light around the edges.

Jesus, he'd missed half the day.

He tried to think. Determined to take on Clare Chance's challenge to get sober, his resolve had remained in place until Saturday when he'd driven to Old Faithful. He had intended to present himself, sober, and thank her for saving him, no matter how worthless he felt. Returning without finding Clare, the four walls stared him down. He paced and wondered why he'd gone.

Alone on another Saturday night, while the park housing around him rang with familial laughter; rage surged like a specter through the drafty floorboards, seizing his throat.

How had he thought to live with Susan in her grave?

Going to the kitchen, he had reached beneath the sink and drawn forth a half-gallon of Old Crow.

As Steve entered the small living room dominated by Susan's black-lacquered grand piano, the hammering at his door grew louder. Half-full glasses and filthy dishes littered the tabletops. An empty half-gallon of Crow lay on the floor, fallen companion to one beside his bed. At some point, he'd shed his jeans and socks in a heap on the floor.

He did not remember doing that.

His caller was using his fist. "Steve? Are you there?" The male voice had a tinge of Oxford. The small square window in the front door revealed Moru Mzima's dark face, his high forehead edged in close-cropped black hair. The bars over the glass were the last vestiges of when the small building had been Fort Yellowstone's stockade.

With trembling hands, Steve turned the dead bolt and opened the door. Bright light stabbed and the old parade ground across the street blurred.

"Moru."

"I was about to break in."

Steve ran a hand through his hair and found it a greasy mess. "Ya know me," he tried at being casual. "I may be late on a Monday, but don't I
always get there?"

Moru flinched. He glanced into the darkened depths of the living room. "May I come in?"

After standing in the fresh air, Steve noticed the musty, sick smell inside. Nevertheless, he waved his fellow ranger in.

Moru looked doubtful, but he came in and folded his long legs to sit on Steve's brown leather couch trimmed in pine. He removed his ranger's hat, the summer straw model. After looking at the dirty dishes and a half-empty bottle of Seagram's gin that Steve had opened when the Crow ran out, Moru settled for placing the hat on his knee.

Steve shifted his weight from one foot to another, like he always did when he was uncomfortable. Susan had called it his elephant dance.

Moru met his eyes. "Shad Dugan sent me."

Oh, boy. Dugan, who worked directly for the Chief Ranger, was reputed to be a fair man. He demanded exacting work and Steve tried to deliver, through his hangovers and the occasional late morning.

"Dugan said to tell you this can't go on," Moru said levelly. "He's considering referring you to a treatment center to dry out."

Steve gasped as though Dugan were here and had punched him. "Oh, yeah? I suppose he was too busy to come over here and tell me this to my fucking face. He lives three goddamn doors away." Maybe it was a good thing Dugan had sent Moru with this little bomb, because it effectively prevented Steve from jumping one of his bosses and ending his career.

Moru worried his hat, turning it.

Steve felt like hitting something, but there was nothing near except the mirror-like surface of Susan's piano. He put a fist on it, holding himself up.

At the sight of Moru's stricken face, the rage went out of Steve. Moru was Ndebele, from rural Zimbabwe. His good fortune in getting educated in England and making it to the United States tended to make him unfailingly cheerful. Today, he looked sick.

"Ah, Jesus," Steve moaned. His head felt too heavy to hold up, so he slumped until it rested on the piano. Light reflections in the deep shining surface and the sudden realization that he stank of stale sweat made him dizzy.

As Steve concentrated on not throwing up, a steadying hand touched his shoulder.

"I don't want to leave." His voice broke. He wanted to stay in Yellowstone where the land brought peace.

"I am told that you must accept treatment or nothing changes," Moru said in a compelling yet soft tone. "Dugan would have come, but he was advised to send someone you view as your friend."

Moru *was* his friend. Steve was grateful for his coming to the Lake Hotel's bar after the chopper crash. He'd told Steve he'd found him slouched asleep in a wicker chair, wasting the view of water. Without a censuring word, he'd settled the tab and supported Steve on their way out of the lobby.

Moru squared his shoulders. "They said you must check yourself into treatment."

Steve couldn't breathe, imagining himself in a straitjacket, screaming and beating his head against the walls of a padded room. Someone would sit in the corridor recording his tears and profanity with an impassive hand. He should have known this was coming, but there were a lot of walls inside him, one for lying about his drinking, another for his father's slow death from leukemia, and the big iron one he kept

Susan and Christa behind.

Except when it rusted through.

"Why now, Moru? I've had these problems for years."

"You said you were running late for a Monday?" Moru kicked the empty bottle of Old Crow with a vicious swipe of his boot.

"Yeah."

"So, it's not Monday, Steve. It's Wednesday."

🔥🔥🔥

On Wednesday afternoon, Clare wiped sweat from her face with the standard issue bandanna. Thankfully, daylight and hours of toil had driven away the spirits of Frank and little Pham Nguyen. Behind her, a column of troops on their second training day marched through still heat toward West Yellowstone.

Things had gone well with the soldiers, despite their youthful armor of invincibility that reminded her of her daughter. Devon could be counted on to downplay danger, no matter whether it was inhaling cigarette smoke with the glamorous air of a fifties movie star, driving too fast even with Clare in the car, or diving into the shallow end of the Springwood Pool. The day Frank died, Devon had taken one look at Clare's face and hid out in her room. It had stung, as if her daughter hadn't cared or taken it seriously.

Ahead in the pines, Clare caught sight of something colorful and veered left.

"This way." Sergeant Travis pointed.

"I know." She tried to keep an edge out of her voice. "I merely wanted to see what was there." Around fifty yards away, a bright drape fluttered from a tree.

Without waiting for Travis's reply, she struck out walking toward the banner. As she drew nearer, the cloth became a faded housedress, drying in the wind. Several tents that might once have been yellow were pitched around the ashes of a campfire. A woman with braided black hair sat on the ground mending a pair of trousers.

Clare stopped and Sergeant Travis stepped on her heel. With a muffled oath, she held out a warning hand. "Migrant camp." This sheltered oasis seemed fragile.

Travis frowned.

"They come to work the summer season," Clare explained. "There's not enough housing in town so they live in squatters' camps. When the Forest Service finds them, they move until they're rousted again."

The woman scrambled to her feet, still clutching the pants. Even at a distance, Clare saw that her eyes were wide.

"Let's tell her to go, then," Travis said loudly.

"Leave her alone," Clare returned.

Travis's eyes were on a level with hers, a fact that obviously added to his Napoleon complex. He seemed to be evaluating whether she regarded her statement as an order.

"I'm heading to town." She turned and walked away, passing the curious group of soldiers. In fifteen minutes, she came out of the trees onto pavement at the west end of Yellowstone Avenue and heard the tramp of boots behind her.

West Yellowstone had the spare look of many a northern

community. Trailer homes and small, weathered houses sported bare yards growing nothing but stacks of firewood and parked snowmobiles. Clare suspected the place would look better beneath the softening blanket of winter.

In front of Fire Command, she arranged to meet Travis and the soldiers inside the park the following morning, when they would dig line on their first real fire.

Instead of leaving, Travis followed her toward the building. "I thought I'd report those migrants to somebody in the Forest Service."

Perhaps because she was from Texas and used to workers from south of the border, Clare was dead set against Travis. "Sergeant," she began. "Those poor folks mind their own business. They need the work and the town needs them during the summer season." The worn, yet freshly washed dress, and the way the woman mended the pants rather than let her husband or son wear them out . . .

Travis's chin came up, but before he could reply, she rushed on. "Second, and most importantly, the Forest Service and Park people have more than enough on their platter. My God, do you think you . . . the Army . . . would be here if the fires weren't out of control?"

The latch clanged as Travis pushed past into the building. "I'll let the authorities decide."

Clare followed him into the command center.

Gathered around the maps, at least thirty men were meeting. Fire behavior expert Ken Roberts had the floor, holding up his Texas Instruments calculator containing the program he had developed, appropriately named PREDICT.

Garrett, seated in the front row, had told Clare about the program. The three main factors used in predicting were fuels, weather and topography. It sounded simple, but fuels could be anything from grass to four hundred-year-old trees.

"Back in July," Roberts lectured, "the thousand-hour fuels had dropped to twelve percent moisture content. I refer to the practice of using four-foot lengths of lodgepole pine that would take at least a thousand hours to dry as an index. To give you an idea of how low that moisture content is, it's the same as kiln-dried lumber."

Clare imagined the forest as one huge stack of kindling.

"This week the numbers have dropped to below ten percent."

A new plastic overlay had been added to the fire map with a dashed red outline that encompassed a large area that had not yet burned. "According to our estimates," Roberts said, "the hundred-fifty thousand acres already consumed could potentially double before the season is out."

Clare felt as though she'd been punched. If Roberts were right, she might be another three weeks getting home to Devon.

"Okay, everybody." Garrett held up a hand. "There'll be a press conference in an hour. We'll release the predictions hammered out here."

Sergeant Travis clumped over to the maps.

Clare went to the kitchen refrigerator. She downed a six-teen-ounce bottle of cold spring water and opened another.

Garrett followed her. "What do you think of their predictions?"

"It's frightening to think we're going to face that much

more." She removed her hard hat, set it on the counter, and riffled her sweat-damp hair.

"It's going to get a whole lot worse than anybody imagines. Roberts's program is designed for surface fires, not crown fires. When you get winds like we're having and the fire leaps up into the treetops, all bets are off."

She gripped the plastic water bottle. Garrett had seen a lot and if he thought it was bad, she believed.

"How's it going with the Army?" He shot a glance at Travis. "Okay."

"That fellow giving you a hard time?"

"What makes you think so?"

"A hunch."

Clare smiled both at Garrett and the sight of Travis retreating from the center without speaking to anyone about the migrants. "How'd you guess?"

"You forget I'm in the minority, too."

She drank deeply of chilled water and looked up at Garrett's dark face. "You're right, I do forget."

He poured coffee and stretched to pluck a pack of Fig Newtons from a high shelf. She surmised from the way he cached his sweets that it was an honor when he offered one. She took a cookie and ate it while Garrett downed five. Scanning the room, she confirmed that he was the only black and she one of the few women present. "Speaking of minorities," she ventured, "my family tree is supposed to trace back to the Nez Perce."

Garrett studied her. "Most folks like you don't acknowledge red or black ancestors."

Clare flushed. "The local bookstores have only a few books about the Nez Perce."

"Try the archives," Garrett suggested. "At Park Headquarters in Mammoth."

❦❦❦

Steve's hands shook as he placed a stack of yellowed papers into a manila folder.

"Right in here." Walt Leighton's voice sounded in the outer room as he ushered someone into the basement archives.

Steve checked his watch and found it nearly five. The time reminded him that the sun was over the yardarm.

What in God's name was he going to do? He longed for the years when he'd been a man who appreciated a good red wine, for the time before his life had been shredded in a falling, flaming instant. Drink was impossible to kick on your own. He'd stopped hundreds of mornings, only to start again the same night. The hell of it was that if he wanted to stay in Yellowstone, he had no choice but to take the cure.

On the other hand, fire's assault on the land he loved made him determined to stay until the crisis ended.

Steve opened a new folder and considered a reprint of Jarred Ayad's article, "An Alternate Route for the Nez Perce through Yellowstone." He knew the Nez Perce story well, how in the summer of 1877 Chiefs Joseph, White Bird, and Looking Glass had refused to go onto the reservation outlined by the U.S. government. After hotheaded young men of the tribe avenged several murdered Nez Perce by killing white settlers, about seven hundred people set out on a freedom flight to Canada. The Army had pursued them through Yellowstone.

"Back here we have our library of books and videotapes." Walt's footsteps sounded loud in the narrow aisle between floor-to-ceiling shelves. The person who followed did not walk as heavily as he. "It's time to close, but since you drove all the way here, I can stay open a while."

"Where would I find information about an old homestead?" The husky voice might belong to a man or a woman. "Someplace close to the Tetons around 1900?"

"Not here, I'm afraid," Walt said. "You might ask at Grand Teton National Park, or at the Historical Society in Jackson. In the meantime, feel free to look around."

Walt retreated toward his office while the other late visitor to the archives shuffled along on the opposite side of a shelf of geology books. A moment later, Steve looked up to find Clare Chance frowning at him, her brows startling wings. Her face had darkened from the sun since he saw her last week.

"Dr. Haywood," she said, "you look like hell."

Clare did think Steve looked terrible, but she immediately regretted saying it. The paper he'd been studying wavered as he laid it down. Pale stubble on his chin outlined where he'd missed a patch shaving.

"You don't look bad yourself." Steve smiled. Despite the puffy bags around them, his gray eyes lighted. If he stayed off the sauce, he might turn out to be a decent looking fellow, with that blond hair and solid looking build.

"Thank you," she said.

He tilted the straight wooden chair on two legs against the basement wall. This was the first time she'd seen him in his ranger's uniform. Above his head, afternoon light shone through the window where he'd placed his summer straw hat on the sill.

"How's the fray?" he asked.

"Almost a hundred-fifty thousand acres." Because misery loved company, she went on, "The fire experts are predicting twice that."

Steve's dry-looking lips pursed into a whistle.

Clare looked at the stack of journals and books on the desk before him. "History?"

"The Nez Perce War of 1877."

She'd been a jock in school rather than a scholar, but she'd listened when her family's tribe was mentioned. That was her history, her blood that had made that trek. "My family has some Nez Perce in it."

"Walt's the historian." Steve gestured toward the front room. "But I've been searching the records about the Nez Perce. I'd be happy to share what I know."

Two hours later, she sat enthralled by the images he painted. If her great-grandfather had ridden with the Nez Perce on their freedom flight, he would have been seven years old. Mentally, she compared her callused hands to the tough planes of flesh that even a child must have wielded in those days. Superb horsemen and proud, even the young people had assisted in driving the herd.

"Those were difficult times." Steve showed her a book with black and white photos of tribal leaders and groups on the reservation. Was one of those barefoot boys her great-grandfather William Cordon Sutton? Even with his fine English name, society must have viewed him as tainted by his halfbreed mother's blood.

Steve pushed the papers away. "I'm starving." He looked at her as if deciding. "Let me buy over at the hotel restaurant." Casual, not like asking for a date.

He stood and extended a hand. Golden hairs flecked its back and his square-nailed fingers looked sturdy.

Clare slid her hand into his. As a scientist, he didn't bear the calluses that she did and she hoped he didn't notice. A tremor in his fingers reminded her once more of the splendid waste he was making of his life.

Her temptation to continue their conversation passed when he said, "A cold one would do about now."

"Thanks." She moved toward the door. "But I believe I'll get on the road."

CHAPTER NINE
August 4

In her cabin at Old Faithful, Clare lay in bed with the same trepidation she felt each night, fearing dreams of death awaited. It was past one and she had to be up at the usual four-thirty. After driving back from Mammoth, she should be asleep, but it was difficult. Some nights, she read until late, and others, she walked. Last Friday she'd been able to read under the spotlight of a full moon.

Escaping into a book was one kind of therapy, but after a while, she forced herself to put it aside. On her walks, she absorbed the peaceful surroundings and wondered where her life was going. In many ways, she was reminded of when she used to walk to school and weave elaborate fantasies of what she was going to be when she grew up.

At five, she had wanted to win Olympic gold, already interested in swimming and other sports. At ten, the goal was to be a famous heart surgeon like the men in South Africa and Houston who saved lives. When she'd passed the fire station and had her face washed by Cinders their Dalmatian, she had never imagined ending up in a place like that.

But her summer nights' dreams dredged forgotten memories of stopping in at the station and sampling stews concocted by a kindly older fireman who reminded her of Frank. Of becoming a sort of Bellaire Fire Department mascot and riding a ladder unit in the Fourth of July Parade. Of hearing the alarm and seeing the men—no women then—pile on their equipment and drive away to the blended wail of sirens. She had watched them until they were out of sight.

This evening at Old Faithful, Clare had made the two-mile round trip to the Morning Glory Pool through a gray landscape lit by stars. On the way back, she'd had a private viewing of Castle Geyser's pale foaming rush against the darker sky. For the first time in years, she'd thought about having someone to walk with her.

In the early days of their marriage, when Houston's summer heat gave way to sultry evening, she and Jay used to take strolls. Cicadas sawed their sharp song and water bugs skated on Buffalo Bayou's low water. At first, Jay carried Devon in a pack against his chest and later he pushed the stroller. As their daughter grew, she'd run free, taking fifty steps to one of her parents', flitting to investigate a rose or chase a lightning bug.

Devon had been the first to drop out of their walks, pleading homework, but Clare suspected TV. Then Clare moved from P.E. teacher to basketball coach with evening games and practices. As their lives diverged, those ritual strolls had slipped away almost without her notice.

Come to think, on nights when Jay was home, he'd carried on alone. Looking back, she wondered if he'd been meeting Elyssa Hendron or some other woman years before she suspected.

Over a week, and she hadn't heard from Deering. Another man who'd dropped in for a brief test drive and evidently decided to purchase another model. Normally, that didn't bother her, but with him, she'd felt a spark. On the other hand, maybe he was busy flying for another charter service. Women were allowed to take the initiative nowadays, too. Someday when she was at West Yellowstone, she could go to the airport and see about getting a message to him.

It was a shame about Steve Haywood. Where Deering was bold and cocky, Steve had a kind of vulnerability that made her want to put a smile into his eyes.

❧❧❧

Steve opened his eyes to darkness. As the familiar shadows of his bedroom furniture seemed to harden before his eyes, he clung to wisps of dream.

When all else disappeared, the ghost of a sweet face remained. Not Susan, but Clare, who'd looked earnest and caring when he'd opened his eyes beside Yellowstone Lake. He focused on her, nut brown from the sun, tousled short hair falling over her forehead. He'd really wanted to have dinner with her, but what could he expect after the wonderful impression he'd made thus far?

Rolling over, he realized that he wasn't going to be able to get back to sleep. Even in darkness, he envisioned the picture of Susan on the bedside table.

What would she think if she knew he dreamed of another woman?

His bare feet found summer's grit on the hardwood hall floor as he headed for the kitchen without turning on a light. There the window revealed a streetlamp's bluish glow between the rows of park housing and storage buildings. The clock on the fifties-vintage stove ticked, its hands pointing to three-forty.

Susan lay beneath the earth, dust to dust. Her lithe body, her spirited hands that coaxed music from everything, including, and most especially, him--that was but a memory.

He opened the cabinet beneath the sink. The last bottle in the house was the gin that had been on the coffee table when Moru came by. Steve preferred whiskey or bourbon, but he swallowed anyway, a deep convulsive contraction. And again.

Susan was ancient history, some black-and-white daguerreotype, no more alive than a picture of Chief Joseph of the Nez Perce or the stark image of charred trees against the night.

Ashes to ashes. The liquor burned and he drank again. The pungent aroma was hot with alcohol and laced with the exotic licorice, lemon, and juniper that gave gin its distinctive nose.

Why are you doing this to yourself? Clare's eyes were pools of sadness that had reached to include him.

Susan would have wanted him to live, not to sleepwalk through his existence.

Steve gripped the edge of the sink with one hand while he poured, hearing the gin gurgle down the drain.

❦❦❦

"Up early, Steve?" Ranger Shad Dugan said from behind his desk.

It was just past six. In full uniform, Dugan had probably been working since five, moving his mountain of paperwork. A big sandy-haired man with a ruddy face, Dugan had over twenty-five years in park management and told everyone that red tape was the worst part of his job.

"We need to talk," Steve said.

Dugan removed his tortoise-shell reading glasses and indicated a chair.

Steve sat and held his coffee in hands that already trembled. That didn't usually hit until noon, but pouring the booze down the drain instead of his throat came with the consequence. "Moru came to see me yesterday."

Dugan nodded. "What'd you decide?"

This was going to be tricky. How to explain that he wanted to change, but the last thing he needed was one of those funny farm places. The ones where you were miraculously cured as soon as the maximum number of days on your insurance expired.

"I know I've got a problem," he began, "and that something's gotta give."

"That's a start." Dugan might have been playing poker, for all the expression in his eyes.

"Here's the thing, though . . . I want to stay in the park this summer. With the fires, I feel like I'm needed." Steve tried to go slowly, but the words tumbled out. "I would hate to see the natural burn policy scrapped without a proper review."

"There'll be plenty of time to fight over that when this is over. Until then, you can consider it put aside."

"We'll need information about burn patterns and how they affect the different vegetation types. Some of the research Moru and I are starting on burns and their recovery should finally come to fruition."

Dugan sighed and turned his mug in steady hands. "I was afraid you'd say that."

Fear clutched at Steve. That padded room was looking more real by the minute.

His boss swiveled toward the sun coming over the long shoulder of Mount Everts. Slanting cliffs of thick outcrop marked the face of the mountain that bordered the east side of Gardner River canyon. The river wound down to join the rushing Yellowstone in the gateway town of Gardiner. In 1959, the United States Geological Survey had settled on two different spellings for the river and the town.

Dugan steepled his fingers and let the silence lengthen. Then he cleared his throat before speaking. "I thought about what I'd do if you wanted to stay."

Steve's heart thudded. If he got canned, where would he go?

"I can't blame you." Dugan turned back to him, unsmiling. "Nothing like these fires has ever happened in Yellowstone and I wouldn't want to miss it, either." He stood and walked from behind his desk. On the wall hung a clipboard, holding the fire maps that had been released daily since July 25 by the Unified Area Command. Dugan put a finger on a spot in the northeast quadrant of the park, midway between Canyon and Tower Roosevelt. "I've got a man on Washburn that needs relief."

Mount Washburn, southwest of Mammoth, rose to ten thousand feet, a natural vantage point for a fire tower. "You can go up," Dugan offered, "but I need someone I can count on to call out every new smoke. Cold turkey on the booze."

"I'll go today." Steve tried to sound confident.

Dugan clapped a hard hand on his shoulder. "Let me warn you. If anybody who talks to you on the radio thinks you're drinking, I'm gonna send a chopper and pluck you off that mountain." His broad face might have been carved of Mount Everts' sandstone. "You won't stop until you're out of Yellowstone for good."

Clare watched the troops from Fort Lewis dig line on their first trip into Yellowstone. If she breathed deeply, there was almost a hint of moisture in the air, but that was illusion, the last of the morning dew evaporating in a forest of 'kiln dried lumber.'

On the North Fork front, the fire burned quietly through duff. Tendrils of smoke curled, the only sign that combustion was taking place beneath the carpet of needles.

There was no need for Clare to be on edge, but another bout of nightmares had her keeping a close eye on her charges. Garrett Anderson had chosen a training area that should be safe, even if the prevailing winds kicked up strongly. Her plan was to work through midday and be out of range when afternoon heat took the lid off the pressure cooker.

It was training, but somebody could still get hurt.

After Frank had been buried, Clare had not returned to the station, making only one weekend trip to work at the Texas A & M fire school. Since Buddy Simpson, her boss there, had made the call to Garrett Anderson, she felt she owed it to him not to plead the stress that was keeping her away from the station house.

Even so, she had awakened early on Saturday morning for the two-hour drive and hoped for a weather cancellation. When she arrived in College Station, the sky, blue-white with Gulf Coast humidity, promised a scorching day.

By the time she finished briefing the volunteer fire department of Toro Canyon, Texas, it was at least a hundred degrees. Each labored breath felt like the air was strained through a wet towel. Although she wasn't going to fight the fire today, she dressed out alongside the others. Well-worn running shoes were exchanged for rubber boots, the fire coat of rough Nomex, snapped and clipped. Her short hair, already sweaty at the back of her neck, went under the Houston Fire Department helmet where it would swiftly saturate.

The loading terminal was only one of a number of scenarios used for training firefighters from all over the state. Behind the tanks stood the mock-up of a train. Down the road were authentic replicas of a ship's deck, an eighteen-wheeler, and a faux apartment building. Each exercise had a staging area, an open-walled shelter used for lectures and storing the students' gear.

Clare had done most of the exercises and she knew well

the feeling that the dragon was about to bite you on the ass. She saw it now in the faces of the Toro Canyon team; a heightened awareness while trying to look like they could give a shit.

She steeled herself and turned the propane valve to light the loading terminal. With a whoosh of ignition, orange flames billowed around the metal tanks and catwalks, accompanied by the open-throated roar of escaping gas.

Six firemen wearing heavy canvas coats, turnout pants and rubber boots tightened up on the hose. The man in front popped the valve and a fog of spray kept the flames away from them.

The team moved forward in a phalanx with their helmeted heads tipped down. One step, two, they counted in unison, until they were almost beneath the tank's overhanging catwalk. Fifty feet away, another group of firefighters wielded their own hose, focusing a stream on the rear of the tank.

No matter how many times Clare watched an exercise on the simulators, it was never the same. Even with identical physical equipment and fuel, the air temperature, humidity and winds made all the difference. Now, on the two-story control tower that overlooked Brayton Field, an orange windsock signaled a wind shift.

"Back it up, back it up," she shouted to the first team over the roar of the fire. "Do it now!"

The group on the hose retreated, one steady, controlled step at a time, toward a flight of metal stairs leading fifteen feet up to an elevated walkway. Before they could get out of range, flames billowed down over the catwalk rail and enveloped the first three persons on the hose. The man in front jerked his head like a dog shaking off water.

"Power cone," Clare ordered.

He twisted the nozzle from the fog setting to a narrower stream. Clouds of steam rose and wiped out her view of the team.

After what seemed a long time, but was really three seconds, the heavy-set fireman who had manned the front of the hose staggered into the open. Big Jerry Dunn, the Toro Canyon Chief, stripped off his hat with its clear acrylic face protector and dropped it. He clutched his hands to his face.

The exercise fell apart. Clare ran to shut off the valve and the last of the fuel burned more quietly.

The Toro Canyon boys helped Jerry to a wooden bench beneath the open-walled shelter. She bent to look at the burn that covered his lower left cheek and chin. "Second degree."

Thank God. In the moment when she'd seen Jerry abandon the drill, she'd imagined the worst. Another man down on her watch, and these guys probably knew she'd been the one with Frank Wallace when he died. News traveled fast in the community of fire.

What could she have done differently? She'd turned the valves the prescribed angle to release the propane at the appropriate pressure, had called the change from fog to power cone when the wind shift called for a stronger stream.

Jerry got up heavily and took off his canvas jacket and turnout pants to reveal jeans and a navy T-shirt that proclaimed *Love a Firefighter* in white letters. He gulped water out of a paper cone Clare filled from an Igloo jug and dumped a cupful over his sweat-soaked reddish hair. Jerry was perhaps thirty-five, but he looked like a big kid.

Opening her emergency kit, she felt the men's eyes on her back. She straddled the dusty bench next to Jerry and pulled out a piece of gel-soaked gauze. Everyone here was as qualified as she to administer this kind of first aid, even if her Houston training and experience outstripped being volunteers in a smaller town.

Gently, she swabbed the dust and sweat away from Jerry's burn, being careful not to break the dime-sized blister that had swollen at the center of the reddened patch on his cheek.

Jerry looked at Clare. "Tell me more about what we should have done out there."

"Like I told you in the briefing, communicate, communicate."

"That fire was pretty noisy." Jerry furrowed his forehead. Beads of sweat stood on his skin and Clare felt droplets trickling down her side.

Fifty yards away, smoke began pouring through chinks in the metal shutters of a two-story brick building. It made her think about her own trip through that sealed mausoleum, a place she'd gotten into and thought she would never escape. Suffocating smoke turned out the lights and a hand on the hose was the only lifeline.

"Think about the search and rescue exercise you did in the smoke house," she told Jerry. "You and your teammate were in constant communication. 'Checking the corner, nothing here, moving left, at the doorframe . . . ' Even though you could see the loading terminal better, it didn't take away the need for shouting to the guys on the other hose."

Jerry nodded, but he didn't look like he'd heard anything except a platitude.

"Seriously," Clare said, wondering again if they had heard she was the one with Frank when he died. Some of them might even have attended the funeral. "When you're out in charge of your crew at Toro Canyon, remember that safety is the number one priority, just like the Red Cross teaches in their lifesaving courses." Along with college competitive swimming, Clare had been a water safety instructor. She'd guarded at a Texas camp, watching kids and water moccasins mingle from a creosoted dock, rainbow slicks on the sluggish river.

"The last thing you want to do, Jerry, as a lifeguard, is to jump in the water and put two persons at risk. In fire, the same rules apply, even when there are victims in a burning structure."

Straight from the manual. It sounded good in the bright summer sun, but when flames had licked the sky from burning apartments, she had felt the same spirit that always seized her before cleaving the water in a racing dive.

She and Frank had never considered leaving Pham Nguyen to die.

CHAPTER TEN
August 5

The next morning found Clare wondering how to spend a day off. She began by running a few miles on Old Faithful's trails, but her restless energy did not dissipate. Caught up in the momentum of firefighting, she found time on the sidelines a waste.

Midday found her in the West Yellowstone Smokejumpers' Base visiting with her new acquaintance Sherry Graham. One of a small minority of women in the elite rank, Sherry was putting the final touch to a parachute pack on a long waxed table when the base alarm sounded.

The first shock of the noise gave Clare a surge of adrenaline. She had to tell herself it wasn't for her. With the outward calm she recognized from her own work, Sherry finished affixing a piece of masking tape with the date, her name, and certification number. She'd told Clare it took years of training before a Smokejumper earned the right to pack a chute.

Putting her finished product onto the shelves covering one wall of the workroom, Sherry said, "I'm spotter on this run.

Wanna go?" A smile brightened her round face.

Clare shoved off the counter and felt the familiar excitement that she'd not experienced in over a month. "Right behind you."

She followed Sherry's sturdy frame past two men repairing chutes on industrial sewing machines, through the three-story loft where chutes hung when they weren't packed for use, then down the hall decorated with photos of past seasons' teams. Just like at the fire station, the first stop in any run was the restroom, in case it was a long time to the next opportunity.

In the ready room, Sherry and two male jumpers rummaged in wooden bins for Nomex clothing.

"Clare, this is Randy's rookie season." Sherry introduced her to a young man buttoning his shirt over compact, taut-looking muscles. "He's studying Forestry at the University of Montana."

"And Hudson." Sherry went on to a short, stout man with hands like a prizefighter's.

"Pleased to meet you, ma'am." A scatter of gray marked Hudson's temples. "I'm a career jumper. Wait tables on Maui, spring and fall. Winters I run snowmobile tours." He described his vagabond life with pride.

The jumpers pulled two-piece, beige Kevlar suits over their fire retardant clothing and stuffed their pockets with granola packs and Hershey bars. Hudson stowed a dog-eared copy of Virgil's *Aeneid*. Their parachutes went on next, secured with a network of black straps cinched up tight over their shoulders and around their thighs. As spotter, Sherry would be coming back without jumping, but she also put on the complete outfit with main and reserve parachutes in case she fell out of the plane.

Clare watched, comparing their gear with her turnouts, air pack, and axe.

The pilot, a lanky dark-haired man with a red handlebar mustache, smoked a preflight Winston. "We're headed to the northeast corner of Yellowstone to a plume sighted from outside the park," he told Clare. "If they're only sending two jumpers, this one's gonna be a cakewalk."

Sherry had her gear on first and while they waited, she told Clare about the Smokejumpers' running contest to land closest and cleanest to whatever target the spotter chose. How if they landed in a tree they wanted to spread their canopy square over the top, so they didn't slip and slide down through the limbs, or 'burn through' as they called it.

Despite the advent of helicopter use in firefighting, the jumpers were never picked up. After they'd felled and buried burned trees and waited until the ashes were cold, they hiked out to the nearest highway. On these treks that sometimes took several days they carried out everything they had jumped in with. In training, the brutal march with over a hundred pounds separated successful candidates from washouts.

All three jumpers secured blue helmets with protective metal grates over their faces. Looking to Clare like space warriors from a sci-fi movie, they headed toward their waiting twin-engine Beechcraft B99.

While they checked equipment, Clare climbed in and sat forward on the bench seat. Tape-reinforced corrugated boxes strapped to metal tracks cramped her knees. She'd been told they contained water, food, Pulaskis, shovels, and sleeping bags.

The heavily laden Smokejumpers piled aboard. As the turboprops spooled up and the plane began to taxi, Clare realized the rear door had been removed. Sherry sat in front so that she could gauge the approach to the fire and decide the best landing target.

The jumpers clipped their static lines to a cable along the floor, so if anyone fell out the line would open their primary chute.

When they reached the end of the West Yellowstone runway, Hudson said, "Hi, ho." Through the metal mask, Clare saw a big smile on his ruddy face. He hummed a bit more of the Seven Dwarfs song about going back to work. It made Clare think what her first day back at the station in Houston would be like . . . she'd probably be whistling in the dark as well.

The engines revved into a whine. Wind rushed through the open door and the noise forestalled further efforts at conversation. Clare had always enjoyed flying and found the sensation of lift-off with fresh air in her face exhilarating.

Once aloft, she had a good view of the gently rolling terrain around the town, with mountains to the west and east. To the south, she identified Yellowstone's boundary by the line where the timber clear-cuts stopped and unbroken forest began. She recognized the area where she had taken Sergeant Ron Travis and his troops for training. In a few days, she'd have a new group of soldiers and she hoped the cocky bantam leader would have a difficult time on the line. He'd continued to be outright rude, even as she held her tongue.

The plane banked around and headed into the park. Within minutes, the terrain began to climb and they sighted the craggy pinnacles of Bighorn Peak. To the east, towering columns of smoke built skyward from the Fan Fire. Hudson bumped Clare with his elbow and shouted, "The Fan started on June twenty-fifth, back when they were letting lightning-caused blazes burn. Looks like maybe they should have let us at it."

Sherry called, "How about the North Fork? We got there twenty minutes after it was spotted, but it was seventy-five acres gone. We had to abort."

The smoke they were headed for wafted from a canyon on Bighorn Peak. Within the valley, the midafternoon air was turbulent.

Sherry conferred with the pilot through headphones. Finally, she pointed and nodded, then climbed back between the Beech's front seats, squeezing past Clare and the others. As she began to shout her briefing from aft of the open door, the plane lurched in a pocket of rough air. "The drop site is downhill from the smoke, about three hundred yards. A clearing along the ravine looks grassy, so I'd suggest it as your target. Since the air's tricky I've asked for a recon pass before you jump."

Hudson leaned to looked at the rising smoke. "That doesn't look like a two-man job."

"Radio if you need reinforcements," Sherry told him. "We're short all around this summer." West Yellowstone was the smallest of the Smokejumpers' bases, with fewer than twenty trained and ready to parachute.

They flew up the drainage and made the first pass over the target at about a thousand feet. To check the wind Sherry tossed a pair of weighted streamers, fluttering banners of pink and yellow that drifted smartly up the canyon.

Clare studied Hudson's face through the grille on his helmet. He was a pro, yet as they flew, his songs and jokes had quieted. Now that he'd seen the fire, his expression was taut.

They came into the valley again and Sherry called, "Randy, you're on deck."

He crouched in the doorway, Hudson behind him. Sherry checked Randy's chute to make sure a red thread was still in place, signifying no one had tampered with it since a certified packer had placed it in queue. Here was where the element of trust came in, as men and women jumped with chutes packed by other team members.

It was the same in the department. When Frank had asked her to back him up on the hose, he'd placed his life in her hands.

"See you in a few days," Randy told Sherry. He sounded a little shaky, even for a rookie. The Beech's engines seemed to whine more loudly as it entered the steep-walled valley. Sherry had told Clare that when they exited at one hundred ten miles per hour, it was like hitting a wall. The jumpers preferred their other plane, a Twin Otter that flew at a more sedate ninety.

Clare's heart pounded as though she were the one about to jump out of a perfectly good airplane.

Sherry tapped Randy on the calf. He vanished through the doorway.

Behind the plane, his thirty-foot round canopy, striped in blue, yellow and white, opened like a graceful flower. The static line flapped and Sherry drew it back inside along with the deployment bag that had held his main chute.

Looking out the window, Clare saw Randy's parachute, floating toward the spiky green forest. She couldn't see the clearing Sherry had spotted.

"Hudson," Sherry called.

A tap on the leg and he left an empty doorway to the sky. Clare expected to see his canopy unfold, but he disappeared without a sign of deployment. Sherry hung on and stuck her head out the door to look back. The wind whipped strands of her brown hair free from her helmet.

"Four . . . five . . . " Sherry shouted. "Reserve!" Her cry came with the unfurling of Hudson's secondary parachute, a smaller twenty-eight foot round that lacked the steering capacity of the main.

The Beech hurtled up over the wall of rock at the canyon's head. Clare didn't see the men land. As they circled back, she put her weight behind shoving supply boxes down the tracks toward the door. Sherry checked the fifteen-foot diameter cargo chute and stuck her head out the door to see whether she could drop the load in the targeted clearing.

With a heavy drone, the plane dove earthward. Huge rocks and the sharp texture of the pines had looked much more benign from higher up. Just when it seemed that they would crash, the Beech's nose lifted and they flew up the ravine at two hundred feet. If Clare had thought it turbulent before, she'd not realized how wild the ride could be. The pilot flew the big twin-engine plane like a fighter, dipping and turning to follow the terrain.

"There!" Sherry pushed and the cargo tumbled out, its chute unfurling just in time to prevent the boxes from smashing.

As they gained altitude and flew over the valley one last time, Sherry pointed out the jumpers. Randy had landed in the clearing, along with the cargo. Hudson's smaller chute hung on the side of a tree, not far uphill.

"Should have capped it," Sherry said. As the plane banked away from Bighorn Peak, she grinned. "All over for them now but the drudgery."

Clare relaxed and watched the mushroom clouds from the larger fires as the sun-warmed air allowed the convection currents free rein. Each day, she had to remind herself that a building thunderhead did not promise rain.

Sherry reached for her Bendix radio with a frown. "Come in?"

An excited male voice came over the airwaves. "Hudson's bleeding bad!"

"Randy?" Sherry asked.

"He landed in a tree and burned through. Fractured his femur and severed an artery."

Sherry looked forward at the pilot and Clare saw her rapid calculation. "We'll have to radio for a chopper."

🔥🔥🔥

Deering smoked a Marlboro and looked around the broad West Yellowstone ramp. The usually secluded area at the north end of the runway had undergone dramatic change in the past few weeks.

The tanker traffic had become constant and the Smokejumpers were making frequent runs. After almost two weeks on the ground, Deering still couldn't believe that no one wanted him to fly.

The chop of rotors approached. By the Island Park logo, a gold-rimmed oval with a black helicopter, this one belonged to Demetrios Karrabotsos. Deering's yearning ache gave way to anger at Steve Haywood for carrying tales.

The Huey's pilot, a bowlegged man Deering did not recognize climbed down, went to a Dodge pickup, and drove off.

Deering put out his smoke. Looking around to make sure Karrabotsos was not in sight, he began a leisurely walk toward the helicopter. The nostalgic fuel smell made him hurt inside.

From the corner of his eye, he noticed the Smokejumpers' plane coming in hot from the runway. The white Beech with orange stripes careened up in front of the base building. Almost before it stopped, a small woman in khaki shorts and a tank top leaped out of the open rear doorway. Deering recognized Clare Chance, sun-pinkened and animated.

"There!" Clare pointed at Deering. She broke into a run toward him. "We need you to fly us into the park to rescue an injured Smokejumper."

The old familiar surge propelled his heart and the rest of him into action. He turned, as if to leap into the cockpit.

Clare slammed her fist into the palm of her other hand. "Let's go."

Deering felt like she'd punched his stomach. Without an aircraft, he was worse than useless.

🔥🔥🔥

Clare waited for Deering to move, but he stared at the Island Park helicopter like he didn't know what it was.

"It's not mine," he said dully. She knew his helicopter had gone in the lake, but thought he was flying this machine. Then she realized he wore jeans and a T-shirt rather than a flight suit.

Adrenaline surging like she was at a fire, she looked around the ramp.

"The pilot drove off," Deering said. "You might find the owner in that trailer. Unless he's out flying."

"I'll go, Sherry," she told her.

"I'll get our rescue gear." Sherry ran away toward the base.

Clare set out for the trailer. Even with his long legs, Deering lagged her.

Three charter companies shared the rental trailer on the edge of the ramp. The Island Park logo was in the middle below Yellowstone Charter's red and black lettering and above the bold blue triangle of Eagle Air.

Clare raised her hand to knock. Deering said, "Just go in."

She opened the door. "Excuse me." She stopped, stunned at the facial scars on the man behind the desk. She recovered. "I'm looking for whoever owns that Huey out front."

"That would be me. I'm Karrabotsos." Calmly, he sipped coffee, keeping his salt and pepper head bent.

A muscle in the side of her jaw tensed. "The Smokejumpers have a man down on Bighorn Peak."

Karrabotsos looked at her tank top and shorts. "You're not a Smokejumper."

"I'm a firefighter and EMT from Houston. I flew with the Smokejumpers today as an observer." She tried to sound professional. "Our pilot radioed and found that all the choppers in the area are either specialty-rigged or farther away than yours."

Even after hearing the story, the older man's expression was unyielding.

"If you're worried about getting paid, I'll pay you myself." Her voice went hard.

"You don't know what you're talking about, little lady," Karrabotsos rasped. "I'd be pleased to help, but I can't." Putting both hands on the edge of the desk, he pushed back his chair to reveal a cast on his right foot. "Dropped a box of fire camp rations and broke three bones."

"What about your pilot?" Deering asked. "Can't you get him back here?"

"He's gone to Pocatello. Had a call that his five-month-old baby is in the emergency room."

"For God's sake, let Deering go," Clare said. "The jumper severed an artery in his leg."

Karrabotsos's gaze locked with Deering's. A glance at the two of them said there was something very wrong.

"Look," she said. "How can you sit by while this war escalates from burning trees to threatening the men that fight it?"

Karrabotsos shifted his eyes back to hers for a long speculative moment.

Finally, he turned back to Deering. "You understand that I don't want to do this," he said, "but if we're going to save that man's life, you'll have to fly."

Although it had been less than thirty minutes since Clare had been in the high valley on Bighorn Peak, everything looked different.

Where the Beech had swept over at one hundred ten miles per hour, Deering maneuvered the chopper more slowly. Despite Sherry's repeated attempts to raise Randy on the radio, they had not established communication since landing in West Yellowstone.

"Where?" Deering asked through their headsets. The wind's rising fury made the Huey shudder and dance.

Sherry peered through the rear window, her cupped hands against the glass. "Can't see them."

The pink and yellow streamers they'd dropped to test the wind had threaded through the tops of the pines. Clare caught a flash of blue below and realized that it was either Randy or Hudson's helmet. "There they are."

"I'll let you off in that clearing." Deering pointed to the

landing place where the cargo boxes lay. On a fifteen-degree slope, the open space was bisected by a dry rocky channel that probably carried snowmelt in spring.

Deering brought them lower. The Huey's engines whined and the tail rotor chopped small limbs, raising the pungent scent of evergreen.

"It's okay, ladies," he said calmly. "Just making a little lodgepole salad." When the skids were about three feet from the ground, he directed, "Better hop off here. If I set her down, we'll never get out."

Sherry removed her headset and shoved open the rear door. A blast of wind caught Clare in the face where she sat behind Deering. She tried to calm her jitters, comparing jumping out of a hovering helicopter to something she knew. Like working the high ladders or rappelling down a building, one of the exercises she taught at A & M.

On impulse, she touched Deering's shoulder. Sinew and bone moved fluidly beneath her hand as he controlled the chopper. His eyes stayed forward. "Hang on until I steady her."

There was no choice here, any more than in Houston when she had to go into a burning building. She tossed her headphones into the rear seat.

Sherry was already out the door, crouching on the skid with one hand around the vertical support. She leaped, landing on the uneven slope in what Clare recognized as the parachutist's roll. Scrambling to her feet, Sherry held out her arms to catch the folding stretcher Clare tossed.

Hot wind from the rotors beat down. Clare hung on the downhill skid, maybe ten feet above the ground.

More limbs fell from the trees. Rotor wash flattened the grass. She jumped.

The pit of her stomach lifted. Feet first, she hit and collapsed to absorb the shock. Sherry was already heading uphill, her back barely visible through the whirling cloud of dust.

Clare followed. The Huey's engines went to a higher pitch and then the sound gradually receded.

The trees grew thick, with no more than a few feet between them. Clare's bare legs and arms were soon covered in black dirt and resin. Wearing light hikers rather than her thick fire boots, she kept slipping on the pine straw.

She had lost sight of the fire, but the smoke reminded her she wasn't wearing fire retardant clothing. It hadn't seemed important when every second counted to get to Hudson.

Randy's relief at seeing her and Sherry was evident on his small, tight features. He had opened Hudson's Kevlar jumpsuit and his hand pressed high on the injured man's leg, shutting down the femoral artery in the groin area. Below the break, blood soaked the beige coveralls.

Hudson lay still. His right leg canted at an oblique angle above the knee.

"Is he conscious?" Clare asked.

"Unfortunately." Hudson opened his eyes.

She smiled and bent close. His pupils looked normal, constricted in the forest's filtered sunlight. "We'll get you out of here as soon as possible." Turning to Randy, she instructed, "Keep pressure on."

"Uh, oh!" Sherry pointed. Not thirty yards away, small flames licked at the duff beneath the trees.

"Maybe you better do something about that," Clare suggested as mildly as she could.

Sherry was off, running toward the supply boxes. Randy stayed in place, an uncertain look on his face. With a glance at Hudson's grim expression, she instructed, "Go ahead and let go. I need to see what we've got."

He removed his hand. A bright, arterial stream pulsed with each beat of Hudson's heart.

Clare shot another look at the fire. There wasn't time to clear a firebreak. Ditto for stabilizing the bleeding and straightening the leg into the proper packaging for transport.

"Randy!" she demanded. "Give me that line you guys use for rappelling."

He pulled a coil from the calf pocket of his jumpsuit.

"Cut me four feet."

He withdrew a folding knife from his jumpsuit pocket.

"A tourniquet," Clare told him as he cut, "just until we get on the chopper."

Sherry was back, carrying shovels and Pulaskis. The fire had taken another five yards.

"Change of plans," Clare said. She tied a constricting rope on Hudson's leg just above the break. Sherry unfolded the stretcher.

As soon as the bleeding slowed, Clare put a hand on Hudson's chest. "We're gonna have to move you. Are you aware of any other injuries?"

The blue helmet swiveled negative.

Clare wished she had another choice for her patient.

SUMMER OF FIRE

♦♦♦

It was flying with the door open, Deering realized, that drove him mercilessly back to the Ia Drang valley. As soon as Clare and Sherry had shoved back the heavy metal frame, the wopping had invaded his skull.

The tight little clearing on Bighorn Peak looked for all the world like one of the LZs Deering had gone into 'slick', sweating because his ship didn't carry guns and the gunships were someplace else when there were wounded to be ferried.

He flew the Huey around the high valley on Bighorn Peak, trying not to think about going back down there. No time for dread, though, for he sighted three people carrying a stretcher on the treacherous slope.

Mentally Deering measured, even though he'd already been in the clearing once. He figured five times the rotor diameter of forty-eight feet. Though he'd hoped the injured man was in decent shape and he might not have to set down, the blood he saw staining the victim's coveralls called up Plan B.

Deering had told Clare they wouldn't be able to take off if he landed, but he'd been in tighter spots, and under enemy fire. He would never forget the sound of bullets striking metal. The high-pitched ping had made him jump the first few hundred times until he realized that if he heard, it had missed him.

Deering saw Clare shield her eyes from the sun. Her steady look said she trusted him.

He went in.

The second approach produced fewer impacts with the trees, for he'd done quite a bit of wood chopping already. As he hovered at about three feet, Clare motioned to the others to bring the injured man forward.

Deering waved her off and landed on the flattest spot he could find. Even so, the Huey canted strongly to the side.

Clare was last aboard and Deering got a look at the fierce concentration on her sun-browned face. The door slammed. Sherry's hand gripped his shoulder. "Go!"

Now was the time when déjà vu would come in handy. Deering ran up the RPMs and picked the Huey up about five feet, guiding the hover backward until the tail rotor slashed the pines. At some level, he registered that Clare and Sherry had acquired their headphones and were discussing a shot of morphine.

With a few hundred feet of open space, Deering lifted the tail and gathered speed. There wasn't enough room to accelerate in a straight line so he went into as tight a turn as he could.

Flying in a circle around the clearing, he managed on the third go-round to achieve lift speed, about twenty miles per hour.

The aircraft lurched, then leaped into the sky.

He changed frequency to let West Yellowstone Control know he was coming, then let Sherry talk with the Smoke-jumpers' base. A larger team of six had been dispatched to dig a line around the fire.

Concentrating on flying, Deering handled the Huey with a mingled sense of strangeness and long familiarity. Although it had been nine years since he'd flown a UH-1, once he held the controls it had surged back.

After Sherry completed her report, Deering radioed Demetrios Karrabotsos.

"Clare says the jumper's stable, just out cold from the pain and morphine," he relayed. "She clamped his artery while we were shaking all over the sky. If I ever need a medic, you call her."

Before Karrabotsos could reply, Clare said strongly, "If you ever need a pilot, you call this guy."

Deering gave her a smile he was sure would make Georgia go ballistic. Clare returned it.

He headed for West Yellowstone. In front of the Smoke-jumpers' base, an ambulance waited. Alongside stood a tight group with notepads, cameras and at least two video units.

"The press is here," Deering announced.

"Who called them?" Clare asked.

He powered down, flipping switches. As the ambulance attendants rushed to the chopper, he finished shutting down and climbed out. It felt odd to be standing on the tarmac in jeans instead of his usual flight suit.

"We'll follow them to the hospital," Sherry told Clare. "I'll get the other guys who aren't on deck." She and Randy headed off toward the base building with its tall parachute loft.

Ignoring the press, Deering started to relax. A cold drink, maybe a steak this evening.

Then he noted that Clare's forehead still furrowed. Her small hands made fists as the gurney wheeled toward the pulsing blood-red emergency flashers.

He thought of telling her that Hudson would be all right, but he didn't know that.

Billings Live Eye captured the Smokejumper being lifted into the rear of the ambulance in blood soaked coveralls. A red-haired woman reporter in a jeans jacket pressed a microphone at him, but Hudson lay motionless.

Deering looked down at the top of Clare's tousled head and felt his adrenaline rush subside. He put a hand on her shoulder and remembered her touch, just before she jumped into the clearing. "Do you think he'll be okay?" He massaged the tightness in her neck muscles.

Her fists slowly relaxed. "Should be . . . if the leg is the only major injury."

He'd not thought of that. With the departure of the ambulance, the reporters headed toward them.

"Mr. Deering! Could we have a word?"

"Carol Leeds, Billings Live Eye," said the redhead. "How does it feel to be a hero?"

Deering broke into a grin.

"Mr. Karrabotsos said this was your first day flying with his company," Carol Leeds went on.

Sonnavabitch.

Across the ramp, Demetrios Karrabotsos balanced in the open trailer door. He propped against the frame with one hand and gave Deering a thumbs-up with the other.

A pony-tailed video cameraman crowded in and filmed.

Someone from the *West Yellowstone News* raised a Nikon. "How about a photo, Mr. Deering? Of you with the helicopter."

"Damn right!" He gave his best shit-eating grin and slung his arm around Clare's waist. What the hell, maybe he would ask her to dinner.

🔥🔥🔥

"Congratulations on getting back in the air." Clare raised her wine glass and clinked it against Deering's Coke. He was flying tomorrow and he'd been smiling nonstop since she slipped into the booth opposite him at the Red Wolf Steakhouse.

"You're one hell of a pilot," she went on.

When he was happy, he didn't look nearly as gaunt. The bruise on his cheek had faded from purple to a rainbow of yellows and greens.

Deering cracked his glass against hers again. "You were pretty spectacular out there yourself. Karrabotsos was disappointed you were just here for the season. Said West Yellowstone could use somebody like you."

The praise felt good. She'd waited at the hospital until Hudson came out of surgery. His prognosis for a full recovery had lifted her spirits so high, she felt she'd been drinking champagne for hours instead of starting her first.

In the dim light of a miner's lamp above their table, the evening slipped away. A little more wine. Good red meat, the kind the body craved after hard work.

Deering speared a thick bite of sirloin. "There aren't many women in fire."

"More every day," she told him. "There were gals in the volunteer departments in the Houston suburbs back in the seventies, but HFD took a little longer."

"You ask me, it's a nice change."

After three days of Sergeant Ron Travis having no use for a woman firefighter, it was refreshing to have the pilot watch her with admiring eyes. Deering wasn't exactly good-looking, but his taut intensity attracted. He talked with his slim-fingered hands, one of which bore a fresh scar.

"What'd you do there?" She reached and touched a finger to the spot.

"Oh, that? A little skin cancer." He was cavalier, but maybe a bit worried. "The doctor said I shouldn't have any more trouble if I stay out of the sun." His mouth twisted in a way that said his cockpit was always sunny.

The sunscreen lecture that Clare gave Devon on her way to the pool rose to her lips. She bit it back and forced her eyes away from those expressive hands. He didn't need her advice, and it felt too intimate to start taking care of him. She'd done everything for Jay and look where that had gotten her.

When they came outside, Clare saw lights in Fire Command. She wondered if Garrett Anderson was still at his post and if he'd taken time for a decent meal.

Deering stood close, but he wasn't invading her space. "You don't want to drive back into the park tonight. Come sleep in Demetrios's third bedroom." Although his tone was innocent, his alert eyes betrayed an interest in getting her under the same roof.

Going with him wasn't something she'd do in Houston, but the psychologist had encouraged her to embrace the summer; the way a child swallowed whole a trip to camp.

Part of her wanted to go along a darkened street with Deering's arm slung around her shoulders. With all that had happened today, and that wonderful heavy meal that Deering had refused to go dutch on, she needed a soft pillow and some shut-eye. As good as she felt about Hudson's rescue, she might even be able to sleep without nightmares.

Deering brushed back her bangs, a light touch that could turn to something else.

Warning lights and sirens said he was getting too close too fast. On her way back to bunk with Sherry, she thought it was one more reason to hate Jay Chance for making her wary of men.

CHAPTER ELEVEN
August 10

Five days later, Clare dug line on the Red Fire. South of Grant Village, she and a group of soldiers worked the edge of Heart Lake in the shadow of steep-sided Factory Hill. One of her guidebooks said the early explorers had named it because the hot springs' steam looked like a New England manufacturing town.

The meditative effect of work and a breeze off blue water gave her time to reflect on turning down Deering's offer that might have led to ham and eggs together in the morning. In the days since, she'd had time to regret rabbiting on him and to wonder if she'd see him again this summer.

Since Hudson had broken his leg, Clare had visited him twice in the West Yellowstone hospital. With a plaster cast from hip to ankle, he had chafed at being sidelined.

It was interesting the way different people reacted to adversity. When Deering had told her in the Bear Pit that he needed to get back in the air, she'd known he was one of those who climbed right back on the horse that threw him.

She envied his ability to shrug off trouble. Her lack of confidence after Frank's death was just beginning to be replaced by a renewed sense of purpose. Participating in Hudson's rescue had been a real boost.

This afternoon's training involved soldiers she'd been working with for several days. Watching a parade of faces that changed from incomprehension to confidence was another factor in easing her anxiety.

There was one problem, though. Sergeant Ron Travis, instead of moving on with the first group of soldiers, had been assigned to work with her for the duration.

With a check of her watch, Clare called for the end of the day. Conversation broke out as they hiked the half-mile back to their truck. Pulaskis and shovels were tossed into a pile.

Clare massaged her aching back, but she was getting stronger every day. It felt good to lift without effort and to keep up with the young male soldiers. It did irk that Sergeant Travis relegated himself to the role of supervisor, for all hands were needed. Just because they were training didn't mean their fire lines were without value.

As she wiped sweat from her forehead, she reflected that her dislike for him went deeper than that. The code of the firefighter was to do the work. If somebody asked for your axe, you did what needed to be done rather than pass it off. A person without equipment was worse than useless. Travis's Pulaski, issued eight days ago, rested behind the troop carrier's front seat.

He lounged on the open tailgate of the truck, looking cool despite the afternoon's heat. A bottled water in his hand made her want to snatch it and pour it over her sweating head.

"A good day's work," she said, loudly enough for the troops to hear. Although she started training with a tough-guy attitude, she thought it important to add praise as their ability increased.

Travis did not second her.

As the soldiers loaded their equipment, Clare spotted a pickup coming up the rutted trail with Javier Fuentes at the wheel. Since she'd taken on instructing soldiers, she no longer worked with the other volunteers from Houston.

A short distance from the troop carrier, she and Javier swapped stories while she downed the lukewarm bottled water she'd gotten from the truck. "How'd a cold Coke go?" Javier produced one from a cooler and she savored the effervescent explosion in her smoke-ravaged throat.

Javier's eyes grew serious. "How're you doing?" he asked in a way she thought referred to Frank's death.

"Getting by. You?"

He flashed a smile born of youthful resilience and testosterone. "This is something else up here." After a drag on his own Coke, Javier went on. "You know, if he'd lived, Frank would have come with us. Hell, he'd have fought fires till they forced him into retirement."

From the corner of her eye, Clare noted Travis listening. "Lose somebody in a fire, Chance?"

Javier jumped in. "Big apartment complex in Houston, wood shingle roof fully involved." His hands pantomimed leaping flames. "She was right in the middle of it when the ceiling came down and killed the other guy on the hose."

He must have thought he was doing her a favor, pointing out her bravery.

Travis shifted his eyes to Clare. "So if we get in a pinch, I can't count on you?"

Javier's bronzed young face frowned. "No, man, see she was lucky to get out . . ."

The soldiers were scheduled to drop her at her cabin, but Clare cut in and asked Javier, "How 'bout a lift to Old Faithful?"

❦❦❦

Clare seethed in the passenger seat as Javier drove. Coming to Yellowstone had not been the escape she had imagined.

Javier turned down the radio feature on the September match of *Stars and Stripes* vs. New Zealand's entry for the America's Cup. "Sorry about that back there."

"Not your fault."

They approached the turnoff for West Thumb. "Pit stop?"

"Never pass up an opportunity," Clare agreed.

When Javier turned into the parking lot, afternoon light had turned the water midnight blue and the wind whipped whitecaps. Her throat constricted at the memory of the day they had rushed to the beach, looking for survivors.

She hadn't seen Steve since she'd turned down his dinner invitation. At the time, he'd been hung-over and she'd thought it the right decision. On the other hand, he'd been perfectly clear and very knowledgeable about the history of her Nez Perce ancestors.

Clare opened the passenger door and started toward the restrooms.

"What's going on?" Javier pointed offshore where a sturdy vessel with a prominent pilothouse and broad deck rode at anchor. The workboat was the type Clare was used to seeing in the Gulf of Mexico, hauling equipment for the oil industry.

Following Javier down the walk, she was nearly run down by Chris Deering. He brushed past her with a purposeful stride.

"There you are." Deering shook hands with an Asian woman wearing a red suit and matching pumps. Her wedge of sculpted black hair rippled in the breeze until she looped it gracefully behind her ear.

A twinge shot through Clare, aware of her own dirty hair and filthy yellow shirt. Soot streaked her arms.

"Call me Suzanne," the woman offered in a flat Midwestern accent.

Deering's eyes lighted as he saw Clare. "You're just in time to watch my helicopter rise from the deep. Turns out she's only in eighty feet of water."

A surge of gladness at his smile put her off balance. She shaded her eyes and looked out over the water at the workboat.

"They've got divers down now, placing flotation," Deering explained, including both women by looking from one to the other. "Clare Chance, Suzanne Ho of First Assurance Aviation Underwriters."

"Let's go and watch." Deering put a guiding hand beneath Clare's elbow. "Can you stay?"

Javier joined them.

They went down the curving boardwalk past mud pots. Most were stagnant matte circles of drying, cracked clay, but one spattered thick glots. Where bleached earth marked prior spring activity, a lone buffalo with a dusty coat posed next to a dead pine.

Suzanne Ho tapped along on high heels, ignoring the springs and wildlife. "So, Mr. Deering, you say you lost control after you flew through a cloud of smoke."

"The air turbulence was murder." Deering pointed to where the fire had burned down to the lake. Stark skeletons of trees and their ash created a colorless landscape.

Clare stopped. She was struck again by the memory of blistering heat beside the chill lake, of kneeling beside Steve's motionless form. Hot and cold . . . life and death, while she waited to learn which card he had drawn. "That's where I found Dr. Haywood."

Suzanne frowned.

"Look!" Deering said quickly.

The surface of the lake boiled. Rotors emerged, followed by a dark blue fuselage. Last to surface was a pair of pontoon-like floatation devices that the divers had attached and inflated from an air compressor.

"It's not that far from shore," Clare said.

"It looked like forever." The edge on Deering's tone said he'd wondered if he were going to make it. "When I was out there swimming by myself."

She'd seen him rescued and wondered how Steve had made it to shore. "What about . . .? " A sharp look from Deering stopped her.

"What about Dr. Haywood?" Suzanne Ho finished.

Small waves slapped below the boardwalk. Deering didn't say anything for a long moment. Such a silent beat that Clare suspected he hadn't mentioned Steve to the insurance company. "What about Haywood?" he finally asked.

"You never spoke of a passenger. Yet, when I was getting your treatment records from Lake Hospital, the doctor told me. Apparently, Haywood checked himself out within a few hours of the accident."

"Yeah, to get stinking drunk," Deering gritted. "I was trying to keep this simple, but you want to know about Steve Haywood, I'll tell you. He lost his wife and baby in a plane crash and turned into a hopeless alcoholic who hates to fly."

Clare gasped. She knew Steve had a problem, she'd seen him drunk and with hands atremble after a bender, but Deering's words pelted like ice chunks. Steve's family dead? Deering hadn't said whether Steve was also on the plane, but his fear of flying made it sound as though he had been.

Suzanne listened with a serious look on her narrow face.

"When Steve got aboard that day, he was scared as hell," Deering went on. "We started to go down and he jumped without a life jacket."

Clare listened open-mouthed. Despite his problems, Steve must have had a strong will to live if he'd made it to shore without flotation.

Javier stood at a discreet distance, his big hands shoved in his pockets.

"I'll need to interview him," Suzanne said in a tone that Clare thought carefully neutral.

"You'll have to hike up Mount Washburn, then." Deering looked pointedly at Suzanne's dress suit and heels. Clare couldn't see Ms. Ho undertaking the expedition.

"Haywood's on the mountain to dry out," Deering finished.

CHAPTER TWELVE
August 11

In the east central part of Yellowstone, Looking Glass Lake shone beneath a sliver of new moon. The wind sighed through the lodgepoles, a stand of old growth that had been kissed by the sunrise for four hundred years. Here and there among the trees, silver ghosts stood sentinel, dead on their feet from the ravages of the pine bark beetle. Long trunks of lodgepoles that had succumbed to winter's winds and the weight of heavy snow littered the forest floor.

A freshening breeze rippled the lake surface. On the beach, a pair of coyotes raised their muzzles.

A flash of light augmented the starlight and a low rumble descended. Ahead of the front, a squall line swept down, churning a path into the waters.

The sky went dark.

The wind increased, first to thirty and then blew at a steady forty miles per hour. The temperature dropped twenty degrees. Whitecaps whipped and splashed the beach. The coyotes trotted into the trees.

SUMMER OF FIRE

Lightning split the night, a long finger that stabbed sideways and illuminated the towering cumulus. Thunder rolled in the mountains. Wind-driven waves began a steady pounding.

With a sharp crack, the next bolt smashed into a live tree. Vestiges of moisture boiled and the trunk exploded, scattering shards of raw yellow wood. In the lee behind a log, a tentative smoke wisp coiled and was whisked away.

A bull elk moved through the woods, swiveling his rack at the unsettled night. He paused to rub his flank against rough bark, scratching luxuriously.

The next arc came down, a short, hot, blast that blinded the bull. He bolted, narrowly missing a dead tree. For a long moment, it seemed as though this strike would have no more impact than the last. The elk slowed his headlong rush, then gathered his dignity and walked more slowly toward the shore.

His nostrils flared as dry pine burst into flame.

No new smokes.

Steve radioed in his six a.m. report. To the east, the Clover-Mist's smoke brightened from gray to pearl, reminding him of dawn in the Great Smoky Mountains.

At his grandfather's cabin on the North Carolina-Tennessee border, he used to get up early and go onto the front porch. Holding the rough wooden rail, he had watched the seemingly endless ranges of mountains, blue swells like ocean waves. Sometimes on wintry days he couldn't tell the difference between fog rising from the bottoms and wood smoke from backcountry chimneys.

Steve loved the soft, deeply weathered eastern mountains. With their ripeness of rotting leaves and mossy boulders, they were steeped in an overwhelming aura of richness.

When he went west for the first time, a college student on his way to fight fires, he'd discovered a raw new world of rock, sage, and towering heights. The thin atmosphere had seemed insufficient then, compared to the heavy humidity of the Carolinas.

Now the Yellowstone air was a tonic.

When he'd come to Mount Washburn, he had cursed Shad Dugan for sending him and himself for not smuggling in a bottle. The first night he had been unable to stay on his cot. The jerky thudding of his irregular heartbeat had coupled with a violent trembling that telegraphed to his befuddled brain that he was cold, even while he sweated.

Oh Jesus, if only he believed there was somebody he could ask for help. No one had radioed for many hours and he wondered if Dugan had engineered giving him privacy for the worst of it. Gradually, control came back, until he was able to sleep a few hours. After three days, his hands had ceased their trembling. Yesterday, he had savored beans and bacon through a resurrected sense of taste.

This small, square tower might have been set on top of the world, with a view that encompassed a hundred miles. As the sun struggled to break through, Steve sipped strong black coffee and imagined that the curling tendrils on the horizon rose from the campfires of the Nez Perce, ghost travelers from the past.

It had been a long time since he'd considered breakfast, preferring to get through his hangover first. Today, he felt like having fried eggs. He turned toward the supply box but became aware of a change in the familiar landscape.

All the monitored fires were posted on his map, updated daily through communication with Fire Command. If something new caught his eye, he had his Osborne Firefinder, a combination telescope and transit mounted on a column in the center of the room. He'd check the trajectory and compare it with the coordinates of the known devils. The final location would be determined though triangulation from more than one lookout.

Binoculars in hand, Steve tried to decide. At about ten o'clock, between the definite smoke of the thousand-acre Shallow Fire and the smaller plume from the hundred-acre Fern, was what appeared to be a new signal. He'd seen last night's dry lightning on the ridges, felt the cooler wind of the front and suspected conditions were right.

Swiveling the Osborne on its post, he put his eye to the telescope and compared the bearing of the suspected newcomer with the known positions of the Shallow and Fern.

He thumbed the radio mike. "West Yellowstone, this is Washburn. New smoke to southeast, vicinity of existing Fern Fire. I make it near . . . " He consulted the topographic map. "Looking Glass Lake."

"Roger, copy, Washburn."

Recognizing the voice of Garrett Anderson, Steve asked, "Don't you ever sleep?"

"Got a room at the Stagecoach Inn ah don't see much." Despite the radio's thinning effect, Garrett's deep baritone resonated. "When we get an exact fix, we'll send the Smoke-jumpers. As her daddy, do you care to name our newest fire?"

Steve looked out through the sparkling windows and studied the faintly rising wisps. Full day had dawned, the promise of morning richly recognized. From behind the eastern wall of smoke, a solid orange disc rose.

"If I hadn't been in the right place at the right time," he proposed, "I'd never have seen it at all." Carefully, he drained the last of his coffee. "Let's call this one Chance."

Clare stepped out of Old Faithful Lodge and found herself alone with the geyser and the morning. Water gushed away from the flattened cone where an eruption had just ended. Sipping coffee from a Styrofoam cup, she followed the boardwalk. At just past six, the only people she'd seen were a few joggers and TW Services workers.

She extended her free arm over her head to stretch out her side. She'd already run two miles in the gray dawn light, trying to erase the fact that she'd dreamed again of losing Frank. How many times had she been through it now, a hundred, a thousand, in sleep and awake? Each night came with the fear of a dragon, waiting in darkness.

Clare deep-breathed and tried to focus on the contrast between the remembered holocaust and the placid solitude at Old Faithful. The inn rose in stately majesty, an impossibly overgrown Swiss chalet. Bare flagpoles studded its roof deck, but as she watched, a member of the bell captain's staff raised the flags of the United States, Wyoming, Montana, and Idaho.

Forest ringed the geyser basin, in contrast to the two hundred thousand acres now blackened within the two million acre park. It was hard to believe that the experts' prediction for the rest of the season had been blown to hell in one week. Garrett's private forecast that the rules did not apply to crown fires had been right.

Clare went down into the narrow valley of the Firehole, where low water slipped smoothly over rocks. Despite the coolness, she could already feel the promise of heat in the day. For a nickel, she'd play hooky and let Sergeant Ron Travis dig his own way around the front of the North Fork.

She gripped the bridge rail. Javier hadn't meant to slip up and talk about Frank's death, but it was too late. Now Travis's generic sexist behavior had turned to a specific lack of trust.

She pushed aside thoughts of the little martinet and thought of her daughter back home. Lately, she'd had trouble in catching Devon at Jay's house, but when she did, she got the expected listless boredom.

Last night had been different.

"Have you met any nice boys?"

"Boys!"

"Okay, young men, then."

Devon was silent for a second too long. "I spend all my time at the pool. Where would I meet anybody?"

Clare's intuition pricked. "How about at the pool?"

"Ma!" Devon had cried tightly, sounding near tears. "Get off my back!"

Clare could almost hear her own mother admonishing her to get to Houston on the next plane. Quickly, before Devon got in some kind of trouble.

Usually Clare brushed aside Constance's anxieties, but today she wondered. Should she pack it in? Give up the most exhilarating experience of her life?

If Devon were younger, Clare would go home, might never have come at all. But one thing in her daughter's constant and irritating refrain rang true. Devon was nearly eighteen, and many girls were wives and mothers by the time they reached that age. God knows Clare had not been much older when she'd married Jay and had Devon. She sighed at the thought of the minefields that lay ahead of her daughter.

Just across the Firehole, Clare spied a cow elk cropping grass. As she considered moving closer for a better look, her Motorola radio seemed to awaken with the day. "Good mornin'," a deep male voice resounded. The elk swiveled its head.

"What's this, a wake up call?" Clare came back at Garrett Anderson. "I'm not only up, I'm meeting Travis and his troops at Madison in half an hour."

"Nope. The North Fork's too edgy," Garrett said. "I've called Travis and given the troops a day off. You too."

Clare knew the vagaries of fire in confined structures or the training field, but Garrett had an uncanny talent for predicting how it would proceed in the open. Reading the flames like tea leaves, he told when and where the next advance would be with far greater accuracy than those entering vegetation, moisture, and terrain data into handheld computers.

From the beginning, Garrett had nailed the progress of the North Fork. Now over thirty thousand acres, it was a sneaky bastard that had a finger pointed at scenic Firehole Canyon Drive, not far from the Madison Campground. If Garrett thought the troops didn't belong on the fire front today, she thought it just as well.

"Say." He was jovial. "You may have a secret admirer."

"What?" She wondered if Garrett might have run into Deering last night in West Yellowstone.

"I think Steve Haywood up on Washburn just named a fire after you."

Clare laughed and signed off. Within seconds, her face settled into more somber lines.

She recalled that little hesitation in Steve before he'd asked her, ever so casually, to have dinner with him. She didn't know what his love life was like, but at times, he acted as awkward as a teenager. Lord, if she'd known about his family, she'd have been more kind.

On the other hand, pity was the worst reason to take up with somebody.

Morning sun touched the highest peak of the inn. The day stretched before her, full of the promise that she would not have to wield a shovel or wind up blackened and coughing from smoke. The thought of clear air reminded her of Jackson Hole when she'd first arrived. She could drive to Grand Teton Park and ask for information about the early settlers. If they knew the Sutton homestead, she might find her grandfather's birthplace before nightfall. There was also the historical society that Walt Leighton had told her about. What if her great-grandmother's journal had been on file there all these years?

On the other hand, that was an all-day trip even without fire apparatus causing traffic jams. Deering had invited her to West Yellowstone this evening for dinner and she wanted to be back in time.

Her attraction to Deering had not diminished, but she couldn't forget the venom in his voice when he'd spoken of Steve.

When she came within sight of the Mount Washburn Lookout, Clare saw that Steve had visitors. He stood at the base of the tower in his ranger's uniform and summer straw hat, pointing off toward the Grand Canyon of the Yellowstone. A man and woman with well-worn backpacks studied the half-mile deep chasm, stark ochre against the green mat of forest.

As Clare drew closer, the hikers headed off across a rocky field. Not twenty yards from where they walked, three bighorn sheep stood as though carved in stone.

Even after the tourists were out of sight, Clare watched Steve from a distance. He removed his uniform hat and ran his hand through blond hair that shot silver in the sun. Squinting, for he wore no sunglasses, he turned to climb back to the lookout.

As she approached, Clare allowed her boots to crunch on

gravel. "Well?" she asked.

"Well what?" Steve's gray eyes lighted. He looked tanner and fitter, without such deep bags beneath his eyes.

"I climbed all this way to find out if you named the Chance Fire after me." The end of the road was two miles below, the trail up an ancient roadbed from the parking lot at Dunraven Pass.

He gave a warm, clear laugh. "I'll never tell."

Although she allowed a smile, it gave her a funny feeling to know that Sherry and the other Smokejumpers might be courting danger on her namesake.

"After all, I owe you thanks," he moved closer, "for saving my life."

Clare flushed, remembering how she'd thrown his thanks in his face. "I was rude and I apologize."

"You were right."

Into the little silence, he rushed, "I get some guests up here, but not many I offer lunch."

Ignoring the small visitor center, they climbed the stairs to the tower. He prepared canned tuna salad, expertly dicing celery and apple into the mix. "Sorry the bread's a little dry," he apologized, placing the sandwich before her.

Clare found the food a masterpiece, or perhaps she had a healthy appetite from her hike.

After eating, they walked the summit meadow where red Indian paintbrush, mountain bluebell, and bright pink Lewis Monkeyflower bloomed. Smoke boiled in all directions, but on the mountaintop, the air was clear. On a flattened boulder, Steve pointed out great grooves where glacial ice had carved its name into solid rock.

Clare smoothed the surface of a striation, her fingers close to Steve's.

He wasn't looking at her, but at the vista of green forests and golden valleys, patch-worked with black. "Lots of folks think we're witnessing destruction instead of rebirth." There was a deep chord in him when he spoke of the land. "When Shad Dugan put it to a choice, leave Yellowstone or get sober, it all came clear to me. If a million acres burned I'd still want to stay."

Without thinking, she closed the few inches between their hands and touched his. Should she tell him she knew of his family's death or let the afternoon wear on without a shadow?

Steve twined her fingers in his and lay back to study the sky. "You should see this place at night. Between the smoke plumes, a million stars shine."

Clare let herself down beside Steve, her shoulders against sun-warmed rock. "On a clear night in Houston, you're lucky to see Venus and Orion's belt. If the clouds are in, the sky becomes such a hazy red that I've wondered if a big fire caused the glow."

"Do you miss Houston?"

Above Mount Washburn, high clouds scudded. Their sharp white on blue was different from the washed out look of the Texas coastal sky. "I don't know about living anywhere else."

"I grew up in North Carolina. People can make a change when they have to."

She wondered if he meant his moving to Yellowstone, or maybe coming to the mountain. He ducked his head a bit and she liked that shyness in him. Not shyness, exactly, for he'd been perfectly poised doing the ranger thing.

Minutes stretched into an hour. The quiet felt companionable, the only sound the wind stirring the stunted white pines.

To check her watch, Clare had to take her hand from Steve's. A glance that she tried to hide said she'd stayed too long to make her date with Deering in West Yellowstone. Part of her was sorry, for Deering was the first man who'd made her aware of herself as a woman in a long while.

But today Steve made her feel special, too. Briefly, she considered telling him about Frank's death. With his own history of loss, he might be a good man to talk with.

Even as she thought how to begin, she discarded it, as she'd decided not to speak of his family. Reluctance to share her shame ran deep.

Just as she didn't care to tell she'd also been married . . . and lost a man she'd once loved.

CHAPTER THIRTEEN
August 13

Georgia Deering looked at the silent telephone in the hallway of her house. She had not talked to her husband in three weeks.

She went out, down the high stairs of the Victorian, and walked the few blocks to Lava Hot Springs's Main Street. Window boxes of petunias decorated the Wagon Wheel Restaurant. Proprietor Howard Silvernail waved from behind his antique glass case filled with gum and mints.

Georgia ducked to avoid some of the T-shirts rigged on a clothesline outside Hannah's Souvenirs. The Portneuf Inn across would be her competition when she and Deering opened their B & B.

At a table of books outside the public library, she selected three Dr. Suess for her nephew's three-year-old. It wasn't too late for her and Deering, with her turning thirty-nine, but it felt that way with Deering's older brother John being twice a grandfather.

Off the main drag, Georgia climbed up into residential

streets, a mix of neat old brick and wooden houses. Most of the yards had that rich emerald lawn and burgeoning rainbow of summer flowers that seemed impossible during Idaho's long winter. She turned in at the wrought iron gate in front of John and Anna Deering's two-story. Lace curtains fluttered, welcoming. Stone steps led up to the porch.

It was hard to believe that twenty-one years had passed since eighteen-year-old Georgia had come to dinner at this house where her married friend Anna lived. She had squeezed in next to the wall beside John's brother, who was on his way back to Vietnam for a second tour. He flew helicopters and said he planned to make a career of it. That scared her, but she had no doubt that if she fell for a pilot she could persuade him to stop flying.

Deering had passed her the potatoes and before the evening was over had driven her up into the dark, pine-smelling forest. He'd pulled off at a pocket-sized turnout, cut the engine and lights. It had been quiet while they savored the night.

They got out. He took her hand and helped her through a forest awash in silver moonlight. A winding swath of thinned grass climbed beside a gurgling stream. A little farther, a meadow surrounded a pool.

Georgia bent and found that it was a thermal spring. Deering's spare frame hunkered down beside her. "Warm, like you," he murmured. In a breathless instant, his lips brushed her neck and the world changed.

Anna Deering came to her screen door in jeans and a big denim shirt that hung to her knees. She and John had returned last night from Yellowstone, a vacation planned before the fires. The somber look in her normally bright blue eyes and the way she bit her bottom lip said she had talked to Deering.

Here it comes, Georgia thought. When it came to family, sides were taken when trouble was only a sniff on the wind.

Anna pushed open the door. The spring made the same aching sound it had for years. "Oh, honey," she choked.

Georgia's tears came; the ones that had eluded her when she lay dry-eyed and stared at the transom over the bedroom door. Wracking sobs shook her while Anna shush-shushed as though Georgia were a child. Finally, they sat on Anna's flowered sofa that she'd gotten re-covered after her children were raised.

"He hasn't called in three weeks," Georgia gulped.

"He told us you hoped they'd never find his helicopter."

"I didn't mean that. I was upset."

"Georgia," Anna said flatly. "This last has brought it to a head, but you've been trying to manipulate him out of the sky for twenty years."

"He risks his life to ferry buckets of water to fires that nobody can stop. What's the use in that?"

Anna went to the rolltop desk and retrieved a folded newspaper. "I picked this up on our trip."

Georgia took the *West Yellowstone News*. The photo took up half the front page.

He stood with his arm around a petite woman in shorts and a tank top. In jeans instead of his usual flight suit, his stance spoke of pride, as did the grin on his face. Behind him was an olive-drab helicopter, the kind he'd piloted in

Vietnam.

Georgia unfolded the paper and revealed the inch-tall headline. Hero Rescues Injured Smokejumper.

Even with his own Bell out of commission, the man couldn't stay grounded.

The paper said two tours in Vietnam had given Deering the jungle savvy to maneuver the Huey in the closest of clearings, getting the Smokejumper to medical care before he bled to death from a severed artery. The woman, Clare Chance, was a firefighter EMT who'd been on the flight. Georgia studied her casual top, one shoulder awry where Deering had his arm around her.

It was quiet, save for the ticking of Anna's grandfather clock.

It had been a long time since Georgia had seen a smile like that on her husband's face. He looked like a little boy posing for the camera with one hand propped on the chopper door like it was a teammate. What she didn't like was that his embrace of the woman had the same look to it.

She smoothed her hand over the picture, careful not to let the sweat on her palms smear the newsprint.

"He's in West Yellowstone working for Demetrios Karrabotsos," Anna said from the kitchen doorway. "Island Park Helicopters."

Where in hell was Georgia? Deering listened to the twentieth ring and looked at the Huey where he'd left it beside the Madison River. It appeared to be a normal summer day with wading fly-fisherman casting lines, but a group of fire-fighters had taken over the campground amphitheater for a training exercise.

Having finally worked up his nerve to call, he needed to hear Georgia's voice. As the phone kept ringing, his heart thudded. For a guy who liked excitement, this wasn't any fun. After thirty rings, he slammed the pay phone back on the hook. One of three yellow-shirts waiting nodded and stepped up to the open kiosk.

Deering crossed the road and leaned against a picnic table. He had always called Georgia at least once a day, even four years ago in Alaska when he'd had to stand in line for the only phone in a hundred miles. He'd gotten to bed at three and thought about being home warm with her in bed, while the glow on the horizon said the sun had barely dipped beneath it. Then back in the cockpit at four-thirty, where he'd do his preflight, drinking a cup of harsh black coffee and longing for Georgia's freshly ground Kenya AA with a touch of cardamom.

He wondered what he would have said if she had answered. She should apologize, for what she'd said about his helicopter was damned near inexcusable. He'd flown other peoples' equipment for years, scraping and saving for a down payment on his own machine. When his Bell had finally come in, he'd bought Dom Perignon because it was the most expensive and dusty bottle at the liquor store. Georgia had been all smiles until she realized he was serious about her breaking it on the skid.

SUMMER OF FIRE

Just thinking about his wife hoping he'd lost his most prized possession jolted him back to outrage. His *Georgie* wasn't a business, but an extension of him. If he didn't get the insurance check soon Georgia might get her wish.

In the dull sheen of afternoon, the Madison looked like molten metal. Only a few miles south, the Madison-to-Old Faithful Road was closed because the North Fork had spotted across the Firehole River. Word had it that the campground would be threatened within days.

That North Fork was getting to be one ugly fire, started by a thrown cigarette, which reminded Deering that he badly needed a smoke. He reached into his flight suit pocket and drew out a Marlboro.

The haze now produced the daily effect of a partial solar eclipse. The surreal half-light disoriented every bit as much as the celestial event. As Deering smoked, a reddish disc of sun appeared, the color of Georgia's hair.

He ground the butt beneath his boot heel.

Slowly, he drifted toward the amphitheater of split log benches where a wiry boy in the ubiquitous yellow shirt and olive trousers lectured to about forty people dressed the same. With a smooth motion, the instructor swung an air pack over his shoulder, the tank hanging upside down. Reaching behind, he cracked the valve and demonstrated breathing the air under positive pressure.

After a moment, the full facemask raised and Deering recognized Clare.

"On the fire lines these won't be available," she said, "but in case you're around the villages and need to go into a burning building we want you to know what you're doing. Remember that fire doesn't have to touch you to kill you. Most people in house fires die when superheated air and gases start at the ceiling and work down. They breathe in thousand degree air and sear their lungs."

She paused to acknowledge a raised hand. "Yes?"

"Will we be safe on the fire line?"

Deering watched her consider.

"Firefighting is a dangerous business," she admitted. "Some folks think that those of us who choose it are crazy. Now, you didn't make that choice yourself, but you did join the volunteer Army, so I can only assume that you're willing to do what your country sets you to . . . in this case, fighting fire." She looked around. "Any questions?"

There were none.

"Now it's your turn." The barrel-chested soldier she passed the pack to followed directions, swinging it high over his head and bringing it down onto his back.

Deering watched until she had helped each man and woman, adjusting a strap here and there. When the lesson broke up, he waved.

"What are you doing here?" She came toward him between the rows of rustic benches.

"What pilots do best." Deering liked the way her long-lashed eyes widened with her smile. "Waiting."

"For what?"

"This afternoon I'm supposed to fly hot meals to the Mink Creek spike camp." He took a deep drag on a fresh cigarette, thinking she looked good in trousers, even oversize ones drawn in with a belt. "You stood me up the other night."

"I got held up on a mountain." She brushed her hair off her bronzed forehead and offered no other explanation. Watching her manhandle the air pack had brought out the contrast between her compact yet strong frame and Georgia's softness.

Perhaps if he and Georgia hadn't been estranged, he wouldn't be thinking about what Clare's taut body might feel like against his, but this summer nothing was as it should be.

He gestured toward the Huey. "Want to go for a ride?"

From the left seat, Clare watched Deering run the rotors up until the chopper lifted off the grass beside the Madison River. It hovered at three feet, then he pushed the cyclic stick forward and added power by pulling up the collective and rolling on throttle. The helicopter accelerated across the grassy meadow until it reached about twenty knots, and seemed to leap into the air.

Below, the forest was green as far as she could see, but as they went on, Yellowstone Lake came up with the burn around Grant Village. The blackened swath brought back her dread as she had scanned rough waters and wondered if all hands had gone down with Deering's helicopter.

He landed at Flagg Ranch, the first private enterprise on the road south after leaving the TW Services empire. While he went to check on his cargo, Clare went into the gift shop. Idly, she fingered a cedar box painted with Old Faithful erupting against a green hill.

Maybe the box could hold Devon's concert tickets or keepsakes. On the other hand, considering how her daughter's tastes differed from her own, she wondered how she might please her. The girl was seventeen going on seventy, playing like a child one moment and disdainful of anything that smacked of youth the next.

Before Clare had selected anything, Deering came to get her.

Once airborne, they headed northeast for forty miles. Deering circled the chopper around Turret Mountain on the north side of Howell Creek, banking to give a view of the steep-sided peak. Then he dropped down between the valley walls.

"There it is." He brought them in to land near a mismatched array of colorful tents and camping gear staggered along a meadow bisected by a mountain stream.

"How long will we be here?" Clare reached for the door handle.

Deering stripped off his headphones. "How long would you like?"

Several hours later, Clare saw him through the throng of yellow-shirts, his olive drab flight suit distinguishing him from the hundreds of firefighters in line for dinner. She waved from her volunteer position inside the medical tent and turned to lay another strip of moleskin on yet another blister. Beside her was a cardboard box filled with discarded, bloody socks left behind by Apache and Navajo firefighters.

Heading to meet Deering, she sidestepped a patch of grayish phlegm on the ground. After foot injuries, bronchitis from smoke inhalation ranked high on the list of ills. Not to mention back problems. Lifting the air pack had aggravated her recurring lower back pain.

Deering ducked beneath the tent flap. He carried an orange stuff sack and a pair of yellow sleeping bags. "I found a crack in the Jesus nut on the Huey."

"Christ," she quipped. "What does that mean?"

In the moment when her words were out, she saw his face settle in serious lines.

"It holds the rotors onto the ship. It breaks, you go down."

Clare looked at the sleeping bags. "How long will it take to get a part?"

When she looked back at Deering, his gaze did not meet hers. "They don't have it at West Yellowstone. I'll have something flown in tomorrow."

"I'll need to radio Garrett since I'm supposed to meet the troops at Madison." Things had to be kept flexible when the fires did the unexpected.

"What time?" Deering asked.

"Noon." The wind riffled the canvas walls of the tent.

He smiled. "No need to call in. I'm sure I'll have you at Madison before noon."

She decided to enjoy the evening. Except for, "Is that one tent I see in your hand?"

"Last one in camp. We'll have to share like scouts."

He made it sound simple, but near midnight, Clare sat in the tiny two-man tent. Deering had excused himself to visit what he called the 'portable convenience.'

Her boots and socks already rested at the head of the zippered bags lying side by side. Together, she and Deering had watched the forest on Turret Mountain being consumed. A big fire at night was even more mesmerizing than staring into a fireplace, or at a single candle's glow.

Ever changing and ever the same.

Out here at the edge of the park, without any homes or property threatened, she could relax and watch the spectacle of nature untrammeled. Deering had stood behind her, a light hand holding each of her elbows. Although she'd rolled the sleeves of her shirt down against the night wind, she was aware of his touch.

Sitting alone in the tent, she suddenly thought that she was playing the fool. He probably wasn't even thinking of her. She shrugged and unbuttoned her shirt, then wriggled out of her pants.

"Look there." Deering pulled back the flap.

Clare dove into the sleeping bag. Once covered, she turned onto her stomach and peered out. The Mink Creek glowed along its front like a brilliant diadem. The wind had picked up, blowing down Turret Mountain.

"The fires are supposed to lie down at night," Deering observed. "This year they must have been behind the schoolhouse when the rulebooks were passed." He sat to unlace his boots.

Clare watched, aware that beneath the covers she wore only a lacy scrap of turquoise bra and panties.

Without looking at her, Deering shimmied out of his flight suit and folded it efficiently at the head of his bag. He lay down wearing plaid boxers. The glow of a Coleman lantern outside was just bright enough to give an impression of his body, slender and high-strung with a sprinkling of dark chest hair.

The camp sounds diminished, the day workers going to sleep while the night shift labored out on the lines.

Placing his hands behind his head, Deering lay quietly, but there was taut tension in his stillness. The smooth wall of the tent angled down six inches from Clare's face and she became conscious of her breathing. After a minute, the effort of inhaling and exhaling made her feel as though she were suffocating. With Deering lying virtually naked next to her, she rolled toward him to get her face into clearer air. She kept her eyes closed.

"Clare?"

"Hmm?"

This was really too much, the two of them stripped to their underwear and pretending they didn't know the game. Not since she was nineteen had she lain next to a new man and felt the way she'd thought was for the young.

But she did remember.

Deering rolled to face her and propped his head on his elbow. The orange light made his hair look as though it had red highlights.

She shifted restlessly.

"Your back hurt?"

"I get muscle spasms."

"I give a mean backrub."

There it was. It was quiet in the tent.

Then, faintly, "I'll bet you do."

In the dimness, Deering's eyes were hard to read, but she

saw an unmistakable spark that said it wouldn't stop at a backrub. Her heart pounded like a hammer.

He waited, watching her.

It had been too long since she'd met someone she would even consider, too many years without the feel of another body against hers. That was the worst part of being alone, losing the unspoken communication of touch.

From outside came music and laughter, underlain by the constant voice of the Mink Creek.

Damn Jay Chance, for making her draw back from men. She'd told herself she stayed free because the men weren't up to standard, and because Devon needed her. Well, Jay certainly wasn't taking notes, Devon wasn't here, and the look in Deering's eyes asked her to roll the dice.

If she turned away, would she be able to sleep, lying close and thinking what if? When she went back to her solitary bed would she long for the hot dark grappling that seized her imagination even now?

Deering's hand lay on his stomach. She couldn't see the skin cancer scar that made him vulnerable, but he and she were no more and no less at risk at any given time. She'd been thinking of fire as a particular threat because of Frank, but couldn't Deering's chopper crash? Hadn't it already?

Clare lifted her hand and touched the faint remnant of the bruise on his cheek. Deering's fingers covered hers, pressing her against his sandpapery beard. Their eyes met and the nearest Coleman lantern sputtered out.

Rolling onto her stomach in the sleeping bag, she rested her head on her arms. Bare shoulders, striped with turquoise straps, were offered.

Deering reached for the zipper of her bag, drawing it down so slowly that she knew she could stop him anytime. The wall of the tent made a shushing sound as he brushed his head against it. He straddled her.

His touch started out impersonal, like a professional masseur, but his fingers were knowing. He massaged lower, moving to the small of her back where the tightness was most acute. She jumped as his fingers found a knot and kneaded.

Minutes passed and his hands familiarized themselves while a creeping, bone-deep weakness spread through her. It wasn't the raging heat from the early years with Jay, but she wasn't nineteen anymore. Deering shifted his weight and pulled the sleeping bag down farther, placing himself astride her bare thighs.

Footsteps passed by outside. Deering stilled his hands.

Clare held her breath.

His lips beside her ear, he whispered, "We should have pitched the tent a bit farther from civilization."

She nodded. He bent and pressed his chest to her back. Skin on skin took her back, five years gone since anyone had touched her there. Tonight it seemed both yesterday and forever as she found her way. He drew her earlobe gently between his lips.

She gasped.

"If we're going to do this," Deering murmured, "we need to stay quiet."

He slipped his hands along the sides of her breasts. Boldly, he moved his body against hers.

"If we're going to do this," Clare returned in a whisper, "we need . . . "

He stretched to reach the zippered pocket of his flight suit and drew out a small sealed packet.

Something went still inside her and she rolled onto her back. "Did you plan this?" she asked quietly.

Deering raised his hands in a gesture of surrender. "A good scout is always prepared."

What did it matter if he had considered the option? Hadn't she?

Deftly, he unhooked the front clasp of her brassiere. "Admit it," he entreated. "It would be hell to stop now."

From outside the tent came a shout. "Blowup!"

"Goddammit!" Deering's voice sounded vicious, like Clare's own stab of anger. How dare fire interrupt what she'd so carefully committed to?

She and Deering dressed rapidly without looking at each other. He opened the tent flap to put on his boots. In the Mink Creek's eerie light, his sharp profile was set as he patted his pocket for a Marlboro. In the flare of the match, she was astonished to see what looked like pain in his eyes.

Clare pulled on her boots without lacing them and scrambled out of the tent. Looking at Turret Mountain, she was shocked by the Mink Creek, driven downslope so rapidly that she could see the front moving through the treetops. Smoke mushroomed into the night sky, blotting out the peak. The back of her neck prickled beneath a brush of breeze blowing toward the fire. In minutes, she knew it would become a gale feeding the convection cell.

A hundred yards away, on the opposite bank of Howell Creek, a group of night shift hotshots wearing helmet stickers that identified them as Californians, emerged from the woods. In brisk single file, they carried shovels or Pulaskis. Bringing up the rear, the sawyers carried chain saws.

The middle-aged woman at the head of the column slogged into the creek, pulled off her hard hat, and dipped up water to pour over her short gray hair. She cupped her hands to her mouth and bellowed again, "It's a blowup!"

A dark-haired man of considerable girth appeared. Clare recognized Hebert Patout, the spike camp commander who had greeted her and Deering earlier in the dining tent. Hebert had patted his stomach and forked up another mouthful of ribeye. "This steak, now, she is not so good. When the fire season end, you come to me and *ma frere* Mousson's restaurant in New Iberia, then we feast?"

Now Hebert looked up at the burning mountain. *"Mon Dieu,"* he muttered, tucking his shirt into his pants.

The breeze freshened and became a steady wind, sucked toward the fire by convection. Hebert produced a small, hand-held anemometer, the three cups atop the control box rotating rapidly. It reminded Clare of a toy, but the reading of thirty-five miles per hour was no child's play. Although the Mink Creek was over half a mile away, Clare bet it could reach the camp in less than an hour.

The woman who led the hotshots reported rapidly to Hebert. The laid-back gourmand with whom Clare and Deering had dined was transformed. "I'm calling an evacuation." The big man clapped a hand onto Deering's shoulder and ordered, "We need your chopper, now."

Clare waited for Deering to say the Huey was out of commission. Instead, he took off downhill at a run.

Within a minute, someone was banging a spoon against a metal coffeepot, the universal camp signal for 4:30 reveille. By Clare's watch, it was one-fifteen. The nylon walls flapped as if the tent were panting. Three short blasts on an airhorn sounded an alarm that could mean anything from a grizzly in camp to the approaching fire. A bullhorn added to confusion. Cutting in and out, the shrill feedback made the message sound like, "Fire . . ." followed by at least ten garbled words, and then, " . . . all hands . . . vacuate."

The Mink Creek spotted ahead as lone trees a hundred yards from the main body candled. In the meadow beside Howell Creek, members of the night shift mingled with the crews that had been rousted from their sleeping bags.

The bullhorn operator got it under control. "Abandon all gear, leave everything except your fire shelters. Proceed to the helipad for immediate evacuation."

A lone chopper began its runup. Another machine added an urgent scream to the Mink Creek's rising roar. Clare looked for Deering in the throng.

One chopper rose into the blood red sky, then another.

When Clare arrived at the helipad, she looked for the Huey Deering had flown, but it was not in the cleared space beside the creek. Word spread quickly that the game plan was to ferry all hands two miles downstream to the broad meadow at the confluence of Howell and Mountain Creeks.

"Plenty of time," someone said, and another, deeper voice

replied, "Bullshit, Monahan."

A Bell 206 Jetranger landed in a wash of wind to take on another load without cutting power to the rotors. Seven people crowded aboard and the Bell was airborne within sixty seconds.

Clare tried not to count the number of persons ahead of her, but as the fire wailed to a screaming crescendo, she found herself murmuring, "Forty-one, forty-two . . . "

"The son-of-a-bitch is not supposed to run downhill." Clare recognized the speaker as one of the sturdy Apaches she'd treated that afternoon. The white gauze bandage she'd taped high on his cheek was still in place.

She and everyone else knew that heat rises, therefore fire does not burn down a mountain. Unfortunately, this summer's fires and their microclimates did not understand the laws of nature, or perhaps man's understanding was faulty.

Clare touched the square pouch slung onto her webbed belt and was not reassured by the compact folds of her fire shelter. The flimsy material reminded her of the space blanket one of her friends had taken to carrying in her car when she moved to Denver. Clare had no more faith in the tissue-thin material keeping someone from freezing than she did in the fire shelter preventing her from roasting alive.

Another chopper came in low, hovered and landed on the flattened grass. With a start, she recognized the green Huey and Deering in the cockpit. He was flying with the cracked Jesus nut, risking the rotors flying off in mid-flight.

Was he ever afraid, Clare wondered? She'd learned in fire that while a healthy dose of fear kept you on your toes, too much was debilitating.

She had avoided watching the advancing fire front. Now, she turned and faced it, feeling the night grow warmer. The Mink Creek no longer looked beautiful. Up close, it bore a thousand brilliant teeth, snapping and biting at the darkness.

It was coming for her. Razor-sharp, it would slice through her flesh like a hot knife.

She looked for Deering, knowing that if he saw her at all, she was a mere face in the waiting crowd.

Coming in for a fourth landing at Howell Creek, Deering held tight to the controls. The Huey took a beating, slewing sideways toward rushing water while he tried to maintain a hover.

He scanned his instruments. Fuel okay, RPM steady, and if the goddamn wind held off . . . Below, the last of the firefighters turned their faces up towards him.

A sudden gust blew him past the LZ, almost into the creek.

Rolling on throttle, he gained airspeed and lifted off again, circling back until he was upwind of the helipad. Quickly, he rolled power to the off position, pushing right pedal to reduce the anti-torque produced by the tail rotor. As the RPM decayed, he increased pitch, lowering the collective so that the Huey sank.

The landing was hard.

Firefighters scrambled aboard.

Deering peered through the windshield at the spike camp.

Outhouse doors beat against their hinges. Loose papers blew along the ground. Above the rotor whine was a sound like a 747 screaming toward takeoff.

There was the tent he and Clare had shared so briefly.

The left side door slammed, followed by the rolling slide of the rear ones into place. Deering looked back to make sure the passengers were secure, then checked the person in the front seat.

Clare's white face stared at him, her eyes stark. She said something he couldn't hear and he gestured toward the headset.

She put it on as he performed instinctive motions with his feet and hands, the intricate dance that propelled the aircraft into the sky.

"Will this thing fly?" She gripped his forearm, creamy bone showing beneath the skin of her knuckles. He'd have a bruise.

Rolling turbulence in front of the fire lifted the helicopter and then let it fall four feet. He concentrated on keeping from crashing. Finally, he got it under control, lifted off and headed toward the drop-off. Clare did not let go.

Deering clenched his teeth at the mess he'd gotten himself into. He'd maneuvered Clare into that tent for the thrill of it, and for revenge on his wife for denying his love of flying.

He should be weak with relief that they'd been interrupted before anything more happened.

He wasn't.

Clare's touch reminded him how complicated this was. He should be ashamed of himself and he was, but when he'd held her, she'd changed from a cheap thrill or instrument of vengeance. He was suddenly, acutely aware of her as a human being, as though she'd been made of mist and had taken form.

As they flew along Howell Creek, into the gradually deepening darkness, he knew she deserved the truth. "There's nothing wrong with the chopper," he said grimly. "I lied."

✤✤✤

"It's kind of you to let me wait," Georgia Deering told Demetrios Karrabotsos as he handed her another Styrofoam cup of steaming coffee. At two-thirty a.m., it was dark and quiet in the control tower of West Yellowstone Airport.

"It's no trouble," the owner of Island Park Helicopters replied. "Are you sure you wouldn't rather wait at my house? You could let Deering wake you when he gets in."

"I've had too much coffee to sleep," she lied.

She studied Karrabotsos's scarred face and wondered how he had been burned. Deep lines around his eyes said he was maybe sixty, old enough to be a veteran of more than one war. He'd been gruff at first, but swiftly offered kindness. She couldn't tell if he knew things were bad between her and Deering, or if he merely offered the chance to pretend.

Likely, he didn't know anything. He hadn't even seemed to recognize her name when she'd shown up at the Island Park Trailer around eight, just in time to find out Deering was overdue. It had given her a chill she was still vainly trying to shake.

One thing she could tell was that Karrabotsos was worried,

too, the lateral grooves in his broad forehead deepening as the hours passed.

Georgia tried not to think about that cute EMT that Deering had his arm around in the newspaper photo. She'd always considered flying to be his mistress. Did she have to worry now about other women?

Controller Jack Owen was pulling night duty, occasionally speaking in reassuring tones to one of the pilots still flying on instruments. Outside the control tower, the north-south runway was a sparkling bracelet of diamonds, surrounded by the sapphire lights of the taxiways.

"I can't imagine what's got Deering off the air unless his radio is out." Karrabotsos repeated the litany he'd chanted for hours. "He flew to the Mink Creek spike camp this afternoon with their dinners. The winds must have kicked up bad to make him stay over."

Georgia smiled. She'd only met Karrabotsos this evening, but she already believed him a solid man that independent Deering would be okay working for if he couldn't operate his own machine.

The thought of flying brought her up against what she'd been trying to avoid all evening. Chatting with Karrabotsos had almost kept her mind off it, but it was getting so late and Deering had been off the air so many hours. If she were alone, she wouldn't be able to beat back tears.

Jack Owen sat up straight and listened intently. He ran a hand through his brown hair, aggravating his already prominent cowlick. "I'll pass it along. You're cleared to land."

Georgia clutched her coffee cup too hard. Hot liquid

slopped over and burned the soft skin between her thumb and forefinger.

"Mink Creek Camp had to evacuate all hands," Jack told Karrabotsos. "Deering's coming in now with your Huey."

❦❦❦

Clare gripped the armrest as Deering set the helicopter down at West Yellowstone.

Bursting with the desire to blurt exactly what she thought of him, she kept silent while a stout middle-aged woman with one of the catering companies waved thanks and headed toward the terminal.

With his head down, Deering gave complete attention to the aircraft.

Clare pitched her headphones into the floorboards and climbed down, stretching her legs to reach the ground. She waited, fists planted on her hips.

He seemed to take an interminable time turning off switches, reading gauges and writing on a clipboard. Finally, he removed his helmet and got out, brushing back his hair from his forehead. He reached to the breast pocket of his flight suit for a Marlboro and walked away from the helicopter. A match flared, a small glow against the floodlights illuminating the ramp.

Clare stomped after him. "You lied about the chopper, to spend the night with me."

"That's right." His dark eyes were steady.

Suspicion dawned. "I suppose that wasn't really the last

tent in camp."

"No."

Clare started away from him with a hard ache in the back of her throat.

Deering grabbed her arm and turned her. "Clare, wait." He pulled her against him, so tightly she could feel his flight suit zipper against her stomach. "It's not that simple . . ."

"What else have you lied to me about?" It shocked her, how the fires and the danger seemed to have heightened everything from desire to despair. She wanted to slap him, but she didn't. She'd never raised a hand to Jay, either, not even at the end.

Instead, she turned and ran. Near the terminal, she passed a small woman with red-gold hair, who also seemed to be in flight away from the tarmac.

CHAPTER FOURTEEN
August 15

Above the North Fork's burned out wake Deering flew the Huey toward the red rim of the world. He was dragging from another fifteen hour day and ready to set down in West Yellowstone. It would be nice to tuck into a juicy steak at the Red Wolf and swap some lies with Karrabotsos.

Upon reflection, tonight he didn't think it would satisfy.

It had only been two days since he'd seen Clare, but his life was divided inexorably into the time before . . . and the time after. Her flesh had been as he'd imagined, lean and needy when he slid his body over hers. It was only a technicality that they hadn't actually . . .

For over twenty years, he'd never considered being unfaithful. Not when other guys sampled the delights of Southeast Asia's fine-boned women. Not when he'd flown fire in Southern California where every woman looked like a movie star. And not on a hot night in an Oregon fire camp, when an attractive brunette named Helen had made it clear she was available if Deering said the word.

He had headed for his solitary sleeping bag without saying it.

As he flew toward West Yellowstone, the first star hung above the North Fork's smoke. It was magical how that always happened, the way he could be staring right there and not see it, as though it waited until he blinked. This lone bright jewel against a deepening azure field made him remember when his Dad would hold him on his hip and point to the sky. "Make a wish on that one, son, the first star you see."

Part of Deering wished he could press Clare beneath him and find relief for the urgency she'd awakened.

In the western sky, another star joined the first.

Part of him wanted to be home with Georgia.

❦❦❦

Clare stared at the hazy sky from Madison Campground and tried not to rustle her sleeping bag. Beside her, one of the women soldiers slept heavily, breathing through her mouth. Her sinuses were probably as screwed up as everyone else's from the smoke.

After a long day on the North Fork, Clare had decided against hitchhiking to Old Faithful. She did not care to have Sergeant Travis think she had abandoned her trainees.

They'd mopped up all day; turning ashes with their Pulaskis and putting out hot spots with the backpack tanks known as piss pumps. Grueling and demanding, but not dangerous. At the end of it, the press had been on hand while she provided first aid for minor burns and the usual foot maintenance.

Two days since she'd done the same at the Mink Creek spike camp and gone to bed in the same turquoise pants and bra, washed out last night in her cabin's small sink.

She wanted to despise Deering, but it was like he'd said. Not that simple.

It wasn't like her to jump into . . . a sleeping bag with a man she knew no better than she did him. At the time, though, it had seemed an inevitable, impulsive part of summer. It was as though she'd left behind her sense of stability, the self who wanted to keep things set for her daughter.

If Devon moved out when she turned eighteen, what would Clare have to focus on? Not two months ago, she'd have answered without hesitation that the Houston Fire Department would receive her undivided attention. Now she wasn't sure about anything.

What would she do when she saw Deering again? Cut him dead, or let his eyes entreat her? Just thinking of his long torso sliding over her back started heat coursing in her. If not for the blowup, she would have turned over beneath him.

If only Deering hadn't lied.

Looking at the filtered stars, she remembered Steve Haywood's love for the night sky over Yellowstone. In a way, the simple touch of his hand had been more moving than Deering's sensual overtures. In Steve, she felt the same deep and lonely melancholy that often overtook her late at night.

Clare took a deliberate breath and closed her eyes. Against the backdrop of her eyelids, she saw the endless undulation of flames.

SUMMER OF FIRE

❦❦❦

Atop the Washburn lookout, Steve turned the pages of an interview with a Nez Perce warrior. The man related seeing his mother trampled to death by a white man driving a wagon through her property. The interloper had been cutting wood for fence posts when she challenged him.

Steve knew about seeing your loved ones die. With Susan and Christa gone, he was a man without an anchor. He lifted his mug and grimaced at the acrid bite of cold decaf.

He pushed aside the kerosene lamp he preferred over harsher battery-operated lights and stepped out onto the walkway surrounding the lookout. Over the rail went the last of his coffee and he set the mug down. When the long summer twilight of the Northern Rockies gave way to velvet darkness, he found that substituting decaf or sipping at water did not satisfy his habit of having a glass in his hand. He still wanted a drink.

A check of his watch said he had read long into the night. Three o'clock and all seemed well, but to the northeast, the Clover-Mist illuminated the underside of smoke clouds. Overhead were the stars, but even with a new moon, the Milky Way's trail was muted. He remembered it that way from when he was stationed at Interior in D.C.

There, his future had been laid out like Washington's street system, wide smooth thoroughfares to success. A house with a green lawn that sloped to the Potomac, the start of Christa's college fund, a recent promotion that came with a government car.

Life was narrower now and rough as a wilderness trail.

The reddish sky reminded him how Clare said the Houston lights also washed out the stars.

Where was she tonight? When she'd come to the mountain, the sight of her had set off a bubbling simmer of well-being that he hadn't felt in a long time. She'd touched his hand.

At the rate things were going, she'd go back to Texas and he'd never see her again. That was probably just as well, but the prospect left a little aching void in his chest.

Due north, a light flickered in the sky as though a switch had been thrown and quickly extinguished. A gust hit the tower and the window glass shuddered. Steve's cup leaped off the rail to shatter against the deck.

He sniffed the air. There was no hint of humidity, but maybe this storm would be the one to bring the blessing of rain. With the dry wind in his face, he hoped.

CHAPTER FIFTEEN
August 20

Saturday dawned with a still heat that Clare felt inside the Smokejumpers' dorm. Through the open window was the ubiquitous pine forest that surrounded West Yellowstone. In the lower bunk, Sherry snored softly.

In this night's dream, Clare and Frank had been together on the North Fork. In her teaching mode, she'd shown him the proper use of Pulaski and shovel to make an effective fire break. The dry scent of duff rose as she struck, turned sod, and moved on.

"Like this?" The tool in his hand became his crash axe.

Frank looked at it and laughed, stocky and strong in his yellow shirt. The smile did not touch his empty-looking eyes. "Pretty easy duty."

"Wait until you've done it for sixteen hours," she came back at him like she always did.

"Ha!" He was weightless, floating magically and leaving a perfectly executed fire line. "I get done here, we'll have us a weenie roast over what's left of the North Fork."

He drifted up a ridge. She followed. "Hold on, you don't know these fires . . ."

Floating through the trees, Frank lifted like a helium-filled balloon Clare had accidentally released at her third birthday party. As the distance between them widened, acrid tears stung her lids.

Scrambling, she fought her way uphill in awful slow motion. There was no sound in the forest save Frank's fading laughter and the warning cry of a Clark's Nuthatch. It cocked its intelligent gray head at Clare. "Run away," the bird said clearly.

She struggled after Frank, cresting the ridge just as flames surged over the top. They roared liked an open blast furnace, living fire, with long fingers that plucked at her retardant clothing. Red and yellow, kill a fellow, but how smooth and seductive the hands . . .

Born of man, Frank transformed into fire. "Come on, Clare." He beckoned, his eyes blank as coal. "I'm waiting for you."

♦♦♦

Clare crossed the wide expanse of Yellowstone Avenue and slung her pack into the troop transport outside Fire Command. She was tired before the day had begun.

The troops milled on the sidewalk, some inhaling a last cigarette before the drive. Sergeant Travis stood by the passenger door, his booted feet planted. "Little late this morning, Chance?"

After lying awake for an hour, she'd fallen back into a deep and torpid sleep. Waking with a start, she'd found Sherry gone and sunlight filtering through pine needles.

She ignored Travis and started to climb aboard, but he jerked his head toward the building. "Garrett Anderson wanted a word with you."

She stared across the lawn. A sleek raven reminded her of the bird that had spoken in her dream. "Any idea why?"

Travis shrugged. "He thought maybe you'd want to cancel today. Something about the weather kicking up." He managed to make it sound like she was chicken.

Fear was a part of fighting fire, the pale underbelly no one cared to expose. From the training field to the midnight call, mum was the word. Call it a belief in bad luck, or maybe it didn't go with the macho image, but the last thing anyone talked about was the ever-present specter of fate.

Anger had been eating at Clare since she awakened from her latest dream of fire. Now came determination that she would not let fear alter her schedule, or her life. With a look at the clear sky and reasonable if a bit lively wind, she said, "If it kicks up later, we can always back out. The guys in the air and on lookout will give advance warning."

"I'm sending a chopper to pull you off there," Shad Dugan radioed Steve Haywood on the Mount Washburn lookout.

Steve's stomach knotted. He wished Dugan had let him drive up the mountain, but his boss had insisted he be dropped off. "I can hike down to the parking lot and you can send a truck."

"That'll take too long. We've had a tourist report of a massive elk kill. I want you there within the hour." Dugan's tone was final.

It was nine-fifteen a.m., with a brisk dry wind out of the north. The airwaves were alive with exchanges that bore out Garrett Anderson's dawn prediction; that today would be the worst yet. No rain since Memorial Day and here came another dry front with a forecast of up to eighty mile-per-hour winds.

Hoping that this excursion might be his ticket back to the real world, Steve packed his gear, gulped a second cup of coffee and went to wait outside. The usual daily weather pattern was already shot to hell. Instead of morning smoke lying in the lows, boiling convection cells rose like thunderheads off every major fire in sight. Haze crept over the flanks of the mountains and cut visibility to ten miles.

Steve's palms were wet. Before he was ready, the dreaded whopping approached.

The helicopter came in, an olive drab Huey with an intimidating military look. The wash of wind from the blades flattened the dry grass around Steve's feet. His heart raced and he bit the inside of his cheek to get some saliva flowing.

The skids were down.

The pilot reached across and opened the passenger door. Steve ducked his head and hurried to climb aboard. Putting on headphones, he heard a western drawl, "No way this was my idea, *Doctor* Haywood."

"Deering!" Steve gripped the door handle. He almost got

out, but Shad Dugan wouldn't buy cowardice.

Before he was strapped in, the chopper lifted rapidly over the treeless patch of summit. Within fifty yards, the slope dropped away and they were flying at a thousand feet.

Steve's stomach rebelled. He clapped his palm across his mouth and took a frantic look for a barf bag. Deering lifted his hand from the collective and plucked a small sack from a pocket on the side of his seat.

Steve choked back the acid liquid, but kept the bag close at hand. He'd never been prone to motion sickness, it was just those last ill-fated flights. He didn't need three strikes.

Although Deering appeared to handle the controls deftly, sweat trickled from Steve's brow to his cheek. Looking out, he tried to concentrate on the land.

The Grand Canyon of the Yellowstone yawned, a steep-walled, towered chasm striped in shades of burnt orange. Hydrothermal waters had altered the rock, turning it so rotten that the river easily cut a deep gorge.

South of the canyon was another world. There, the Yellowstone meandered peacefully across the golden, grassy expanse of Hayden Valley, oblivious to its upcoming wild ride.

The Huey turned west into the wind. Steve made a conscious effort not to clench his fists.

"I was directed to drop you at Norris." Deering's voice penetrated the overpowering white noise of the engine.

Steve frowned. Just yesterday, the North Fork front had been five miles southeast of Norris Geyser Basin. He wouldn't have thought it possible, but once more, Garrett Anderson had accurately predicted trouble.

"Look," Deering went on, "about that day we went down . . . "

"I'd rather forget it." Keeping his head averted, Steve concentrated on the horizon and keeping his stomach tamed.

"Believe me, I would too," Deering went on, "but my Bell's rusting in a shed in West Yellowstone."

"Tough." Steve's hands fisted on his thighs.

"If I don't get my insurance money, the salvage company can claim her."

"What's that to do with me?"

"The insurance folks want to talk to you."

Steve gritted his teeth as the Huey flew like it was driving the potholed stretch of road between Madison and Norris. Black smoke roiled off the North Fork and the rest of the sky had a reddish cast.

Deering said, "Getting that money will help get me out of a jam. My wife's pissed off enough."

"I don't care about your personal problems."

"You don't have to worry about them blaming you for screwing up the bucket." Deering persuaded. "I told them I got set by wind off the firestorm."

They were coming in fast. Steve held his breath and tried to make sense of what he'd just heard.

The Huey set down. Steve crumpled the barf bag and threw it in the floorboards. "Blame me?" He opened the door and let in the howl of wind. "When I finish telling them about you," he shouted above the din, "you'll be walking."

✦✦✦

Deering's hands shook as he landed at West Yellowstone. He tried to tell himself that it was because gusts kept buffeting the chopper, but he knew better.

God damn the day he'd first set eyes on *Doctor* Steve Haywood. Within two hours of Deering meeting the man, his helicopter had been at the bottom of the lake. If that Smokejumper hadn't broken his leg, Deering would still be schlepping retardant onto aerial tankers.

As hot as his rage was, he couldn't completely ignore its cold companion, a stony feeling in the pit of his stomach that reminded him where the real fault lay. Georgia was right about him being a daredevil. If only he could turn back the clock, take the time to find a landing spot and make sure the bucket was suspended properly beneath his chopper.

When Deering found out whom he was going to pick up this morning, he'd been half-afraid that Suzanne Ho had taken his advice and hiked up Mount Washburn. Instead, it appeared that the corporate wheels were turning more slowly.

Deering's momentary relief that she had not talked to Haywood had been wiped away when he realized his claim wasn't going to be paid until she did. Now that he knew how Haywood felt, he was sweating large caliber bullets.

Pushing away his unpleasant thoughts, he wondered where Garrett Anderson was. He'd been instructed to pick him up near the charter trailer.

At the sight of the nearby Smokejumpers' Base, Deering thought of Clare and the day she'd helped him in the rescue. The urge to see her again rose as it had with unruly regularity in the past week.

Garrett came up to the Huey from behind and opened the left-hand door. Deering jumped as the wind flapped a copy of last week's *Time* in the floorboards. The cover bore an artist's rendering of the Crucifixion for a story on the movie, *The Last Temptation of Christ*.

"Can we fly in this?" Garrett slammed out the wind, re-establishing the illusion of calm. "I just did. After ferrying a guy from Washburn to Norris, I was dropping incendiaries on the North Fork." The ping-pong ball sized capsules of fuel were dropped to ignite backfires. When the main fire arrived, the area of expended fuel might stop it.

"I heard the tower might call down the planes and choppers."

"This is recon, right?" Deering started flipping switches. "Let's check the wind along with everything else."

Moments later, they flew east along the Madison River at about five hundred feet. In the burned-out sector of the North Fork, National Park Mountain's stark cliffs loomed. Beyond, Madison Campground had been made into a fire camp. Colorful tourist tents had been replaced by olive drab and the RVs by troop transports.

Deering headed northeast and began to see areas of active combustion mixed with untouched vegetation. This mosaic created a patchwork effect. As they approached Norris, where Deering had dropped Steve earlier, the sky grew reddish and hazy. Radio chatter intensified as other choppers flying buckets of water checked in. The day's air controller warned someone about getting too close to the flaming trees.

"We've got battle lines at Norris and on the road to Canyon," Garrett said. "I don't think they can do anything but watch this burn."

A few miles on, a roadblock held up a line of traffic below. In an open field beside the highway, several helicopters sat idle, obviously ordered down by the air controller.

Garrett's thick fingers gripped a handhold as he looked at the grounded helicopters.

Smoke spiraled up, reminding Deering of the afternoon he'd ditched in Yellowstone Lake. He was careful to fly well clear this time.

The North Fork threw off a pocket of rough air. Deering corrected course and concentrated on keeping the aircraft steady.

Garrett peered back at the parked choppers in the drifting orange light. "I'd hoped to check out Silver Gate and Cooke City." The small towns in a high valley outside the northeast entrance had a love-hate relationship with the Park Service. In winter, the highway over Beartooth Pass closed, making the route through Yellowstone their only access. This summer a few hothead residents thought park officials hoped to burn them out.

Another big bump and Deering's hand tightened on the cyclic. Below, a phalanx of firefighters sprayed water on the roof of the Norris Museum, with flames not a hundred yards away.

An updraft lifted and then dropped the chopper, causing Deering to bite his tongue. Swallowing the salt of blood, he said, "We've gotta turn back."

Right now Deering was probably threading his chopper through turbulence, Clare figured. Last night she'd stayed with the Smokejumpers without letting him know she was in West Yellowstone. It had seemed the right thing, and today on the North Fork front, she was certain of it. Her anger at the fires, and at herself, still drawn to a man who lied, drove her like a dervish.

She kept one eye on the rising wind. It was just past ten and in two hours, they'd fallen back three times. In each case, Sergeant Travis had watched fire eat its way toward their line with his jaw thrust out. When embers flew a hundred feet ahead, he shouted and pointed for the troops to run down spot fires.

Gone for Clare was the pleasant exertion of hefting the Pulaski. No more the meditative lassitude of repetition. This day's dry front was a fury.

She wondered what Steve saw from Mount Washburn. With the inversion broken so early, the sky must be filling with spectacular thunderheads rising to thirty or forty thousand feet. "Look out, Chance." Travis pointed behind her with a smug look. If she had eyes in the back of her head, she'd have seen that once more their line had been defeated. No matter that Steve called this rebirth, it was a war.

Steve knelt beside a motionless cow elk. The North Fork had left a stark and colorless landscape, save for scattered cherry embers.

Pines stood stripped of their needles, bark transformed to charcoal. Despite his attention to the elk, Steve kept a wary eye on the snags, for the forty mile per hour wind could bring one down in an instant.

Behind him on the pavement of the closed highway, a group of tourists and firefighters watched from a distance of fifty feet. That wasn't far enough, for he imagined he could feel their eyes on his back. He reached to check the cow for a pulse. Failing to find any, he touched a finger to the open, staring eye and got no reaction.

He bent to look and found the pupils fixed and dilated. He breathed relief, for the last thing the Park Service needed was for the public to witness an animal's suffering. Of course, the press corps was no doubt on the way.

Steve believed in the natural rightness of wildfire and its rejuvenation of the land, but it was damned hard not to take this killing personally. His boots stirred a layer of ash as he walked toward the rest of the carcasses.

There were about thirty, the herd bull, a couple of younger males who had yet to challenge for the cows, and at least ten yearlings and calves. One of the spindly-legged young lay at the base of the tree it had trusted to shield it from the approaching inferno. Steve's throat thickened.

There were a lot of stories about mass kills. Most were false. He had watched buffalo and elk graze with flames not fifty feet away. As fire approached, the animals usually moved calmly out of range.

It was damned uncommon, but something had gone

terribly awry for this herd.

Steve studied their coats. Although they all rested inside an area that had been most thoroughly burned, he saw only a minor amount of singed hair. The powdery ash swirled and he could see the disturbance left by hooves.

Determined to investigate, Steve looked and found he was still in seclusion.

Pulling his folding lock blade knife, he thought this would be the easiest course. The dead calf's coat was thinner and the trachea would not be as tough as in the more mature elk. Intending to steady the throat, he placed a hand on the soft hair and nearly lost his nerve. Tears swelled, blurring the landscape into uniform gray.

Steve blinked hard and swallowed. He ran his thumb along the knife-edge to test its sharpness. If he could just have a drink to steady himself . . .

He made the cut quickly.

Thick soot coated the vocal cords that would never grow to bugle during the rut. Even as the elk had instinctively sought protection by sheltering themselves in the area that had already burned, smoke inhalation had felled them.

Steve wiped his bloody blade on the calf's coat and replaced the knife in his belt pouch. The wind shifted, bringing a strong smell of smoke from the firestorm raging at Norris.

When he was but halfway to the highway, a woman with a microphone came toward him, trailed by the ponytailed cameraman who'd heckled Steve at Roaring Mountain.

There were nearly thirty-five thousand elk in the park, but it would do no good to speak of them today. The loss of these thirty was news.

"Carol Leeds," called the reporter. "Billings Live Eye." The wind snapped her jeans jacket.

☙☙☙

Clare heard it coming through the treetops, a sudden downburst off the North Fork's convection cell. The raging gale bordered on hurricane force.

Snags scattered through the forest went down as though a scythe mowed them.

A shower of embers began. In front of Clare's feet, one landed on a log and burned a small black patch. Within seconds, it burst into flame.

Sergeant Travis was already in retreat, as were the troops. That was good, for if Clare had shouted no one could have heard. Down the line, the group of California hotshots she'd seen on the Mink Creek abandoned their position.

Once in the truck, bouncing along the rutted dirt track, Clare was pleased that Sergeant Travis routinely invoked executive privilege and rode shotgun. It was nice not to listen to his twist on their retreat. It was also pleasant to be in the company of the young people the nation relied on for defense. Wide-eyed at the almost nuclear forces the fires released, they nonetheless recovered quickly. Eager voices expressed determination to get back out there and slay the dragon.

Once again, they reminded Clare of Devon, whose October birthday was just over a month away. It was difficult to believe that her little girl was almost old enough to serve her country, but there it was. Many of these soldiers must have mothers at home; women who worried and watched the nightly news, praying no harm would come to their child. As youthful as they were, some probably had wives and children.

When the troop transport reached the highway, it joined a line of cars and trucks held up by the road closure. Clare switched on her radio and listened to the biggest battle going on in the world this day.

South of the park, downed trees on power lines had started two new conflagrations. One had caused the evacuation of Flagg Ranch, where Deering had picked up meals for the Mink Creek camp. The Clover-Mist, Hellroaring, and Storm Creek fires were torching over a mile of forest an hour. The renamed Red-Shoshone was making another run at West Thumb, causing a new evacuation.

When Clare heard that Dr. Steve Haywood had discovered thirty dead elk, she was sorry for the animals, but glad Steve was off Mount Washburn.

CHAPTER SIXTEEN
August 20

Steve took a deep swallow of the double bourbon he'd ordered from the Mammoth Hot Springs Bar. It seared all the way down. He looked for anyone he knew in the anonymous tourist crowd, telling himself that he was safe here even as he damned it for a lie.

Through the wide windows opposite, he saw the oasis that irrigation had created, a sanctuary for Mammoth's elk herd. A group of perhaps fifteen lay in the soft grass while daylight waned.

Steve imagined what would happen if the North Fork, only ten miles south, burned to here. Over two thousand firefighters were on the lines, but today's blowups made it clear that man was helpless in the face of such natural forces.

If the North Fork came to Mammoth, he wanted to be on the front lines, to cut that bastard down the way it had destroyed those defenseless elk.

Steve took another drink. It didn't burn as much.

If Clare knew he'd succumbed, she'd be disappointed. He

wished he knew where she was on his first evening in civilization. At Old Faithful, West Yellowstone, or was she in one of the myriad fire camps? With the thought, he had a nagging feeling of betraying Susan, even after four years.

He raised his glass and was surprised to find it empty. Sliding it across the bar, he gestured for another.

A hand clapped him on the shoulder. "I bloody heard you were back," Moru Mzima said in his deep, Oxford-accented voice.

Word spread fast on the Mammoth telegraph. A tourist could think it an impersonal place, with thousands of people passing through every day, but those who lived at Park Headquarters knew how small a town it truly was. Here Steve was, back from supposedly drying out on the mountain, with a double bourbon in his hand.

He cursed his judgment in coming to the hotel. He should have driven down the canyon to Gardiner for a bottle. Only the fact that drink came quicker here had swayed him.

"Yeah," Steve said dully, "I'm bloody back, all right."

Sure enough, Moru glanced at Steve's drink. "You made Peter Jennings."

Big fucking deal. Steve suppressed it because Moru did not use foul language.

"A photo of an elk carcass and you."

"Was that all?" Steve drained half his fresh drink. "Nothing I said about how the large animals usually aren't harmed by fire?"

"Not a word. That did get aired in Billings."

"A huge audience there."

"Tonight was the biggest sideshow yet." Moru grimaced. "Leaping flames and sweaty firefighters." His voice took on the officious tone of a TV announcer. "Over a hundred thousand acres burned in a single Black Saturday."

Wanting to change the subject, Steve asked, "Have any of our experimental plots burned?"

He'd been collaborating with Moru on documenting the effects of fire on the plant community. They catalogued the species diversity in a marked-off area, waited for it to burn, and studied the recovery.

"Not unless we got lucky this afternoon with the North Fork," Moru said. "I've got the summer interns I'm working with, Thomas Lee and Kelly Engels, on some new areas in the predicted path of the big fires. Thomas wants to do one by Old Faithful."

"That'll never burn." Even as he spoke, Steve knew he had yet to see the fire maps for this Black Saturday. He would not have imagined the North Fork getting as far as Norris.

Moru smiled. "I think Thomas wants a chance to hang out near a bar and decent restaurant, rather than doing all the remote hikes we've had those kids on for two and a half months."

"I'll help you start more tracts this week," Steve said. "I'm off the mountain."

Thinking of getting another drink, he went on, "Beer, Moru?"

"A cola, please. I must drive this evening."

"How's that?"

"Dugan heard you'd pulled into town and assigned me to

drive you back to Mount Washburn," Moru said. "Tonight."

❦❦❦

As night fell, Clare parked her rental car in front of the Smokejumper's dorm in West Yellowstone. The wind still blew, seizing trash from the catering barrels and transforming the papers into darting white birds.

In the dorm's dining room, Hudson read a dog-eared paperback while he ate. Every square inch of his cast sported a riot of signatures and humorous obscenities, along with a drawing of the Beechcraft discharging jumpers. Sherry's chili had so many crumbled crackers in it that the mix was unrecognizable.

She pointed to the pot with her spoon. "Randy's leftover masterpiece. Had to make a run yesterday before getting any."

Clare helped herself to the fragrant mix of meat, onions, and spice and straddled the bench, just as Deering appeared in the doorway. To his credit, his languid pose straightened when he saw her. While he greeted the others, she used the excuse of being ravenous to shovel food without ceremony.

"Cowboy chili?" Deering sounded friendly, but his lips pressed his cigarette and his eyes suggested Clare could bitch him out later.

"No beans," Sherry said. "You a purist?"

"Beans or no, I'm hungry enough to eat that whole pot." Deering looked around the table. "And thirsty enough to drink a beer. Forecast says we'll be grounded again in the morning. Any takers?"

"I'm in," Sherry agreed. "Hudson'll come. Clare?"

Deering had his back to her at the stove, but his shoulders stiffened while she pondered her reply.

"All right," she agreed. "What else have I got to do?"

Deering turned, bowl in hand, and his tight look said she'd hit the mark.

Fifteen minutes later, the headlights of his pickup illuminated a haze on the highway into West Yellowstone. Clare rode in the center front, pressed between the impersonal bulk of Hudson and the taut tension of Deering.

"That smoke looks like blowing snow," Sherry said from the jumpseat in back.

"I wish." Hudson peered past his propped-up leg.

In West Yellowstone, traffic was backed at every stoplight. In addition to the usual Saturday night in town crowd, there were hundreds of firefighters and tourists. Deering passed the Red Wolf Saloon, and on the second pass around the block, a camper backed out in front of Fire Command.

While Deering helped Hudson, Clare climbed out the driver's side. She looked at the tall, lighted windows in the massive stone and log building. "I'll be along later."

Deering caught up with her halfway across the lawn. His touch found her shoulder.

"Don't."

He removed his hand, but stayed close at her heels. "We've gotta talk."

She went inside the big raftered room with a moosehead over the fireplace. Folding chairs were set up in rows, but there was no one there. From beyond the swinging doors that led into the main command center came a hum of voices. Clare pushed through, and found phones ringing and people talking on radios at nine o'clock at night.

At the fire map, a bearded older man sketched an extension to the North Fork. His marker blackened past the Grand Loop Road and Norris Geyser Basin. As Clare looked at the small patch that represented the Chance fire, several miles southwest of Clover-Mist, the marker slashed across the plastic overlay. Today Lovely and Chance had burned into Clover-Mist. The dark mass obliterated the entire eastern sector of the park.

As a firefighter, she gritted her teeth at so much destruction.

Garrett came out of the kitchen with a cup of coffee and a stack of Fig Newtons. "Share my supper?"

"What in hell happened out there today?" Clare asked. "We couldn't fight fires, we couldn't find a road open."

"We couldn't fly," Deering added.

Garrett shook his head. "Yesterday the total for all the fires was two hundred seventy-five thousand acres. Soon we'll be staring at half a million."

Clare whistled.

"The wind hasn't died down like it usually does at night," Garrett continued. "I'm getting reports from all over of crown fires running. The Superintendent's meeting up at Mammoth to decide whether or not to close the park."

"That would be a shame for folks like the Cullens who own the Red Wolf," Clare said.

"We'll be calling in reinforcements, a couple dozen more

twenty-person crews. And more soldiers for you and Sergeant Travis to carp at." Garrett smiled.

"Marvelous."

"When's it gonna end?" Deering looked at the map.

"There's no hope of stopping this," Garrett drawled. "We'll try to save the buildings and power lines, but until the snows fly, this is gonna be like the Siege of Atlanta."

"How's that?" Clare tried to recall her Civil War history.

"Fight and fall back. These fires aren't going to stop until the rain and snow put them out."

🔥🔥🔥

When Deering and Clare were back outside, he turned to her. "We can join Sherry and Hudson for a drink . . ."

"But?"

"I'd like to try again with you."

She kept moving.

Deering stepped in front of her, so close that she could smell a mixture of soap, citrus aftershave, and tobacco. "I know I lied. It seemed like the only way."

She sidestepped and walked on.

"Okay, I'm sorry."

At the raw sound of his voice, she stopped.

He took the back of her arm in a gentle grip. "Is that what you want to hear? I was wrong to set you up like that. I only did it because I thought we'd be good together."

She considered his plea, weighing how angry she'd been against how many times she'd relived those hasty, hot moments at Mink Creek. Without committing to anything, she walked with Deering in the street beside the vehicles of weekend revelers who'd had to park away from the watering holes. As the lights of the town center receded, his hand on her arm was warm like it had been when they'd watched the Mink Creek burning Turret Mountain.

"This is where Karrabotsos lives." Deering motioned to a house she had passed the day she and Sergeant Travis had found the migrant camp. She recognized the snowmobile parked on the front porch.

"Did you plan this, too?"

"You're the one who starting walking down this street."

She sighed, "So I did."

"Come inside."

She ought to go back to the Red Wolf and have a drink with Hudson and Sherry, but the reddish glow in the sky reminded her of the filtered light in the tent at the spike camp. She'd thought of it, ten times, a hundred, at odd hours of the day and night . . . most often when she lay in her narrow twin bed at Old Faithful and argued the pros and cons of finishing what they had started.

"Please." Deering circled his fingers on the sensitive flesh on the back of her arm.

He wasn't perfect and neither was she.

With a key from beneath a flowerpot, Deering unlocked the front door. Inside, he disappeared into blackness until a faint glow shone at the end of hall. "Beer?"

"Sure."

The refrigerator shut. Bootheels sounded on hardwood.

Halfway up the hall, Deering snapped on a light in a side room, turning him into a tall silhouette.

The can he pressed into her hand was cold and wet. She took a huge swallow.

"Come down here." Deering led her toward the light.

They would talk now. Had he always wanted to fly? Was he a bad boy in third grade? Did he ever get a puppy for Christmas?

Clare stopped in the doorway. Against the paneled wall was a single bed as narrow and lonely as hers at Old Faithful. Deering set his beer on a chest of drawers, took hers and placed it beside his. He stepped closer and tilted her chin up toward him.

It was going too fast, like last time. All she really knew about Deering was that he loved to fly, a daredevil to some, or fool, if you listened to Steve Haywood.

"Wait." She stopped him with a hand on his chest. "We need to talk."

He covered her hand with his, pressing her fingers. "For Christ's sake, you wanted it as much as I did."

It still grated that he'd lied.

Deering dipped his head, a move to kiss her. His breath smelled of smoke and beer.

Clare blocked him with her forearm. It was more than just the night at Mink Creek. This evening it rankled that instead of buying her a decent margarita, he'd snagged a beer from the fridge and tried to lay her down before she'd had two sips. Granted, she was out of practice, but she had an idea of how she wanted to feel.

She tried to gather the shreds of her thoughts. "It's just that . . ."

Deering backed away and stared at her. "We're working eighteen hour days. I'm based in West Yellowstone and you're staying at Old Faithful." He waved a frustrated hand. "We've gotta take advantage of the chances we get."

Clare went cold inside. "I get it. You're saying 'let's hop in the sack' and I'm supposed to say, 'Great, I have an hour free on Tuesday'."

She went down the hall, past Karrabotsos's snowmobile, and into the night.

YELLOWSTONE FIRES
August 22, 8:00 a.m.

Here is a list of the fires and approximate perimeter acreages. To date, about 354,470 acres have been affected by fire. However, only about half of the vegetation has burned within many fire perimeters. Throughout the summer, 50 different fires have been started by lightning. Of those 50, seven are still burning inside the park. Fire fighters are working to control them. Any new fires will be suppressed as quickly as possible.

Clover-Mist Fire: 156,502 acres. Mist Fire started July 9. Clover started July 11. They joined on July 22. Shallow Fire started July 31. Fern Fire started August 5. These two fires joined Clover-Mist August 13. Lovely Fire started July 11 and burned into Clover-

SUMMER OF FIRE

Mist on August 21. Crews attacking hot spots on northeast flank. Fire trucks and crews in Silver Gate and Cooke City as a precaution. Pebble Creek Campground is currently closed and is being used as a firefighter camp. Regular U.S. Army troops arriving today to give civilian fire fighters a break. Fire contained at Thunderer, Amphitheater, and on Republic Pass.

Falls Fire: 3,738 acres. Started July 12. Fire within ½ mile of South Entrance Road.

Fan Fire: 22,020 acres. Started June 25. Islands of unburned vegetation continue burning within perimeter. 70% contained by a fire line.

Hellroaring Fire: 33,000 acres. Started August 15. Outside the park, burning to the northeast.

Lava Fire: Started July 5. Contained but began smoking after high winds on August 21. A few fire fighters have gone in to cool it off.

Mink Creek Fire: 21,036 acres in Yellowstone. Started July 11 outside the park in Teton Wilderness. Burning to the northeast into the Shoshone National Forest.

North Fork Fire: 91,700 acres. Started July 22 by human. Now has two fronts: one north of Norris, the other along Canyon-Norris Road. Norris and Madison campgrounds closed and in use as fire camps.

Red-Shoshone Fire: 58,744 acres. Red Fire started July 1. Shoshone Fire started June 23. Joined August 10. High winds caused flare-ups around Grant Village and West Thumb that led to evacuation of Grant Village on August 21.

CHAPTER SEVENTEEN
September 3

"What's your crystal ball say now?" Clare asked Garrett through a mouthful of Fig Newton. On her first day off in two weeks, she'd stopped by Fire Command to look at the full-sized quadrangle maps used for daily press conferences. Since Black Saturday, over two hundred thousand acres had burned inside Yellowstone.

Garrett set down his coffee and slid a hip onto a metal desk. "The moisture content measured in large logs continued to drop through the month of August, now hovering in the seven-percent range. Grasses and small twigs are at two percent. You just look at this fuel wrong and it blows up in your face."

The description made Clare think of Devon, whose eighteenth birthday was exactly one month away. It had been just that amount of time since the day she'd listened to the fire behavior experts' obsolete predictions. Although trying to second-guess her daughter by long distance was as futile an effort, she wondered aloud, "Seriously, Garrett. It's September now. When do you think this will break?"

He shrugged with the weariness of battle fatigue and looked out the south windows toward the nearest advance of the North Fork toward town. "Your nightmare is as good as mine."

She hadn't told him about Frank or her bad dreams. She didn't plan to.

As she turned to leave, thinking of visiting the Smoke-jumpers, Garrett detained her. Rummaging on his desk, he produced a pink slip. "While you were out screwing off . . ." He chuckled.

The message was from last night. Jay had called.

She stared at it like it came from another planet. What could her ex want, unless something had happened to Devon? With a fluttery feeling in her chest, Clare dove for the nearest phone.

Jay answered the home number and she heard a football game in the background. No doubt, he was sitting in his expensive leather recliner in the game room with the surround sound theater.

Clare bit her lip. She'd never been into ostentation, it just seemed that the pleasure cocoon he'd built for him and Elyssa was one more symbol of rejection.

In response to Jay's generic hello, she clipped, "What's happened?"

Jay chuckled. "You worried about me?"

Clare's nails curled into her palm. "I am worried about *my* daughter," she enunciated. "I know you'd only call about her."

"Our daughter." Jay wasn't laughing anymore. "I guess you're feeling guilty by now, knowing you shouldn't be out there."

"What do you mean I shouldn't be out here?" Her voice

rose and she berated herself for not calling from someplace private. The woman dispatcher at the next desk had perked up and was staring through thick glasses.

"I can't do a thing with Devon," Jay whined, quite a trick for such a big guy. "She keeps saying she's nearly eighteen, but she needs supervision. Elyssa thinks she's seeing some guy on the sly, somebody too old for her."

Devon's talk of moving out without an education or a job rang a warning bell. That was how Clare had ended up married to Jay. "How does Elyssa know?"

"She saw them together."

Alarms went off, but Clare stuck to her guns. "You'll have to be a parent for a change."

"Sorry, but Tuesday afternoon Elyssa and I leave for Greece. Our tour doesn't end until September twentieth."

Clare had always asked Jay to take her places and he'd told her he was happy watching TV. "So change your plans."

The woman who'd been listening leaned across. When she grinned, it accentuated that her lipstick had bled into little lines around her mouth. "Give him hell, honey."

"Have you a paper and pen?" Jay asked in the smooth voice reserved for clients and wheedling.

"What for?"

"For flight information. Monday morning I'm putting Devon on a plane to Wyoming."

Everything in Clare seized up. "You can't send her here. Postpone your trip."

"You know better than that."

Clare's mind raced for an alternative.

"It's Delta into Jackson Hole," Jay went on relentlessly. "Monday at two."

Today was Saturday.

Before she could reply, he hung up.

She dialed back and got the answering machine. Elyssa's syrupy greeting went on while Clare gritted her teeth. At the beep, "Damn you, Jay, pick up."

Of course, he was sitting there watching football and laughing at her.

She banged out of Fire Command and told herself that she crossed Yellowstone Avenue quickly to avoid being run down by an Army Humvee. It was no use, as her boots struck the pavement with hard clacks. Her breath came fast and she wanted to break Jay Chance's neck. Not to mention Devon's.

Jesus, what if Devon was pregnant?

If there was somebody in her life, maybe it would be good to get her away from Houston, but West Yellowstone, Canyon Village, and Silver Gate were under siege and Clare was needed more than ever.

A young woman and her pig-tailed little girl sidestepped on the sidewalk to evade Clare's headlong rush. Kids were cute when they were small.

She turned in at her destination. The ice cream store window sported a painting of a five-foot long boat bearing mammoth scoops of ice cream foundering beneath chocolate syrup, crushed strawberries and pineapple. Comfort food, just what she needed to help her forget about Jay and Devon.

She smiled at the young man behind the freezer case. "Banana split."

She'd gotten to know Alonso Mansales, who lived in the forest with the other migrants.

He dipped ice cream, dropped the stainless steel scoop into a container of water, and began to mound toppings. Watching him work, Clare was glad she'd urged Sergeant Travis against reporting the woodland camp to the Forest Service.

Alonso's dark eyes went to the plate glass window. Outside, the sky looked as though it portended rain, but only ashes fell.

Impossibly, the North Fork now threatened to burn through West Yellowstone. If Clare had imagined the Mink Creek as a sharp-toothed carnivore, then the North Fork had become an octopus of the Jules Verne variety.

"We had to move our camp west." Alonso handed over her banana split.

She took a bite from the chocolate end. It didn't taste as good as she'd hoped.

The parade of people outside grew larger, folks on their way to a Town Hall meeting, where they would be met with more platitudes and predictions. Clare was glad she didn't have to get up before the crowd like Garrett would.

Alonso's look was grave. "The fire?"

Words of reassurance rose to her lips, but she stopped short of speaking them. All the predictions had been wrong. "I don't know," she told him. "I just don't know."

Throwing away the ruins of her confection, she stepped into the darkening day and joined the crowd. Nearly everyone walking toward the meeting seemed prepared to evacuate.

"I've got our clothes packed," an elderly man said, "but we

can't afford homeowners insurance. If our place burns, we lose everything."

"They're hosing down roofs out our way," said a woman with a chiffon scarf across her face. She raised her eyes to the falling ash.

The atmosphere of uncertainty, with people talking about losing their homes opened a pit in Clare's stomach. After she sold her house this fall, where was she going to end up?

She figured the two firefighters ahead of her to be swapping lies, but as she drew closer, a big red-bearded fellow declared, "Damned feds, taking over everything in sight."

"Forest service is cut out, too," agreed a slender man whose smooth cheeks and downy hair made him look too young to be a firefighter. "The Type I teams and the military just marched in."

Clare took a closer look and noted from their T-shirts that the men were members of the local fire department, grousing about folks like her and Garrett Anderson.

Inside, the battle lines appeared drawn. The lectern was set up opposite the townspeople. Garrett stood flanked by men with rangers' shining badges and military officials in camouflage fatigues. It looked as though they hoped to reassure the population, but unfortunately, the rear windows faced south. Not three miles away, a crimson tentacle of the North Fork crested a ridge.

"We've got all kinds of resources, helicopters, and tankers," Garrett said into the microphone. "They're clearing a six-blade dozer line west of town and east by the park."

"All this 'let burn' is going to burn us out of town!" A woman with a hard-looking face called from near the stone fireplace.

"Damn right!" someone else shouted.

The tallest of the park officials stepped forward. "I'm Tom King, Yellowstone Superintendent." He looked over the sea of angry faces. A flush suffused his own face beneath a shock of unruly hair. After a pause to let the catcalls go unanswered, King cleared his throat. "On July 27th, the Secretary of the Interior upheld our suspension of the park's 'let burn' policy. Ever since, we've been throwing everything we have at these fires." He nodded toward the military. "Even brought in our boys in uniform, but . . . "

A big man who looked to be in his early sixties took off his orange ball cap and stepped forward. "I'm Pete Cullen, sir, own the Red Wolf across the way. Every time you say a fire won't burn past this place or that, you come back later and say the place is toast."

"We've never seen wildfire act this way," King said. "This season is defying all the models."

The people murmured like a rising wind.

Pete Cullen raised his arm and they quieted. "Me and some folks are doing something. Bringing in irrigation equipment and setting up a great big line of sprinklers on the edge of town."

"We're much obliged to you," Garrett told him, then announced to the room at large. "Mr. Cullen will be up front if any of you good people would care to help him out."

Clare didn't like the little frisson of hope that went through the room. A few sprinklers would have little use against the North Fork. Garrett must have realized. "I hate to say this, but if I lived in West Yellowstone, I'd be thinking about what to take with me in case of evacuation."

"No matter what bullshit you shovel," someone shouted, "you've given up our town."

Garrett's jaw set, but Tom King was faster. "Putting firefighters in front of these fires is like putting your hand in front of blowtorch. You know you're gonna get burned." The Superintendent paused. "We believe that people's lives are more important than property."

CHAPTER EIGHTEEN
September 4

The next day was Sunday, but it saw Clare back on the line with a new batch of troop trainees.

On Cutoff Mountain, inside the northeast corner of Yellowstone, she shielded her face with her gloved hand and used a drip torch to splash flaming diesel onto the forest floor. The dry mixture of needles and bark flared.

Stepping back, she joined Sergeant Travis, who stood in an attitude of command. She'd learned that his father was a career Army officer who had sent his son to military school, starting with seventh grade. In her mind, this helped to explain, but did not excuse his behavior.

Ignoring Travis's pose, Clare watched the burnout eat its greedy way across the slope. With luck, the small blaze would deprive the approaching Hellroaring Fire of fuel.

Behind the backfire and the main body of flames, twenty infantry bent their heads to the task of scraping earth with Pulaskis.

"They make good groundpounders," Clare observed, wiping her forehead with the back of her hand.

Travis surveyed the group that included two Native Americans, one Black, and three Hispanics. Two were women. Despite their differences, they all seemed equally wary. "Fresh off the plane in Bozeman," he said. "We should be breaking them in at West Yellowstone, not on a live fire."

"The North Fork is probably torching our training ground there." Clare thought of Alonso Mansales and his family moving out of the path of the monster. Garrett had suggested she take the soldiers to the Hellroaring, reported to be creeping along under light and shifting winds. Started August 15 at an outfitter's camp north of the park, it had spread south and now covered over fifty thousand acres.

She looked at the sun, half-hidden behind a pall of smoke, and checked her watch. Nearly six p.m., surprising, for the temperature was climbing.

She took a long draught of lukewarm water from her belt canteen and continued to monitor the backfire. It attacked a downed log with sharp teeth of flame. This part of the woods was full of fallen trees that had died from an invasion of pine bark beetles.

Travis groused, "I don't like the looks of this."

In the same moment, the skin on the back of Clare's neck prickled. Much as she hated to admit it, she agreed. It was the quiet, the dead zone where not even the air stirred. Fifty years ago the stories of calm before a blowup had been mythology, but science had corroborated that the dragon held its breath . . . just before it seared the land.

The wind began to pick up. First a puff and then a blow, it brought the acrid smell of singed duff. Atop the near ridge, the main body of the Hellroaring torched a dead tree into a hundred-foot tower of flame.

"This was supposed to be safe." Travis licked his lips.

Clare did not reply. This wasn't like Black Saturday, with nearly hurricane force winds, but she didn't like it. The ground fire rose from a height of one to three feet. Over the ridge crest a steady roar mounted.

A sharp stab went through her at the memory of her dream. The one where Frank had led her to the ridge in time to join him in fiery death.

A falling cinder kindled a spot fire almost at their feet. Billy Jakes, a carrot-topped soldier with bright blue eyes, broke from the line and shoveled dirt. More embers swirled, landing on clothes and smouldering out on the fire retardant Nomex.

"Let's get out of here," Clare decided.

Travis was in full retreat. "If anything happens to these guys, you got us into this."

A half-mile away, Steve was alone on the Pebble Creek Trail, two faint wheel tracks covered in dry golden grass. The deep valley between Cutoff Mountain and the long cliff of Baronette Peak was already in shadow. He was hungry; his lunch of cheese, peanut-butter crackers, and an apple had long since burned off.

It was good to be off Mount Washburn and on to other things.

Yesterday he had radioed Park Headquarters and asked for

Shad Dugan. In a confident tone, he'd said, "I've been up here right at a month. It's time to come down." Outside the fire tower, the view that had once innervated had begun to close in.

"Think so?" Dugan asked dryly.

"Lots of rehabs run twenty-eight. I've done my time." He tried to sound matter-of-fact, but he knew the real reason he was in a hurry to get down. What were the odds that Clare was still in the park?

"Still want a drink?"

"Hell, yes. I probably always will. Walt Leighton gave up smoking ten years ago and says he wants a cigarette every day."

"Think you can turn it down?"

There was the tough question. Would staying longer on the mountain make it easier? He didn't know if Moru had told Dugan about him drinking the one night he'd been near a bar. Probably yes, since the two of them had put their heads together about getting him help.

"If I'm going to take a drink, I'm going to take it. I know the consequences." He also knew that he wanted to see Clare again enough to risk it.

Today he'd been chasing a report that the Hellroaring had killed over a hundred elk. Shad Dugan had flown the area earlier and neither he nor Steve had seen any dead animals.

Although it was past six, Steve heard over his radio that the air war to save West Yellowstone was still in full swing. A few hours ago Garrett Anderson had told him there was only a twenty-five percent chance of saving the town.

The wind picked up. Steve smelled fresh smoke, a distinction he recognized between the scent of charred forest and one burning actively. He swore and headed for his truck. Hoping the product of government maintenance and a hundred-thirty thousand hard miles would start, he made plans for a hot meal at the Storm Creek Fire Camp, a few miles away inside the northeast entrance.

The burning smell grew stronger.

Steve picked up his pace, limping after hiking for hours on his bad knees. A few hundred yards to the west, a sudden flare indicated ground fire leaping into the treetops. He reached for his radio to notify Fire Command, just as a ragged assemblage of firefighters straggled onto the trail.

Clare recognized Steve despite his fire clothes and hardhat. She raised an arm. As dirty and soot-streaked as she was, he probably didn't know her.

"Our trucks are a half mile west," she called over the rising roar as the fire crowned. She looked at the green government pickup parked behind Steve.

"Let's go," Travis shouted in command.

Steve opened the driver's side door and leaped in. Clare and the soldiers piled into the truck bed. The engine nattered, but failed to turn over.

Clare surged off the tailgate and ran around to the front. Wrestling the hood release, she revealed the oil-stained engine.

"Piece of shit," Steve muttered at her side. He turned, saw her, and said, "You again," in an ironic voice.

Silver gray eyes met hers for the barest second and they both broke off to scan the compartment. He prodded at corroded battery terminals and lifted a cap while Clare stood on tiptoe to jiggle the spark plug wires. It did not escape her that Sergeant Travis sat on his ass in the truck bed.

Steve got behind the wheel and tried again. "We'll have to push-start it."

Without even looking at Travis, Clare ordered the soldiers out. They obeyed in quick unison and put their arms to the rear panels. It was no good, as the fire worked its way down to the road, effectively blocking them from heading back into the burned area for safety.

The impulse to run seized her. It showed on every face as heat reached them.

Steve gripped her arm. "Out of time." He reached for the belt pouch that contained his 'shake and bake.'

Dear God, not those flimsy things.

Steve pulled out a wad of silver foil.

Just this morning, she had shown the troops the use of their shelters. Now she waved her arms and shouted for them to clear a spot. It seemed impossible that the tiny tents could keep out the wall of flame that raced toward them.

The soldiers spread out uncertainly, shrugging off their packs. Clare wished she could coach each of them through this. Unfortunately, she was forced to dump her pack and begin clearing a place where she might save her own skin.

While she worked, she noticed that Steve was close to her side, his head down as he dug with a shovel he'd pulled from the bed of his pickup.

SUMMER OF FIRE

A sudden gust thinned the smoke. The troops scraped away at anything that could burn. Clare looked at the Hellroaring and worked faster. Sweat poured down her sides.

A rain of embers caught the dry grass in a dozen places. She leaped to stamp out one small fire, and then another.

The troops fumbled at their belts for their shelter pouches and shook out the pitifully inadequate looking covers. Silver foil whipped as they struggled to control all four corners.

Steve whirled to put out another spot fire with his shovel. Clare put a hand on his arm. "Here it comes."

She stared at the blazing trees for a moment, transfixed. Then she reached for her shelter.

A look of horror spread over the face of her most enthusiastic pupil. Private Billy Jakes hardly looked older than Devon, with freckles and those blue eyes like her daughter's. The wind enlarged a great rent in his shelter, splitting it down the middle.

Glowing embers fell faster. Burning branches blew into the road. Without stopping to think, Clare tore the shelter from Billy's hands and let it blow away like a billowing sail. She reached for her own and pressed it into his hands.

The fire swept through the treetops a hundred feet away, pillars of orange, red and purple. Searing heat blasted Clare's face and the grass at her feet burst into flame.

In the same moment, a tongue of flame roiled out of the woods and licked at the foil mounds where the soldiers had already pulled their shelters over them on the ground. Hands that had been reaching to tuck in flaps retracted inside the balls that looked like baking potatoes wrapped and ready for the oven.

Clare met Steve's eyes. He pulled his tent over his shoulders like a cape and shoved her ahead of him onto the semi-cleared ground, falling half beside and half on top her.

"I wish I had a respirator," she said grimly.

They lay awkwardly, arms and legs bumping and hardhats at odds. The dragon's breath pressed hot foil onto her shoulder and she realized that the Hellroaring was upon them.

Nearly inaudible above the fire's vacuuming scream, someone in a nearby shelter sobbed. Steve had gone down with his sleeves rolled up and his hands bare. She imagined his knuckles heating as the line of firelight brightened the edges of the tent.

He swore viciously.

Clare placed her hands in leather gloves over his, taking the tapes from him. "I've got this end." His boots held the other.

He jerked his hands inside with what she imagined would be second-degree burns. Clusters of crimson fireflies revealed pinprick holes in the shelter. Smoke poured under the edge, bringing tears to her eyes. Crazy currents lifted the material and let fire seep into the uncleared grass.

While Clare held on, Steve repeatedly slapped out small flames, swearing as he burned his hands. Despite gloves, her hands grew hot, especially her left little finger that felt as though she pressed it to an iron.

How could she have become so cocky, thinking things were going well? What if Devon were one of the young people here today?

A roll call was in progress. One by one, the troops called

their names into the din. Halfway though the alphabet, Sergeant Travis shouted, "Jakes? Sound off, soldier!"

The only reply was a barely audible sob.

Hellish orange light seeped through the pinholes. "Stay with it!" Clare shouted. "Whatever you do, don't get up and run!"

The roll call broke down as other voices joined in.

"Hold on!"

"Everybody stay put!"

A sudden, shrill cry made Clare think the pain of her fingers was nothing. It went on and on, a scream of such purely distilled agony that she wanted to put her hands over her ears. Her imagination took flight. A shelter had blown free, the wall of flames devouring its occupant.

Or worse, Clare screwed her eyes shut against the image of someone who'd panicked and thrown off their hope of salvation, a lurching, staggering, falling torch.

🔥🔥🔥

When the screaming finally stopped, she shook with sobs. Her tears dried instantly in the scorching air.

Despite an incoherent comforting murmur from Steve, it all surged back. Surrounded by the blast furnace bellow of the Hellroaring, through her closed eyelids, she could still see the glare of fire, both real and remembered. In the Yellowstone wilderness, someone suffered an agonizing fate. In a Houston apartment house, a roof slanted sideways, twisted, and crushed the man on the hose.

In the past weeks, Clare had gone from denying Frank's

death, underscored by her refusal to return to a station without him, to anger at being left unscathed at his side. Now that rage rose with the fire's fury. Travis had said this was her fault.

"No!" She'd kicked at the flaming timbers over Frank, drunk on adrenaline and determined not to lose.

But she had. Frank was dead and a soldier's silence spoke more eloquently than a cry.

Her fault.

With arms that ached, she struggled to hold the foil that flapped in a sixty mile-per-hour wind. Her leather gloves blackened and she gritted her teeth against her burning hands. The fire built to crescendo, sounding like a jet squadron taking off from an aircraft carrier. Communication between shelters was now out of the question.

Steve's weight felt solid and Clare was glad she wasn't alone like the rest.

The smoke thickened. Pressed as close as possible to the ground, she struggled for oxygen. Gripping the tapes as hard as she could, she burrowed her face into the dirt, sucking air from the porous, sandy soil.

God help her, Devon was coming tomorrow and she had to be there. She couldn't die on this remote mountain, when not ten minutes ago life had been fine.

A little voice whispered that Frank had felt that way too.

❦❦❦

Steve realized that he must have blacked out, for the shaky breath he took was perceptibly cooler. Once he'd had anesthesia, that same sensation of being here and then . . . being here. His head spun as wildly as on a college drunk, back when he'd seldom imbibed.

Outside, the only sound was the diminished crackle of flames.

The quiet after the agonized cries spiraled him back. The still silence that had fallen after the Triworld jet jerked to a halt had been replaced by a quick whoosh and crackling. For the rest of his life, fire would remind him of the night he'd thrown off his seatbelt, thinking to leap to his feet and pull Susan and Christa to safety. Shocked into immobility, realizing they would never need his protection or love again, he would have remained with them. He'd been saved because two fellow survivors saw his plight, fought him from the fuselage, and restrained him from going back in.

At the height of the Hellroaring's passage, he'd wondered, as he had while the plane fell, if this was it. To live through the crash, bury his family, and die in a worthless shake and bake? His redemption had died with Susan and Christa, but in defiance of his denial, at the height of the firestorm, Clare had murmured something that could only have been a prayer.

She lay beneath him, small and still. He lifted his weight off her with an effort, willing his knees to support him. He lifted his right hand, the one less burned, and touched a pulse in the side of her neck.

She shifted slowly, as though waking from sleep. Through the reek of burning, Steve smelled their mingled sweat.

He'd thought of her on the mountain. How she'd studied him with a steady gaze, as if she saw beyond the sodden wretch that drink had made him. That is, that he'd made of himself.

Her high-boned cheeks and generous mouth; that bronzed skin that invited a man to smooth his hand across it . . .

He rasped her name with a smoke-raw throat. She moaned.

His trembling right knee signaled that it was about to collapse.

Her hands disentangled from the shelter and she turned over beneath him. "We made it," she whispered, her tearing eyes triumphant.

A surge of gladness that they had come through . . . together, made him not sorry that he couldn't hold himself up any longer.

His weight came down, his body covering hers, feeling a tautness in her that sang. He did not believe it was his imagination. For the first time since Susan, he knew the touch of a woman, warm and full length, shocking him with its rotten timing.

"Ten hut!" The troops' leader sounded as though his boots were planted beside their shoulders. He'd been useless when they were trying to start the truck, but now he wanted to play commandant.

Steve threw off the shelter in a swift movement, pushed himself off Clare and leaped to his feet.

The world had changed.

The road was a blackened shadow of the grassy strip. Dead pines stood with needles burned off, their bare limbs looking naked and somehow obscene. A layer of white ash covered the ground and a charred smell pervaded everything from Steve's clothes to the pores of his skin.

SUMMER OF FIRE

The troops emerged, climbing unsteadily to their feet. Here and there, someone nursed a burned hand or wrist, but the fire shelters appeared to have prevented catastrophe. The only two women in the group appeared from shelters next to each other, while the bantam rooster of a Sergeant stood with his feet apart, his face pointed accusingly at Clare.

She pushed past Steve, searching. Her face was set in grim lines that told him she was ready for anything, from minor burns to full cardiac arrest.

Steve wasn't.

Clare knelt and lifted a soot-blackened silver sheet with sure hands. Steve stepped closer and smelled something worse than a burned-out forest, a sweetish stench of scorched meat.

Bile rose in the back of his throat. That shiny, blackened crust belonged to no race on earth. White, Black, Hispanic, or Native American, there was no clue left. Fire retardant clothing stuck to skin as though it had melted on. One sleeve still smoked.

A look at Clare's face confirmed the man was dead.

The first time she'd seen a dead person, she'd been shocked at how truly gone life was in the instant that light faded from their eyes. They hadn't let her see Frank, but she'd imagined. His hearty energy turned to one more piece of fuel.

Clare felt the letdown start inside her chest and radiate down her arms. It happened whenever she'd been pumping adrenaline for a long time and there was nothing more to be done.

Sometimes it happened watching someone's house collapse on irreplaceable photos, a child's doll, and the memories that would never be the same. Once a family Golden Retriever had been trapped in a laundry room. When intense heat had beaten her back, she'd thought she'd need support to simply hold herself upright.

She'd gone on.

After Javier had dragged her away from Frank and into the street, after she'd cried with Pham Nguyen's mother, she'd gone down onto the curb. With her head between her knees, she'd felt lower than the gutter beneath her boots.

Beside the dead soldier, Clare was fiercely grateful she was already on her knees, for she would have fallen. Delayed reaction set in, a deep trembling that replaced the wall of detachment she'd thrown up on approaching the downed man. She was aware of the others standing at a distance, waiting to see what she might do. "There is nothing," she said, then realized she'd merely thought it.

Steve offered the radio he'd worn on his belt. Hers was in her blackened pack.

She stared at the box as though she didn't know what it was. Gradually, her training reasserted and with a shaking hand, she clicked the mike. "Firefighter down," she told the man who answered.

Thank God it was someone she didn't know, for if she had to talk to Garrett she'd break down in front of Sergeant Travis and the soldiers. "We need emergency medical care and transport for ... twenty-two. We've got one ... body."

She realized that she didn't know who had died. It could be

any of the soldiers, whether they had called their names before the screaming or not. "We'll have to get back with an ID."

"Christ, who . . .?"

"We've got Joe, Sheila, Mako, Rodriguez . . . "

"Sound off!" Sergeant Travis clipped.

It began as before, proceeding briskly all the way to J.

Private Billy Jakes, who had answered the previous roll call with a sob, did not reply.

"Jakes!" Travis shouted. "You there?"

A low murmur began.

"Jeez, not Billy . . . "

"Sound off, I said."

The rest of the roll continued more slowly, from Lomatewa through Sanchez to Young.

"Ah, hell . . . "

"Billy."

Clare had handed Billy her own shelter after his blew out, but fate had evidently decreed it his day to die. Several of the male soldiers dashed at tears with the backs of their hands, while the two women let themselves cry without wiping their faces.

Dry-eyed, Clare pushed to her feet. She moved among the survivors, checking for burns and other injuries. She watched for signs of shock and instructed a shivering Rodriguez to wrap himself in a shelter.

She stepped toward Sergeant Travis last. His quick emergence from the shelter and attitude of command led her to believe he was not in serious trouble, but she needed to be sure.

As she approached, Travis stiff-armed her back. "Go away,"

he said through set teeth.

It seemed to take a long time for help to arrive from the Storm Creek Camp, even though it was only about five miles as the crow flies. After their initial reactions to identifying Billy, most of the soldiers sat silently on the clean sides of shelters spread on the ground. Their shoulders slumped with exhaustion.

Steve sat beside Clare, looking lost in his own thoughts. Periodically, he cleared his throat and spat mucus into the ash. She did the same at intervals, aware of her raw throat.

The dead man lay at a little distance. No one looked in that direction.

Clare did not need her eyes to see a vivid picture of the face death wore today. Before entering the fire department, the only corpses she had seen were the pale products of an undertaker's art. Masquerading as sleep, death wore pancake makeup.

In the field, it was different. A heart arrested and a woman toppled off the toilet. A middle-aged man died during sex and lay in an awkward sprawl, the sheets soiled with his bowel's release. Billy Jakes's humanity was lost along with his skin. The sour cooked smell and stink of singed hair clung cloying in Clare's nostrils.

About thirty minutes after she'd radioed, headlights approached in the gathering dusk. How fortunate that the burned trees were mostly standing, or the vehicles would not have been able to drive in on the dirt track.

Without waiting for orders from Travis, the soldiers got to their feet and climbed wearily into the back of the Army transport. Travis waited with Clare and Steve while the ambulance attendants made a perfunctory check for a pulse. The senior man shook his head and his assistant brought out the body bag.

When they lifted Billy into it, Clare caught the malevolent flash of blame in Sergeant Travis's eyes.

CHAPTER NINETEEN
September 4

"Good lord, what happened to you?" A powerful-looking woman in a Prescott Arizona Hotshots cap looked at Clare from the next sink. They were alone in the women's shower trailer at the Storm Creek Camp.

"Setting backfire on the Hellroaring." Clare's boots sat side by side on a bench, along with a fresh set of Nomex. She stripped off her stained shirt and trousers and dumped them on the floor. The once-polished stainless mirror gave a blurred suggestion of her blackened face with bloodshot eyes.

Clare suspected that the woman had not asked about her merely because her clothes and skin were filthy, but because of her strained white look beneath the soot. The set of her mouth said she was at the limit of endurance.

"Rose Chee," her companion offered.

"Clare Chance." Because Rose had a kind face, she confessed, "Around six it blew up and we went into shelters."

"Everybody make it?"

Clare swallowed around a hard lump.

Rose waited. From the pocket of her fire trousers, she produced a gold tube, twisted it with an adept hand and applied a coat of crimson lipstick. She pressed her wide lips to even the color.

Clare met her serious dark eyes. "We lost a young infantryman out of Fort Lewis. They were just in and I was training them."

"Jesus."

"Yeah."

Pulling a stack of the paper towels offered for drying, Clare headed to a shower stall and pulled the white plastic curtain behind her. She dropped her charcoal-mottled turquoise brassiere and underpants into the trashcan on the rubber mat. As she reached for the taps, the tears came.

With them surged the memory of harsh questioning after Frank's death. Hadn't she known they should retreat from beneath the burning overhead? Had she given Frank any signal to back off? Had he, in turn, tried to go back and found her blocking his way? How was it possible that the roof had come down without warning, as she suggested?

She imagined the combined firepower of the National Park Service and the Army descending on her. Did not Sergeant Travis express concern at the safety in the area, long before the actual emergency? Hadn't she taken it upon herself to delay a judgment call until it was too late?

For God's sake, the Hellroaring had been tame earlier. She'd given her own shelter to Billy Jakes.

Somehow, she did not believe that would be enough.

They hadn't let her see Frank's body. He'd been brought out of the apartment house in the same type bag they'd closed Billy in; the one that served as equalizer for kings and paupers. Frank's casket had been closed.

Seeing Billy's disfigurement made it real. Clare slid down the fiberglass shower wall and hugged herself beneath the spray. Great gulping sobs wracked her and she hoped Rose Chee didn't hear. Without success, she called on her resource of coolness, the one that permitted her to package the dead.

This happened to the best of them. Some firefighters called it processing, an impartial cover-up for the tears, the rage, the obsessive washing that failed to remove the taint of smoke and burnt flesh. Everybody handled it her or his own way and Clare had congratulated herself at partitioning it when the victims were unknown.

Even after Frank, she'd been in denial. Despite her few bouts of crying, she'd set her backbone in a straight line and run to Wyoming. Now, she let the cleansing water mingle with her tears. Frank was not waiting back at the station the way she sometimes imagined. The good knife he'd brought to chop onions and spices had gone home with his widow. Someone else's clothes hung in his locker.

When she finally emerged from the shower stall, two women were talking excitedly about the prospect of the thousand people in the Storm Creek Camp being evacuated before morning. The fire that had threatened Silver Gate and Cooke City at the east entrance had backed around and was heading for them.

At this latest proof that there was no haven, Clare wondered if what she, and everyone on the lines had gone through today wasn't enough.

Now she faced the prospect of phoning Garrett. Sergeant

Travis had probably bent his ear an hour ago, before the transport carrying the troops back to their base had left. Billy Jakes's comrades had been excused from the fire line.

Clare had decided to stay overnight at the camp, rather than ride to West Yellowstone under Travis's baleful eye. His farewell had been to succinctly turn his back and walk away. Not a word to suggest she might give a shit about what happened to Billy.

With a shock, she remembered that Devon's plane arrived tomorrow afternoon. For the past few hours, it had been wiped from her mind. Now that she knew the fire was coming, she wished she'd hitched a ride to pick up her rental parked at Old Faithful. If the camp was evacuated to Mammoth on the north end of the park, she might have trouble getting to the airport on time.

Near the dining tent, she queued for a pay phone. It would be more private than talking to Garrett over one of the radios.

His deep voice was unchanged and reassuring. "Anderson."

She bit her lip against the horror of Billy's screams.

"Yo, talk to me."

"It's Clare."

"Gal." His voice said he knew. "You okay?"

She sucked in her breath. Did trembling inside qualify as okay? Even though she'd bathed, the scorched stench had permeated her head and she could not shake it.

Garrett spoke into her silence. "These things happen," he said in an uncanny echo of what the folks at the station had told her about Frank.

"Yeah," she managed.

"With your daughter coming, you take some time. Show her the sights," he offered.

"Yeah." She discovered how hard she'd been gripping the receiver only when her fingers relaxed.

"I've been briefed on what happened, but I'll need your story. Are you up to it now while the memory is fresh?" His voice was steady.

"Okay," she agreed. Around her was a throng of yellow-shirts. From eager students to men and women with graying hair, they all risked themselves, as she did.

She just didn't know if she wanted the job anymore.

The Storm Creek Camp's dining tent bustled at ten p.m. Hundreds of firefighters, pilots, and support personnel grabbed a meal before too little sleep and a too-early call.

Despite her aversion to the thought of food, Clare joined the line. A loudspeaker garbled a country tune while servers heaped her plate with greasy pork chops, lumpy mashed potatoes, and canned green beans.

Since the troops had left, the only person she knew at the tables was Steve.

When she paused beside him, he looked up from his Styrofoam plate. His blond hair was clean and, like her, he had turned in his soiled Nomex for fresh. Some medic had bandaged his more seriously burned left hand, and his right was pink in places. Her own hands stung, but she didn't think she needed a bandage.

Clare climbed onto the bench beside Steve. As she settled in, her arm brushed his. "Excuse me," she murmured.

She reached for a plastic saltshaker. Steve passed it, their hands touching briefly. His face, still pink from a day of sun and the heat of the fire, seemed to turn a bit redder.

Looking at her plate, Clare salted, lifted a mouthful of the tasteless green beans, and salted again. Her raw throat protested.

Steve looked at her and the night wind ruffled her hair. The errant gust traveled through the tent, making the sides sway and firefighters grab for their napkins.

Clare met his eyes, remembering that afternoon, his weight on hers in a way that couldn't help but make a man and woman consider. She told herself it was the adrenaline and the danger. Death had been on the wind, passing so close that the shelter's flapping might well have been the Harpy's wings.

Billy Jakes had worn a wedding ring. Had someone called or was his wife still passing a pleasant evening? When the phone rang, she'd answer in a breezy familiar way thinking it must be him . . .

A mouthful of pork resisted Clare's attempt to swallow.

As if he read her thoughts, Steve reached for her hand. He forced her stiff fingers straight. "Don't beat yourself up over Billy Jakes, Clare."

His touch did what a hot shower and Garrett's kindness could not. She found herself able to take a full breath and at least attempt to relax. Her shoulders and back stayed tight.

Steve circled his thumb on the inside of her wrist near her pulse. "There's nothing you could have done," he soothed.

"Done about what?"

Clare looked up to find Deering. His smile said he saw she'd abandoned her bra. He appeared not to notice that Steve held her hand, or that she was close to tears.

She pulled back and faced the remembered intensity in Deering's eyes.

A beat late, he said, "*Doctor* Haywood." Without an invitation, he sat across from them. Evidently, he had been to the showers, too, his hair leaving a damp trail on the collar of a khaki shirt. He wore his aviator sunglasses on top of his head.

After what had happened today, Clare was torn between being glad to see him and plain not caring. She cut a slice of pork and failed to convey it to her mouth.

"I can safely tell you that West Yellowstone is secure this evening," Deering said.

She was too exhausted to celebrate, but glad for the townspeople.

"I must have dropped a hundred buckets of water on the edge of town." Deering acted as though she had not walked out on him. "The downdrafts were so bad I had to tell myself I was going in for a closer look when I was putting on throttle and dropping like a rock." He forked up a mouthful of mashed potatoes.

The last thing she needed tonight was braggadocio.

Next to Clare, Steve shrugged at the hero talk. "I'd have expected you'd be trucking that useless chopper out of town."

"That's a million dollar machine." Deering cut his eyes to Clare as though he hoped to impress her.

"Did your claim get settled?" she asked.

"Or did the salvage folks take your Bell?" The taunting vehemence in Steve's voice shocked her. "You didn't hear about that?" he said. "The salvage company gets it if flyboy here doesn't come up with the money."

Deering slammed a fist on the folding table, making it shudder for ten feet. Curious glances were directed their way. "Okay." His voice carried. "I tried to cover up what really happened . . . for you."

"For me?" Steve glared.

"Guys." Clare held up a hand.

Deering ignored her. "I know your job's on shaky grounds, Haywood. You don't need for anybody to know you fucked up."

"I fucked up?" Clare saw Steve's muscles bunch as though he were about to rise.

"But since you want to play hardball," Deering seemed oblivious to people staring, "I'll have to tell First Assurance I had a passenger who wrapped the bucket cable around the skid. Screwed the pooch."

Clare put her hand on Steve's arm. She didn't know whether she meant to support or restrain him.

"Everybody knows about you, Haywood," Deering taunted. "It's already around how you fucked up again today and lost your truck. How you're scared to fly after that crash with your wife and kid and trying to drink yourself to death."

The music and talk in the tent seemed far away. Clare felt Steve's arm tighten and realized that he clenched his steak knife's handle beneath the table.

Without thinking, she slid her hand down and put a hard grip on his fingers, heedless of his burns. "Don't let him do this to you," she murmured.

The knife fell to the earthen tent floor.

Steve sat back, cradling the hand she'd grabbed with his other. She moved her hand back to his arm and thankfully, he failed to leap across the table for Deering's throat as she half-expected.

Ignoring Steve, Deering turned to her as though nothing had happened. "If the wind doesn't shift, the Storm Creek's coming right through camp. You ought to let me fly you out of here." His tone was proprietary as he reached across to brush her bangs out of her eyes.

She jerked away before she even thought.

And felt Steve's shocked eyes on her. Of course, he couldn't have known she'd been seeing Deering.

"Mister Haywood? " A slight Hispanic man in TW Services coveralls stood behind Steve's shoulder. "I go to the terminal at Gardiner for supplies. Do you need a ride home?"

With another scathing look at both her and Deering, Steve rose. "Thanks, Miguel, I'd like to get home tonight."

"How could you?" Clare threw at Deering. Her voice carried and people were still swiveling their heads to look at them. He shook his head, a play to the crowd that said he thought both she and Steve were the ones in error.

Clare shoved back her plate. A murmur of voices trailed her departure.

She looked for Steve, her steps speeding when she realized there were too many men in yellow shirts. Away from the dining canopy and bright lights, she knew she'd lost him. Standing in the parking lot, she tasted smoke, a pervasive foul taint on every wind.

On a nearby Army tent, a hand-lettered sign proclaimed 'Valley Forge West,' referring to a shortage of boots in the military ranks. The Army boot soles were not nearly as heat resistant as the heavy White's brand boots worn by the fire-fighters. Clare's own feet felt hot inside hers, as though they had not cooled from the roasting they'd gotten during the Hellroaring's blowup.

Rapid footsteps sounded on gravel. She stopped, hoping it was Steve.

"Wait," said Deering.

She set her teeth. Tonight when he'd first arrived, his smile had still had the power to make her feel that extra awareness of him. She had sat there next to Steve and across from Deering and been torn by feelings for both of them, until he had attacked Steve.

Deering touched her shoulders.

She went tense. "Look," she said, "we had to go into shelters this afternoon and I'm completely wired. My daughter is flying in to Jackson Hole Airport tomorrow."

He moved his fingers, massaging. "I can make it better . . . "

"Dammit!" Her voice went shrill. "A man died."

He lifted his hands. From the dining tent, the wail of Crystal Gayle entreated her man. The camp generators droned.

Clare turned on him. "How could you?" she challenged. "What you said about Steve's wife and child . . . "

Deering's eyes showed his own pain. "He's been nothing but trouble for me, ever since he got on board my *Georgia* back in July. Now I'm stuck flying military surplus." Deering pointed to Karrabotsos's helicopter behind the fence erected to deter buffalo and elk from damaging aircraft. "I asked Garrett where you were tonight because I wanted, no, needed to see you. After a full day in the cockpit, I fly over here and find you holding hands and making moon eyes."

The heavy growl of a diesel roared toward them on the bulldozed track leading out to Highway 212. The headlights of the big machine swept over them. When the glare subsided, Clare saw Steve in the passenger seat.

There was nothing to stay for. She couldn't stand that Steve thought she was on Deering's side. And another midnight evacuation would put her God knows where when Devon's plane landed.

She ran toward the truck, waving her arms.

The door opened and Steve pulled her into the cab. When they reached Mammoth, she could get a room at the hotel. In the morning, she would figure out how to get to the airport.

The miles unfolded hypnotically, as the truck made the ten-mile descent down Soda Butte Creek to the Lamar River valley. Traffic was light, for the hotel guests, campers, and soldiers of the fire war had settled for the night.

Clare straddled the seat between Steve and Miguel. She saw little of the country, just the stabbing beams of headlights on the two-lane asphalt and the colorless specters of trees rushing past. To the north, the crimson glow of the Storm Creek and Hellroaring fires lighted the sky.

Down and down, twenty miles until the truck launched onto a span over dark space. A sign identified the chasm as the Yellowstone River. After Tower Junction, they began the climb up the divide that led to Mammoth.

Deering had put his hands on Clare tonight, but the thrill that had first run through her at his touch had vanished. Hell, nothing was the same as it had been four hours ago when she and Steve had crawled into a dugout hole in the ground and listened to Billy Jakes's fiery death.

On the rising slope, moonlight silvered the Blacktail Deer Plateau. A pair of reddish-gold orbs flashed in the headlights, animals abroad in the night.

Past the summit, the road to Mammoth joined Lava Creek Canyon, spiraling down. The center of the gorge was an ominous gash.

How dark was it where Billy Jakes was tonight? He had a wife, maybe even children, she didn't know, but Sergeant Ron Travis had been clear. Clare had led Billy on his final march.

The truck rushed down a roller coaster that carried her stomach. Tomorrow Devon would arrive, coming into the midst of another death investigation involving her mother. She'd shrugged off Clare's feelings of guilt over Frank, just like all the other firefighters. Get back on that horse and ride, they'd all said. Right into the maw of the Hellroaring.

She didn't know if she could go back on the line. Garrett had given her a few days off to show Devon the sights and after that, maybe she'd go home.

As they drove, she felt Steve's thigh and shoulder against her side. A few more miles and he looped an arm around her, drawing her head onto his chest. She rested against him, hearing his steady heartbeat. Deering had said he was a worthless alcoholic and she'd seen him drunk, but that couldn't erase the way Steve had looked at her just before he'd thrown off the fire shelter.

Clare looked through the windshield and watched night rush at them.

CHAPTER TWENTY
September 4

By a freak of atmospheric currents, Mammoth Valley was clear tonight. Leafy cottonwoods underlined to Clare the contrast between this refuge and the stark skeletons of trees all over the park. A herd of perhaps thirty elk posed on the lawn in front of Park Headquarters.

They were more fortunate than the ones Steve had found on Black Saturday. For that matter, through mere luck, Clare and Steve had not been dealt the card Billy Jakes had received.

She climbed down from the truck after Steve. In the street, he said, "You can bunk at my place." She saw how he looked at her rather than at the Mammoth Hotel across the way.

She considered. Still shaking inside at how close they'd come to the edge, she wasn't ready to be alone.

He pointed along the street lined with stately old houses. "I'm down that way."

She checked herself for reluctance. "Your place is fine."

Steve played tour guide. "There used to be a much grander hotel. The National was an enormous wood-frame place, built in 1886." A little nervousness edged in his voice.

"What happened to it?" she asked, still aware of how good it had felt to be snugged against him in the truck.

"It burned."

They passed four two-story duplexes with tall brick chimneys. "Park service employees live here now instead of Fort Yellowstone's officers," Steve said. The next low frame building they passed was fronted by a porch holding an armada of bicycles. "This place used to be park headquarters at the turn of the century. Moru Mzima, a naturalist from Zimbabwe, and his wife, Nyeri, live there now."

Clare looked across the lawn. "And kids."

"Three." Steve smiled. "I sit for them sometimes." He pointed to a smaller building at the end of the row. "My place is next."

"What did the Army do with it?"

"It was the first building in Fort Yellowstone. A guard house to hold ten prisoners." The innocuous one-story building, its wide porch a dark perimeter, did not look like a jail.

Clare stared. "What were the prisoners in for? Picking flowers? Collecting minerals?"

"Poaching. Selling alcohol to the soldiers."

Silence fell.

"So what's it like, living in the stockade?" Clare tried.

Steve cleared his throat. After a little while he said, "Walt Leighton says I treat my home as a prison, especially when I have a bout of . . . bad times."

Deering's words about Steve's wife and child hung between them. A pink tricycle lay abandoned on the lawn. "You have kids?" he asked.

Clare sighed. "Actually, I'm picking my daughter up at the Jackson airport tomorrow. At least I'm supposed to."

"I can try and requisition another truck and drive you . . . but it may not be easy."

"Or I can hitch a ride to Old Faithful for my rental car." Despite the peaceful atmosphere, the night seemed to be at a distance. Because she'd felt safe in the curve of Steve's arm, she went on, "Devon thinks she's coming on vacation, while you and I are watching people die."

He slowed his steps. "What will you do with a little girl here?"

She stopped. "Devon is seventeen."

"No way." Steve whistled softly. "You got pregnant when you were twelve?"

"Thanks," she said. "I don't know what I'm going to do with her. My ex thinks she's seeing an older man and won't deal with it. He and wife number two have plane tickets to Greece."

"That's tough." Steve stepped onto the porch. "I often wonder what would have happened to us if Susan and Christa had lived."

As Steve reached for his keys, Clare watched the patterned silver light that shined through the porch lattice from the streetlamps and a quarter moon. The stench of death was still in her head. Based on experience, it would be there for days, but she sniffed and tried to replace it with the scent of fresh-cut grass and summer flowerbeds.

She needed this sense of normality tonight.

Steve opened his door and flicked a switch that spilled a pool of brighter light.

Moving past him to the focus of the crowded room, she slid a hand onto the black-lacquered finish of a grand piano. Beneath a layer of dust, it felt smooth as silk. She raised the cover and picked out a chord with her right thumb on middle C.

Her fingers protested when she flexed them and she became more aware of her burns. "Do you have any aloe?"

"I could use some myself." He went down the side hall.

Clare played random chords until Steve came back barefoot in khaki shorts and a tourist T-shirt with a moose on it. He offered bottles of green gel and hydrogen peroxide.

She urged him toward the worn, brown leather couch that clashed with the ornate piano. "Let me look at your burn first." When she unwrapped the layers of gauze, blistered skin made her wince.

That wasn't like her. As a teacher and mom, she knew how to minimize life's little hurts. When she worked wrecks, fires, or medical emergencies, she called on a calm façade that sometimes kept victims from going into shock. This evening she was so fragile that this reminder of Steve's vulnerability made her eyes sting.

Keeping her head down, she cleaned the seeping wound and applied a fresh bandage. "Okay." She put the brisk grip-and-release move of a coach on each of his legs.

It was his turn to wince.

She bent to explore first one knee and then the other. Her fingers traced the length of the three-inch scars, matched pairs along the inside and outside of each kneecap. "Sports?" This explained why she had occasionally noticed Steve limping.

"An accident."

She suspected the air tragedy that had taken his family, but he did not volunteer. He made a move to go and she backed away.

In his kitchen, copper pots hung from a wrought-iron rack. Repeated scrubbing had worn the linoleum until the red and gray squares were blurred into a muddy continuum. The dining area, with a pine table between corner windows, overlooked another row of staff housing.

Steve opened the icebox to reveal a rotting cucumber, three cans of Olympia beer and some Calistoga mineral water. "This is the first I've been home in a while. Stick around until I get to a store and I'll make you *coq au vin*."

Clare's opinion of him continued to change. First the piano and now he professed to be a chef. Of course, the tuna salad he'd whipped up on Mount Washburn had been tasty.

She took the beer he offered and drank, the carbonation stinging her raw throat. Uncapping the Calistoga, Steve drank off half of the quart in three gulps.

Clare lifted her Oly and raised an inquiring brow.

"I'm off the sauce." He toasted with his water.

Something inside her lifted at his commitment to stay sober. Being on a mountain was one thing, handing your guest a beer and not having one yourself must be tougher.

She bent to take off her heavy-soled boots. In sock feet, she carried her can into the living room. "Do you know Moonlight Sonata?" She sank onto the sofa.

"I know the piece. I don't play."

That was odd. Everything else here fit her expectation. A set of packed bookshelves held technical books on biology and geology, along with a well-worn collection of popular paperbacks. Bleached animal skulls sat alongside specimens of turquoise, amethyst, and other rocks she couldn't identify.

She set her drink on the pine coffee table and lifted an irregular black stone. It was heavy and smooth, but the concoidal shape tapered to sharp edges.

"Obsidian," Steve said. "The Nez Perce believed it had healing powers."

Holding the rock, she asked, "Do you think it could help me forget today?"

"Only you can answer that."

She stared into the stone's glassy depths. Inside was a vortex, somehow dizzying. Glancing toward the darkness outside the door, she noted the bars on its small window.

Steve took the obsidian from her. "You've been through a lot." He set the rock down. "But there were a few things about today I wouldn't change." His steady eyes suggested he was as aware of her as she was of him.

Clare looked for a distraction. "Your work?" She nodded toward a black-and-white photo of a snowshoe hare huddled at the base of an aspen. On the same wall hung a view of the Grand Teton emerging from morning fog, alongside a baby elk with spindly legs threatening collapse.

"I put in a darkroom beside my study," Steve said.

Something about the process of capturing a wilderness image and putting it into a frame underlined Clare's ephemeral association with the Yellowstone country. Her family had once lived on this land, while she merely visited, welcome to take snapshots, leave footprints, and go home.

Although she ran out of small talk, she felt more was required. "Long day," she began and then realized that she was taking them back to the Hellroaring.

"Very long." He shifted his weight from one foot to the other. The caring in his eyes, overlain by something deeper, decided her.

Curling her feet beneath her on the couch, she confessed, "Today isn't the first time I've had somebody die in a fire with me."

Steve came to sit beside her.

"Frank inspired me every day. He kept the station meals on par with a chichi restaurant. He shorted-sheeted our bunks." She gave a giggle that surprised her.

Steve smiled.

Once more, she felt solemn. "We were together on the hose. When the roof came down, and I lived, I was afraid to show my face at the memorial service."

Steve took her hand. "What happened to Frank and Billy wasn't your fault, no matter how hard you try to take responsibility."

"Get back on that horse?"

"Right."

Sick and tired of hearing that, she withdrew her hand and lashed out. "That's great advice, but do you practice what you preach? Did you book an airline flight after your crash? Have you given any thought to remarrying?"

Steve levered off the couch and stood with his back to the piano, his gray eyes bleak.

Her ears got hot. "I'm sorry. That's none of my business . . .

especially the part about marriage."

For a long moment, they faced off. Then Steve nodded with a gentleness that said he accepted her apology.

Clare wished he were still sitting next to her, but the distance of the room separated them.

Steve glanced over his shoulder toward the rest of the house. "There's only the one bedroom." A catch in his voice suggested he might be thinking of those brief moments when their bodies had pressed together in the fire shelter.

A pulse began to pound in her. "I don't want to put you out."

Extending his un-bandaged right hand, he reached to help her up. "You won't."

His palm was dry, reassuring, and strong against hers. She remembered him holding her in the truck, his heart beating beneath her ear. Someone else's strength was what she craved tonight, to set aside the burden of training young men and women too briefly, before sending them to what today had been death.

She stood. Steve released her hand, but warmth lingered. They went into the hall, leaving the light from the living room behind. His touch on the small of her back almost made her turn, thinking of going into his arms.

She waited. At the archway that led into a darkened room, he left her, padding across the hardwood floor.

When he turned on the bedside lamp, it shone full force onto a picture of a blonde in a black formal dress, smiling lovingly at her photographer. She sat at the keyboard of a grand piano, her hands poised to play.

"Your wife?" Clare asked quietly. The wild pulse in her still pounded, incongruous against the feeling of being dashed with cold water.

"That's Susan," Steve agreed. He sank onto the bed with a dejected look.

Clare folded down beside him. "Why don't you tell me about her?"

❦❦❦

"Fasten your seat belt." The pert Triworld Air attendant couldn't hold a candle to the incandescent beauty of Steve's wife, made ripe by her recent pregnancy. Susan held three-month-old Christa against her breast while he secured her seatbelt.

He'd wondered at the wisdom of traveling with Christa so young and fragile, but Susan had been off the circuit for six months. She'd badly wanted to make the concert engagement in Anchorage.

At last night's performance, she'd been at the top of her form, gracefully introducing three compositions she'd written while on sabbatical. "I call this the *Suite of Life*. The first movement speaks of the passionate glory of conception, the second of the still fullness of waiting. The last celebrates birth, both as completion and a promise that is just beginning."

Steve had heard Susan play it a hundred times in the studio overlooking the Potomac, first a halting, intermittent progression of notes. Gradually, a theme emerged that was day-by-day embellished. Never had it flowed as it did in answer to the questing hush of the Anchorage audience. During the standing ovation, he'd blinked back tears.

In the morning, Susan's agent had telephoned their room at the Captain Cook Hotel. Steve took Christa and walked to the window overlooking Cook Inlet. The tide was out, exposing a half-mile of chocolate mud flat that would be covered again within hours. Ever since Susan had told him she was expecting he'd felt differently, as though he were not just a scientist observing the cycles, but finally part of life's ebb and flow.

Christa's rosebud mouth nudged his shirt. Her tiny face began to screw up as she gathered energy for a squall that would keep Susan from hearing the news from New York. Steve chuckled and offered his finger as a pacifier.

"Guess what?" Susan crowed, putting the phone into the cradle.

"They hated you in Peoria." He kept his face straight.

"The *Times* had a man here last night, happened to be on vacation." Steve heard in her voice there was only one *Times* and that it was in New York. "He phoned in a review of my new work that Charlie says will net me a recording contract."

As the 737 taxied for takeoff in Anchorage, he looked at the barren earth beside the runway and thought how impossibly rich his life was.

Steve realized that although Clare studied him with steady eyes, tears ran down her cheeks.

They sat opposite each other on his bed, crossed-legged like children in a reading circle, but he couldn't read her.

He'd told her about screaming metal and fire. How he did not remember Susan and Christa's funeral because he had attended in a wheelchair, doped to the gills. He'd been lucky, they told him, that he'd taken the impact there and not broken his neck.

How many times in those early days had he wished he had?

"After it happened, I was stationed at Park Service Headquarters," he said. "I'd drive to work on the George Washington Parkway. Planes were always taking off and landing at National, flying low over the Potomac."

"How did you come to Yellowstone?"

"Everyone knew I was having a rough time." He swallowed. "My boss thought that if I had a fresh start someplace I could get back into research . . ." He looked at her squarely. "It was a kindness. And a move to get a problem drinker off their hands."

She nodded. "Do you miss the booze? Crave it?"

"Some days are better than others."

He didn't tell her that sometimes he thought he would die for a drink. What had kept him going so far was waking each morning with a clear head and a load of unfamiliar energy. It was then that he realized he wasn't getting old like he'd thought.

"Has there been anyone else?" Clare picked at a loose thread on his bedspread.

"No." Steve eased back and propped himself on an elbow. He hadn't felt this comfortable with somebody in years. "Living in Mammoth makes it tough. Few single women winter in and the summer staff are transients." He felt her cool appraisal of his excuses. "And, of course, what you said. I'm shy of taking a risk again."

He focused on Clare. "And you?"

"Since my divorce I've just tried getting Devon grown up. That hasn't worked so well either."

They kept talking, words tumbling over each other. He shared confidences he would not have imagined telling anyone, a substitute for what he wanted . . . to take Clare in his arms.

How many times on Mount Washburn had he caught himself spinning a scenario like this? Wondering how they might end up alone. Now he sat not three feet from her on his bed, for God's sake.

What stopped him was Susan's loving gaze from the nightstand.

The phone beside the photo rang, the sound jarring. Steve jumped. Rolling over and reaching for the receiver, he groused, "Yeah?" The bedside clock said two-fifteen.

"Is Clare there?" a male voice inquired.

Wordlessly, Steve handed her the receiver and walked out of his room.

❀❀❀

"You said you needed to get to Jackson Hole Airport tomorrow to pick up your daughter," Deering said. "Sorry, I mean today."

Clare jumped to her feet beside Steve's bed. "How did you know I'd be here?"

"Lucky guess?"

While she considered hanging up, he said, "How are you getting down south tomorrow?"

"With Steve's truck burned, he'll requisition another, or I'll hitch a ride with someone from the fire cache here at Mammoth. Get my car at Old Faithful."

"The south entrance is going to be closed all day," Deering urged.

That meant going over through Idaho, a hundred miles out of the way.

"Come on. If Steve is going to drive you, I'm helping him out. It would be an all day job."

She didn't care to listen to Deering pretend to be nice to Steve, but what she absolutely did not want to be was late picking up her daughter. Devon must be feeling rejected by Jay's taking off to Greece with Elyssa.

Clare decided. "Her plane gets in at two."

"I'll be there first thing in the morning."

As she placed the phone back in the cradle, Steve called from down the hall, "I'll bed down on the sofa." The hard note in his voice said the evening was over.

With a sigh, she picked up the picture of his wife. When Clare was ten, her mother had insisted on piano lessons. Although Miss Bryan had been diligent at teaching the perfect arch and placement of the hands, Clare had never really had any talent.

Susan Sandlin Haywood's sinewy fingers looked perfect.

In the corner of the frame was a miniature of a newborn, the kind they took in hospitals. Christa's tiny pink face crinkled, her mouth open in a yawn.

Tears pricked Clare's eyelids. Here she'd been thinking of going to Steve, when he wasn't over the loss of his wife. Wasn't that her damned luck this summer? Coming to Yellowstone had seemed a grand escape; fight the big fires that made the national news while clearing her head. Instead, she'd screwed up big time. Tried to lead the troops and ended up in a tiny silver shelter fighting for her life.

She climbed into Steve's bed and reluctantly admitted that had things been different she might have shared it with him.

Tossing until three, she fell into a sleep tormented by crimson light, the strobe effect of the flapping shelter, and the charred smell of burnt flesh.

CHAPTER TWENTY-ONE
September 5

Clare awoke with the fear she'd already missed Devon's plane. She dressed and hurried down the hall to find rose light coming in the window over Steve's kitchen sink.

He stood barefoot at the counter in a faded cotton shirt and jeans, putting coffee beans into a grinder. His sleep-tossed hair looked somehow intimate. He gave her a glance and bent to his task, pressing a button and sending up a delicious aroma of fresh ground. The high-pitched whine prevented her from speaking.

When he released the control, silence fell.

"Morning already," she ventured.

He dumped the grounds into a glass pot without ceremony.

After all that had happened between them, she'd been hoping he'd be over Deering's middle-of-the-night call.

The copper kettle on the stove whistled.

Turning his back, Steve poured boiling water. The kettle went back on the stove with a clank. When he moved the coffee pot on the tile-topped counter, it clinked. She wondered if he'd cracked it.

Last night his coughing from the smoke he'd inhaled had interrupted her fitful sleep. Knowing he was awake had made it worse, the two of them separated by fifteen feet and the infinite gulf that Susan's picture and Deering's call had created.

Steve finally looked at her. Leaning back against the counter, he folded his arms across his chest. "What did he want?"

Quick anger shot through her. She'd left Deering to come home with Steve. She'd gone to his bedroom, her heart beating hard . . . and found a dead woman with the power to keep them apart.

Clare crossed her arms over her own yellow-shirted chest. "I told you I have to be in Jackson to meet Devon. The south entrance is closed, so he's flying me down."

"I could have driven you through Idaho." His voice rose.

"I'm not sure we could make it on time," Clare excused. "He'll be here in a few minutes." Now that she knew Steve was this upset, she wished she could change her mind and let him take her.

He slammed his fist on the tiles. "Dammit, Clare, he's a married man."

Her face went hot and the ancient linoleum seemed to tilt. *What else have you lied to me about?* Deering had not answered when she'd asked that at West Yellowstone Airport. "If he is . . . "

"Count on it."

"I was going to ask . . . " She controlled herself with an effort. "What business is it of yours? Last night you preferred to sleep with your memories."

He crossed to her in three swift steps and his hands came

down hard on her shoulders. "What business of mine? Nothing, except that I was a damned fool . . . sitting on that mountain dreaming. And all the time that S.O.B. was on the make, married or not."

A faint 'whump whump' came through the open kitchen window.

Steve let her go and busied himself pulling down a single mug. He pressed the filter plunger to hold the grounds in the pot and poured. He sipped, deliberately.

She searched his face. If she left now, they'd probably never see each other again. That wasn't what she wanted, but the set of his jaw and the rising sound of rotors said it was time to go.

With the clothes on her back and her wallet that had survived the firestorm in her hip pocket, she turned and rushed across the living room. After a struggle with the turn bolt, she stepped into the yard and scanned the sky.

With typical brashness, Deering ignored Mammoth's helicopter pad down the road. The Huey came in low over the picnic tables across the street and hovered above the old Fort Yellowstone parade ground. Deering's sunglasses shielded his face, the rising sun reflecting on the windshield.

Clare looked back at Steve's house. He stood on the porch watching her, his ire mixed with a look of longing that almost made her turn back.

The Huey set down. When she looked again, Steve was gone.

She ran, warmed by anger at both men. Wrestling open the chopper door, she stretched to get into the left seat.

As soon as she was in place and slammed the door, Deering

lifted off. She fumbled for her harness and headphones, while the earth dropped away. Below, the highway from Mammoth to Tower Junction crossed Lava Creek on an impressive metal span, near its confluence with the Gardner.

Over the engine's roar and the steady whopping of rotors, Deering said dryly, "Good morning." Dark eyes shot a sideways look. "I trust you passed a pleasant night."

"Fuck you," Clare said. "Did you sleep with your wife?"

Deering cut power and the Huey started to lose altitude.

"What are you doing?"

"Putting her down."

"What for?"

"So we can talk."

"Talk all you want. I can't hear you." Clare tore off her headphones and dropped them.

They were coming down onto a broad meadow of dry golden grass. She remembered the drive last night when she and Steve had looked out at the high country of the Blacktail Deer Plateau.

Within a rising cloud of dust, the chopper hovered, then landed. A look out at the expanse of empty meadow made her reconsider getting out and walking away. Nothing was going to make her miss Devon's plane.

The rotors wound down. Deering sat with both hands draped over the cyclic stick until it was quiet, save for the hum of wind around the door seals. He took off his headphones and put them between the seats.

She sat stiffly.

When she failed to look at him, he said, "Clare."

She flicked her eyes to his. There was no cajoling, just an infinite sadness that reminded her of when he'd climbed out of the tent at the Mink Creek Camp.

"You're right," he said evenly. "I am married."

"Then what . . .?"

"When I ditched, she said she hoped they never brought up my chopper. She doesn't understand my flying, like you seem to. I was torn up, looking for a way to get back at her."

Clare saw in him what felt like the first solid truth she'd seen. "You love her."

"Yeah."

Now that she knew . . . too late, that she cared for Steve and not Deering, it was easy to say, "Then, for God's sake, what are you doing here?"

🔥🔥🔥

Georgia Deering swam through molasses-thick darkness toward the light. She kicked and pulled until the brightness became a flood of morning sun on the bed. Through the open window, framed by gently blowing lace curtains, she heard the chatter of the Portneuf as it wended its way downstream from Lava Hot Springs.

Gradually, Georgia came fully awake, realizing that she'd overslept for the third time in a week. Ten-thirty usually saw her breakfast of shredded wheat and strawberries finished, dishes on the drain board.

She ran a hairbrush through her unruly reddish curls and put on her favorite white terry robe, well washed and softened.

In the hallway, she paused to straighten the frame of the wedding ring quilt she'd made when she and Deering got married. It hung next to a shadow box of tiny porcelain dolls. When she got to the kitchen, she frowned, for she'd fallen asleep without putting away last night's dishes.

Although it was pushing noon, she didn't yet feel like eating. "Maybe just a cup of tea," she said, and shook her head. "Pretty soon you'll be answering yourself and then what?"

What indeed? She'd been putting off finding a lot of answers, even afraid to ask the questions. Surely, Deering had been curious about her showing up in West Yellowstone, waiting around with Karrabotsos, and then disappearing. Didn't he even suspect she might have seen him with that Clare?

When she'd come home, she hadn't even told Anna. As if not speaking of it could erase Deering pulling another woman against him in the familiar way she'd thought was reserved for her alone.

Moving woodenly to the pantry, Georgia reached for the canister of herbal tea that Deering had helped her make one day earlier this summer. When she popped the tin, the dank smell of chamomile, mixed with the almost sour essence of stale rose hips smote her. She gagged and lifted the trash lid, but it wasn't enough to put it in the garbage.

Barefoot, she crossed the soft grass she'd hand watered during the drought. Beside the river, she dumped the tea, expecting the flakes to float away. Instead, the mixture landed in a clump beside a rock.

Georgia kicked at the pile. She lost her balance and almost fell into the stony streambed. "Damn you!" she cried, not sure if she meant Deering or that woman. To see the last trace of tea wash down the Portneuf, she knelt on the grassy bank and reached to stir the brew. The smell of tea mixed with tannic decaying leaves overwhelmed her.

She leaned over the bank and gagged. Bright morning receded, her world reduced to the space between her hanging hair and the Portneuf. When the storm had passed, Georgia curled up, shivering. She hoped Widow Barcus wouldn't see her lying in her bathrobe on the lawn.

This crystal morning made her think how different it was where Deering worked, of the smoky hell above Yellowstone. Although she'd told herself she didn't care to know what he was doing, she tuned in the news every evening like clockwork.

Last night, Connie Chung had opened, "Tragic news this evening from Yellowstone National Park."

Georgia's heart had begun to race.

"Private William Harrison Jakes, nineteen, of McCall, Idaho, died when a firestorm overtook him and his fellow firefighters. The other members of the group of twenty-three survived beneath Mylar fire shelters, which miraculously shielded them from the fury of the Hellroaring Fire."

Hellroaring.

That was rich. It wasn't enough that fire warriors challenge the gates of hell. No, they had to call the fire the Hellroaring, like kicking sand in the face of Beelzebub.

Georgia's rage made her forget being chilled and sick. She sat up, wiping cold sweat from her face with her terry sleeve.

A faint 'whop whop' came to her.

Deering often came home by chopper, landing at the local

heliport near the high school across the road.

She remained on the ground, feeling dew seep though her robe. The helipad was also used for medical emergencies and by other businesses.

The chopper's sound grew louder.

Reluctantly, she pushed to her feet and walked around the side of the house. Once she got past the area where she'd watered, the dry grass felt sharp on her bare soles.

The helicopter came in low across the football field, olive drab with that same military look as the one in the newspaper photo. There was something else as well; some indefinable nuance in the approach angle that said her husband had come home.

Deering started shutting down. Karrabotsos had sounded surprised when he had radioed for permission to fly to Lava Hot Springs, but had let him go, muttering something about taking better care of that little red-haired gal.

That made no sense for Karrabotsos had never met Georgia.

How simple it had seemed when Clare challenged him. She'd managed to cut through all the bullshit. He did love his wife, had always loved her. No matter how he pretended nonchalance, crashing his helicopter had shaken him to the core. When Georgia hadn't been there for him, he'd turned to the first available woman, the same kind of daredevil behavior he exhibited in the air.

As the rotors wound down, Deering felt the reluctance that

had kept him from calling home these past weeks. Before he stepped down, he reached to the left seat and gathered up a florist's box. In the breast pocket of his flight suit rested a velvet jewel case. This morning when he'd dropped Clare off he'd hitched a ride into the town of Jackson.

With a slam of the Huey's door, he started across the grass. Before he'd gone ten steps, he saw Georgia at the edge of their yard, inside the low, wrought iron fence. Her white terry bathrobe was belted around her, that glorious copper hair curling over her shoulders.

Taking a breath of the wonderfully clear air, Deering waved.

Usually she jumped the knee-high gate, rushed across the street to the landing field, and launched herself at his neck. This morning, she stood still at his approach.

Deering came through the gate and proffered the box. He encircled Georgia with his other arm and aimed a kiss. She turned her head and his lips brushed her cheek.

"Flowers?" she asked flatly.

"Yeah, I know how much you like 'em in the garden . . . "

Her bright head was down and she busied herself with the satin ribbon. The florist had said that long-stemmed red roses were the most romantic statement a man could make. He wished with all his might that he could come home clean instead of with this dirty feeling.

"I'll put these in water." Georgia headed for the house and he had no choice but to follow.

"Hon," he tried. She was already inside the kitchen, rummaging beneath the counter for the vase he'd sent her roses in twenty years ago. Cheap florist's stock, no blown glass, she'd kept it all these years. He realized, shamefaced, that he'd never repeated the gesture.

Georgia filled the vase, wiped it with a dishtowel and set it on the wooden table. It rocked, reminding him that he'd promised to fix that shaky leg.

She arranged the roses, cutting them to different lengths with a crosswise knife cut. This time of year, she usually had that vase full of blooms from her garden. Her task complete, she said, "I was just going to make myself some tea." She sounded as though he were a guest in his own kitchen.

"Tea sounds good."

Georgia brought out orange pekoe. Deering wondered what had happened to the herb blend she usually liked. With her back to him, she put on the kettle and looked out the window.

He reached to his pocket for the jewel box. Georgia was October born, the opal birthstone, and he'd found a simple gold band set with a glowing bluish-purple cabochon.

He held out the velvet case. Georgia took it.

The teakettle whistled.

She set the case on the counter and removed the pot from the burner. Steam rose from the tea, wafting a sharp aroma. Georgia reached for a cup, stirred and pulled the tea bag onto a saucer. He wondered where his cup was.

"Aren't you going to . . .?"

She rediscovered the jewel box and slowly opened the lid.

Now, she'd smile and throw her arms around his neck.

Georgia's mouth twisted. "It's funny." She set the case down without removing the ring. "I read in a magazine last week that when your man shows up with flowers and gifts, he's guilty of something."

Deering felt as though he stood in a cold draft. "You believe everything you read?" He took her shoulders in his hands. Even through the bulky robe, she felt as though she'd lost some weight.

Georgia backed until the kitchen sink stopped her. "I didn't have to read about this. Anna convinced me to come up to West Yellowstone and find you. That nice Mr. Karrabotsos let me wait at the airport in the middle of the night until you finally showed up."

No wonder Karrabotsos knew what Georgia looked like. "So, why didn't I see you there?"

Georgia reached to one of the roses and plucked off the top. The petals fluttered to the floor. "You didn't see me, but you sure saw somebody. You put your arms around that woman, the one from the news photo."

She ripped off the top of another rose and let the petals fall.

Deering felt as though the air were a thick liquid that he swam through. "No." He couldn't think of anything that wouldn't be a lie, and he was through lying. Another rose ended up on the floor. "It's not what you think," he managed.

Georgia put out a stiff arm and shoved the vase she'd treasured for twenty years, and he'd never realized why until today . . . off the table. It tumbled to the floor, bounced once and smashed.

"Go back to her," she said. "Fight your damned fires."

CHAPTER TWENTY-TWO
September 5

Within the peaceful town of Jackson, nestled at the base of a butte, it was hard for Clare to believe that war raged on a hundred fronts to the north. She wanted nothing more to do with it.

After she'd told Deering good-bye at the Jackson Hole Airport, she had rented another car, shopped for clothes that weren't green and yellow Nomex, and checked into a motel. Then she'd walked, window-shopping turquoise jewelry and bronzes, and sat beneath the town square's antler arches.

Deering had gone to try and make things right with his wife, as it should be. That left things all wrong with Steve. Last night, after they'd talked for hours, she'd almost believed the spell of his Susan was weakening. And if Deering's call had made him jealous, maybe that was a good sign. She passed a pay phone, but what could she say if she called? Devon would be here within hours.

Thinking of family and watching the tourist stagecoach circling the block reminded her that she wanted to learn about her ancestors. Such ties extended beyond death, like Steve's to his wife and child. If she didn't have Jay anymore, she at least had her daughter and the people who'd gone before.

Recalling the Yellowstone historian's recommendations, she searched out the Jackson Hole Historical Society. It occupied an authentic-looking log building on a quiet side street. When she opened the door, a bell tinkled.

The man who emerged from the rear room might have been a weather-beaten seventy or a well-preserved eighty-five. His ruddy face beamed beneath a shock of silver hair. "Don't get many folks here." Filled from floor to ceiling with ancient volumes, the dimly lit cabin was not exactly the average tourist destination.

"Asa Dean." Her host peered owlishly through glasses and extended an age-spotted hand.

"Clare Chance."

Some of the books were thick leather-bound tomes with pages edged in gold; others had seen better days. Wildflower books were filed alongside old novels. When she trailed her finger along the edge of a water-stained spine, Asa offered, "A souvenir of the 1927 flood."

"I've not heard of that," Clare said.

"Back in twenty-five, old Sheep Mountain got tired of holding herself up and slid down into the valley of the Gros Ventre." Asa's voice lapsed into the cadence of telling a familiar tale. "Dammed the river and created Slide Lake . . . until the wet spring of twenty-seven. On May eighteenth, the earthen dam let loose and a fifty-foot wall of water wiped out the town of Kelly."

"Were you here then?"

"I was born in Kelly in ought-seven. Moved to Jackson after the flood."

"I had some family that lived near the Tetons. My grandfather left for Texas in twenty-seven."

"Mayhap 'cause of the flood." Asa toyed with his suspenders. "Would you like coffee?"

Clare checked her watch. She'd called the airport and been told that Devon's flight was delayed several hours. "That would be nice."

"Cream and sugar?" Asa stumped into the room behind the library.

"Just black." She raised her voice, for she'd noted her host wore a pair of large, old-fashioned hearing aids.

Asa returned. Coagulated lumps of powdered creamer floated in both brimfull Styrofoam cups. "What brings you to Jackson?"

"I'm a firefighter."

"Whee . . ." Asa set his coffee on a worn antique table, hitched up his pants and sat down. "Many women do that now?"

"Some," Clare said, then admitted, "not many."

"We're hearing they can't stop those fires. Just plain burning out of control, and all you firefighters do is toast marshmallows."

By now, she should be used to peoples' attitude around the park. No matter how skilled the generals and their troops, or how many millions were spent, all they could do was try to keep the fires from damaging life and property.

Clare set her coffee aside. "My family was already in the valley around the turn of the century."

"Not many folks here then," Asa said.

"Their name was Sutton."

Asa nodded. He was silent for so long that Clare wondered if he had heard her. Finally, he said, "Suttons lived out north in what's now the National Park."

"My great-grandmother Laura was supposed to have kept a journal. Nobody in the family has it and I wondered if it might have wound up here."

"We don't have anything like that," he answered immediately.

"How can you be sure?" Clare gestured toward thousands of books.

"Been working here since forty-nine. Know every volume on every shelf."

There were a lot of books, but she figured that in thirty-nine years she could get through them all. "Did you know the Suttons?"

Asa dipped his head. "They sold out to the Snake River Land Company after the flood. Their ranch ended up inside the park, just the way Rockefeller wanted it."

"What do you mean?"

"John D. Rockefeller, Jr. hated the gas stations, billboards, and cheap tourist camps near Jenny Lake. He decided to buy up all the private land and donate it to the country for a national park."

"What's wrong with that?" Clare asked.

Asa scowled. "If you'd been here then, you'd understand. They set up a dummy corporation and kept folks in the dark about what all the buying was for."

"My family sold out?"

"Yup. After the Gros Ventre flood, people were nervous and took whatever offers they could get. Your folks got taken to the cleaners along with my father."

"Do you know the way to their place?"

"Ask at Grand Teton Headquarters," Asa said.

Clare thanked him and headed for the door. She wondered if Devon would show any interest in knowing about the family.

While she killed more time in town before heading for the airport, she felt torn between anticipation at seeing Devon and an ache over what might have been with Steve.

❧❧❧

Two hours later, Clare watched as the 737 taxied up to the Jackson Hole Airport. The small terminal squatted on the sage-covered flats beside the startling wall of the Tetons. Smoke hung in the valley, giving a filtered view of the mighty bulwark.

After twenty or so vacationers had picked their way down the stairs to the tarmac, Clare saw Devon. Her unruly hair was more golden than usual; she must have hit the Summer Blonde too hard. Charcoal rimmed her eyes and her cutoffs and tank top were tight. When Devon got to within three feet, Clare smelled gin.

Before she could berate Devon for getting the flight attendant to serve someone underage, a low male voice spoke from behind her. "How about introducing me to your daughter?"

Her two worlds collided.

"Hey, Mom." Devon tossed off her greeting, and checked Steve out, from his red western shirt and faded jeans down to scuffed leather hiking boots. She raised an inquiring brow that made Clare feel as though she was the one who had some answering to do.

"This is Dr. Steve Haywood." Clare did not meet his eyes. She wasn't prepared for what she might find there. Truth to tell, she wasn't ready for him to see how foolishly happy she was to see him.

"Hello," Devon responded, "*Doctor* Steve Haywood."

Clare could tell by the knowing look that her daughter thought they were an item. Not ready to admit how it made her feel, she stood on tiptoe to kiss Devon's cheek. "Hi."

"What kind of doctor?" Devon asked. "Are you sick?"

"Yeah." Clare figured that about summed it up. "Sick of eating smoke and watching the fires outstrip anything man can throw at them."

She was tired of everything about this wild country, except the man who smiled indulgently at Devon. "I'm a biologist. The past few years I've been counting elk."

"Elk," Devon echoed flatly.

Steve cradled the back of Clare's arm with a persuasive touch. Gone was his mask of anger, replaced by the warmth she remembered in his eyes. That spark she'd felt in him just before he threw off their flimsy fire shelter.

From the corner of her eye Clare saw Devon notice.

"I happened to be in the neighborhood." He grinned. "I wondered if I might buy you two ladies dinner."

"Steak?" Devon qualified.

"The best in town," Steve agreed.

Clare let their momentum carry her to baggage claim and out into the yellow afternoon light. After all, Devon already thought she and Steve were together.

He carried Devon's duffel bag to Clare's rental car and showed off the clunker of a truck from the park motor pool. "A hundred eighty thousand miles and she shudders when I brake. It's a wonder I made it over Teton Pass."

"I'm glad you did," Clare told him.

Devon gave him a funny look.

As he held Clare's car door for her, he murmured, "If I didn't catch you at the airport, I was going to check the motels."

A little stab went through her at the thought of what people could do in motels. This evening, though, she had a duty to her daughter.

🌢🌢🌢

At Jackson's Million Dollar Cowboy Bar, the main room boasted a dance floor, pool tables, and long bars on either side. Glass cases displayed a stuffed grizzly, bighorn sheep, and game birds. When Devon mounted a vacant saddle that served as a barstool, Clare smiled at a wisp of memory; her tiny blond child bouncing a hobbyhorse until the springs squealed.

"I'll have a Coors," Devon directed the young man wiping the knotty pine bar.

Clare lost her smile. "You will not." She ordered Cokes for them both.

"One more," Steve said.

Devon looked softer in the golden glow that illuminated the Cowboy.

Steve slid some bills across the bar to pay for their drinks. Clare liked that he was taking care of them.

"Have you been to Jackson before?" he asked Devon.

She shook her head.

He looked at a faded sepia print of men dancing to a fiddler's tune. "Jackson was a pretty wild place around the turn of the century. There weren't enough women, so the men danced with each other."

Devon flipped back her hair and looked bored.

"No kidding." He kept on. "The guys with the longest hair pretended to be gals."

"They were probably gay."

"Maybe." Steve looked at Clare. "I think most of them were just lonely."

As lonely as she'd been last night when she knew another woman held him from beyond the grave.

"Haywood, party of three."

They followed the hostess to the basement steakhouse. After recommending the ribeye, Steve turned to Devon. "I also have a research project that involves the Nez Perce War of 1877."

Devon looked like she was in history class waiting for the bell.

Steve elaborated. "Your mother said your family has some Nez Perce in it."

"I didn't know that." Devon turned blue eyes on Clare. "I don't look like an Indian."

"No, of course you don't," Clare soothed. "My great-grandfather was a quarter Nez Perce, making you one sixty-fourth."

"Why didn't you ever tell me?" Devon insisted.

Clare shrugged, but she felt uneasy. She'd been acting like the "folks" Garrett had talked about, not wanting to mention their Native American ancestors for fear of being ejected from the drawing room.

With smooth ease, Steve saved her by regaling them with stories about the old days in Jackson's Hole, when the fur trapping of the early eighteen hundreds gave way to turn-of-the-century homesteading and running cattle. Ranching "dudes", guests from California or the east, had gradually taken over, evolving into the tourist industry that sustained the region in the late nineteen-eighties.

Clare relaxed and enjoyed the evening more than she had imagined possible. The steaks were fork tender. She ordered a glass of red wine and hoped it didn't bother Steve as he drank his Coke.

When they stepped out of the Cowboy, Saturday night traffic was thick on Cache Street. A charred undercurrent came to Clare's nostrils, borne on the wind from the Teton Wilderness. The fires had consumed nearly a million acres in the Greater Yellowstone Area. Some called it disaster, as Connie Chung, Dan Rather, and Jim Lehrer entertained the nation nightly with forests in flames. Others, like Steve, believed that fire was natural, old trees giving way to an astounding variety of new life.

"Are you driving up to the park tonight?" He leaned against a knotty pine support.

"We've got a room at the Antler Inn." His obvious weariness reminded her that she was still exhausted from yesterday's brush with death.

Devon knelt on the sidewalk to examine the Cowboy's woodcarvings of stagecoaches. Clare frowned at the hint of swelling breast that showed at the side of her tank top.

Steve shifted his weight from one foot to another and she wished they might have a few minutes alone. "I'll head back north." He pushed off the post.

"Come by the room and call to check on the roads," Clare suggested.

He agreed. She was glad he put his arm around her shoulders as they walked down the boardwalk. Even at Devon's dark look, she did not pull away.

The motel room smelled faintly of prior guests' cigarettes, but was clean and comfortable. Devon flung herself on the bed farthest from the door while Clare removed her boots.

Steve dialed Fire Command and asked for a status report. After hanging up, he said, "It could be tomorrow afternoon or the next day before the south entrance is open."

Clare leaned against the partition that divided the bedroom from the bath. Bluish shadows beneath Steve's eyes told her he hadn't slept worth a damn last night, either.

He moved toward her and put out his un-bandaged right hand. "Come here."

She let him draw her out onto the second floor balcony. The murmur of traffic and the talk and laughter of tourists walking around town had subsided. Even the air had changed, turning oppressive. Lightning flashed above the manicured ski slopes carved into Snow King Mountain.

With a glance at Devon, Clare pulled the door shut but did not latch it. "You can smell the rain," she hoped.

Looking up, she realized that the water falling from the clouds was evaporating before it reached the mountaintop. In Yellowstone and the surrounding National Forests, flames swept on through the night. Fueled by the tinder-dry forest and nourished by wind, the lightning of each rainless front spawned more.

"It's got to end soon." Steve echoed her thoughts.

"All fires go out."

Something in Clare's throaty voice reminded him he was losing the best thing since Susan . . . before it got started. Clare would be going home to Houston and he didn't know how soon.

With his wife, there had been a slow and gentle progression from friendship to intimacy. Nurtured by the cocooned environment of the university and the long slow semesters, they'd had the luxury of time. This summer he felt like he'd been chasing even an hour with Clare, mostly in vain. When she had flown away with Deering this morning, he'd watched her go with a sense of what could only be called desperation.

Maybe he'd been a fool, as he'd told her, to sit on Mount Washburn and imagine. Maybe he'd been doubly the fool when he'd tossed the cold remains of his coffee in the kitchen sink, packed his kit, and leaped to the wheel of the ancient

Park Service truck.

He turned and found her closer than he'd thought, almost against him. With bare feet, she hardly cleared the top of his shoulder. He wished he were drunk, loose enough to slide his hands up her shoulders, then reversed that, fiercely glad he had all his senses to appreciate her.

Her eyes were a little red, but so were everyone's who'd been on the line. Her lips' slight chapping moved him more than Revlon red. Did her curve of smile invite, or had it been so long since he'd made the first move that he'd forgotten how?

He decided on the old "nothing ventured, nothing gained" gamble, and bent toward her. She looked up at him and he believed she was receptive.

"Mom," said Devon, three feet away in the doorway.

Steve stepped back. His face went hot while a flush stained Clare's cheekbones.

Although physically a woman, Devon studied them with a child's suspicion. "Have you got the keys? I left my bags in the car."

Clare fumbled in the pocket of her jeans. The key secured, Devon headed for the staircase.

Steve wanted more time with Clare, but he decided it was not to be. "I'd better look for a room, then." His married friends had told him how god-awful kids were on your sex life.

Below, Devon dragged out her duffel and backpack and slammed doors. He saw Clare scan the street where a couple of "No Vacancy" signs were visible. "You'll never get a place at this hour."

"Yeah," Devon agreed, as though eavesdropping was perfectly fine. "This town is packed."

So he'd drive up to one of the Teton overlooks and sleep in his damned truck. If one of the rangers rousted him, he'd flash his badge and convince them that Steve Haywood was not drunk for a change, just too dog-tired to drive. He'd try not to think that last night Clare had slept in his bed while he'd repeatedly retrieved his pillow from slipping through the sofa's armrest.

He could hardly believe his ears when Clare's husky voice stopped him. "We have two beds. Why not stay with us?"

Ten minutes later, Clare climbed in beside Devon, who appeared to be already asleep in the spot against the wall. She'd thought of asking Steve to go for a walk, but they were both exhausted.

At least now, they had tomorrow.

Keys and change jingled when Steve placed them on the round table near the window. That sound came from another life, when Jay used to stow his stuff on the glass-topped dresser in their bedroom.

Steve faced the window and she heard the snaps of his western shirt. He loosened the cuffs and shrugged out of one sleeve, stopping to scratch his back. Off with the other and he turned out the hanging light over the table.

With wonder, she realized that she had spent the entire evening without thinking of Billy Jakes, her upcoming interrogation, or the question of whether to quit fighting fires. From across the three feet that separated the beds, her eyes met Steve's. One arm was pillowed beneath his head and the other beneath the covers, but for a moment, she felt as though he reached out to her.

CHAPTER TWENTY-THREE
September 6

The river terrace dropped away, revealing an inner valley where the Snake River flowed in three winding, braided channels. On the bank, Clare saw at least a dozen leaning cabins with red metal roofs bleached by the sun.

"There's the Bar BC," Steve offered. "Dude ranch for armchair cowboys of the teens and twenties."

When Clare had told Steve over breakfast omelets that she wanted to try and find her family ranch, he had immediately started making plans. Even Devon had surprised her by saying she'd like to go.

They'd convoyed to the airport and dropped off Clare's rental, then driven through sage meadows and crossed a bridge over the rushing Snake. At the Grand Teton Visitor Center, a silver-haired ranger offered directions to the landmark Bar BC and the nearby Sutton homestead. "They're just ruins," he warned. "We don't have funding and the goal is to let the land return to its natural state."

The Bar BC was better preserved than Clare had thought from the way he'd spoken. Despite their derelict appearance, most of the buildings stood intact behind rail fences. The exception was a bare foundation with a river-rock fireplace where she imagined ghosts danced on moonlit nights.

Steve turned the noisy truck onto a faint track at the base of a bluff. Willows and aspen grew thick in the bottomland. As the trail grew fainter, they backtracked several times. Finally, Steve brought the truck to a halt beside a small ravine lined with granite boulders. "Can't give up now."

He struck out on foot down the bank and into rushing water. Clare splashed behind him, wetting her boots and jeans. Past the ravine, she had to watch for burrows, twisted roots, and the rounded pellets of elk droppings. The bottomland smelled of evergreen, the woodsy tang of sage, and something cinnamon-like. "What smells like Christmas?"

Steve pointed out a tree with light-brown bark. Its narrow leaves had yellowed from the dry season. Pulling a clump that looked sticky with pungent sap, he brought the spicy aroma to her nose. "Cottonwood."

They walked the faint memory of a trail around a bend. There, leaning log walls and a trio of ruined cobblestone chimneys made Clare draw in her breath. Remnants of jagged glass studded the window frames, and the wind roamed freely through what might once have been a cozy refuge. The sagging door swung on its hinges.

Hurrying footsteps sounded and Devon rushed up panting through her open mouth, her lips slicked with a red so dark it looked almost black.

Clare stepped onto the porch where someone had laid a mosaic of river rocks. Above the door, a weathered set of elk antlers spread bleached branches.

The cabin's interior smelled of the pine log walls. Save for metal andirons and a kettle on the hearth, the main room was empty. Irregular gaps in the wood floor showed packed earth beneath. In the other room, a potbellied stove stood close enough to cast warmth onto the bed. Looking at the rusted frame, Clare imagined that here was where her family had once lived and loved.

Her grandfather Cordon had grown up surrounded by the awesome beauty of wilderness, yet he had moved to Houston and gone into the oil business. Standing in the homestead, she wondered why anyone who lived here would leave this country. Even the flood of Asa Dean's story should not have deterred the hardy folk of the frontier.

Of course, her try at this wild country had resulted in disaster.

"Mom," Devon called from the main room.

"What?"

Clare looked in and found Steve watching Devon with a raised brow. Her daughter bent over in her already abbreviated cutoffs, rocking a loose hearthstone that chinked. "It's probably buried treasure," she suggested with childlike enthusiasm.

"Don't be silly, the place is falling apart."

To her surprise, Steve defended Devon. "You never know until you look."

He pulled an andiron from the fireplace, knelt, and strained to lift the heavy rock. The powdery scent of earth emerged, along with the sharp edge of tarnish that Clare recognized from cleaning her mother's silver tableware.

Steve lifted out a box a foot square and six inches deep.

For a moment, she thought he would open it, but he offered it to Devon.

She seemed taken aback and looked to Clare as if for permission.

"Go ahead, dear."

When Devon raised the blackened lid, the hinges broke. She looked startled, and Clare said, "It's okay."

Reaching in, Devon drew out a compact, leather-bound book. Gold leaf edged each yellowed page. Inside, *Ex Libris* and the name in spidery brown ink.

Laura Fielding Sutton.

Clare's mother had been right about her great-grandmother keeping a journal. It was difficult to believe that the delicate book had not been ruined by rain or melting snow. The silver box's bottom had tarnished through, making it a ruined shell.

Devon riffled the tissue-thin sheets. They were a bit warped, with a tendency to stick together. A clear round hand sprawled, occasional splotches revealing that Laura had tended to press her fountain pen too hard. How long ago must this have been written, fifty years, eighty?

With a steady look that revealed the woman she might become, Devon passed the book to Clare.

July 23, 1925

Six a.m.

From this high meadow on the Grand, dawn silhouettes the scar on Sheep Mountain where the Gros Ventre Slide took place a month ago. When the mountainside gave way, I saw curious plumes of rising dust. Trees danced and undulated and the hillside peeled away to raw earth. Finally, I heard an unearthly low rumbling as though a train passed.

When the earth lay quiet, a mile and a half long gash wounded it.

Engineers have assured that the slide is stable and that the Gros Ventre River can simply go on flowing around the side, but I wonder. There are stories of major earthquakes in just the last century and the Yellowstone country is violently unstable.

High above me on the Grand, morning kisses the highest peak with rose. The light brightens and sweeps down, illuminating more of the mountain with each moment. The sunrise comes to me and warmth touches my face.

Yesterday afternoon a summer rainstorm passed, quick cold making us reach for oilskins. As rapidly as it had blown up, the squall gave way to sunset. Ruby light pinkened scattered snow-fields and the high glaciers glowed.

Cordon built an evening fire and paid attention to the young woman he brought along. Francesca is lovely and sweet, an immigrant from Italy. When I put on some beans, sliced bacon, and added brown sugar, Francesca suggested that a pinch of dried mustard would add flavor. Our younger son, Bryce, back from another of his wanderings, started coffee and struck up conversation with the guests we brought up to the campsite. I hate the term "dudes." Before we sought the warmth of our bedrolls, we watched for shooting stars. One traced a long line over Idaho.

We went to bed with an added sense of anticipation. This morning we strike out, not for the ranch and the valley, but for the summit of Grand Teton.

The rest of the words blurred. Flesh of Clare's flesh, Laura Sutton had climbed the peak that soared to the sky. And there in the meadow of flowering yellow balsamroot walked a new generation in Devon.

Steve passed Clare a clean bandanna. She sniffed and blew her nose.

Mildly, Steve observed, "By rights, that book belongs to the National Park Service." Then he grinned. "I don't think anyone would mind if you hung onto it."

Clare tested one of the porch posts with the heel of her hand. It seemed solid and she leaned against it. "I'm sorry I got weepy." She tucked the kerchief into her pocket rather than hand it back soiled.

"Keep it," he offered. "Something to remember me by when you get back to Houston."

She did not miss the catch in his voice, just as Devon reached the cabin's front steps.

Driving through a long corridor of pine on the Rockefeller Parkway, headed toward Yellowstone, Clare could not resist the urge to open the diary again. With the sunlight strobing on the pages, she read a passage dated two years later.

May 19, 1927
Three a.m.
When the warning came from Ranger Dibble, saying that a wall of water was bearing down on Kelly, many people did not believe.

This evening was a horror. Past dark we searched for survivors amidst the mud and rubble left when Slide Lake broke its dam. I helped our neighbors from Mormon Row lay out the dead in the church. While I helped carry buckets of water to wash the dead, Cord was on the detail of men constructing coffins.

Near midnight, young Cordon insisted that his father and I return home and rest. Before we left what remains of Kelly, only four buildings standing, he promised to eat something and rest. I suspect he has kept searching by lantern light. Francesca, the girl he has been after, was helping out at the school today and has not been seen since before the flood. I only hope that Bryce was delayed in returning from his journey and was far from here.

At the Bar BC they asked for news of the dead and those missing. I don't think that either Cord or I wanted to be alone yet, for we stayed late drinking coffee and talking with Struthers Burt.

I should sleep, but I keep listening for Cordon's Model A. It is as though if I hope hard enough he may bring us Francesca, weary yet well. I am sure that if I close my eyes I would see the wall of water, bearing the trees and rocks of Slide Lake Dam, houses, fencing and livestock.

Devon put an arm around her shoulder. She'd been reading over Clare's shoulder in the truck's front seat. As Clare dug out Steve's bandanna again, she said, "It's okay, Mom. If she hadn't made it, we wouldn't be here."

"Except that your grandmother's name was Anne Lamar."

"Oh . . . yeah." Devon chewed her lip and stared again at the page, while Clare wondered if the diary would unravel the mystery of the missing Francesca.

❦❦❦

In late afternoon, Steve pulled under the massive porte-cochere of Old Faithful Inn. They had stopped along the way at several waterfalls. Overlooking the Lewis River's rugged canyon, Devon had gaped at the blackened landscape where the Red-Shoshone had wreaked ruin.

As Devon slung her backpack over her shoulder and opened the passenger door, Clare said, "Just a minute . . . " She swallowed the rest, for her daughter was out and heading toward the walkway encircling the geyser. "Our cabin is number sixteen," she called after her.

In late afternoon, the loading zone was chaos. Rainbow bags and designer leather lay strewn over the wide sidewalk. A bus arrived, blowing diesel exhaust.

It was difficult for Clare to reconcile this air of normality with the fact that beyond the public window dressing, Pete Cullen and his West Yellowstone volunteers were moving in irrigation sprinklers. Since their town was no longer threatened, the equipment was being brought into the park to protect power lines. When Clare had spoken to Garrett this morning, he'd cautioned that another grasping tentacle of the North Fork reached for Old Faithful.

Although she had phoned him with the best intentions, she had hung up without telling Garrett that she was going home. No matter how many ways she tried to phrase it, the words had choked in her throat.

Steve rested both hands on the steering wheel. His left hand still wore the bandage she'd put on for him the other night at his house. An unbidden image of his strong, yet gentle fingers sliding over her skin almost made Clare gasp. She hadn't felt this way with Deering.

Another bus pulled in behind them. Steve glanced in the rearview mirror. In just a minute, she would get out and thank him for the ride. He'd drive away without having explained his trip to Jackson, all because her daughter was too damned effective a chaperone.

The bus driver hit the air horn.

Do something, but for God's sake don't let him leave.

Wordlessly, Clare brushed Steve's cheek with the back of her hand. He'd brought his kit into the Antler this morning and shaved, leaving his skin smooth with a hint of blond stubble. He gave her a long look. "I can't drive if you do that."

A second horn blast and he said, "I guess I'll have to park and get us some dinner."

CHAPTER TWENTY-FOUR
September 6

No matter how many times Clare watched Old Faithful Geyser, she never tired of it. Despite the fires, tourists from all over the world crowded closer, speaking the universal language of expectation.

The circular walkway ringing the geyser was at least fifteen feet wide, standing room only with the rows of wooden benches already occupied. Clare looked for Devon, but didn't see her.

The waiting crowd stirred as the first signs of steam poured from the roundish mound of white rock in the center ring. Across the mineralized soil on the far side of the geyser, a small group of tourists clustered. Not ten feet from the elevated walkway, a shaggy bull stood with his head lowered, creating a buffalo jam.

Another blast of steam burst from the earth, a white cloud streaming against the hazy summer sky. Steve's hand rested at the small of her back.

Above the spectacle, the long green shoulder of a ridge stood at least three hundred feet high, a backdrop for the geyser's hundred-fifty foot show. Towering and triumphant, the foaming rush peaked and began almost imperceptibly to subside. Too soon, the exalted ritual turned to streams of hot water finding a path away from the central cone.

The sounds of the crowd muted. People turned away before the last gallons spilled over the terraced earth. The small channels narrowed, running in rivulets down to join the Firehole River.

As Clare and Steve headed for her cabin, she caught a glimpse of Devon dropping a cigarette and stepping on it with her clunky boot. Beside her, a tall man in his mid-twenties produced a lighter and lit her next smoke while she shoved the pack in her bag. He looked down her tank top and laughed at something she was saying

A sick feeling seized Clare. She'd given her daughter the birth control lecture a long time ago, but Devon had never volunteered and she'd never directly asked whether she was sexually active. She could imagine Elyssa being smugly certain of the worst.

As she watched Devon flirting with someone she'd just met, Clare wondered if she'd been naïve.

"Home sweet home." Clare opened the door of her small dark cabin and went in ahead of Steve. Cool air and a musty smell greeted her, a sign that the sun never really reached through the pines decorating the row of employee housing. Late afternoon light filtered through the flyspecked window, illuminating faded paint in a dark shade of brown. Twin beds shoved against opposite walls had less than three feet between them.

"Nice place." Steve raised a brow.

Clare grinned. "I've slept in worse spots this summer." In a tent with Deering, but they hadn't actually slept, in a sleeping bag on the ground at Madison. "Even in the plain old dirt I've fallen asleep."

Steve tossed Devon's overstuffed duffel onto the floor. "I doubt if your daughter will be as forgiving of the accommodations." His tone suggested he'd noticed the dark looks Devon had been giving him.

What could she expect? This was the first time Devon had ever seen her mother with a man other than her father. Clare sank onto one of the beds and lay back on the brown ribbed spread. "Sometimes being a mom wears me down."

Steve rubbed the back of his neck and looked thoughtful. "I don't know. If Christa had lived I think I'd be looking forward to even the teen years."

"I'm sorry." Clare sat up. "I didn't think. "

"Don't worry about it." He sat on the opposite bed with a hand on each knee. "I owe you an apology, too."

"For what?"

"For trying to mind your business. You and Deering are adults."

She'd figured he'd forgiven her when he showed up in Jackson, but it was good to hear. "You were right about him being married."

"I had it from the horse's . . . " His expression suggested he meant the opposite end from the mouth.

"I know you don't like him," she rushed on, "but he's had a hell of a time this summer. Especially with his wife since the crash."

Steve's face went stony. "Which he has no doubt convinced you was my fault?"

"Not at all. I know the captain is always in charge." Clare slid closer to the edge of her bed and leaned toward Steve. "I believe Deering does too."

"Could have fooled me."

This wasn't working out like she'd hoped. She hadn't intended Steve to think she was hearts and flowers for Deering's tough luck.

Steve went on, "You have to admit that trouble at home is an old excuse for roving."

Clare wondered if Jay had used that one, telling Elyssa his wife didn't understand him.

She faced Steve across the space between the beds. "Let's not argue about Deering. When he flew me to Jackson, he told me he still loves his wife."

Steve's shoulders looked tight. "So, where do you and he stand?"

Clare shook her head. "I'm not in the picture. I told him he should go back and fight for his wife if that's what he wants." She'd been fighting for Steve and so far, he didn't seem to get it.

She put out her hand. His eyes went to it and his hands relaxed atop his legs.

"Clare," he said softly.

She wondered how many times he'd said "Susan," before his wife died, like breathing in and out. The way she'd said, "Jay."

"Steve," she answered. Was she ready to feel that way about another man's name?

He moved across and slid his weight onto her sagging bed beside her. Her pulse tripped.

From the corner of her eye, Clare caught a movement at the cabin door.

Steve swore under his breath, not quietly enough, for Devon's penciled dark eyebrows formed a vee. Clare scrambled to her feet along with him, aware of how this must look.

"What have you been doing?" She went on the offensive. "I told you half an hour ago where the cabin was." That was enough time to get into trouble; look at how close she'd just come with Steve.

"What would I be doing?" Devon ducked her head and shrugged a sullen shoulder. "What were you doing?" She nodded toward the rumpled bedspread and snapped on a light, destroying the cozy twilight.

"Devon," Clare warned. "We're talking about where you were."

"I was walking around, for chrissake." She flung her backpack onto the bed opposite Clare's. "If you think I'm lying, why don't you just read my goddamn mind like you always think you can?"

"I can read you," Clare agreed. "When you dip your head and give that little shrug I can never believe a word you're saying."

Devon made fists. "Yeah, well, Annalise MacIntyre was in Charter Hospital and they taught her in group that family should never use words like *always* and *never.*"

"They said to *never* use them?"

"Funny, Ma."

"Clare." Steve put a hand on her arm. "I think I'm gonna take off."

She glanced at her daughter and back to him.

"Don't mind me." Devon threw herself onto her bed and buried her face in crossed arms. "You two go on with your romance." Her shorts hiked up to reveal a crescent slice of pale buttock above tanned thighs.

Steve turned away, his face flushed at her and Devon's squabbling. Or maybe he was too nice a guy to look at her daughter's backside. Clare followed him to the door.

He stopped and turned. "You take care of Devon."

Even if she did need some time for managing the temper tantrum, she didn't want him to leave. "Steve . . ." She heard the urgency in her voice.

He reached to cradle her cheek. "I'll come back in a while. Maybe we can get that dinner."

Gravel crunched beneath his boots as he walked away. Reluctant to go back and argue with Devon, Clare watched Steve, with his sturdy shoulders and slightly awkward yet determined gait, until he was out of sight. Against the last light on the western horizon, the black silhouette of an ash fell to earth.

In the confusion of her inopportune desire and Devon's animosity, she'd almost forgotten about the fires.

With a sigh, she turned back to the door. The scant glow of the bedside lamp illuminated tousled golden hair on the pillow. It reminded Clare of when Devon was little and she'd tuck her in at night.

How could you know what was going on with your child? From the first moment of awareness, they began a tug of war with their parents that ultimately resulted in the fledgling flying from the nest.

Clare leaned against the splintery wooden doorframe. "We need to talk."

"I'll smoke if I please. I'm almost eighteen." Devon spoke into the pillow gathered beneath her face.

"It's not the smoking." She came inside and stood between the beds. "It's this business of you wanting to move out after your birthday. Elyssa said you might be seeing someone . . . older."

"Annalise's grandma was eighteen and her grandpa thirty-eight when they got married."

"Times change." Clare tried to sound reasonable. "Look at war years, when a lot of people get married because they don't know if they will come back alive."

Devon rolled over and sat against the wall, drawing her knees against her chest. Her boots soiled the covers. Clare ignored it and focused on blue eyes. "When you go to work at the fire station," Devon accused, "I don't know if you'll come back."

Clare felt as though she'd been struck. Devon had always presented a teen's indifference when she left for her shift. Even when Frank had died, she'd kept her distance and Clare had resented the hell out of it. "Don't change the subject. We're talking about your life."

"You don't want a daughter." Devon swiped at a fat tear tracking through a smeared mess of powder and blush. "You and Dad would rather have a wind-up doll you can send back and forth when you get tired of it."

Clare went to the room's wall sink. Carefully, she washed her heated face, appreciating how cold the water was here compared to Houston.

"You've got something going with Steve," Devon challenged. "What do you care about me?"

In the small spotted mirror, Clare saw the flush rise to stain her already sunburned cheeks. The mirror also revealed the belligerent look on Devon's tear and mascara-streaked face.

Clare laid her washcloth on the rim and took hold of the cool porcelain of the sink. How useless counting to three was in practice.

"From the way Steve looks at you," Devon flung, "I'll bet he knows what you look like naked."

Clare whirled and stabbed her finger at Devon. "That's it. As long as you live with me . . ."

"I'm old enough to take care of myself."

If Elyssa were right, Devon was about to make the same life-altering mistake that Clare had made at little more than her age. In perfect hindsight, she saw rushing into a relationship with Jay Chance as her poorest piece of judgment. Too angry not to, she moved forward until she stood over Devon. "You mean old enough to get some man to take care of you."

The impact of Clare's words showed on Devon's face as though she had thrown a handful of gravel. Her own shock made her mind go blank as the tiny cabin and the narrow space between the beds seemed to close in.

Devon leaped up. "Fuck you!" she screamed. Both hands caught Clare in the chest, a solid blow that shoved her backward to land on the small of her back against the bed frame. Sharp agony narrowed her vision, but she was able to see Devon push through the cabin door and run away.

Steve was surprised to see lights in the Visitor Center. More ash drifted down as he stepped up to the door.

It was locked. Inside, he could see a meeting under way in the auditorium behind the interpretive exhibits. In the front row, Steve recognized Ranger Butler Myers, with a tired yet tense look on his horsy, bearded face.

Steve tapped the glass.

Butler unfolded his long frame from the chair and came to the door. "You got a nose for trouble, Haywood."

"How so?" Steve hoped Butler wasn't referring to his drinking.

"Come in. We're gonna need all the help we can get."

Duncan Rowland, the Incident Commander of the North Fork, held the floor. The slim, dark-haired man in a ball cap nodded to acknowledge Steve and went on with his briefing.

He indicated a map that showed the North Fork looking like an octopus, with a rounded head to the northwest and arms that reached in all directions.

Rowland pointed to a new tentacle. "This area has defeated all our efforts. Observers on the fire line are watching the wind in case we need to call an evacuation."

"Shutting down the complex would be unpopular with the traveling public," Butler drawled. "They like to get up close and personal with these fires, take their pictures."

Rowland removed his cap and twisted it. "We're not gonna know any more for a while," he said. "I recommend everyone hit the sack early."

Steve had been thinking of driving home to Mammoth tonight after he bought Clare . . . and Devon, dinner. Now he must stay, even if it meant sleeping in his truck, for all hands would be needed tomorrow.

Rowland completed his warning. "There aren't any decent breaks in topography or fuel between here and the North Fork. Without a change in the weather, all hell is going to break loose."

Clare lay curled on the bed in her cabin. The nausea that had gripped her when her backbone slid down the metal bed frame had passed, but she didn't feel like moving. Nothing . . . nothing like that had ever happened between her and her daughter.

Why couldn't she have mustered the self-control she used in training? Elyssa had never liked Devon and she was the source of this rumor about the older guy.

"Clare?" Steve stood in the doorway.

She wanted to jump up and throw her arms around him, but it seemed too difficult.

"What happened?" He came and knelt beside her.

"Devon and I had a difference of opinion."

"A bit more than that, I'd say." His mouth twisted. "I shouldn't have left."

"You couldn't have known." How could he have known?

Steve pulled her to her feet and against him. She pressed her cheek against the softness of his faded red shirt, smelling a hint of male sweat and feeling safe.

"Has anything like this happened before?" His hands felt sure on her back.

Clare blinked back tears. "Never."

"I guess she doesn't much care for me."

"It's not you," she protested against his chest. "That's just how it started."

He folded her closer and his heart beat against her ear. "We're going to get you some dinner," he said.

"I couldn't eat."

"You need something," he urged. She did indeed need something. It wasn't food.

She shook her head again to dinner. "I need to wait for Devon."

"I'll go, then." He started to move away. Her hands tightened on his shoulders in a way she hoped he could not mistake.

The flash in his eyes happened suddenly, yet she felt she'd been waiting for it a long time. He dragged her back against him and they found their fit, her head tipped up against his shoulder. She felt as though her body was defined by its contrast with his, more compact and softer where her breasts were crushed against him.

Their mouths met and melded. A great relief went through her and she let out the breath she'd been holding. They felt good together, a scary thing in the midst of the maelstrom surrounding them.

Her focus shifted from her own response to his. Running her palm up the back of his neck, she slid it into his hair. He gave a sharp gasp and she moved to press her lips to the hollow at the base of his throat. Until this moment, she'd been competing with a memory. Now she was the one in his arms.

She laughed in soft victory, flushed with the power to give him pleasure. This wasn't a thing like the amorphous hunger that had seized her with Deering. This made her feel both exhilarated and secure, despite her conflict with her daughter.

Steve deepened their kiss and his hands became more urgent. She wanted this with him, because of the chords of need he touched in her.

In the same moment that she realized Devon could come back at any time, Steve pulled back gently. "I hate to say this," he said in a voice thick with regret, "but after what happened with Devon, you don't want her to find me here tonight. Especially, since I can't trust myself to keep hands off."

He was right, much as she hated it. There was no doubt that if he stayed they were going to end up on one of the beds in a most compromising position.

"There's more," he went on. "I just crashed a meeting at the Visitor Center where they're considering an evacuation."

"Oh, God. What if Devon doesn't come back?" Clare almost hoped she had hooked up with some guy who'd feed her and drive her away from here, rather than have her wandering cold and alone in the dark. Her backpack lay abandoned on the bed, so she had no money or ID.

"There's nothing we can do tonight," Steve said. "I'll sleep in my truck and check back in the morning. If she doesn't show by then we'll put out a missing persons report through the Park Service."

She stood at the cabin door and hugged herself while he walked away. A car passed, its headlights illuminating his back as he headed purposefully up the narrow lane between the cabins.

In case Devon came, Clare left the door unlocked. For hours, she strained to hear approaching footsteps or the creak of the latch. Outside, the wind rose to a moan.

Devon was out there somewhere while the octopus continued to spread its arms through the night. Punching her pillow, Clare tried to tell herself that she could take the front line against the beast, though Billy Jakes's death made her want to give up the fight.

A branch scratched the cabin window like fingernails on a chalkboard.

With a sigh, Clare turned on the light, found her great-grandmother's journal, and opened it at random. The entry was dated after the flood in 1927, but Laura was recounting a story about fleeing a forest fire that burned in Yellowstone around the turn of the century.

That steep west slope on Nez Perce Peak must be unchanged by years, still the Devil's own playground of sharp and treacherous boulders that shifted beneath our feet. In the suffocating dark, I thought that each step might be my last before falling away in a slide of serrate lava rock.

Even Cord's arms failed to warm me through our night on the rock face. Sleep eluded and the pungent smell of burning wood came to us on the wind.

In the morning, we achieved the ridge top. Our place was marked by an ancient, twisted pine, reaching gnarled limbs into the smoky morning sky. The tree seemed to grow from a cairn of boulders that men might have made. I wonder now if perhaps the Nez Perce piled the stones about the old tree's base as some kind of sign.

The sight that greeted us on the east side of the divide was astounding. Like the raging heart of a furnace, fire swept toward us through the tops of the trees, leaping from one to the next in the space of a single heartbeat. I know not how far we ran along the knife-edge to the north before we dropped down onto the steep slope. Trees exploded as though hit by cannon fire. Sound poured over us like nothing I have ever heard, a full-throated yet hollow roar that struck terror.

Clare knew that predatory call. She'd heard the voice of the Shoshone when she and Steve had cowered in the lake with shards of wood showering from exploding tree trunks. At the spike camp, she'd waited for the chopper with a desperate effort at calm, all the time believing the Mink Creek screamed her name. The Hellroaring had spared her, but taken its offering when Billy Jakes had panicked.

She continued to read.

I wish I could say we were saved through action on our part, some clever sleuthing of cold cavern air, but we fell into our refuge without seeing it. In a dank lava tunnel with a cone of dirty snow unmelted from last season, smoke nearly suffocated us.

We lived, yet are guaranteed no more and no less than anyone who takes their hold on life for granted. I don't want to remember, but these awful days after the flood take me back to when darkness nearly overtook me. A dreadful time when I believed that despite our love, Cord and I would never find a place to be together.

Clare shivered and closed the book. She'd lived alone for years, but this summer had blasted her complacency like a tree exploding from wildfire's heat. First Deering had awakened long dormant physical needs, but it was more than that. Now her soul craved the kind of tenderness that Laura must have found with her Cord. How incredible that a single kiss from Steve could create this monstrous hunger for all that they could be to each other. The temptation to try and find him was almost overpowering.

The thought arose that they could have been together all this time. The branch tapped again and she started, conjuring ideas that he knocked . . . and an image of him leaning lazily against the doorframe, looking down at her.

She would lift her hand and beckon him inside. How his eyes would light as he came to her.

Clare lay in the lamp's shaded glow and imagined stoking the sparks he had kindled.

Old Faithful's parking lots were nearly empty. Thousands of

day visitors had moved on, leaving seven hundred hotel guests and a few hundred employees who lived at the complex.

Steve got out of the truck's cab. Favoring his right knee, he climbed into the bed of the pickup. From beside the shovel and axe that rangers carried year-round for fighting fires and digging out of snow, he pulled an olive drab down sleeping bag, sealed in plastic to protect it from weather. The truck bed was not exactly soft, but the front seat was too cramped for his bad knees.

Thinking of Clare, warm in bed in her cabin, Steve unrolled his bedroll and got into it. Toward morning, it would get down in the low forties or high thirties.

He lay on his back and looked at the sky. Clouds skidded past, or were they clouds? The whiffs of fresh smoke he'd been catching all evening now came with annoying frequency.

The North Fork was on its way, loaded for bear.

Steve hoped Clare would find Devon before trouble got here. Despite her animosity toward him, he'd seen the charm as well as the conflict in the child-woman. With her parents divorced and her father's remarriage one that obviously excluded her, it was no wonder she had lashed out at her mother over him. Despite Clare's concern, he figured she'd probably show up back at the cabin when it got cold enough.

He wondered if he had been a fool this evening. Instead of leaving, he could have drawn the paper shades and turned the bolt. He flashed on images of Clare naked—a mystery to be unveiled.

With his arms beneath his head, he watched a sliver of moon appear to fall endlessly, the billowing shadows rising to meet it.

It was like that with Clare. He felt as though he'd left his life behind, falling free like the moon through the heavens. As sleep rose to meet him he dropped into a dream in which he was not quite the fool he'd imagined.

YELLOWSTONE FIRES
September 7, 8:00 a.m.

Here is a list of the fires and approximate perimeter acreages. To date, over 633,000 acres in Yellowstone National Park (and over * * * * acres in the Greater Yellowstone Area) have been affected by fire. However, only about half of the vegetation has burned within many fire perimeters. Throughout the summer, 52 different fires have been started by lightning. Of those 52, eight are still burning inside the park. Fire fighters are working to control them. Any new fires will be suppressed as quickly as possible.

****1,066,010 acres

Clover-Mist Fire: 238,300 acres. Mist Fire started July 9. Clover started July 11. They joined on July 22. Shallow Fire started July 31. Fern Fire started August 5. These two fires joined Clover-Mist August 13. Lovely Fire started July 11 and burned into Clover-Mist on August 21. The SW flank is near Turbid Lake and may reach the East Entrance Road. A major run occurred in the Jones Creek area within 2 miles of Pahaska Tepee. Engines and crews were sent to the area for structure protection. The fire could reach Pahaska today. 1352 firefighters, 35 engines, 7 bulldozers, and 3 helicopters.

Fan Fire: 23,325 acres. Started June 25. The fire is reported as contained. One crew is completing mopup. 25 firefighters, 1 helicopter.

Hellroaring Fire: 57,470 acres (estimated 8,500 acres in Yellowstone NP.) Started August 15. A planned backfire did not occur due to unfavorable conditions. The backfire will be tried again today. Crews burned out around Buffalo Plateau cabin. Tuesday night this fire joined with the Storm Creek Fire. 628 firefighters, 5 helicopters.

Huck Fire: 56,345 acres. Started August 21. Caused the evacuation of Flagg Ranch. Spreading SE into Teton Wilderness and N across the Snake River into Yellowstone National Park. Fire had pushed around Pinyon Pk. into Gravel Ck. Fire is exhibiting erratic behavior. 640 firefighters, 6 engines, 5 helicopters.

North Fork Fire: 145,800 acres. Started July 22 by human. Split from Wolf Lake Fire at Gibbon Falls. The fire has spotted to within ¾ mile of Old Faithful Area. The area is being evacuated this morning. Sprinklers have been installed under powerlines. A major run to the NE occurred in the Mt. Holmes area. West Yellowstone and Island Park areas had little activity. 1608 firefighters, 39 engines, 22 bulldozers, and 6 helicopters.

Snake River Complex: 205,800 acres. Red Fire started July 1. Shoshone Fire started June 23. Joined August 10. Falls Fire started July 12. Red-Shoshone joined the Mink Fire on August 31. Acreage includes Continental-Ridge and Mink Creek fires. Fire activity was generally light yesterday. Some small spots are being worked today. Winds were mostly light. Mink Fire crews were successful in keeping the fire in the Yellowstone River drainage. Fire is most active in Pass Ck. and Silvertip Ck. 703 firefighters, 16 engines, 6 helicopters.

Storm Creek Fire: 65,000 acres. Started July 3. A spot fire has moved just N of Silver Gate. Fire is also within one mile of Cooke City. All non-essential fire personnel and all area residents have been evacuated. No structures were lost overnight. <u>Hgwy 212 from Tower Junction to the Sunlight Basin Cutoff (Hgwy 296) is closed.</u> 1236 firefighters, 48 engines, 4 dozers, 7 helicopters.

Wolf Lake Fire: 61,200 acres. Divided from North Fork Fire at Gibbon Falls. The fire is advancing NE into Carnelian Ck. and in the area of Dunraven Pass and

LINDA JACOBS

Mt. Washburn. Line on the S held well. Line around Canyon Village also held. More engines arrived form California. 675 firefighters, 30 engines, 3 helicopters.

CHAPTER TWENTY-FIVE
September 7

"Park service," A woman's voice filtered through the cabin door. Clare rolled out of bed and her feet found the cold floor. The bed with Devon's duffel bag and backpack was still empty. "Yeah?"

"Sorry to disturb you, but this is official business."

She threw on a T-shirt and sweat pants. Outside, morning was a gray streak against smoke hanging in the Firehole Valley.

The young woman at her door wore a ranger's uniform, complete with a brimmed hat of pale straw. Despite the chill, she was sweating, her chestnut hair damp where it showed at the temples. "We're evacuating Old Faithful. The North Fork fire is threatening . . . "

"Oh, dear."

"There's no cause for alarm," the ranger said. "You have until ten a.m. to leave, but I would start right away."

Minutes later, Clare found Steve in the parking lot. He lay curled inside a sleeping bag in the back of the Park Service truck. One arm was over his head, reminding her of when she'd found him on the lakeshore.

He must have heard her boots on the pavement, for he opened his eyes. This time he looked neither confused nor shocky, but gave her a steady smile that lifted her spirits until he asked about Devon.

She shook her head.

He wriggled out of the bag in his jeans, shirt, and sock feet. With a glance at her Nomex clothing, he said, "I've got a spare set to change into." He pulled on his boots, and grabbed the folded shirt and pants from his bag.

As he let himself down from the tailgate, he cringed when he put his weight on his right leg. She put out a hand and he let her help him.

Swiping a hand through his hair as a comb, Steve led her toward the Visitor Center. Although it was not officially opening time, she could see through the windows that a number of people were crowded inside. The woman ranger who'd knocked at Clare's door stood surrounded by at least six elderly women.

"What do you mean, evacuate?" one stout dowager demanded.

"We were on a bus tour," said another, a small-boned woman with the hump of advancing osteoporosis. "I think they left without us."

Clare followed Steve through the gift shop to the information desk. There, a ranger with a strained look on his bearded face tried to answer questions from at least three people at once.

Steve hailed, "Hey, Butler."

"Is the fire really coming?" a pudgy woman in Birkenstocks asked.

"Can we stay and watch?" A boy around six tugged his father's polo shirt.

Steve's hand closed over Clare's shoulder. "Butler Myers, this is my friend Clare Chance. She's with the firefighters from Houston."

Butler nodded absently and started to deal with another agitated traveler. Finished with the social niceties, Clare grabbed the ranger's arm. "You've got to do something. My daughter is missing."

He spoke over his shoulder to a female ranger who looked about twenty. "Take over, Jen."

"Let's go over here, ma'am." Butler drew Clare past a seismograph to the rear auditorium. Steve came along, still carrying his fire clothes, and turned on the lights in the vacant room.

From his breast pocket, Butler drew a small notepad and pen. "I'll need your daughter's name and a description."

Clare thought how many times she'd taken information from people in crisis. With the tables turned, she took a breath and tried to stay calm. "It's Devon, Devon Chance. She's a couple inches taller than I am, blond hair, shoulder length . . . "

"I'm sorry," Butler interrupted. "Did you say taller than you?"

"About five-six."

"How old is she?"

"Seventeen."

The woman ranger Butler had called Jen stuck her head in the door. "The wind's kicked up. Thirty-to-fifty on the heights. That puts the North Fork here in a matter of hours."

"Please," Clare said. "You've got to find Devon."

"How long has she been missing?"

"Since last night." It seemed like a lot longer.

"Where did you last see her?"

"At my cabin. Number sixteen on the back side."

"Then how did she get lost?"

Clare hesitated. "We . . . that is . . . " She thought of lying, but it wasn't in her. "We had a fight and she ran away." Her back still smarted from the rough edge of the bed frame.

Butler ruffled his beard with his hand.

"She's a good kid," Steve put in. Clare could have kissed him for it.

The notebook lowered. "I'm sorry, ma'am, but at her age law enforcement would not track your daughter as a runaway."

"Someone could hurt her," Clare insisted.

"We've been busing folks out of here since seven," Butler said. "She was probably on one of the first ones." His voice had an upbeat tenor. Clare knew that tone; she used it herself on the job. "I'm sure you'll find her, ma'am." Butler touched the brim of his hat, gave Steve an apologetic glance and hastened back toward the front desk.

Clare sank into a chair and put her face in her hands. Steve sat beside her and said, "Devon is old enough to take care of herself."

"How can you say that?" Clare turned on him. "She didn't show any judgment when she ran away."

"Point taken, but Butler's probably right. If she's running, she's already gone."

For the rest of the morning, Clare and Steve tracked back and forth across the complex. From the post office and Snow Lodge on the southeast to the Hamilton Store and Conoco station on the northwest, they scanned the common areas, both indoors and out. Just past noon, they took a seat on one of the vacant benches surrounding Old Faithful.

"Now what?" Clare asked.

"We hope she's in West Yellowstone or Mammoth with other evacuees," Steve said. "If so, she'll ask around and find Fire Command or Headquarters."

Clare hoped it would be that simple.

She looked over at Steve watching the opening of Old Faithful's show. Strands of his hair blew over his forehead and the collar of the yellow shirt he'd put on. She thought about smoothing them. The memory of being in his arms last night came back as they watched the geyser.

The deep familiar growl of a fire truck sounded behind them. In the parking lot beyond the Visitor Center a group of structural firefighters mustered.

Steve rose, "I'm going to the snack bar and see if they're still open. Get us something to eat."

Clare nodded, watching the firefighters. She recognized Javier Fuentes, standing out above the crowd in the same moment that he saw her. He came to her with his long-legged gait, dark eyes bright. She reached up to hug him.

She'd seen him off and on during the firefighting effort, but today his embrace reminded her that he'd done the same after Frank had died. Javier had picked her up from the gutter and taken her from the scene, given her strong coffee, and refused to let her succumb to feeling guilty.

Her arms tightened convulsively.

"Hey, hey? What's this?" he asked.

A sob burst from her, startling them both.

"What in hell's happened?" Javier drew back to look at her.

"We lost a soldier the other day. A guy I was training."

"That's tough." Javier checked her face again. "Ah, God, Clare, you can't do this."

"Who says I can't?" she exploded.

"I say," he insisted. "You refused to come back to the station. You wanted to rush off up here so I decided to come, too. But you can't run away from the fact that it's a dangerous goddamn business."

"I'm thinking of getting out of it," she said grimly.

Javier's eyes went wide. "You can't. For every student of yours who dies, there are the rest you taught something to save their life . . . and the lives of others. I'd back you up on the hose any day."

Behind him, one of the firefighters pointed to the southwest, where a towering column of smoke looked like a nuclear weapon had exploded over the horizon.

Javier pointed toward the inferno. "We need every hand we can get." He lifted hers and looked at them. "There are a hell of a lot of folks alive today because these are some of the best hands in the business."

The roiling firestorm was the kind of enemy that called for somebody, anybody, to rise up and fight. Clare shook her head. "I can't."

"The hell you can't!" Steve said from behind her. She thought he'd gone to the snack bar.

She turned. His eyes looked like flint chips.

Javier dropped her hands and stood back.

Her eyes held Steve's for a long moment while his softened. His look of encouragement spoke volumes, but he simply said, "Frank and Billy would want you to." Putting a quick grip-and-release on her shoulder, he walked away.

Javier waited.

Clare stared at the pavement, sprinkled with little marble-sized chunks of obsidian. As she had done so many times, she ached for a sign from Frank. Was it possible that he was irrevocably gone? Could all those people who believed in ghosts and portents from beyond be wrong? She closed her eyes and sent her own message winging, knowing it was yet another futile one-way effort.

By now, several others had joined her and Javier. Clare heard, " . . . planning to foam the cabins."

Another man said, "Hose down the roof of the inn."

Straining memory, she could see Frank at work, his back to her while he lifted and dragged a hose. All their training, repeating drills until reaction became instinctive. Working at A & M and at the fire academy in Houston, they had faced fake situations, but the flames had been real.

The North Fork was out there and this was definitely not a drill. In her mind's eye, Frank never turned to look at her, but wasn't it enough to know that if he were here, he'd lead the charge?

Steve approached and gave Clare a Coke and two Hershey bars. She popped the top and drank. "Thanks. I should have had supper, or at least some breakfast."

He shifted his weight from one foot to the other. "I've run into some fellow scientists," he said slowly.

Clare saw three people waiting for him outside the cafeteria. A tall dark man talked with a younger Asian fellow who wore glasses. A girl a few years older than Devon sat cross-legged on the sidewalk. She rooted in her backpack and came up with a cigarette pack.

"My neighbor Moru," Steve said, "and our summer graduate students. They could use my help cataloguing some areas in the path of the burn, but if you need me . . . "

"I don't need you right now." She touched his arm so that he would understand the "now" aspect of the statement. Later, she reserved the right to need much more.

Clare turned and faced the southwest, staring directly into the face of the North Fork. Silhouetted against the smoke, tankers dropped retardant and helicopters ferried water.

"You help your friends," she told Steve. "I've volunteered to join these guys."

CHAPTER TWENTY-SIX
September 7

For the second time this summer, Deering found himself flying blind, trapped inside turbulent smoke. Luckily, he'd already released his load of water and was turning back toward the Firehole River to refill the bucket.

Deering hoped that Mark Liebman in the lead plane had not seen him. Flying into zero vis was strictly verboten. He corrected course, pulled up and to the right, which should have brought him into clear air. Instead, he was still within the cloud.

He straightened out to avoid putting the chopper into a tight spiral that would result in flying in circles. Using his compass, he flew in the opposite direction from which the North Fork was approaching.

Seconds passed. Deering fought to keep the craft steady and checked his altimeter. He tried not to dwell on the fact that there were a number of aircraft in the area, all flying VFR, or visual flight rules. If someone else blundered into the cloud, there could be a midair.

He stared through the windshield. The murk snugged right against the glass.

This was bad business. Today showed all the signs of being another one like Black Saturday. If the wind kept rising with the dry cold front, Old Faithful Inn was going up.

"Okay, Deering," Mark Liebman radioed in his habitually cheerful manner, "no playing peek-a-boo."

"The hell you say," Deering gritted. Was there a barely perceptible thinning of the smoke?

Before he could decide, a harsh droning drowned the Huey's engine noise. As Deering broke in a patch of clearer air, a C-130 tanker flashed past. The enormous plane dove earthward, on approach to dump retardant.

Deering's hands stung as adrenaline rushed to them. The Huey plunged, caught in the vortex from the tanker's four great propellers. Struggling to arrest the dive, he realized that smoke kept him from seeing the ground and that he could smash into it at any second. He kept his eyes glued to the artificial horizon and altimeter, trying not to think about instant annihilation in a fireball of fuel.

In the midst of maybe dying, he couldn't help but think of Georgia. He'd thought of her that day in Yellowstone Lake, too, when he'd longed to be home.

He cajoled the controls and forced himself not to imagine the ridge top studded with treacherously sharp pine trunks, God only knew how far below. Finally, the Huey began to respond.

Once in open air, Deering was able to see he'd been only a few hundred feet off the deck. He let out a shaky breath and wiped his sweating palms, one at a time, on his pant legs. Thank God, he wouldn't have to tell Georgia he'd crashed twice in one summer. He thought of her arms around him, and found that the stinging in his eyes was not all from smoke.

As he headed toward the Firehole to pick up more water, along with the tattered remnants of his self-control, the radio crackled with a message from West Yellowstone Air Control. He was wanted to meet Garrett Anderson and fly recon.

All the way west, he kept expecting controller Jack Owen or Mark Liebman in the lead plane to ground everyone. For the first time in his life, he was ready.

Once on the West Yellowstone tarmac, Deering climbed out of the Huey and slammed the door.

"Hey," Garrett called from beside the fence near the Smoke-jumpers' Base.

Deering waved, but did not alter his course toward the charter trailer. Inside, Demetrios Karrabotsos sat at the Island Park desk with the phone against his salt-and-pepper head. Deering knew he'd be out flying later, for the cast had come off his foot the day before yesterday.

Down the narrow hall, Deering went into the office of Johnny Arvela of Eagle Air. He dialed, his hand trembling like it had on the collective when the C-130's wake buffeted him.

On the third ring, Georgia said hello in a small voice that said she wasn't smiling.

"Please," Deering said, "don't hang up."

She didn't, but neither did she speak.

"Babe, I'm sorry. Sorry for everything about this summer. That I . . . chased another woman. Jesus . . ." He gripped the edge of the metal desk. This was harder than he'd imagined. "I went after her . . . but nothing happened, not what you think, anyway."

Still silence on her end.

"I'm begging you to forgive me." He was sweating like a whore in church. "Let me come home. I swear I'll make it up to you."

"Did she throw you over?" Georgia dripped ice water.

"No! I'm the one who wants our life back together. Babe, I can't do this anymore without knowing you're there for me."

The hum on the line underscored that she was far away. The trailer shook as someone came up the steps.

"When?" Her voice sounded small.

The pressure changed in his ears as the outer door opened, then slammed. "As soon as I can . . . " From the front room, he heard Karrabotsos talking and Garrett's deep baritone.

"What does 'soon' mean?" Georgia asked.

"Tonight," Deering promised, "I'll be there tonight." He'd breathe the blessed smokeless air and listen to the Portneuf's peaceful chatter.

Heavy footsteps came down the hall. "Deering?"

"A minute," he called, and more softly, "I love you, hon. I'll see you this evening."

Garrett rapped on the door. "Where are you? I thought you were taking a leak."

"Who's there with you?" Georgia went suspicious.

Garrett opened the door and boomed, "We need to get in the air."

"I see," she said.

"See what?" Deering held up a hand at Garrett, who nodded and pulled the door closed.

"I have to go, Georgia. The North Fork is going to hit Old Faithful today and I have to fly Garrett Anderson . . . "

"It's always the same, isn't it? No matter what I need from you, there's always a fire somewhere that's more important."

For a moment, Deering thought she'd hung up, but there was no dial tone. He heard muted strains of music from the little stereo he'd given her a few years ago to listen to while she quilted. There was a subtle change in the sound, as though she'd put the receiver down on the table and walked away. "Georgia!" Deering shouted.

She hadn't hung up, but he did, slamming Johnny's phone onto the cradle.

He sat for a long moment with his head in his hands. He had to fly. His livelihood depended on it, and whether Georgia liked it or not, hers did too. He'd make this one flight, he bargained, like he'd planned, and then go home to her. He'd made a promise.

When he came out, Garrett was polite enough not to ask questions. They walked in silence to the Huey, where Deering did his preflight and runup and hoped his hands weren't trembling noticeably.

Devon thought that if Clare were still at the geyser basin, she would be out there with the firefighters. Through the glass rear door that led out of the Old Faithful Inn lobby, the sky looked even darker than it had when she'd come inside just after one p.m.

Her mother's accusations still made her chest ache. For years, both her parents and Elyssa had believed the worst of her. According to Annalise McIntyre, whose folks had dumped her in the loonie bin for acting out inappropriately, group therapy was full of "dysfunctional families."

Last night when it had gotten too cold and scary, Devon had sneaked, shivering, into the hotel. Near dawn, a patrolling security guard had rousted her from a couch on the lobby balcony. "Go on now, miss, we don't have no sleeping in here."

He'd thought she was a vagrant.

This afternoon the smell of smoke permeated even inside the Inn. Members of the press came out from filming the vacant dining room. With a small shock, Devon saw they wore white napkins tied around the lower half of their faces as filters.

"You think maybe we should get out of here?" she asked a red-haired woman reporter in a jeans jacket. Maybe she and her ponytailed companion with the video would give her a ride out. She'd looked for Mom until all the buses had gone.

The reporter shook her head and headed with the others toward the stairs. Devon checked out their conversation.

"Superlative vantage point . . . "

"Special exception . . . "

Devon ducked into the cavernous dining room with wagon wheel chandeliers and a huge fireplace. Like the others had, she grabbed a napkin off a table setting. Hurrying to keep up, she chased the press upstairs.

On the third floor, she followed the journalists as they stepped over a chain and went up rickety-looking stairs through the open atrium. Devon didn't look down as she climbed. At the top was a tree house, complete with gingerbread scrollwork. Out through a door so small she had to duck, and onto the inn's roof. Forceful gusts of wind struck. She stopped and stared at the column of smoke pouring up from the fire that seemed to be just beyond the horizon. One more set of wooden stairs took her to the widow's walk astride the highest peak of the inn.

A mounting roar announced the approach of a plane from the west. Flying low, the tanker dumped a load of red liquid in a long sweeping pass. A rosy fog hung, streamers emerging from the bottom of the cloud as it fell to earth. The smoke lay down and Devon breathed relief.

In a moment, it swirled up black with the fire's renewed fury.

The North Fork couldn't be half a mile away.

With the rising wind and deepening darkness, it grew colder. On the opposite side of the roof, the ponytailed man videotaped the people wearing napkin masks. Even though the smoke stung her eyes and throat, Devon clutched her own napkin in a sweaty hand.

The woman reporter began taping. "This is Carol Leeds, Billings Live Eye," she intoned importantly. "Only a handful of tourists remain to watch the geyser's show at Old Faithful Inn this afternoon, where formerly there were hundreds of spectators." A double ring of empty benches surrounded the geyser. "The evacuation was announced at dawn. All morning, busloads of visitors and employees have pulled away from the loading zone in front of this landmark hotel. This does not mean that all is quiet, though, for firefighters have ringed the inn."

From below, they sent flaring arcs of water to break on the roof and sheet down. Farther away, another group covered small wooden cabins in foam that looked like shaving cream.

Devon looked for her mother, checking for a firefighter who was a lot smaller than the others. Last night she'd slipped up and admitted to being scared when Mom went to the fire station. Pretending it didn't matter had been part of her defense. That had worked pretty well . . . until back in July when Mom came home and said she'd seen a man die. Thinking it could have been Mom who had burned to death had shocked Devon, so much she hadn't known what to say.

She'd said nothing. Gone to her room and cried. Come out later with her eyes kohl-rimmed to hide the evidence.

If her parents hadn't cared enough about her to stay together, she sure wasn't going to let them know anything bothered her. Her Dad had prissy, flat-assed Elyssa who sat on his knee and acted like Devon had bad breath when she went to hug her hello. Now, Mom had taken up with some Steve guy who lived thousands of miles away.

That scared her more than anything else. She'd seen Mom go on some dates since the divorce, but there was something very different about the way she looked at Steve.

And he at her.

The sky grew more garish by the minute. The sun appeared as an occasional bloody disc. Behind the southwest ridge,

Devon caught a glimpse of orange, the barest tongue of color licking forth and then being swallowed by smoke.

The reporter continued. "The employee dormitory stands in the shadow of the larger inn." The cameraman filmed the dark shingled barracks. "If it survives this day, the summer workers will not be back until spring, for the Park Service has determined that no matter what happens, they will close the Old Faithful complex for the season."

Devon heard the roar of a plane, but she couldn't locate it. Another flame leaped the ridge, and she realized that the sound was coming from the fire, an unearthly shriek that sounded as though she were standing in front of a jet engine. There were plenty of firefighters here, but the fire didn't look as though anybody could do anything about it.

Some still tried. Helicopters ferried back and forth, dipping their canvas buckets into the Firehole River, then flying to dump their loads and return. As the North Fork crested the ridge, the choppers looked like angry insects, impotent before the screaming monster.

🔥🔥🔥

Deering took off into the wind and was reminded of Black Saturday when he'd flown Garrett and been forced to turn back. As before, they flew into the park along the Madison River, with blackened forest beneath. To get to Old Faithful, he made a wide swing northwest around the fire front. He still felt shaky after his close call with the tanker.

Garrett sat stolidly in the left seat, swiveling his bald head.

From the Hellroaring at the far northeast corner of the park to the Snake River Complex in the Teton National Forest, the entire horizon had exploded with mushroom clouds.

Deering tried to concentrate on flying. He came in toward Old Faithful from the northwest, crossing the Firehole and flying along the open meadows crisscrossed with boardwalks. Garrett pointed to the lower parking lot where several TV vans were parked, satellite antennae on their roofs. "Look at those bloodsuckers. Hoping this place burns so they can get their shot at the big time."

A sudden downdraft gripped the Huey and the negative Gs increased. Deering rolled on throttle and steered to get out of the convection system before the fire front. He wished he could take his attention off flying and check Garrett's face. They said these fire generals had nerves of steel.

The helicopter jittered and shook.

Of course, a lot of folks thought Deering had brass balls, as well, but he could feel . . .

The thing was, he didn't want to feel. Not to think about how old this chopper was, and how flying it suddenly reminded him of the turbulence over the Chu Pong massif just before he'd sweep down into the Ia Drang Valley. "Fuck you, GI." The sound of VC Charlie, latched onto their frequency, just as Deering was about to make a tight approach. Below, in the landing zone carved out of jungle canopy, he'd take on injured soldiers no older than he was. Looking back, they'd all been kids.

Flying over Old Faithful, the trembling started in the pit of Deering's stomach. It spread up through his chest and down his arms until he had to grip the controls hard, trying not to let his sweating palms slip. It had been a long time since he'd felt the old battle fear and it didn't make sense.

Or maybe it did. The prospect of life without Georgia scared the living shit out of him.

He forced himself to concentrate on the turbulent sky and realized that Garrett was speaking through the headset. " . . . thing working?"

"Yeah, Garrett?"

"Guys down there. It looks like they're getting cut off."

Deering looked where Garrett was pointing and tried to focus on a group of four yellow-shirted people on the ground. They were inside a roped-off area that surrounded a small meadow. Two knelt in the weeds and the others were standing, writing on clipboards. "They don't seem to realize," Garrett said in a worried voice.

Deering couldn't afford this, absolutely must not fall apart in front of Garrett Anderson. If he did, his fire charter days would be over. He inhaled through his mouth and let it out slowly, imagining that he was blowing out the knots inside. Some people had panic attacks, going mindless in the middle of their kitchen, but it had never happened to him. He'd thought it a sign of weakness.

The night he'd come home from Vietnam, Georgia had cooked his favorite Greek meatballs, poured stout red wine from a jug, and lighted candles on the porch that overlooked the Portneuf. Drawing her against him in the creaking metal glider, he'd made a mental note to put some WD-40 on it in the morning. The old place had gone to hell without a man to take care of such things.

"Aren't you happy to be home?" She snuggled close and he felt the warm curve of her breast.

"Of course."

"You seem . . . preoccupied."

He'd left that damned jungle, a godforsaken place where men's feet rotted in their boots and souls were etched, on the other side of the planet. Unfortunately, he already knew that distance had failed to silence the jerky cacophony of shot-out rotors, the rattle of incoming machine gun fire, and the screams of nineteen-year-old Johnny Washington who'd died in the seat beside Deering.

"Don't you feel better now that nobody's going to shoot at you?" Georgia looked at him with soft green eyes, her hair a red-gold cloud around her luminous face.

He opened his mouth to tell her how wonderful it did feel to be safe, but he stopped. It was then, at that peaceful moment with the river running by and a sliver of moon peeking through the top of a cottonwood that Deering realized.

Waking up in the morning without the prospect of combat was dead boring.

It did not make sense, therefore, that on this afternoon over Old Faithful, he should be hyperventilating and sweating like a grunt under fire.

"Are you all right?" Garrett asked.

"Must have gotten hold of some bad chow," he managed. Turning to the man in the left seat, he lifted a hand to wipe his brow. "I'm gonna have to set her down."

CHAPTER TWENTY-SEVEN
September 7

Clare watched the Huey's rotors wind down on the Old Faithful Inn parking lot.

"They're bailing out of the sky," Javier Fuentes said. He kept the hose from the foam tank trained onto the employee cabin near the one where Clare was staying.

With a worried glance skyward, she realized that no other planes or helicopters were in sight. Without air support, the battle could be lost.

The chopper door opened and she saw Garrett Anderson climb out. He headed across the parking lot to a man she recognized as Duncan Rowland, Incident Commander of the North Fork. Clare said to Javier, "I'm going to find out what's happening."

She ran to Garrett.

"Hey, gal. This is one bad mutha, " he shouted with a baleful glare at the North Fork.

Fire swept over the southwest ridge while cinders the size of a man's hand pelted the parking lot. Rowland, a slender man with narrow features, listened to his Motorola. "This is it," he told Clare and Garrett, yanking off his ball cap and throwing it down. It tumbled away like a soccer ball.

Press vans were retreating from the perimeter, filming as they drew back to the open space beside the inn. Everyone in sight wore a bandanna or some kind of cloth tied over his or her face.

With a start, Clare realized that there were eight or ten people on the widow's walk atop the inn, small stick figures at this distance. More press, no doubt, daring danger the way her daughter liked to do. She wished she could warn them off, for if the eighty-five year old wooden building billed as the largest log cabin in the world went up, they were going to be shit out of luck.

The eerie orange light deepened to the reddish-brown of dried blood. Clare had to remind herself that the air itself could not burst into flame. As more burning brands sailed sideways, it was apparent that even the relative haven of the parking lot was not a safe place.

Behind the Hamilton Store and the Snow Lodge, the top of a two hundred foot wall of flame hove into view. Clare stared at the monstrous apparition.

East and west, the North Fork burned there as well, its long tentacles encircling the inn. Where was Steve? He'd gone into the forest and there didn't seem to be any part of it that wasn't burning.

And where, oh God, was Devon?

The wind that had been blowing toward the blaze shifted and bore down more directly on the Inn. Clare felt as though she stood in front of an oven, reminding her of the day she and Javier had driven through the tunnel of flame at Grant Village.

Duncan Rowland turned to his car, opened the trunk and drew out a fire shelter.

Clare fingered the pouch on her belt. Surely, that wouldn't be needed here on the parking lot, but the flame front was throwing up huge fireballs that raged for seconds before they disappeared. If one of them spotted forward . . . She shut her eyes, but she could still see the Hellroaring . . . no, it was the North Fork.

Eyes open, she pulled on her goggles from around her neck and fended off the flying bits of forest. Javier ran up to her and they both realized in the same instant that the crew protecting the Snow Lodge, Hamilton Store, and some storage buildings was woefully inadequate to the task. It was all she could do not to run away, but she hurried across the parking lot with Javier, toward the North Fork.

A cinder driven sideways by the wind caught her in the chest. As she brushed it off, she realized that if she had not been wearing Nomex, her clothing would have caught fire. She ran on toward what looked like the gaping mouth of Hades.

At the edge of the lot, she and Javier joined a pumper crew that was hooking up to a hydrant. "What can we do?" she shouted into the wind.

"Back us up!"

The men dragged the hose toward flaming trees not fifty feet from the nearest building. Clare and Javier made sure the line did not catch on the bumpers of the few cars still on the lot. If the inferno reached them, their gasoline tanks would add fuel.

The heat was worse here. She pulled her bandanna higher over her face and wished she were up front where the water was. The humidity from the spray would be welcome relief to her parched throat.

As fire torched the nearby pines, she realized that they would lose this battle within minutes. From here, the North Fork need only spot across the parking lot and the inn would be in flames.

"We need another line," Clare told Javier. She ran toward an engine parked at the base of the inn. The roof sprinkler system came on, letting water wash down the sides of the building.

As Clare sprinted past the grounded helicopter, she realized that Deering was the pilot. She hurried on, gasping for breath.

Getting to the engine, she grabbed a firefighter's arm. "Help us on the perimeter."

The man's eyes went wide behind his smudged visor. "Are you kidding? We're to stay by the inn."

Clare looked back the way she'd come and realized that the North Fork had reached the storage shed. In the same moment, she saw a ranger running toward the crew she had left. He waved his arms and shouted, pointing away from the shed.

It was clear that the person he was screaming at did not understand, so he balled his fists together and then threw his hands apart in a gesture that conveyed an explosion.

The crew began to run, leaving the perimeter abandoned. She could tell that Javier didn't see her as he ran for the largest open space to shelter.

"Can I help here?" Clare shouted to the man spraying the inn's roof.

"I think we've done all we can," he returned.

She ran for the chopper Deering sat in. Pulling herself up into the passenger seat of the Huey, she slammed the door.

Breathing hard, with a stitch in her side, she felt the futility. It was stuffy in the cockpit, but not as crazy as being out in the screaming gale. "Will we be safe here?" she asked.

Deering stared through the windshield. "We're a ways from anything flammable right now, but if the inn starts to go up, we'll need to abandon ship."

"Okay." Clare turned to study his pale face. "You look sick."

Deering's eyes were smoke-reddened. "I really am sick . . . or something. Garrett and I weren't scheduled to land, but I . . ."

Clare put a hand on his shoulder. He shook as though he were on drugs, like some of the ODs she'd run to the ER in Houston. She'd told Deering there was nothing for them, to go back to his wife, but she hated to see him falling apart like this. "Have you seen Georgia?"

The chopper rocked as a gust struck it. More cinders pelted the windshield.

"I botched it." He sounded broken.

Clare sat up straighter when she saw Garrett Anderson running toward them. He slid open the rear door and the wind whirled inside. Climbing into the back, he said, "Deering, the way the fire's moving, I'm sure that it's cut off those guys we saw counting plants or something." He raised his index finger and circled it to mimic rotors. "Let's pick 'em up."

Clare swallowed. Steve had gone to do something in the woods with his fellow biologists.

She waited for Deering to start flipping switches.

The chopper rocked again. "Can't do it, Garrett," Deering said. "In this wind, we'd crash."

Devon jumped as an explosion reverberated across the Geyser Basin. Fire raged on three sides of the inn and darkness had fallen in midafternoon.

The North Fork swept steadily toward her perch on the roof of the inn. A building at the edge of the parking lot burned unchecked, after the firefighters who had been spraying it had retreated.

Another rumble rolled across the valley. "What is that?" Devon asked.

"Probably fuel storage tanks," the tall cameraman with the ponytail replied. He hefted his video unit to his shoulder. "It's time to get off this firetrap."

Below, a helicopter sat on the parking lot. Its door opened and a small figure climbed out. Something about the determined walk of the person dressed in fire clothes made her scream, "Mom!"

Clare, if it was she, joined another man and headed away from the hotel. They looked strong and purposeful like all the firefighters, while Devon shook with fear. She must have been crazy to come up here.

A gust hit her like a fist. Her hand opened and the white

napkin lifted and blew away.

God, she was falling, her arms windmilling toward that lousy knee-high rail. Heights had made her mindless since she was old enough to peer from the stair landing and scramble back for dear life.

She landed hard on her wrist and elbow. Lying on the rubber roof mat, she fought nausea while pain brought tears to her eyes.

Reaching her trembling good hand to the railing, she pulled herself up. A single dizzying glance over the edge told her if she had been next to the downwind side, she'd have tumbled fifty feet down the steep roof.

Her heart hammered. Looking at the faraway porch where she would have fallen, she suddenly realized that the shingle roof was ablaze.

Devon shrieked and nearly wet her pants. She ran for the stairs behind the ponytailed cameraman. Down one flight and just before she reached the door leading inside the inn, a flying cinder caught her in the chest. Feeling its sting below her collarbone, she raised a hand to slap it away. In the same instant, the singed foulness of burning hair filled her nostrils.

The cameraman, already halfway inside the inn, turned back. His video landed on the decking with a crash. Swiftly, he pulled off his jacket and wrapped her head and shoulders.

The burning heat on her skin sent agonized pulses that threatened to send her to her knees.

Her rescuer dragged her through the portal and inside the dim space beneath the roof. Devon stammered, "Thanks," and shoved the jacket at him. She ran down the steps toward the tree house. Already a blister was rising on her chest above the curved neck of her tank top.

She had to find her mother. Mom would take her someplace safe. She'd bandage her burn and her wrist that was swelling and hurting more every second.

It seemed to take forever to stumble down flight after flight of stairs. Outside the inn, grit and ash bombarded her.

Raising her arm to ward off the onslaught, she looked for the chopper. An inferno surrounded the inn in every direction, while a clutch of tourists with their backs to the strong wind watched an eruption of Old Faithful. The ridge that formed a green backdrop behind the geyser was fully aflame.

Devon ran to the helicopter. "I'm looking for Clare Chance," she shouted, as the man in the cockpit swung open the chopper door. "She's my mom."

"Yeah," the slim, dark-haired man in an olive-drab flight suit answered without interest.

"I need to find her," Devon insisted. "She was just here."

The pilot removed his sunglasses and she saw that his eyes, surrounded by a sunburst of lines, were red. Of course, everybody's were because of the smoke, but he looked wracked out. He studied Devon wearily. "I can't help you." She saw him take in her burned chest and irregular, singed hair. "You okay?"

"I will be when I find my mother."

✿✿✿

Clare followed Garrett across the parking lot, surprised that she had trouble keeping up.

"Those people you saw," she said. "I think one of them might be Steve Haywood." Having the inn in peril was one thing. If the North Fork threatened Steve and his friends . . .

"The guy who was drying out on Washburn?" Garrett grinned despite his speed. "The one I thought was sweet on you?"

A quick flash of last night's all too brief embrace made Clare return, "He's off the mountain now." She got into the spirit of joshing in the face of danger, an old habit of hers and Frank's. "Did I mention how kind it was of you to tease me about him over the public airwaves?"

"Always happy to oblige."

As they headed across the complex, Garrett's continued banter helped keep her mind off his ominous statement that he believed Steve and the others had been cut off.

It was bad enough that she couldn't find Devon, but there was no reason to believe she'd been caught out on the flat by the North Fork. An inveterate urban kid like her daughter would have been trying to pass for twenty-one in the bar rather than taking a wilderness hike.

Steve and his fellow biologists were another matter. She imagined them out there absorbed in their work, while the fire came on.

🔥🔥🔥

Steve surveyed the forty-by-forty foot area they had staked

out, partly sheltered by a community of mature lodgepole. The trees exuded chemicals that discouraged the entry of other plant species into its neighborhood.

The balance of the tract had been cleared of forest by the pine bark beetle. A few snags stood, but most had gone down and were in an advanced stage of rot, providing homes for communities of fungi, grubs and termites. Growing lushly around the fallen were crested wheatgrass gone to seed, spreading fronds of bracken fern, and dense patches of red clover. A Monarch flitted around the clusters of late-blooming goldenrod.

Fly away, Steve told the butterfly. The rooted could only await the inevitable.

"Twenty-eight, twenty-nine, thirty." Moru finished his count of common Indian paintbrush in precise tones. He looked toward the sound of the approaching fire and broke into a smile. "I believe this one will burn."

Summer intern Thomas Lee looked at the darkening sky through thick glasses and pressed his lips together. Steve thought Thomas wanted to head out, but didn't want to be the first to suggest it.

Kelly Engels wiped sweat from her freckled forehead. "Let's beat feet!" She tightened the cinch on her untidy ponytail, stowed her clipboard in her pack, and waited expectantly.

As Steve's focus shifted from the plant community to the North Fork, a rising roar made him wish they had worked faster. Moru got to his feet with a worried look.

Kelly swiveled her head. "It's jumped the highway!" she shouted. She took off, Thomas at her heels.

Moru was running now, too, leaping over logs behind Kelly and Thomas. Steve chased them, running awkwardly on his crippled knees. Behind them, the North Fork howled like a predatory animal.

Steve and Moru had fire shelters on their belts, but he hadn't seen any on Thomas and Kelly. Maybe they had them in their packs, for at this rate they were going to need them. He hated the thought of going into a shelter for the second time in a week, but there it was. And from the wind velocity and the sound of it, the North Fork's firestorm would burn far fiercer and hotter than the Hellroaring. If they were overtaken, they'd probably die.

Trying to think of a way out, he considered the layout of the complex. If they worked their way to the left, they might get ahead of the fire's path and break into the open near the employee cabins.

The smoke grew thicker. Ahead, the visibility was down to just under a hundred feet when Thomas slewed to a stop, holding his out his hand. When Steve pulled up beside him, he felt the fire's heat. As Kelly and Moru joined them, a flash of orange appeared through the trees.

"They'll be heading for the easement," Garrett predicted. From his neutral tone, she gathered he saw long odds against their making it.

This wasn't goddamn fair. Last night she'd dared to believe that Steve was making a new start after losing Susan and

Christa. A fresh beginning that she might have a stake in.

Her little voice whispered that life . . . and death . . . weren't fair.

Garrett looked at the hellish red twilight and broke into a flat out run. Clare's bandanna covered the part of her face not protected by goggles, but she felt the stinging impact of wind-borne cinders.

Not far from the south edge of the parking lot, the wide, treeless swath of easement headed into the forest. Clare strained and picked out four yellow Nomex shirts. They weren't even wearing hard hats and she assumed they hadn't believed the North Fork would move this fast.

She picked out Steve and uselessly added her scream to that of the fire. He waved an arm to signal that they were heading her way.

Clare started toward them, but Garrett grabbed her sleeve. "I wouldn't."

Although she'd come to appreciate his wisdom, this time she tried to pull away. "Steve!" she cried.

Garrett's fingers held like a vice. "Rule number one," he ground out. The commandment she'd preached to Jerry Dunn of Toro Canyon, about not jumping into the water to save a drowning victim unless you had the right equipment and were certain of conditions.

The one she'd ignored while struggling to uncover Frank, the one Javier had disregarded to drag her from danger. She struggled to get free, to go to Steve, but a wall of flame roiled up over the trees on the easement's west side. Heat waves distorted the air.

Garrett pointed to the pipes running down the center of the corridor with sprinkler heads at intervals. "The irrigation system!"

Pete Cullen and his West Yellowstone volunteers had brought their equipment to protect the power lines, but no water flowed. "Why isn't it on?" Clare shouted.

"Don't know."

She located the fireplug where the pipes were tied in to the four-inch connection. "I hope there's pressure." She ran for the nearest fire truck, parked thirty yards away. Instinct told her that she was running for Steve's life.

No one was near the vehicle, a grim sign that this perimeter, too, had been abandoned, so quickly that nobody had moved the truck. She checked the back where the hose clamp was, but the plug wrench wasn't in plain view. Moving to the side, she unlatched the shining silver cover of the nearest locker.

Nothing inside but air packs, with spare bottles clipped in place above. Clare started for the other side of the truck and realized that the wrench was on the rear step. She'd just failed to see it.

When she grabbed the two-foot steel spanner, she heard a man call to her and realized that someone was coming to save the truck. Without waiting to explain, she ran back toward the easement.

At the fireplug, she didn't dare take time to assess Steve and the others' situation. The look on Garrett's face was enough as she read, "Hurry," on his lips. The sound was torn away by the North Fork.

Clare fit the wrench head over the five-sided lug on top

of the fireplug. She took three turns with her right hand to tighten the grip of the jaws, leaned into it, and prayed.

❦❦❦

It was too late to outrun the fire, Steve realized. The North Fork relentlessly filled in the portions of black canvas not yet painted. He'd seen Clare across the burning barrier, for a bare second, but she was out of sight now.

He and the others had one last chance. To leap through the low, burning brush of the easement and sprint through the unburned woods to the Firehole River . . . immerse in the cold water and let the fire rage over their heads.

Steve began to run, hoping that his fire retardant clothing would prevent major burns. Within a few yards, his knees reminded him that he had already done far too much insult to his old wounds this day. Each step was as though a blade stabbed through his calf and emerged from the top of his thigh. He felt the heat, just ahead where he would have to plunge into the flames.

Clare waited for him, so close, and yet cut off by the enemy they'd been combating all summer. With a surge of anger, he decided that he, by God, was not going to die this way. For the first time in years, he had something to look forward to.

As he redoubled his efforts, he suddenly felt something he believed was impossible. Stinging droplets pelted him, spraying his face and forearms. It was rain, no, of course, it wasn't; great black clouds were in the sky, but it sure as hell wasn't raining.

He stopped, stunned. Falling water mingled with his sweat and dripped down his neck to his collar. Moru held out a hand, palm up, and watched the drops land on his pale palm. The smile lines at the corners of his eyes and mouth grew deeper.

The conduit down the center of the easement spewed great fountains. Where water landed on the fires, a cloud of steam arose.

🔥🔥🔥

Clare saw them running along the pipeline. After thirty yards of slogging through thick brambles, Steve lagged the others.

The tall man gasping for breath waved thanks when he passed Clare and Garrett. The two young people didn't stop running even when they were in the clear. As Steve staggered onto the pavement, his legs buckled.

Clare knelt beside him. "Give me a hand, Garrett."

He bent to help.

Steve struggled to rise on his own, but Garrett grabbed him beneath his arms and pulled him up.

"Can you walk?" Her voice carried that element of business she used in emergencies, but she heard a trembling kind of timbre that said she was running on empty.

"Not sure," Steve managed.

"Put your arms around us," she urged, "just in case."

Garrett hunched down so that the disparity between his and Clare's heights would not throw Steve off balance.

"I wish to God those sprinklers had been on," Clare said.

"It would have saved me nearly having a coronary."

Steve's arm tightened around her shoulder. "You?" He gave a grin that turned into a grimace when he put weight on his right leg.

"Power lines can be restrung," Garrett said. "I'm sure they needed the water pressure to defend the inn because it can't be replaced."

"Did it . . .?" Clare stopped. Had all their efforts to save the building she loved ended in a smoking ruin? She ran to the plug and turned off the flow, hoping it might help keep up pressure at the inn.

Ahead, the other scientists stared at something in the distance. Clare moved forward to see around the pines that blocked her view and she saw through the red haze. The inn was still there, with flags snapping on the ramparts.

Yet, all was not the same. A blackened ring would surround Old Faithful, long past all their lifetimes.

CHAPTER TWENTY-EIGHT
September 7

I n Karrabotsos's Huey, Deering acknowledged radio communication. If this was a blanket call to set down, he was way ahead of them. Controller Jack Owen knew it.

"Deering," Jack spoke directly to him. "I need you on Nez Perce Peak to pick up some hikers. Word is they're trapped on a ridge by fire."

"I'm trapped on the ground by one," Deering replied. "You got any idea what's going down at Old Faithful?"

"I thought the worst was over."

"I can't take off in this wind." He repeated what he'd told Garrett. "I'd crash."

Clare's daughter had blue eyes that weren't a thing like her mother's. They went wide. Maybe he shouldn't have used the 'c' word, but he did want to make his point with Owen. "Where's Johnny Arvela?"

"Way north. Look, those hikers were spotted by a fixed-wing over an hour ago. God knows what's happening up there."

Deering wasn't ready to fly again, but with a sinking

feeling, he gauged the wind's velocity and direction. In the past few minutes, it had shifted so that the full brunt did not bear down on the inn. "Where is it again?"

"Either Nez Perce or Saddle Mountain. The pilot wasn't sure. Two or maybe three guys."

Clare's kid clutched his arm. "Can't we get out of here?"

A few minutes ago, it hadn't seemed possible that the inn would not burn, but now the roof merely smouldered. It looked as though the firestorm's front had passed, already cresting the ridge with the lookout.

A nasty ache rose in his throat. The wind was still a hazard, each gust rocking the chopper, but it was subsiding rapidly. "Okay," he told Jack. "It looks like the worst is over here, but I was flying Garrett Anderson."

"I'll see that he finds out where you are."

That settled it, except for Clare's daughter. "Look . . ."

"Devon." That was going to be a nasty burn on her chest. She cradled a swollen wrist and hand that was turning blue.

"Look, Devon, I've got to fly out of here now. You need to find a medic."

"Take me with you!"

"I thought you wanted to find your mother. She's here somewhere."

"I've looked for her all morning. I don't have any money to even get something to eat." Her voice was a wail. "Besides, everything's closed."

Deering calculated. He shouldn't take on a passenger like this, especially for a rescue mission. But there was no way he could fly and open the rear door if the hikers had to board while he hovered. No telling what kind of terrain they were on, but Jack had mentioned a ridge.

He decided to relent. He could easily carry three hikers and Devon and she might be useful. The trip out to the eastern part of the park wouldn't take long, and he'd have her in the hands of a West Yellowstone medic within the hour.

"Okay," he told her. "You can hook up with your mom at Fire Command."

"Now, what in the . . .?" Garrett Anderson frowned. Clare thought the annoyance in his voice odd, when he should have been pleased to see the inn unscathed.

Away across the parking lot, the Huey's rotors turned, the engine revving up in a whine. Only a few moments before, they would not have been able to hear it over the screams of the North Fork.

"Where in hell is he going?" Garrett pulled his Motorola from his belt and tried to raise Deering in the cockpit.

"I thought it was too windy to fly," Clare said.

"It's still touch and go." Garrett groused.

"I've flown with Deering," Steve began.

Clare heard the venom in his voice and silenced him with a look.

"Yeah?" Garrett asked suspiciously.

Steve started to speak, but Clare cut him off. "I was with Deering the day he rescued a Smokejumper on Bighorn Peak, and the night he ferried over fifty firefighters out of the Mink

Creek spike camp, just ahead of a firestorm. He did one hell of a job."

Garrett stepped away from them and used his Motorola. "Hello, West Yellowstone?"

As soon as they were alone, Steve's hard look challenged her defense of Deering. After last night, she'd thought they had that straightened out.

"Steve, Deering is a good pilot, with guts. Are you certain that your feelings about flying aren't getting in your way here?"

Their eyes held, but before either could speak, Garrett was back. "Buddy, it's gonna be one hell of a drive," he said to Steve, "but could I trouble you for a lift to West Yellowstone?"

"Sure. Moru is driving the kids back to Mammoth." His gray eyes remained on Clare. "You coming?"

She thought of Devon and shook her head. "I have to find my daughter. She's been missing since last night."

Garrett jumped on the new emergency with the same alacrity she'd seen in him since July. "Okay, I'll need a description, and a photo if possible. We'll get it out to all the rangers and the heads of the fire crews as well, since most of the park is closed to tourists."

"I've got a picture in my bag at the cabin."

"Get it then, so we can head out," Garrett said.

It wasn't far, but before she'd covered half the distance, she saw smoke coiling up from behind the first row of rough wooden roofs. A pale swirl compared to the black tower over the North Fork. Despite layers of foam laid on thick, at least seven of the small dark buildings had burned.

Approaching on leaden feet, Clare found she didn't need her key. The ceiling had collapsed, covering the smouldering ruins of the twin mattresses. Burned and half-burned timbers lay about like pick-up sticks, some precariously propping up portions of the roof. She almost leaned against the door-jamb to support herself, but felt the heat of charred timber just in time to pull her hand away.

She was losing it. Almost two months of inhaling enough to equal two packs a day, and she had had enough. If . . . when she found Devon, she was going to take her home.

The things she'd bought in Jackson were on her bed, with Devon's picture inside her checkbook. Peering though the drifting smoke, she saw the synthetic bag, a melted lump of plastic. Thankfully, she carried her wallet in her trouser pocket.

Her foot crunched on fallen shingles as she advanced carefully into the cabin. The inn might have survived, but how old was this building that had seen many seasons of employees and their families come and go? With a thickening in her throat, the ruin reminded her of the falling down homestead of the Suttons.

There was more to lose here than a photograph of her daughter. Clare had only begun to know Laura Sutton through words penned long ago and she wanted more. To know the hardships and triumphs of a life that had ultimately led to her creation.

The small table where she'd left the book still stood between the beds. There was nothing on it except the lamp, lying on its side with the shade burned away. She started to move toward the table, stepping over fallen boards.

Her foot slipped on the pile of rubble and she fell against the bathroom wall. Looking down, she saw that her boot had uncovered the diary. With a sigh of relief, she snatched it up and headed back to where Steve and Garrett waited.

"There's Nez Perce," Deering told Devon.

Straight ahead of the Huey rose a high peak with a broad, jumbled slope of blocky rock facing them. Sharp ridges splayed out in three directions. The summit was above timberline, with scrubby grass growing in the fractures between dark rocks.

Jack Owen had said the hikers were being trapped on a ridge by a fire. Seeing a rising smoke column behind the mountain's shoulder, Deering zeroed in on a potential area.

He put the chopper into a dive. Then he leveled off and flew along the west spine. From a few hundred feet away he noted that the rocks were as big as houses. There was no sign that the hikers were sheltering on the barren slope.

"Help me look for these guys," he told Devon through their headphones.

She swiveled her blond head. From the corner of his eye, Deering noted long tanned legs in tight shorts and surmised that Devon's father must have been a big man. Her mother was certainly a lot smaller.

He climbed again, heading up to the ridge crest. The top flashed past and the forest on the east side dropped away beneath. There was the fire, eating its way up the slope.

Deering swung in a wide arc and came back. This time he flew only about a hundred feet off the promontory, fighting the wind that swept up from the valley and mixed dangerously above the spine.

Devon's hands were twisted together in her lap.

The narrow ridge dropped away on either side. The west was barren talus, the east studded with evergreens, the tops of their tall trunks below a rocky patch near the crest. Deering began to whistle tunelessly through his teeth.

He tapped the radio button to call Jack Owen, but the wind surged up from the west slope. Even with both hands fighting the controls, the chopper swept over the east side of the ridge.

Deering couldn't fucking believe it. He struggled to stabilize, to achieve some lift. It wasn't happening.

Jesus, why had he brought Clare's daughter? In twenty-twenty hindsight, that was another of his brilliant hotshot moves.

The tail rotor caught the trees and the Huey whipped around. The main rotors sliced at the tops of the pines. The upper part of the slope was steep, dropping away so that there was at least a hundred feet to fall.

All he could do was watch it happen and wait for impact.

The chopper nosed over. It seemed to take a long time, yet he also had the impression of tree limbs flashing past.

Clare's daughter screamed.

Rocks rushed up. The windshield shattered.

For an instant after impact Deering kept falling, then his seatbelt and shoulder strap seemed to crush his chest. Metal screeched on rock as the rotors smashed to a stop. The Huey came to rest on its left side and he thought it was over.

Then the chopper seemed to feel the slope. Very slowly, it began an almost gentle roll.

Through a haze, Deering registered that he had to do something. Help, they needed help. He reached to the radio, "Mayday, Mayday."

Things speeded up fast. Once over, the chopper's ceiling became the floor. His seatbelt eased, then tightened.

"West Yellowstone, come in. Mayday." It was bad enough that he'd crashed twice in one season, but he'd promised Georgia he'd be home tonight. In a just few hours, he was supposed to be eating Greek meatballs and opening a nice jug of red. Everything would be back in place, including his wife in his arms.

The chopper continued its roll. He'd once had a nightmare like this, about being in an elevator that escaped its shaft and swung in a dizzying arc.

He had to get the message out, so that at least Georgia would know what happened.

"Mayday, Mayday."

The familiar words reminded him of landing under fire. The tattered shreds of falling foliage marked where bullets ripped the lush green jungle. How many times in years since, had he dreamed the controls failed to respond to his handling? No matter how he pushed the pedals or moved the cyclic and collective, the Huey hovered, directly in the line of fire.

Another trip upside down and then upright. He tried to

focus in the midst of tumbling chaos and saw the shattered state of the machinery in the dash.

"West Yellowstone, I am down on Nez Perce Peak," he tried. Dead air told him all he needed to know.

CHAPTER TWENTY-NINE
September 7

Clare did not look back as they left the burned-out heart of Yellowstone. Garrett drove in deference to the pain in Steve's knees and she sat between them in the front seat of the tired Park Service truck. In her lap, she carried her great-grandmother's journal.

On both sides of the Grand Loop Road, flames glowed crimson in a ten-mile stretch between Old Faithful and Madison Junction. If these dry weather fronts didn't break soon, the entire two million acres of Yellowstone would end up like the trees that were torching tonight.

July 25th seemed a year ago instead of six short weeks. At Grant Village, she had never seen anything like the tunnel of flame on the narrow, deeply forested road. Tonight, she was deeply weary of watching fire's relentless advance.

Garrett had radioed Ranger Shad Dugan about Devon and received a more satisfactory response than Butler Myers had offered during the siege at Old Faithful. All over the park, radios were crackling to life with a description of a blue-eyed blonde.

Somehow, that didn't help. Even with a day's high in the eighties, nights grew cold. In just a few hours, the bloody sun would set for the second time since Devon had left in shorts and a tank top. A shrill admonition echoed from when Devon was two and Clare's mother found her clearly unable to mother her own child. "Don't you let that precious darling go out without a jacket!"

A jacket . . . when it might already be too late.

They rode in silence for miles. Clare felt sorry for Steve who grimaced each time the worn out suspension took on a pothole.

Garrett tuned the truck's radio to the press conference that North Fork Incident Commander Duncan Rowland was conducting at Old Faithful. With a deeply obvious sense of relief, Rowland revealed the inn's narrow escape. He reported the loss of fourteen cabins along with a gasoline tanker truck and storage shed, and gave thanks that no one had been seriously hurt.

When the press conference ended, Garrett shook his big head and snapped off the radio. They left the fire behind and drove through the false twilight of smoke.

Leaving the park's deep forest and broad meadows beside the Madison River was as startling as plunging into cold water. West Yellowstone shone with neon signs advertising Exxon, the Red Wolf Motel and the Saloon next door. When he passed Fire Command, Garrett did not slow. "I thought we'd go on to the hotel. We've got a block of rooms."

From Yellowstone Avenue, he turned onto Dunraven Street,

passing two troop transports. Farther down, the Stagecoach Inn, with Swiss style dormer windows on the second floor, covered an entire block.

Inside the high-ceilinged lobby, a group of uniformed military had staked out the conversation pit before the fireplace. From the hotel bar came the raucous talk and laughter of enlisted men and firefighters. Business boomed even if the townsfolk were livid about lost revenue from the fires.

Garrett shouldered his way to the check-in and doled out keys. Clare noted that Steve's was 218 to her 220. Nodding toward the bar, Garrett said, "We can get something to eat in there after we freshen up."

Clare turned to speak to Steve, but he was limping toward the broad staircase without saying whether he would meet them. Garrett caught up and assisted him while Steve leaned with one hand on the polished wooden rail. She started to follow, but figured on seeing him later.

Caught without belongings for the second time in three days, Clare bought toiletries and a T-shirt with a grizzly logo in the small shop off the lobby. After a moment's deliberation and weighing her own negative reaction to Deering's coming prepared to Mink Creek, she picked up a discreet small box of condoms. She wasn't sure yet about sleeping with Steve but a powerful wave of temptation surged.

With the box in her bag, she wondered if Steve had been a Boy Scout.

Going upstairs, she appreciated the Stagecoach's rustic flavor with its western style artwork and bronzes, imagining a visit when the carpet was not stained by the tramp of sooty boots.

As she put her key to the lock, she noted that Steve's room was indeed the one next door. Once inside hers, she heard the rush of his shower through the connecting door.

Clare placed Laura Sutton's diary carefully on the chest of drawers. She pressed a hand flat to it as if communing and thought how nearly she'd come to losing her tenuous connection to her great-grandmother in this afternoon's fire. Her hand came away a little sooty so she got a tissue and wiped the leather.

Stripping off her dirty clothes, she went into the bathroom.

Back in July, her reflection had stared at her in the College Station Ramada Inn. At the time, she had believed her day running training sessions at Texas A&M had been a difficult one. Her cheeks had been pink and full from the day's heat, her muscles reasonably fit from lifting weights at the fire station. They had called it an emergency when Jerry Dunn of Toro Canyon had been burned, a minor second-degree blister.

Tonight the woman in the mirror was a stranger.

With skin as nut-brown as her Nez Perce ancestors, her face had gone gaunt and the cords in her neck stood out. Her breasts looked smaller than she could remember since puberty and her hipbones defined her flat stomach. More dark roots and a bit of silver showed in her hair.

Somehow, the blond highlights didn't belong to her anymore. In the lobby shop, she had purchased a manicure kit, hoping to clean up the ragged edges of her cuticles. Instead, she used the tiny scissors to attack her bangs.

A pile of clippings mounted on the porcelain sink. With each cut, Clare felt as though she left behind the woman she had been in Houston, emerging like a butterfly from its chrysalis. She imagined that the natural dark shades in her hair were her great-grandfather's gift of heritage.

When she had finished, she stared at a ruffled little boy's cut. What she saw in her eyes still scared her.

🔥🔥🔥

In the Stagecoach's Barrel Bar, the knotty pine walls bounced back the sounds of a country music duo playing guitar and keyboard. Clare had caught their act one night with Sherry and Hudson. Then she'd felt differently about the exuberant exhilaration of the fire crews, listening eagerly to each new story of beating back a fire front, getting run out, or rescuing someone in trouble.

Wearing clean fire clothes, Garrett waited for her at a table. He looked at her new T-shirt and the filthy pants she'd put back on. "Something for you from down the street." He nodded toward a fresh yellow shirt and olive trousers folded neatly on the chair next to him.

"You've saved my life." Clare thought of going to change right away, but she was starving. The Coke and candy bar she'd had was a long time ago.

She sank into the wooden chair opposite Garrett.

His serious black eyes held hers. "You doing okay?"

"Better when I find Devon."

Steve came to them through the throng in jeans and the western shirt he'd worn in Jackson. He gave her a quick once-over that included her haircut, but didn't say anything.

She and Garrett ordered frosted mugs of beer and Steve a Coke.

Garrett placed his big hands flat. "I found out where Deering flew off to this afternoon. He went to check out a report of some hikers trapped by fire on a ridge." His expression was graver than she might have expected.

"No one was hurt?" she hoped.

"We don't know. After Deering flew out toward Nez Perce Peak, he never radioed back. It got dark before they could send anybody to look for him."

Clare gripped the cigarette-burned edge of the table. "Oh, God. Do you think he's all right?"

Steve shifted in his chair and made a face that could have expressed pain or a reaction to her concern for Deering.

Clare's mind flashed to the gilt-edged book on her dresser upstairs. "My great-grandparents were caught by a forest fire on Nez Perce." What if Deering was on that same peak, down for the second time in a summer? He'd told her of his wife's fears.

Pizza came; the frozen kind that got soggy when heated. Clare chewed without tasting. Garrett tried to keep up conversation, but while Steve obliged with talk of the ecosystem's burn recovery she fell silent. Every minute that passed made it less likely that Devon was trying to get a message to her.

Before they parted for the evening, Garrett told Clare, "I promise I'll phone your room if I hear anything about Devon, no matter what time."

"Or if you hear from Deering." She couldn't help saying it.

Steve pushed up from the table. His chair squealed on the

wooden floor that was littered with peanut shells. "I'll catch you folks in the morning." His voice was neutral, but Clare detected coolness. He made eye contact with Garrett and passed over her.

As Steve took his leave Garrett told Clare, "The park people and law enforcement in the border towns will keep looking for Devon." He put out his hand and hers disappeared into his firm grip. She drew strength from his calm certainty that things would work out.

By the time she reached the long upstairs hallway, she heard a door close near hers with a hard note that sounded final.

Biting her lip, Clare went into her own room and slammed her fist against the back of the closed door. What the hell was the matter with Steve? She thought they'd straightened things out about Deering last night.

She killed the hotel room lights, but it wasn't dark. A red glow from the neon hotel sign filtered through the drapes like the eerie night beauty of the Mink Creek. Thankfully, the blowup had stopped her and Deering from having sex. She couldn't call what they'd been about to do making love.

In the half-light, she stripped off her boots, socks, and pants. Wearing only her T-shirt, she climbed onto the king bed and stretched out.

Dammit, she and Steve could be good together. Her breath caught as she remembered the urgency with which he had pulled her to him last night. How his lips had felt smooth against her chapped ones. He'd made her feel connected, something foreign now that she was used to making her own way.

She sensed her heart beating, not faster, but she could feel her pulse as though she was more aware of life flowing through her. Her hands rubbed the quilted, paisley-print bedspread, heating with the friction. Steve's skin would be warm if she stroked her fingers over his back.

With a final adjustment, the tumblers fell into place inside her. The moment when she went from 'what if' to certainty that she wanted to make love with him. There would be time for second-guessing back in Houston if she was wrong about them, but what a lost opportunity if they never tried.

Clare spread her arms and legs and imagined that Steve's weight pressed her as it had in the fire shelter when his eyes had sparked a message. She looked at the connecting door that led to his room.

Steve shed his denim shirt and boots and sat on the bed he'd hoped to entice Clare into. That wasn't happening because it was always Deering, Deering, Deering. What a great pilot Deering was, she'd said. It was Steve's fucking problem that he was afraid to fly.

He'd had time to go over that one a dozen times on the drive from Old Faithful. If Garrett hadn't been there, he'd have told Clare how it pissed him off.

He should say to hell with her.

The urge for a real drink, not some sugary concoction, surged. What if he went down to the bar for a bottle?

He reached for one of his boots and started putting it back

on. Clare would be gone soon, back to her real world while he continued his role of 'the widower who needs a good woman' in Mammoth.

Steve stopped, his hands at the laces. If he went downstairs, if he started drinking again, Shad Dugan would exile him.

Poised on the edge, he weighed the smoky glow of a good scotch against Mammoth beneath a clear winter sky. White drifts, piled as high as houses, casting blue shadows on the snow. Freezing air stung his nose and lungs while he made the short walk from the old stockade to the administration building. The bar on the door clanked as he pushed into warmth and found Moru Mzima pouring coffee and checking out the cherry pastries someone's wife had baked.

He'd climb the worn stairs to his small corner office, awash in morning sun and cluttered with stacks he called his piling system. He always savored days devoted to research. Only in winter when park visitors were few could an interpretive ranger find that kind of luxury.

After a few days spent snowed in, the space between the walls always seemed to narrow. That was when he and Moru would head off on snowmobiles into the park interior. Jouncing over the washboard surface formed by the machines, they were warmed by insulated snowsuits, gloves, and helmets, even while traveling fifty miles per hour through subfreezing air.

On the return, he never failed to thrill at the way the world changed at the innocuous notch that edged the vast white expanse of Swan Lake Flat. In the narrow apex of Golden Gate Canyon, the road began a seemingly endless spiral, through

the jumbled giant blocks of white travertine called the Hoodoos, sidehilling beside a sweeping vista at least thirty miles
up Blacktail Deer Plateau. Winding past the terraces of
Mammoth Hot Springs and the old military cemetery, onto
the parade ground and . . .

Home.

Clare had been the catalyst; the seed to renewed hope when
she'd challenged him not to destroy himself. Now he determined to stay sober for all that was important in his life.

He slid off his boot and it clunked to the carpet. To under-
line the point he pulled off his socks.

In the bathroom, he dashed double handfuls of cold water
on his face. He had lost the spare tire and his muscles were
defined from the summer's work. His hair wasn't ever going
to get any thicker, but what there was bore gold sun streaks.
His face was bronzed and the puffy bags beneath his eyes
had disappeared.

Coming out of the bath, he stopped and looked at the connecting door. Clare was behind it, wearing that silly grizzly
shirt or maybe nothing at all. His breathing deepened, or
maybe it just seemed the air grew dense. This new, heavy atmosphere defined his body, making him aware of all his sensations. The carpet felt soft beneath his bare feet. His jeans
rode low, looser in the past weeks, well-worn cotton against
his skin. He ran a hand over his stomach and chest and stared
at the thin panel that separated him from Clare.

She was probably in bed now.

He began to pace, as best he could in the small room, a few
feet toward the nightstand, about face and around in front of

the silent TV to the other side of the bed. If he had any sense, he'd turn on the set to distract him.

He kept moving.

The king bed looked vast and empty, while just beyond that wall Clare was equally alone. On each circuit, he had to pass the door, not once, but twice.

He would never know what had been between her and Deering, but she'd told him it was over. She could have stayed at the Storm Creek camp with the pilot the other night, not gone home with him to Mammoth. She could have let him leave that night in Jackson, instead of sharing her and Devon's room, sleeping trustfully near him.

Last night, she'd come into his arms. His hands felt full with the pulse of wanting to touch her again, to feel her bare skin full length against him.

Steve slowed his pacing. He was never going to sleep knowing how close she was. He found his palms pressed flat against the door. Slowly, he bent and put his ear against it to hear if she had put on the TV. All was silent.

If he opened this side, ever so quietly, he could see if she had her lamp on. Before he could change his mind, he twisted the turn button on the lock and pulled the door open. The knob-less facing panel looked odd, beveled like a door, but one without promise. If he knocked, she might tell him to go away. Perhaps she would not.

He told himself that it didn't make sense to start something that was doomed to end with them separated by half the continent.

But for him it was already begun. After four years on ice, it was time to start living again.

❦❦❦

With her hand on the knob of the connecting door, Clare jumped at the soft knock. Relief turned her knees to jelly as she opened the door.

Steve leaned against the jamb as though he had all the time in the world, but she felt the fallacy in that; saw the tautness in the muscles of his bare arms and chest. Her heart pounded.

"Steve." She backed up, flustered. Her hand went to the pulse at the base of her throat. "Why didn't you tell me downstairs that you wanted to talk to me?"

He hooked his thumbs inside the belt loops of his low-slung jeans. It hitched them down to reveal his navel, encircled with a whorl of golden hair. "We can talk if you like . . . but . . ." His gray eyes were smoky.

It seemed at once a long time and yet might never last long enough, while Steve simply looked at her. His gaze drank in her breasts beneath the grizzly bear T-shirt, down to where it draped boyish hips she'd hated in high school. The way he crooked a brow said he didn't think her hips were a bit like a boy's.

He came to her in three swift strides as though he'd forgotten the pain in his knees. Her mouth opened beneath his as if they'd had years of knowing each other rather than a single kiss.

Her fears for Devon were still with her, could never be far from the surface, yet Steve compelled her to lose herself and be shored up with his strength.

He deepened the embrace and she felt his need. His hands defined her in a way she had never thought possible. This might be another brainless decision of the body, the kind of stupid mistake she'd almost made with Deering, but how strong this sense of right.

She was vaguely aware of him stripping off his watch and dropping it onto the bed behind her. That simple gesture touched her as he tried to protect her from being scratched by the buckle.

One of his hands slid down her back and found the bottom of the thin T-shirt. She thought with longing of turquoise lace, tossed into a trashcan at the Storm Creek Camp. Raising her arms, she let him draw the single garment over her head.

She stood before him as naked as the desire in his eyes. She'd imagined them taking it slow; savoring each step that had been too long denied, but her hunger was as fierce as his.

"My God," he said with undisguised appreciation. He was beyond savoring the view, shucking his jeans and underwear in a single motion to reveal his impatience.

She brushed her palms across his chest and he pulled her to him. The warmth of skin against skin made her shudder deliciously. "Remember when you were younger and this was a huge deal?" she whispered.

He stroked her bare shoulders and lowered his mouth to her ear. "I don't know about you," he nipped her lobe, "but for me, it's as special . . . and as important, as ever."

"That's what I was getting to." She ran out of words as he took her mouth. They went down together onto the bed, she on her back. She was ready, so ready, and he knew.

She reached to touch and found him powerful and equally prepared. He poised above her, seeking, and their eyes met.

He smiled.

As he pressed into her, she felt tight around him, another sign that it had been too long. Her hands roamed and discovered skin as smooth as she'd imagined. He smelled clean, yet the earthy scent of musk rose as she met him. His breath was fast against her cheek and he moaned. The sound of his voice drove her harder.

Dear God, it had never been like this. The urgency of his touch spoke to a sweet sense of yearning in her. This man, this place, this improbable set of circumstances, even her fear for Devon, combined to carry her along like a sweeping wave. Faster and hotter, Steve built to a frenzied motion. Sweat-slicked, driving, driving, until he said in her ear, "With me, Clare."

She was there. A feeling so piercing and intense that tears filled her eyes, while the clench of her sent him to the brink.

Steve awakened in darkness with his arm around Clare, her body against him so that they fit together like a puzzle ring. Those intricately woven bands were a lot easier to take apart than they were to put together.

Yet, how complete he felt. The neon glow coming in around the drapes made him give thanks that it was not morning.

Nights alone sometimes seemed interminable, but he wanted this one to last.

He remembered telling Clare, not once, but several times, of the glories of winter in Yellowstone. He'd shared the splendor of the Lower Falls, frozen into a three hundred foot cone of ice, Norris Geyser Basin steaming like a small city, and the sight of a mother moose breaking a path through March snow for her newborn calf. He'd not realized himself what he was doing, but with Clare warm and firm beside him, he admitted that he wanted more than this night.

She stirred and murmured his name. He loved the way it sounded, as though he were rediscovering value long forgotten. Today, she'd saved his life by turning on those sprinklers, and when he reached the parking lot . . . and her, he'd felt like a player rounding home base. How stupid he'd been to get hung up on Deering when she had been waiting for him.

Clare turned into his arms, her mouth finding his unerringly in the firelike glow from the windows. Impossible, but he wanted her again. Would keep wanting her if the way he felt tonight was any indication.

They moved together, less frantically than the first time. He was not as desperate for touch long missed. The memory of Susan, the luxury of their time together, was pushed aside by the sweet ache that strove and climaxed with his and Clare's mingled cries.

When they lay together, hearts pounding, he knew he'd been right to open that door. Like the spring crocus from the soil, reborn in a single night, he said hoarsely, "You make me feel alive, like I haven't been for years."

SUMMER OF FIRE

🔥🔥🔥

Steve's words made Clare realize she'd had her life on autopilot since Jay had left.

Sure, there was plenty of Brownian motion like molecules vibrating in a science lab. She'd become a firefighter and helped others, gotten Devon through high school, but what had she done for herself?

"When you knocked I had my hand on the doorknob," she confessed.

He chuckled, their bodies still joined. "After how childishly I acted about Deering, you were ready to do that for me?"

"For you . . . and for me."

With his weight pressing her into the mattress, it was hard to remember her reservations. She reveled in sensation until he caught his breath and rolled off her.

Then she came back to earth. He'd had a Coke this evening while she and Garrett sipped at beers, but could he stay on the wagon?

It went deeper than that. Being in bed with him was no guarantee he was getting over Susan. Men and women thrown together during fire season met, coupled, and parted by the hundreds.

Neon light from the window was joined by the faintest graying of sky. "Oh, God," Clare said. "Morning and still nothing from Devon."

"I'll help you," Steve's hand gripped hers. "Whatever happens, you don't have to face it alone."

CHAPTER THIRTY
September 8

Georgia Deering came out of the bathroom, wiping her face with a damp washrag. Feeling better after throwing up, she was almost hungry for bacon or sausage instead of her usual cereal and fruit.

"How long have you known?" her sister-in-law Anna asked from her place at the kitchen table. Her blue eyes were bright with what looked like merriment.

"Known what?"

Anna laughed and sipped the coffee she'd made, taking over Georgia's kitchen the way she ruled the roost in her own house. "Aren't you the one who's wanted to get pregnant for years?"

Georgia lowered the rag to her side and stared at Anna. She felt a quietness inside as though the world had paused and she with it.

Then . . . *of course.*

Last night, she had awakened alone as she had since July. Outside the bedroom window, cottonwoods etched charcoal against the slate sky. In a few weeks, the shadowed moon would grow round. So many times she and Deering had lain and watched the trees transform from blackened lace to silver filigree. Moon by moon, they'd marked the years.

Now, with each passing moon she was no longer alone.

"How far along are you?" Anna persisted.

Georgia considered. With Deering gone, she had not even consulted her calendar. The last time he had been home was the second weekend in July. "Nearly two months. I've lost weight, not gained."

"Of course you have," Anna agreed. "I used to do that when I had morning sickness."

Georgia groped for a kitchen chair and sat. "He called me yesterday, said he was coming home last night." Speaking of it brought back the ache she'd felt, straining for a sound in the darkness. Waking and hoping she had missed the chopper's landing and that any moment, his key would turn the latch.

"Where is he then?" Anna asked.

"I don't know." Her cheeks flushed. "I'm afraid I wasn't very nice when he called."

"You two are beginning to make me lose patience."

Georgia tried to ignore Anna's steely glare. It wasn't as though Deering was innocent. "He admitted to chasing that woman. Clare, the paper said her name was."

Anna did not relent. "Does he love her?

"He said he loves me." The kind of tears that stung filled her eyes. "I want our lives back together."

"Well then . . ." Anna prompted.

Georgia put a palm on her still-flat stomach and tried to

imagine a baby in there. What would Deering say when he found out? Lately, they had given up even talking about it.

Anna went on. "It's past time you came to your senses. Deering's going to fly no matter what you say. And if you love him . . ."

"I do." Flashes hit her of a whirlwind courtship that had enticed her to forget he was a pilot. Of wedding white and the sweetness of her first married kiss. Of a man who'd worn his military uniform to marry before heading back to Vietnam.

"If you love him, you need to realize that that boy," Anna nodded toward Georgia's midsection, "is gonna want to fly with his daddy more than anything."

Georgia had always thought if she had a child, it would be a girl. Someone small, pink and sweet smelling. Kendra would be a champion quilter and biscuit maker, winning ribbons all the way to the Idaho State Fair.

For the first time, she considered the possibility of a boy. Georgia had never known the rough and tumble of a brother, but she'd watched John and Anna raise their raucous brood. If she and Deering had a boy . . . or a girl . . .

You'll want to fly with your daddy. She smoothed her stomach.

The telephone rang and her heart started to pound. She answered, "Hon?"

"Mrs. Deering." The deep voice was made soft by a Southern inflection. "This is Garrett Anderson with the West Yellowstone Fire Command."

She wished she could turn back the clock, crawl into bed and go to sleep. Maybe she would dream that Deering had his arm snug around her. "He's not here," she managed.

"Yes, ma'am, I know. I'm calling to tell you that he flew out yesterday afternoon and we haven't heard from him."

Georgia dropped the phone from nerveless fingers and heard it clatter and ding. She was vaguely aware of Anna picking it up and talking to the man on the other end. Last time Deering had been AWOL she'd seen him come back . . . with that Clare.

But he'd sworn that was done. Yesterday, he'd promised to come home and if she'd mistaken the love and remorse in his voice, she was never going to trust her instinct again.

Anna put down the phone and the look on her face said it all. This time they didn't think he was held up at some spike camp by the wind. They never would have called unless they thought he'd gone down.

Clare struggled from her dreams and picked up the telephone in mid-ring. The clock beside her bed at the Stagecoach said it was nearly nine.

"Yeah," she managed in a sleep-ravaged husk. She glanced over her shoulder and saw Steve stretched out beside her with the sheet draped over his bare hip. His mussed hair spoke of midnight pleasure and his eyes said he'd not had enough.

"It's Garrett," said the distinctive voice on the phone.

"Yeah." Clare ran a nervous hand through her newly shorter hair.

"Some good news. Those hikers were sighted down in the

Lamar Valley by Johnny Arvela when he was flying in around sunset. I just got word." His somber tone said there was more and it wasn't pretty.

"That is good." She twisted the phone cord and noted a patch of beard burn on her left breast. A surreal feeling split her into two women, one who wanted to hang up and crawl back into a cocoon with Steve, and a mother screaming inside for news of her child.

Garrett went on. "The rangers at Old Faithful questioned the firefighters after the North Fork passed. When Deering's chopper took off, a number of persons said they counted two passengers."

A shudder went through her. Steve touched her arm. If Deering was down somewhere in the mountains . . . "Who would be with him?"

"I'm afraid that this morning your buddy from Houston, Javier Fuentes, heard about the search. He called in to say he saw a blonde with curly hair beside a helicopter, talking to the pilot."

"Oh, God."

Steve's hand tightened.

"Fuentes thought it might be Devon. This was during the height of the firestorm."

Clare opened her mouth to say that there were a lot of blondes, but Javier knew Devon. A pit of cold fear opened in her chest.

"The smoke is pretty thick this morning," Garrett said. "They'll be starting the air search as soon as they can."

SUMMER OF FIRE

❀❀❀

Demetrios Karrabotsos led Clare and Steve across the tarmac at West Yellowstone Airport. Tankers and helicopters were lined up at the ready, their crews standing in groups killing time with fire gossip. Karrabotsos scanned the gray sky. "This temperature inversion should clear in another half hour."

He sipped from a Styrofoam cup, grimaced, and tossed the last inch of coffee onto a wild rosebush edging the airport ramp. "Fresh caffeine, my treat." He headed toward the crowded catering tent.

Ever since Garrett had suggested Devon was with Deering, Clare had been dwelling on what he'd said last night. Deering had been called to the scene of a fire, where people were supposed to have been trapped. Why had hikers even been permitted into the backcountry?

The orange juice she selected, in a plastic cup with foil top, tasted sour.

She tried to focus on Steve and Karrabotsos's small talk, but her mind spun scenarios.

Deering and Devon had crashed in a fireball of aviation fuel. They'd lost power and come down in the burning forest. They had landed, thinking they saw the hikers, and been overtaken by fire on the ground like Steve and his fellow scientists had nearly been.

How she wished Devon had left the park on one of those buses and was somewhere in Montana.

Karrabotsos evidently knew the dangers of fire. Those scars on his face bore the slick look of burns. Realizing she'd been caught looking at them, she averted her eyes.

"Vietnam," he said. "Chopper crash."

"And you still fly."

Black eyes fixed her with a look of disbelief. "You can't let something like that scare you off."

Thinking of her own experience in losing faith, she was fiercely glad she'd fought the firestorm at Old Faithful. Having done that, she still wasn't sure she could return to the station in Houston. Being out there in the parking lot was far different from fighting fire in close quarters. What if someone who trusted her to watch his or her back ended up in a tight spot? Could she be sure she'd act without thinking to save them?

Karrabotsos cast another look at the brightening sky. "May as well start my preflight."

Clare imagined the Huey disappearing into the haze. She'd sit around the airport with Steve and drink endless cups of black bitter coffee, wondering what was happening to Deering and Devon.

She set her jaw. "I'm going with you."

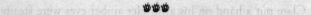

Steve swallowed and looked across the ramp at the helicopter Karrabotsos planned to take. Another Huey like the one Deering had flown. Just the sight of it started a griping in his gut.

He admired how the tough part of Clare continued to assert itself even as she warred within over her friend Frank and the young soldier Billy Jakes. She could handle this while he stayed behind.

The way she spoke to Karrabotsos and did not even turn to him said she couldn't imagine him willingly getting aboard the helicopter. Competent pilots would accomplish the search and Steve couldn't bring anything to the party.

Competent? Clare thought Deering was a good pilot and he'd crashed twice. Craggy veteran Karrabotsos must believe the same for he'd hired him. Hell, the older man had been burned in a crash, yet he was one of the most respected in the air charter business. Even after going down, he thought the idea of being deterred by it preposterous.

Steve tried to deep breathe, but the sensations he'd felt on this tarmac back in July surged up. Heart pounding, sweating palms, and a fierce anger that he had to fly, although it had been his decision. Again, on Mount Washburn when he'd flown on Black Saturday to save his place in Yellowstone. He'd had to grab a barf bag for the same nausea that gripped him now.

Deering and Karrabotsos might keep getting back in the air, but Steve couldn't do it.

Clare put a hand on his arm. Her amber eyes were steady and without blame. "You wait for us."

He didn't deserve her. How could he spend a night like the one they'd shared and not stay by her side for this? If, God forbid, Devon was hurt or . . .

Clare might end up the first responder on an unimaginable scene.

In the deepest part of night, he'd held her to him and wanted more. At the first sign of dawn, he'd made a promise that she would not face this alone.

Hadn't he coached her to get back to fighting fires?

Hadn't she challenged him to embrace life again?

He stared hard at the helicopter. "I'm going too."

Clare looked out the Huey's left front window at the park's staggering beauty. Despite the nearby ravaging by fire, the unburned banks of the Madison teemed with game. In a few minutes Old Faithful passed beneath, the jumping off point for the search.

In the pilot's seat, Karrabotsos turned his helmeted head from side to side, scanning. Steve sat in the rear seat with a hand on Clare's shoulder. She wasn't sure if he offered support or was holding on because of his own uncertainty.

Yellowstone Lake reflected the gray sky. There was the scorched shore between Grant Village and West Thumb where she'd found Steve. His hand tightened as they flew over.

The mosaic of burns slid past beneath the aircraft, a grim reminder of the fire reported on Nez Perce when Deering flew out. If they found the wreck of a chopper, would she have the strength to go in as a medic, checking for survivors when it might be Devon lying bleeding and battered?

Or worse.

The Absaroka Range rose before the chopper's windshield,

mocking her with its remoteness. No rapid Life Flight to the Houston Medical Center. No world-class trauma ER ready to receive.

From behind Clare, Steve pointed out the grassy meadows alongside meandering Pelican Creek. Just downstream, the waterway joined the broad expanse of Yellowstone Lake. "Those flats down there are prime grizzly habitat," he told her through the headphones.

It was a good front and she suspected how much it cost him.

"I'm glad you came." She raised her hand to his and squeezed.

Karrabotsos flew east. He talked on the radio with the other pilots helping in the search.

They swept up over a low, treed pass and into what Steve pointed out as the Lamar River Valley. "The Nez Perce camped in the widest meadow where two rivers come together. Plenty of pasture for their horses." Half hidden by haze, the valley might have been a pleasant place, except where the Clover-Mist Fire had left it blackened.

They lost altitude and the valley came into sharper focus. There was no sign of a helicopter on the open ground.

Ahead, a massive peak loomed. Its crest was sharp, with great spines of dark rock sticking out from the summit like stiff fingers. "Nez Perce," said Steve. The west slope of chock-a-block boulders must have been where Laura Sutton wrote of spending a cold and uneasy night. Her journal remained in Clare's room at the Stagecoach.

They flew nearer and Karrabotsos studied the terrain. "I don't see anyplace a helicopter could land." The jumble of great, dark rock looked even more treacherous up close.

Clare's stomach swooped as the Huey banked and flew along Nez Perce's deeply forested east flank. It was here that the Clover-Mist, the largest fire in the park, actively cut a swath through the trees. Smoke roiled up from the flame front.

"See that?" Steve pointed above the fire near the ridge crest. "The way the trees there are not quite as tall?" There was at least five feet of difference in the trees' height, along a curving line up a ravine. "There was a forest fire here in 1900," he went on. "Looks like it's going to burn again."

My God, that was where Laura Sutton had been trapped with fire sweeping up toward her. The pilot flew low enough that the ridge crest was above them. "It looks to me as if Deering isn't here," he said.

Outside, the haze grew thicker.

"I'd like to look around a wider area," Karrabotsos suggested.

Clare felt as though bands squeezed her chest, keeping her breathing shallow. She tried a deeper inhalation, but had to force it. They flew north toward the rocky summit of Saddle Mountain, barely visible through the smoke.

Karrabotsos radioed Johnny Arvela of Eagle Air. "What's the vis up your way?"

"No good," Johnny's voice came over the air. "I'm gonna have to set down at Cooke City and hope the fire doesn't come through town. They almost lost Silver Gate yesterday and they're not in the clear yet."

"I don't like the looks of this here," Karrabotsos replied.

The bands became a vice as Clare watched a gray blanket of smoke swallow the Lamar Valley. The altimeter read ten thousand and this part of the park was studded with peaks between ten and eleven thousand feet.

Karrabotsos began to climb, ten-three, then ten-five. Steve's damp hand pressed her shoulder and she placed hers over it again.

"Two choices," the pilot said. "Find a safe place to set down or go up to twelve thousand and fly on instruments back toward West Yellowstone."

"What about other planes or helicopters?" Clare asked. "How will you avoid them?"

He did not answer.

Steve swallowed, the sound audible in the headphones. "Your call, Clare."

There way no way she wanted to try for West Yellowstone, not if they could get safely on the ground. She knew that Steve felt the same and her heart swelled at his sacrifice.

It was a foolish long shot, but if they set down, maybe they could still look for Devon and Deering. Trying to tamp down anxiety and sound matter-of-fact, she said, "The summit on Nez Perce looked pretty smooth."

Karrabotsos banked sharply and headed back south. Clare strained to see the peak through the thick air. If they crashed, would there be two choppers down on the same mountain?

She turned in her seat and met Steve's eyes. "I'm sorry I got you into this."

The apprehension in his expression mixed with determination. He pointed over her shoulder. "There's the mountain."

Clare tried to relax her tensed hands when she saw that the crest of Nez Perce had broken through the murk.

Karrabotsos's calm exterior remained unchanging as he radioed his intent to West Yellowstone. He brought them in carefully against the wind sweeping the bare promontory. Rotor wash threw up reddish dust and rolled gravel away from their landing.

When the skids touched, every muscle in Clare's body was as taut as piano wire. Behind her, Steve sighed and she tried to exhale her own tension.

Outside, drifting white eddies resembled a damp mist. For a moment, she thought she saw a darker patch of smoke down along the north ridge, but before she could point it out, she lost sight of it in the haze. That didn't make sense, anyway, for the Clover-Mist was burning on the mountain's forested east flank.

The rotors wound down and finally stopped.

"Gonna stretch my back." Clare opened the door and got out onto the dark reddish gravel. The wind hit her full on, plucking up dust plumes from the tundra-like surface and whipping them away. Steve climbed down from the rear seat, groaning when he put his full weight on his right leg. She saw that he tried to move fluidly as if the last thing he wanted was sympathy. Karrabotsos opened the chopper door, but remained inside talking on the radio.

The smoke thinned and Clare caught another glimpse of what looked like a spot fire along the ridge. It didn't look right though, for the smoke was inky black.

"Down there," Steve said. "Looks like . . ." He stopped and she figured he didn't want to suggest it might be a fire set from the Huey's fuel.

"Yes, it does." She turned back to the chopper. "First aid?" She must have been brain-dead this morning, for she should have gone to the Smokejumpers Base and gotten a trauma kit.

Karrabotsos nodded at a metal box behind the rear seat. She unclipped it from the bulkhead and despaired for what it contained; gauze, tape, a few aspirin, and a useless cold remedy.

"Wait for me," Steve said.

She started down the ridge and quickly outstripped his pace. When she glanced back Karrabotsos was following, moving even slower as he favored the foot he'd broken earlier in the summer.

Clare headed for the spiny promontory, placing her feet with care on the loose volcanic gravel. The mountaintop resembled a cinder cone like Sunset Crater in Arizona where she'd also found the downhill easy. Coming back, it would be a step up and a slide down.

Surrounded by murk, she moved down into a zone of stunted, wind-ravaged trees surrounded by waist high brush and thick grasses. From down the east slope below treeline came the resinous smell of a fresh burn, and she heard the dull roar of the Clover-Mist.

Over the sound, there might have been a faint cry.

Clare stopped to listen, but it was not repeated. She swallowed around a parched patch in the back of her throat.

She climbed down farther onto hard rock that formed crooked stair steps. Out onto the ridge now with a drop off on either side, she picked her way with exquisite care. Drawing closer to the black pillar, it became clearly distinct from the wildfire below. The premonition that it was the smoking remains of a crash site grew stronger while the bands around her chest threatened to snap her in two.

From above and behind, Steve's voice came to her. "Clare, wait for us."

She knew he meant to spare her being first on the scene, but that was no good. If there was anything to be done, she needed to be there. Once more, she bargained in vain for a well-equipped trauma kit to fall out of the sky. Cooling gel for burns, an air splint for fractures . . .

She caught a glimpse of something in the trees below the ridge crest and she wasn't ready. *God, don't let it be them. No, let it be them.*

Her heart leaped. The twisted wreckage of rotor blades was unmistakable.

She wished she could turn away from this, to let Steve or Karrabotsos take the lead and have the first knowledge.

Then she went still inside. A firefighter approaching a scene, she went into the minute-by-minute mode that people described from accidents. Evaluating, calculating.

The ruined chopper hung tangled in the trees. Not burning. The fire had clearly been set atop the rocky ridge, a pile of green pine boughs and seat cushions from the helicopter.

They weren't dead, then.

She broke into a run, heedless of the treacherous footing. She cupped her hands and shouted. "Deering!"

That cry she'd heard before, only faintly, came again.

She lost her balance and nearly went off the side. As she clung to the sharp rock, her palms scraped with white patches turned pink with seeping blood. A wave of nausea welled.

Breathe, breathe.

When she straightened, there was movement below. It resolved into Deering as he climbed out onto the ridge crest wearing his flight suit. He stood at a respectful distance from the fire and waved both arms over his head.

She made it the rest of the way and he grabbed her in a bear hug.

"You're okay?" she asked.

"Just sore. Clare . . ."

"Some people said that Devon . . .?" Her mouth and throat had transformed to the Sahara.

"Mom?" a voice quavered from down the slope.

Clare sagged against Deering. His hands kept her upright while she vowed never to let her daughter out of her sight again. "Stay there, honey."

Her boots slipped on rock and gravel, while incredible blue eyes beckoned. It didn't matter that they'd fought or that Devon had run away.

Sitting on a tarp spread on the ground, Devon had an olive wool Army blanket draped around her. She held one swollen wrist cradled with her other arm. With a supreme effort, Clare held back from hugging her.

"Let me see." She knelt and pushed aside an empty can of Vienna sausages.

Devon's expression was a little shocky. With a careful hand, Clare brushed back the blanket and a singed wing of hair to see what was beneath the loosely taped gauze on her chest. Releasing the tape that Deering must have applied from the chopper's first aid kit, she examined the wicked burn. Part of it had blistered and a patch showed the discoloration of third-degree.

"At Old Faithful," Devon said faintly. "My hair caught fire."

A great hematoma cut diagonally across her shoulder. Seeing seat belt bruises in car accidents made Clare surmise this came from the chopper crash. She checked Devon's collarbone for a fracture, but there was no flinch at mild pressure.

On her left temple, Clare found a contusion that had swelled half an inch. "Is your vision clear? Have you had any trouble staying awake?"

Devon shook her head. "What you see, Mom." Tears welled and she lifted the cradled wrist a half-inch. "I fell on the roof at the Inn."

Clare's stomach clutched as she remembered the people on the widow's walk, daring the firestorm's fury. She bent her head and noted that Devon's fingers were cold and a little blue. Definitely, she had a bad sprain, maybe worse.

"Can you climb just a little way?" She tried to sound upbeat.

"I think so." Devon sounded dazed and with that bump on her head . . . Clare helped her up and wondered if she would be able to support her up the hill, for her own legs felt unsteady.

Steve and Karrabotsos arrived together, both limping, but looking game.

Deering faced the older pilot. "I'm sorry, man." He gestured toward the ruined helicopter. "I know you didn't want to hire me . . ."

Karrabotsos gave him a level look. "I never do anything I don't want to do." He surveyed the topography. "Wind currents can be murder in a spot like this."

Clare helped Devon to the ridge top. Steve clapped an arm around her shoulders. "You found your gal."

She gave him a smile through the sting of tears she'd held back while being a medic. With one arm around him and the other around the taller Devon, she managed, "She'll always be my little girl."

"I'll just scatter this fire on the rocks," Deering suggested.

Clare turned to help, but Karrabotsos pointed back the way they'd come. "Won't matter."

Driven by the wind, the Clover-Mist had worked its way up the slope close to the ridge crest. It leaped ahead in the trees, heading for the summit on a diagonal that had the potential to intersect their path. Beside Clare, Steve cursed.

If her great-grandmother had not survived a fire on this very mountain, she and Devon would not be standing here today. Grabbing her daughter by her uninjured arm, she urged her onto the trail.

Deering took the lead. He moved well, but looked more pale and depressed than when Clare had seen him at Old Faithful. Between Deering and Clare, Devon climbed like a robot, one sturdy bare leg in front of the other. As the slope grew steeper, sweat darkened her hairline. Behind Clare, Steve limped grimly while Karrabotsos brought up the rear, favoring his lame foot.

The wind shifted and brought the fire's path more directly toward them. The stench of burning grew stronger. Clare eyed the patch of brush and scrubby trees they had to cross to reach the summit.

The flat-out race made her think of other times when

people had been caught in the open and tried to outrun a fire. In the worst disaster the Smokejumpers had ever experienced, thirteen had perished in 1949 at Mann Gulch, Montana. Once fire had chased them out of the trees and onto the grassy slope, they had never had a chance.

As the ridge widened onto a more open hillside Deering slung an arm through Devon's. They moved up and slightly ahead of the fire.

After a single glance over her shoulder, Clare refused to look again. The survivors of Mann Gulch had been lucky to slip through a rocky crevice and emerge above the fire.

There was no place of safety like it in sight.

Their hope lay on the treeless summit. It was only another fifty yards, then twenty-five, but the men at Mann Gulch had been overcome mere seconds from safety.

As fire attained the brush, its sound sharpened from a dull roar to a snapping. Clare helped Deering with Devon and the first aid kit fell from her hand. It landed with a clatter and bounced down about fifteen feet, then wedged into the rocks.

Clare abandoned it.

The straggling group struggled on. How slim the margin between life and death, how fine the edge they trod. Everyone said she'd been lucky when the roof came down on Frank, a few feet and a hair's breadth from horrifying cremation. Had he had time to know this screaming rush that drove her? Had he watched the rafters begin their slow deformation and felt the choking certainty?

Don't look back, she thought, but knew Steve had fallen behind. A scream built inside, but she could do nothing for him with her daughter staggering and about to fall short of the finish line.

Above, Deering made it to bare gravel. Clare shoved up out of the weeds, gasping and supporting Devon with an arm around her. Her impulse was to keep running from the fire, but on safe ground, she looked back.

With one good leg, Karrabotsos had gotten ahead of Steve with his two bad knees.

"You making it, Haywood?" Deering called down.

Steve's wooden pace slowed and then he stopped. Clare imagined heat searing his back and thighs, burning his skin as though his Nomex clothing was made of paper. He swayed forward and planted both hands on the slope, pain twisting his features.

"Steve!" That shrill scream was her voice. She couldn't move with Devon's arm heavy over her shoulders.

Deering plunged back into the waist-high brush. Like a skier, he made a series of sidehill leaps, steadying each landing with a grab at the tough grasses. The fire was less than a hundred feet away when he reached Steve and slung an arm around his back.

Clare's heart pounded while Steve redoubled his efforts. Deering speeded him along, half dragging him when he faltered. They passed Karrabotsos when he lacked fifty feet to safety, but now the heat blasted like a blowtorch and the foul taste of char filled the back of Clare's throat.

Deering kept pulling Steve toward bare rock.

Clare stared at Karrabotsos. Not fifteen feet below, the pilot wasn't going to make it. Her arm was still around Devon, supporting the most precious thing in her existence.

As though he spoke in her ear, Frank's voice said distinctly, "Go!"

Without thought, she shoved her daughter uphill and leaped toward the inferno.

Fire swirled around Karrabotsos. An errant prayer came to Clare, that this was going to be like passing a finger through a candle flame. Perhaps if they moved fast enough . . .

She grabbed him by the arm. He gave a shout, more a scream.

"Go!" she echoed the voice in her head. "Go, go!"

For an instant, they teetered together on the verge, but she dug in her boots and pulled. The soft gravel gave. She raised her leg and tried to get elevation, and managed to keep half their gain. The next time she put her foot onto a tuft of tough grass, then another. Teeth clenched, she wasn't letting fire have another soul.

Everything seemed to be in slow motion as she dragged Karrabotsos up and out of the flames. The world was on the other side of wavering orange air that shimmered and distorted. In the last few feet, Deering grabbed Karrabotsos's other arm and they made it to clear air.

The acrid, animal aroma of singed hair stung Clare's nose in the same instant she felt Devon's hands slapping at her head. Thankfully, the wind had whipped the flames away from her skin.

Steve flailed at Karrabotsos's burning hair as the pilot collapsed to his knees. His fire retardant flight suit was in good shape, but his face showed bright scarlet. "God, that hurts," he moaned.

With the burns he'd already suffered, this was going to be nasty. "Okay," Clare snapped. "Let's get him on board."

She and Deering pulled Karrabotsos to his feet and assisted him up the unstable gravel slope. It was just as she'd feared, tough and treacherous footing. Behind, Clare noted that Steve and Devon were helping each other.

When they reached the chopper, Deering maneuvered until Karrabotsos could sit in the doorway on the deck and scoot backward. White lips pressed together as he slowly made it inside.

Clare helped get him situated with Devon on the rear seat in the back of the Huey. She placed herself between them to keep an eye on both.

"I'm sorry I lost the first aid kit," she said.

"Nothing in there that would help." Although Karrabotsos's burns were blistering, he bore them with the stoic air of a man who had seen much worse.

Clare turned to Deering. "Get us in the air!"

He moved toward the front seat.

Steve looked at the skid and the step up to get inside with a reluctant expression. Flying over the mountain's sharp rocks and steep slope must have brought back a frozen peak in Alaska, where he'd faced the worst a man should have to. Now he waited once more to fly with the man Clare knew he despised.

With a painful grimace, he climbed in. Wrestling the handle, he slammed the sliding door home, and met her eyes. "Hell of a job you did back there."

"I had help."

Steve probably thought she meant Deering helping him outrun the flames. Sure enough, he shot a glance at the man in the right front seat putting on headphones.

How many times had she bargained for a sign from Frank? She'd wished to believe the dead sent signs to the living, but had never thought it possible.

She still didn't. That voice, so like Frank's, had not come from beyond, but from inside her. She'd trained with him, drill after drill, back when she was green. He'd kept her moving, taught her not to let the dragon's voice distract her from the goal. He'd bandaged the burns she'd earned and then let her tend to him. Everybody in the station had sensed their unbreakable bond.

No, he hadn't come back from whatever new adventure he was surely on. She had simply known what he would have said as certainly as she knew her own name.

She stared out into the sky, into an image of Frank's smiling eyes. "Thank you," she whispered.

CHAPTER THIRTY-ONE
September 8

Deering looked at the Huey's controls and thought he would be sick.

Not again.

Not after ditching his *Georgia* in Yellowstone Lake. Not after the panic at Old Faithful and landing in disgrace. Not after crashing with Clare's child on this remote peak.

Last night, he'd lain beside the wreckage of the Huey Karrabotsos had trusted him with. Hearing Devon's labored breathing, he had hoped she'd be all right. He'd given her the only blanket and lay down back to back with her to preserve body heat. With a rock hard beneath his spine, his temples had pounded where his pulse had turned timpani. He'd pulled back his sleeve to reveal the lighted dial of his Timex.

He wasn't blind, then.

Lying on the remote mountain with a sour taste in his mouth, he'd realized that while he slept he'd been on another black excursion to Vietnam. One of those trips across space and time that spirited him away when he closed his eyes. No matter the passage of years, he still rested fitfully, as though staying awake would keep the demon at bay.

All the way up the mountain, Deering had counted on Karrabotsos to fly them out of here.

The vis was terrible with the smoke rising off the Clover-Mist, but if he took off to the northeast, he'd probably be able to get them free. With Karrabotsos and Devon both needing medical assistance, he'd have to risk flying on instruments to West Yellowstone.

A good plan, but he clutched the cyclic stick as though he had tunnel vision. Fresh sweat that wasn't from the climb broke out on his forehead and felt cold in his armpits.

On that afternoon back in July, over Yellowstone Lake with wind whipping in the door, Deering had fought the dizzying sway of the sling load beneath his helicopter, acting as yin to the aircraft's yang. He'd wanted to believe that Steve Haywood was to blame when the heavy bucket had engaged his Bell in a tug of war, a pair of pendulums in dynamic opposition.

"Let's go," Steve said from behind him. Deering sensed the impatience in him and in the other passengers who hadn't spoken.

Still, he sat. Last night he'd made a promise, sent a message through the night to Georgia, swearing to God that if he just got off this mountain alive, he'd never take the controls of another helicopter.

Steve bent his head between the seats and stared hard at him. "Come on, guy. You can cry in your beer about crashing when you get home. Now, it's time to fly."

A man who hated him, who was terrified of flying . . . and yet Steve's voice was strong and upbeat.

"When did you figure that shit out?" he muttered. Sonnavabitch, if Doctor Haywood didn't sound like he was ready to go for another ride with him driving.

"All kinds of strange things have happened this summer." Steve clapped a hand on his shoulder. "Go with the flow."

What the hell.

Deering took a deep breath and started his preflight.

Clare felt the skids touch down at West Yellowstone. The ride had been white-knuckle all the way. Karrabotsos seemed to be in a lot of pain but doing as well as could be expected.

That was more than she could say for Devon. Although her daughter was sitting up, the look in her eyes said that once danger had passed she had retreated within. She cradled her damaged wrist close to her chest.

Clare's forehead and cheek stung, but it didn't feel like she was going to blister. Her hair, already short, came away in singed corkscrews when she ruffled her hands through it.

Steve slid open the chopper door to admit the paramedics. Clare related Karrabotsos's status, cautioning them that he'd been burned before, while the attendants transferred him onto a stretcher.

A look around revealed that they had landed near the main terminal of West Yellowstone where she and Deering had set down the night of the Mink Creek blowup. Just as he had that evening when she waited to grill him about his duplicity, he was shutting down the aircraft.

Today she wasn't angry, despite that he'd crashed with her daughter on board. The Army blanket that had been around Devon's shoulders, the can of Vienna sausages, and the gauze over her burn all spoke of his kindness. She'd seen his hesitation at the controls on the mountain, heard what had passed between him and Steve and knew he was beating himself up as surely as she had when Frank and Billy Jakes had died.

All the passion and anger that had been between them had burned out, but she touched his shoulder. "Thank you for taking care of Devon," she said simply, "and for getting us back here."

Steve let himself down from the door and landed with a groan. Despite his infirmity, he helped Devon.

When her feet hit the pavement, she folded down and sat. A faint look of surprise crossed her face and then faded. Clare clambered out and knelt beside her. "Hon?"

Devon did not answer.

❦❦❦

Deering came out of the examining room into the hall at West Yellowstone Hospital. The doctor had pronounced him free to go, with advice to take it easy for a few days.

That was an understatement. Since the crash, his muscles had been stiffening like a strap of wet rawhide in the sun. All he could imagine was going back to his bed at Karrabotsos's house and finding solace in the dark comfort of sleep.

Had someone, perhaps Karrabotsos, called and told Georgia that he was missing? He hoped she didn't know yet, for he wanted to be the one to tell her. He might have dodged the bullet, the fires might burn on, but he was out of this particular war for the duration.

When he'd returned to Vietnam after a leave between tours, he'd ridden part way back on the carrier Lexington. The naval aviators had flown training missions night and day, the roar of jets and the smell of exhaust fouling the warm tropical sea. Deering had waited in a damp twilight mist with a crowd of seamen while a downed pilot was brought aboard. Whispered word passed that it was his second time to put an A-4 Skyhawk in the drink.

The pilot walked off the rescue helicopter under his own power, a stocky kid with hair so blond and short that he looked as though he'd shaved his head. Several enlisted men and an officer tried to speak to him, but he brushed them aside on his way to the edge of the flight deck. Deering held his breath, for if the pilot intended to jump no one was near enough to stop him.

Still dripping wet, the young aviator plucked gold wings from his uniform and flung them into the sea.

Deering looked up and down the hall, thinking that there was something he should do before he left. Back in July, Clare had shown up in his room at the Lake Hospital by mistake, but their lives had been entwined since that moment. He wanted to find her and make sure that Devon was okay.

His boots were loud on the tile floor as he headed toward the lounge and nurses' station.

He was just opposite a swinging door marked *X-ray - No Admittance* when someone pushed the portal wide and nearly collided with him.

"Whoa . . . "

"S'cuse me."

Steve Haywood, still dressed in dirty Nomex, leaned on a pair of aluminum crutches. The fluorescent lights hummed harshly, casting a pale wash over the windowless walls and Steve's pain-lined face.

There didn't seem to be anything more to say. Deering moved to go.

"That was some decent flying you did today," Steve said evenly. "Not to mention dragging my dead ass up that hill."

Deering stopped. "I didn't think you believed I could pour piss out of a boot."

"I didn't."

"So?"

"Clare suggested that perhaps my view of you was colored by my . . . past experience with flying."

For the first time, Deering imagined what it must have been like for Steve to survive while his wife and baby lay mangled in the plane's wreckage. How excruciating would it be if Deering never saw Georgia again?

"I've been thinking about that day we went down in the lake," Steve went on. "That whole business with the wind off the fire and trying to use the bucket to help those folks . . . well, who's to say we didn't both do the best that was humanly possible?"

"Who is to say?" Deering asked carefully. "First Assurance?"

Suzanne Ho was still out there, unwilling to authorize his claim until she talked to his passenger.

Almost casually, Steve shrugged, "Insurance companies are a pain in the butt." He flashed a small grudging grin. "Ya done good today."

The two men fell into step. The brighter light at the end of the hall silhouetted a small woman, her red-gold hair a halo.

Deering inhaled sharply.

From beside him, Steve said, "Is that . . .?"

"Oh, yeah."

Georgia's eyes looked enormous in her pale face. "Garrett Anderson called me at the hotel and said you were here. I drove up this morning."

Deering's steps quickened. He buried his face in the side of her neck and wrapped her tight against him. She pressed close and slid her hands inside his filthy flight suit.

Relief suffused him, as profound and complete as any he had ever known. Her touch said she'd forgiven him Clare, and if fortune smiled, their lives could go on.

"Hon," she said brokenly. "We're going to have a baby."

Only a moment before, he'd been stupid with fatigue and, surely, he still was, but at the sound of her voice, he took off without benefit of wings. "A kid!"

The surge of elation surprised him. He thought of Clare's daughter, nearly grown, and yet she'd longed to find her mother when trouble struck at Old Faithful. Would he and Georgia be able to raise a loyal and loving child like that?

Deering became aware that his wife was waiting with her breath held for him to express something other than surprise.

How would he feel after the first shock subsided? He and Georgia weren't young; he'd be nearly sixty when the kid started college . . .

But Lord, what a chance to start again. His brother had grandchildren and whenever Deering held one of the tiny mites, it gave him the thrill of possibility. Thinking of life's changes reminded him of his gift to Georgia, the one she'd waited for over twenty years.

"That's great about the baby." He spread a hand over her warm tummy. "I'll have lots of time to spend with him . . ."

"Him?"

"Or her. I'll be home since I'm giving up flying."

"You're what?" She looked at him with disbelief.

"I'm going to retire."

Georgia pressed his hand to her stomach. "But this little one's going to need college money."

"I'll find something else."

"Like what?" She pulled back with hands on hips, his much-loved little harridan. "I know you've crashed twice, but look at the good you've done." She didn't stamp her foot, although he felt like she had. "That Smokejumper you saved . . . and Garrett said how you got those people off the mountain today when Karrabotsos was burned."

"For Christ's sake, Georgia, you've been on my ass to stop flying ever since I can remember. Can't you just be happy you finally won?"

She smiled. "I thought I'd never hear you say it." On tiptoe, she brushed a kiss across his cheek. "It was my fondest dream, but," her whisper made it real, "promise me you won't decide today."

There would be time to think later. For him and Georgia to try and find their way through the briary mess this summer had become. For now, he held her, just held her.

"Babe," he whispered. "Let's go home."

❀❀❀

Clare sat in the waiting room and cupped warm Styrofoam. The coffee was the same bitter machine brew she'd sipped at the Lake Hospital back in July. Today in West Yellowstone, she waited to find out whether Devon's wrist was fractured or merely sprained.

Trying not to think about the frightful blank look on her daughter's face when she'd collapsed on the tarmac, Clare wondered where Steve was. When Deering had driven them down in his truck behind the ambulance, Steve had been taken away in a wheelchair.

This morning at the airport, she'd never expected him to fly. Even if he had promised she would not be alone, she had not imagined him getting onto a helicopter with her.

She slouched against the uncomfortable straight-backed chair. Steve had stood by her, but on the mountain, she'd let him down. She'd stood on the safety of rock while Deering leaped to his rescue. Although she could plead the excuse of Devon's weight hanging on her, she did not believe that would suffice. Ahead of her still lay the interrogation surrounding the death of Private William Harrison Jakes.

Clare sighed and looked around the empty room. An

abandoned jacket lay in a chair and a blanket and pillow marked where someone had passed the night waiting for news of a loved one. A television high in the corner played the evening news with footage of the fires behind Peter Jennings's shoulder. The usual firefighters on the march, the obligatory chopper picking up a load of water, the flying tanker dropping colorful retardant. This was where she'd come in, seeing romance and adventure in a line of sweaty firefighters trudging up a forest road.

As much as she longed to explore where she and Steve might have gone, it was time to take Devon home to Houston. Her heart ached, but when it came to blood, a mother's choice must be for her child. Somehow, she had to convince Devon that she was too young to try and make it on her own.

As to firefighting, she had yet to decide. At Old Faithful, Steve had said Frank would want her to battle the North Fork.

But Frank had been a war-scarred veteran with over twenty years in the department. He'd told her that his grown son was proud of his old man, not scared like Devon had been. If Clare's work brought continued pain to her daughter, she'd have to cash it in and dust off her teaching certificate.

Clare opened her eyes to find Steve leaning on crutches in Devon's hospital room doorway. He wore his jeans and western shirt.

"How long have you been there?" She straightened the

recliner beside the bed where Devon slept and stretched to release the kink in her back.

A slow smile spread over his face. "Not long. You must have felt me looking at you."

Clare wished she believed in telepathy with this man. She rose and gestured Steve toward the brown vinyl chair she'd slept in. He remained on his feet.

Outside the window, all was dark except for pole lights in the parking lot. Clare's watch said it was nearly midnight. "Is Karrabotsos all right?" she asked.

"Doing well, considering. This time around he'll be looking at more skin grafts." He looked at Devon, who lay with blond lashes sweeping her cheek, her arm in a cast. "How is she?"

Clare reached to smooth back Devon's hair. The singed section had been trimmed, leaving her with a lopsided haircut that made her look very young. "No concussion from the crash. Just the burn and a crack in the radius above her wrist."

Steve advanced into the room with the awkward swinging gate of a person on crutches. "I know you well enough to figure you're tearing yourself up over what happened with her."

He'd been her constant cheerleader, telling her to never back down and she was getting sick and tired of it. "I should never have come here," she said. "Devon would be safe at home if I hadn't."

"That's enough!" He straightened and put more weight on his legs.

Devon sighed and turned her head. She was on Percodan, a strong painkiller that would help her sleep.

In a softer voice, Steve went on, "If you hadn't come, I

would never have met you. You saved my life more than once this summer, and I couldn't believe it when you pulled Karrabotsos out of that fire."

She shrugged. "Training and reflex."

Steve rearranged a crutch and grabbed her hand. He turned the palm up and looked at its calluses, scrapes, and half healed burns. "I was there when your friend Javier from Houston said you had the best hands in the business."

"All right, I'm fucking good at what I do," she threw at him. "But I'm a mother, too, and from now on Devon won't have to be afraid of me getting hurt or killed. I'm taking her home and quitting this business." Saying it out loud cemented the decision she'd made in the waiting room.

"I'm not going to listen to that." Steve propped his crutches against the wall and pointed a finger at her. "You think you can control your life by crawling into a hole. That you can protect Devon from what the world is going to throw at her by smothering her. Well, I've got news for you, Clare." His mouth twisted. "Shit happens. If you don't believe that, just ask a guy who's been there."

"Susan," she said flatly.

"Susan," he agreed "and Christa." He looked at Devon. "You can try and run her life, but ultimately, she's got to figure things out for herself, like we all do. Don't make any quick decisions you'll regret."

Clare sighed. Who wouldn't want to exert some control after watching the fires burn unchecked for months? After a summer in which two men had died on her watch?

A flicker of pain crossed Steve's face. She touched his arm.

"You need to sit."

"I need a lot of things." His eyes lit with an awareness of last night's stolen hours, and he lifted a hand to stroke the serrate haircut the fire had left her with. When he touched her neck, it made her aware that comfort wasn't all she wanted from him.

Here come the tears, she thought, yet oddly enough, she didn't feel a thing like crying. She thought he might kiss her, but she wasn't ready for Devon to open her eyes to that. She fingered the front of his red shirt with western snaps. "You must have gone to the hotel."

"Deering gave me a lift."

"Is he still here?" She hoped Steve wouldn't get the wrong idea again, but she needed to know that Deering was okay.

"His wife came to take him home."

"I hope they work it out this time."

"They seemed pretty happy to see each other." He spoke easily of the man he'd once wanted to fight. "Before he left he asked me to tell you goodbye . . . and thanks."

Deering had found his home and life again, but what lay ahead for her? After she sold the house in Houston, what then? Although a job waited for her at the station with Javier and the others, she felt she'd moved beyond it.

Steve's hand moved over her hair. With a ragged limp, he moved closer.

"I should have asked how're you doing." She gestured toward his knees.

He dropped his hand to his side. "They X-rayed me and said another round of scraping and washing the joints out might help if I want to do it this fall." He lifted a shoulder. "Some things I've been living with a long time."

Suddenly she couldn't stand his steadfast grieving for Susan any longer. If he hadn't been hurting, she might have shoved his chest. "You tell me how to live my life . . . you with your shrine in your bedroom. If we hadn't been in a motel, last night would never have happened."

"That's not fair." Gray eyes bored into hers.

"You don't play fair telling me to buck up. Every time your knee hurts you think about the bum rap life served you." Her breath came fast. "The doctor said Devon could leave in the morning. I need to make arrangements for our flight."

"No." Steve's throat moved with his swallow. "Come here."

If she let him hold her, how much harder it would be to leave. The worst part of going back to Houston would surely be the memory of last night.

"Please," Steve said hoarsely.

With a glance at Devon, who still appeared to be sleeping, Clare went into his arms. It was as good as she remembered, better, for Devon was safe. She pressed her cheek against Steve's chest and listened to the steady beat of his heart.

If this was good-bye, then she was going to be a crybaby about it. The tears she'd not shed waited behind a dam about to break. She burrowed her head and tightened her grip on him. How unjust a world where something as beautiful as this was to her was merely a summer interlude for him. "Steve," she whispered, "I . . ."

He shushed her by pressing two fingers to her lips. "Shhh."

She gave up, for there was nothing left to say. They would

promise to call and write and visit at Thanksgiving, but by then their separate worlds would have re-absorbed them.

"I've been thinking about a lot of things," he said.

She'd been thinking, as well. Too much. This sweet ache had no place when the best thing that had happened to her would end when her plane took off.

Steve bent and pressed his lips to hers, setting her tears free.

"Devon's not ready to travel," he murmured at her ear. "Why don't you both come home with me?"

CHAPTER THIRTY-TWO
September 9

Clare sat between Steve and Devon as he shifted gears on the long grade up from Yellowstone's northern gateway to Mammoth Hot Springs. They'd driven the long way around from West Yellowstone through Bozeman, rather than the shorter route through the park.

The rushing Gardner River ran between steep cliffs where, on Steve's advice, Clare kept an eye out for bighorn sheep. The higher mountains were barely visible through a yellowish haze.

"I don't like the look of this smoke," Steve said.

Clare pressed a hand on his arm, warning him not to disturb Devon.

He fell silent.

Talk of evacuation had been on the air in the Pic and Save Market in the park's northern gateway town of Gardiner, Montana, when they had stopped for groceries. She had not reported it to Devon, who had waited for them in the truck. When the tiny village of Mammoth appeared, Clare could only see a few buildings, the rest obscured by drifting cottony tendrils.

By the stone barn housing the Mammoth Fire Cache, there were at least twenty fire engines. She swore under her breath at the long arms of the North Fork that now stretched from one side of the park to the other. They should have checked conditions at Fire Command before striking out, but she had so wanted to bring Devon to a safe refuge.

There was Steve's place in the old stockade. He shut off the engine and limped around the rear to pull the passenger door open for Devon.

"I can do it." Devon swung around and stepped out. Steve steadied her.

Clare scrambled down behind her. "Do you need another pain pill?"

"No." She shrugged off Steve's hand. "I can walk." Clare suppressed a smile at her daughter's pride.

Steve's crutches lay in the truck bed. "Damned things are more trouble than they're worth." He snagged a bag of groceries and stumped toward his back porch. Clare plucked a second sack, aware that Devon followed slowly.

Steve's porch was full of man stuff. Shelves lined with open toolboxes, cans of lubricant spray, and coils of rope covered one wall. Inside, the kitchen was as immaculate as when Clare had run out on Steve drinking coffee the other morning. Devon came in looking curious.

Clare helped Steve put away the groceries, passing canned goods to the pantry and items into the fridge. She and Jay used to do these simple domestic chores together. As she picked up a jar of basil and accurately opened the cabinet that housed the spices, Devon accused, "You've been here before."

"I have," Clare turned to her, "but it happens that was a lucky guess."

Devon looked skeptical.

"Are you okay or would you like to lie down?" Please, don't let Devon think she was trying to get rid of her.

"Down," Devon agreed, although her eyes were clear, the last pain pill having evidently worn off.

Steve closed the fridge. "You gals take my room." His eyes flicked to Clare's, the barest glance that was swiftly gone.

In the living room, Devon trailed a finger across the shining surface of the grand piano. When they reached Steve's room, she stopped halfway to the bed and stared at the picture of Susan at the same piano. Clare watched her give an appraising glance at shining golden hair and black velvet, and then look at her mother with butchered hair, rough yellow and olive fire clothes, and thick boots.

Steve rummaged in the closet and came out with a stack of pillows and a comforter. "I'll take these out to the living room so I don't have to bother you later."

"Who's that?" Devon blurted, pointing at the picture.

"She was my wife," Steve said evenly. "Susan's passion was music . . . and Christa, our little girl. That was taken at the hospital when she was born."

"Where are they?"

Clare bit her lip to keep from chiding Devon. After the way she'd yelled at Steve in the hospital about not being over his wife . . .

"They were killed in a plane crash four years ago." He looked from Devon to Clare and said softly, "I wasn't."

The memory of how good it had felt in Steve's arms when he'd asked her home came back to warm Clare.

Devon made it to the bed and sagged onto it.

Steve headed for the door. "I'm gonna take a walk around and see what's going on. You make yourselves at home."

That word again. His body brushed Clare's in the doorway even though there was plenty of room to pass. She watched him limp down the hall and out of sight toward the kitchen.

When she turned back, Devon was studying her.

"Are you sure you don't want another Percodan?" Clare offered the pill because it was something she could do. Steve would call it keeping control.

"Okay." Devon got into bed.

Clare brought the pill and water and smoothed the rumpled covers. That done, she touched her daughter's cheek. Her little girl, once as clear as rain, had become so dark and deep she didn't know how to reach her.

Cornflower eyes brimmed. Clare leaned and plucked some tissues from a box on the nightstand. Her hand passed in front of Susan.

Devon fiddled with the cast on her forearm while her tears flowed. Clare put her arms around her; an awkward fit, and felt her own eyes grow wet. "Mom." A gasp. "I'm sorry for knocking you down, for being so stupid."

"I forgave you a long time ago." Clare patted Devon's back and felt her twitch. "I'm sorry I accused you of something Elyssa was spreading. I should have asked before jumping to conclusions."

"I wish I had somebody, but I don't." Devon sniffed. The guys I like best go for other girls, and older guys are a little scary. Except for Harry."

"Harry?" Clare tensed.

"Annalise MacIntyre's big brother. He's like my brother too. He gave me a ride home the other week and Elyssa saw us. When she went ballistic, I let her think whatever she wanted."

Clare smiled through her tears.

"Steve is okay." Devon disentangled herself and pulled back.

"When did you change your mind about him?"

"I heard you two talking in the hospital. I was awake." Devon looked down and picked at the bedspread. "Yeah, I know, why'd I ask who was in the picture if I knew?"

"Maybe you wanted to hear his answer."

Devon nodded. "Steve said I needed to figure things out for myself. Well, I have been thinking."

She would never have thought any good could come of Devon's night on a dark and lonely mountain. "Thinking about what's next?"

Devon sniffed again and swiped her uninjured arm across her nose. "I was thinking of getting a place with Annalise. She can't stand living with her folks anymore and she didn't want to go it alone. But just before I left Houston, she said she was going to go to A & M in January."

"College?" Casual, just the right note.

"Dad always said he'd pay," Devon ventured.

"You said you were finished with school." If she were just going to party with her friends, it would never work out. "Are you going just to be with Annalise?"

Devon lifted the tissue Clare had given her and blew her nose. "You say there's nothing out there 'cept flipping burgers unless I go to school, or train for something . . . like bein' a firefighter." Her voice was a little slurred as the Percodan began to take effect.

"Not that, hon . . ."

"Yeah. You were talking to Steve about giving it up . . . but, Mom," her voice grew fainter. "you're a pyro."

"That doesn't mean it's right for you."

Devon smiled sleepily and snuggled down in the covers.

Clare tucked her in and sat beside her until she slept. Relief at knowing there was no man in her daughter's life made her feel absurdly happy. With her contacts at the fire school, and Jay and the Hendrons, perhaps Devon might yet have the college days Clare had missed out on.

When she came out of the bedroom, it was dim and quiet in Steve's living room. She checked her watch and found it half past four, too early for it to be so dark.

She switched on a lamp. Polished ebony glowed, but when she smoothed the piano's top her finger came away dusty. A closer examination made her suspect the dust contained some soot.

After brushing off the piano bench, she sat and poised her hands, the way Miss Bryan had taught her when she was nine. She played, the perfect ivory making it possible to find the way without stumbling. She hadn't known she remembered, but as she progressed from a soft opening to a more confident tone, she recalled that it was one of Chopin's

Preludes. Music poured into her from the keys, rather than from her mind down a system of nerves. Heedless of Devon's sleeping, she made her way toward the end of the work, a triumphant crescendo.

The final notes lingered like a subtle mix of fine spices. When the last vibrations died, Clare dropped her head and leaned her forehead against the cool wood of the music rack.

One way or another, Devon had said she'd be moving from under Clare's roof. She wasn't yet comfortable with that, but Steve had tried to tell her that Devon had to make her own way. Ranger Butler Meyers had made it clear that even a seventeen and eleven-twelfths runaway wouldn't be tracked down by law enforcement.

Clare recalled her own youth. A faded shadow of her eighteen-year-old self faced her mother with Jay's arm around her. "I'm old enough to do what I want." Constance had folded her hand even as she would have to. She could only hope that college would work out, rather than a job in fast food. Or getting some man to pay the bills, the insult that had made Devon knock her on the floor.

The yearning ache that had centered in her chest wasn't unpleasant, but she wanted Steve to come back.

The faint vibration of an approaching vehicle resolved into the guttural growl of a diesel coming into Mammoth from the east. Clare got to the kitchen in time to see a red ladder unit pass behind the house. Wind tossed the treetops and moaned around the ancient wooden window frames, driving the smell of char inside.

She frowned. Mammoth's natural bowl shape was probably

collecting smoke from miles away, but she'd not seen a fire extents' map since Wednesday morning. Black Saturday and the siege of Old Faithful had shown how much could happen in a short time.

A sedan bearing the insignia of the Boise Interagency Fire Center drove in and parked beside the row of firefighting equipment. When Garrett Anderson climbed out and headed with swift purpose toward the Fire Cache, Clare left the house and followed.

YELLOWSTONE FIRES
September 9, 8:00 a.m.

Here is a list of the fires and approximate perimeter acreages. To date, over 816,225 acres in Yellowstone National Park (and over 1,198,00 acres in the Greater Yellowstone Area) have been affected by fire. However, only about half of the vegetation has burned within many fire perimeters. Throughout the summer, 52 different fires have been started by lightning. Of those 52, eight are still burning inside the park. Fire fighters are working to control them. Any new fires will be suppressed as quickly as possible.

* * * * *

Clover-Mist Fire: 304,100 acres. Mist Fire started July 9. Clover started July 11. They joined on July 22. Shallow Fire started July 31. Fern Fire started

August 5. These two fires joined Clover-Mist August 13. Clover-Mist fire camp was not evacuated as reported earlier. Structure protection in Crandell area is still a priority. Twenty buildings, trailers, and shed were lost, although many vehicles were saved. Pahaska Tepee is reported as being OK. Mop-up continues in the Squaw Ck. area. Acreage increases were in the Jones Ck., Papoose Ck., and Squaw Ck. drainages. 1700 firefighters, 69 engines, 12 bulldozers, and 3 helicopters are on the fire.

Fan Fire: 23,325 acres. Started June 25. The fire is reported as contained. One crew is completing mop-up. 25 firefighters, 1 helicopter.

Hellroaring Fire: 62,340 acres (estimated 9,500 acres in Yellowstone NP.) Started August 15. Most of the acreage increase resulted from backfires. Storm Creek continues to advance in the joint burn area and move down Slough Ck. 562 firefighters, 5 helicopters.

Huck Fire: 88,300 acres. Started August 20. Caused the evacuation of Flagg Ranch. Yesterday's backfire was successful at keeping the fire on the N side of Pacific Ck. Fire activity was low yesterday due to inversion weather conditions. 798 firefighters, 2 engines, 8 helicopters.

SUMMER OF FIRE

North Fork: 229,400 acres. Started July 22 by human. Split from Wolf Lake Fire at Gibbon Falls. The major activity was on the NE where the fire burned past Indian Creek Campground. Resources are being moved to the area to deal with the anticipated advance of the fire into the area S of Mammoth. Mop-up and structure protection are continuing at Old Faithful and West Yellowstone. Additional line construction is being done to the W of the park near West Yellowstone. 1570 firefighters, 49 engines, 22 bulldozers, and 6 helicopters.

Snake River Complex: 210,300 acres. Red Fire started July 1. Shoshone Fire started June 23. Joined August 10. Falls Fire started July 12. Red-Shoshone joined the Mink Fire on August 31. Acreage includes Continental-Ridge and Mink Creek fires. Emphasis will be on keeping fire out of the Lewis River Canyon. Crews continue to work on the South Entrance road, which will remain closed. Mop-up continues. 564 firefighters, 16 engines, 1 dozer, 6 helicopters.

Storm Creek Fire: 81,000 acres. Started July 3. Residents were allowed back into the Cooke City-Silver Gate area, but were evacuated again because of the concern over high winds today. The fire continues to move easterly into the Beartooth Wilderness. A finger of the fire has reached the backburn at the NE Entrance. The SW flank is still hot and is moving toward the Hellroaring Fire. 1172 firefighters, 35 engines, 4 dozers, 6 helicopters.

Wolf Lake Fire: 70,400 acres. Divided from North Fork Fire at Gibbon Falls. No major runs occurred Thursday. Fire continues to spread toward Tower and Lake. Fire is on three sides of Canyon, although firefighters have prevented any structures from being burned. Tower and Roosevelt are well protected. Planning for the defense of Lake continues. 720 firefighters, 40 engines, 2 dozers, 3 helicopters.

In the United States, 68,396 wildfires have burned 3,799,550 acres in 1988.

In the command post of the Mammoth Fire Cache, Clare and Garrett looked over the morning's fire map. Constructed through infrared imaging, the study continued to be released daily to appease the army of media. Although the outline of the North Fork did not appear to be within striking distance of Mammoth, the copy indicated that resources were being moved in.

A young man from one of the engines spoke over the clatter of printers and ringing of phones. "We just drove in from the south. The North Fork is up on Swan Lake Flat, coming fast."

Garrett nodded. "We're just waiting for the latest weather, but I'm guessing that the front is moving faster than expected."

SUMMER OF FIRE

Ben Mallory, a sixtyish man who headed the cache, handed a flimsy sheet of paper to Garrett. "Four p.m. update."

Garrett scanned it, the furrows on his forehead deepening. "We'll be battening down the hatches here by midday tomorrow." Looking back at the fire map, he withdrew a pen from his pocket and sketched a slender and deadly tentacle of the North Fork that pointed directly at Mammoth. "If we get the predicted winds, we'll see fire behavior like we've never seen before."

Clare swallowed. "What next?" she asked on behalf of a circle of listening firefighters.

"Evacuation?" someone asked. "Wouldn't hurt to get the civilians out of the way."

"That's up to the Chief Ranger," Garrett said. "I'm sure he doesn't want to disrupt his people's lives any more than he has to. Tomorrow morning should be plenty of time if folks need to move out."

"We'll beat it," someone said.

A chorus of agreement arose. In spite of herself, Clare caught the contagious excitement. She wasn't going to fight this battle, but thoughts of the North Fork heated her blood.

"Hey," one of the firefighters called. "How does the government put out a fire in your kitchen?"

"They backburn your living room," another hollered.

Clare gave a tight grin.

There would be backburns set around Mammoth tomorrow, a risky endeavor at best. The fire near Grant Village had been deliberately set to deprive the Shoshone of fuel, but had gotten away from firefighters. Tuesday's near miss at Silver

Gate and Cooke City on the east end of the park had been due to a runaway backfire.

Maybe Devon was right about Clare being a pyro, for she could almost feel the drip torch in her hand and smell the pine pitch. She'd learned this summer that despite the dryness, trying to ignite the seedlings of Douglas fir was nearly impossible, so she'd targeted pine and duff.

One of the firefighters was showing the others a cartoon of the National Park Service emblem with its tree and mountain emblazoned on an arrowhead. In this version, the tree was a blackened stick. Clare smiled. After a few days away, it felt good to be back.

"Everybody take ten," Garrett called. "Shad Dugan is coming over to map out where the crews will set up."

The group headed for the coffee urn and began passing Styrofoam cups. "Something to drink?" Garrett asked Clare.

"No, thanks."

"Fig Newton?"

She laughed.

"They're in my car," Garrett said. "Why don't we take a walk?" He led the way out of the command post past the crowded radio room and the warehouse depleted of Pulaskis, rope, shovels, and webbed belts with canteens. The cache was mostly stocked for wildfire fighting, with a small unit for calls in the village. The biggest local fire danger was the Mammoth Hot Springs Hotel across the way, or it had been until today.

When Clare and Garrett went out, the world looked brighter. A stiff wind had blown out some of the hanging smoke, giving a filtered view of the surrounding mountains. The sun looked angry, a violent red disc suspended over the white terraces of the hot springs. As they crossed the lawn between Park Headquarters and the first big house on Officer's Row, Garrett asked, "You see any news last night?"

"Nothing but a few minutes of Peter Jennings. I caught it in the hospital waiting room while they were X-raying Devon. Democrats trying to give the spin that if they were in charge, nothing like this would have happened."

"*Nightline* agreed that people will argue about fire management policy for years," Garrett said. "How is Devon?"

"Cracked wrist and a chest burn she got from a flying cinder at Old Faithful." Ashes drifted from the sky as premature darkness resettled over the day. "She'll be okay once I get her home to Houston."

Garrett stopped in the street and looked at Clare. A flicker of his eyes took in her ragged hair. "How're you doing?"

She recalled their unfinished business. "I'll be a lot better when they've finished the Hellroaring investigation."

His dark brow furrowed as they moved onto the lawn with scattered picnic tables. "I've already taken statements from Sergeant Travis and the troops. And you told me about it the other night."

They reached the old parade ground that was thick with sage. Clare stopped beside a fence around a fumarole. Watching the steam rise and whip away on the wind, she dared to hope, "Is that it?"

"That's it."

She held the wooden rail and rode a surge of elation.

"I know you won't let an accident like what happened to Private Jakes run you off." Garrett was offhand.

She opened her mouth to tell him she'd quit, but said, "How do you know that when I don't?"

"A tough gal like you didn't let the death of Frank Wallace get her down."

Clare went still inside. "All summer, I've kept up a brave front, never thinking you knew."

"Buddy Simpson at A & M told me. He thought coming up here would do you good."

"So did the department psychologist."

Garrett leaned his bulk on the fence rail. It creaked and he stood straight again. "Getting back in action is always the best thing."

"Now you, too." Clare let go of the rail and crossed her arms over her chest. "I've been hearing that from everybody all summer."

"Because it's a fact."

Hadn't she thought that, herself, back in July when she scanned Lake Yellowstone and wanted to help the anonymous victims of a helicopter ditching?

Garrett went on, "Before you get away from us, I want to ask what you think about wildfire work."

Clare weighed the hours spent in the fire station in Houston against the mountain vistas the Smokejumpers enjoyed in West Yellowstone. The siren's wail as the engine negotiated eight lanes of traffic on Westheimer Road, versus the sunlight strobing in an avenue of trees. Going into an apartment to pull down the ceiling with a pike pole, or digging line in the pine smelling forest, with the ever-changing flames crackling a few yards away.

Both were honest hard work.

Billy Jakes had met a terrible end on the Hellroaring, but it was God's own truth that she saw more death in the city from wrecks and coronaries than she could ever find in the forest. For the first time since she'd made her decision, she hesitated. "What about wildfire?"

"I want you with me at the Interagency Center in Boise."

Clare glanced over her shoulder toward the small frame building Steve called home. Boise was a lot closer to Yellowstone than Houston. "Talk to me," she said.

Garrett smiled. "Before you commit yourself to Boise there's one more thing you might want to know. Ben Mallory is retiring here at the Fire Cache early next year. They'll be needing somebody too."

Are you moving to Yellowstone? Clare heard Devon's voice in her head, as clearly as when her daughter had asked the question earlier in the summer. She looked again at Steve's place, where the light from the lamp she'd left on in the living room glowed. "I'll think about it."

Black smoke billowed from behind the high smooth shoulder of Bunsen Peak.

🔥🔥🔥

Steve left the administration building and limped across the lawn toward Park Headquarters. Maybe he should have brought along those crutches.

With an angry look at the smoke haze, he found it difficult to believe it had only been seventy-two hours since the North Fork's Incident Commander had pronounced that fire would sweep through Old Faithful. Now the Chief Ranger was weighing the wisdom of evacuating Mammoth. In contrast to the seasonal ebb and flow, headquarters was the year-round community that directed people and goods to the rest of the park, like a heart pumping blood.

Steve passed Carol Leeds from Billings Live Eye and the ponytailed cameraman who'd heckled him at Roaring Mountain. They were filming the collection of fire trucks and apparatus in the yard.

The outside basement door of headquarters gave its usual protest at opening, but finally let Steve into the hall outside the archives. To his surprise, the lights were off behind the wire glass windows. Walt Leighton and Harriet must have closed early to pack for the evacuation.

Pale illumination from the above ground basement windows gave Steve a view into the familiar room lined with filing cabinets. To him, these records were so much more than yellowed paper and fading ink. They were people's lives, transcribed with loving care, so that future generations might know their legacy. He thought of Clare's ancestral diary that they'd found in Grand Teton Park. He needed to look at that and make sure a copy was made for posterity.

An approaching fire engine rumbled. Ranger Shad Dugan had said that by morning there would be at least forty units onsite. Steve glanced at the sprinkler head on the ceiling. Beneath the stone building, the archives were largely insulated, but what of the historic wooden buildings of old Fort Yellowstone? By this time tomorrow, the place Steve called home might be ashes.

His knees protested as he exited the building and headed toward his house.

Next door, Moru Mzima came out and set a loaded cardboard box on the open tailgate of his Chevy wagon. "Bloody glad to see you," he called. "I heard just now that you were in another nasty scrape yesterday."

Steve clasped Moru's extended hand. "It's been one hell of a summer."

Moru shifted his tall frame and nodded toward the half-full rear of the station wagon. "The North Fork's not to reach us till tomorrow, but . . ." He cocked a dark brow at the restless limbs of the cottonwoods. "In the morning I will send Nyeri and the kids to stay with friends in Bozeman."

"Good idea." Steve would have to send Clare and Devon away, too. He planned to stay, for even a gimp could patrol the evacuation by truck.

"You must get packing," Moru advised.

"I'll do that now." Steve took off toward his house at as brisk a pace as he could manage, pausing to dry-swallow two ibuprofen when pain told him to take it easy. He passed within twenty feet of a lazy group of elk. These local animals seemed so tame that he could only hope they would move off their chosen turf if the North Fork burned through.

Steve went up the back stairs of his house and into the kitchen. The house had that silent feel he always came home to, and he had to remind himself that today he wasn't alone.

"Clare?" False twilight made the kitchen dark.

Devon was supposed to be sleeping, so he stopped calling and went into the living room. Here a lamp cut the gloom. Steve went into the short hall and listened for the murmur of voices. A board creaked beneath his boot. The bedroom door had been left off the latch.

Clare's daughter lay on her side with one hand beneath her cheek. The shorn part of her curly hair exposed a profile smooth and untroubled like a child's. A little tug in his chest said that Christa would have been a blonde too. Although Steve thought he'd opened the door quietly, blue eyes opened and focused on him. "Is Mom here?"

He shook his head. "She may have gone over to the Fire Cache."

Devon gave a faint smile. "She can't stay away, even when she says she's gonna." She closed her eyes as though she was still exhausted.

From the nightstand, Steve picked up the frame containing the pictures of Susan and Christa. In the living room, he stripped off the backing and removed them, then set the empty silver frame on the piano.

Down the hall, he opened the spare room that he used for a study and darkroom. Aluminum foil covered the windows and an Indian blanket was rolled to block the light from under the door. His negatives resided in a metal box, indexed by year and subject matter. He placed the box in the hall.

From a nearby shelf, Steve plucked his master's thesis and doctoral dissertation, the copies that had been signed by his major professors. He tucked the photos of Susan and Christa inside the back of his dissertation on forest ecology, contrasting the Southern pine assemblage with a deciduous control.

Books in hand, he stood thinking what else was irreplaceable. His textbooks were out of date. His favorite novels could be found in a library. His furniture was ordinary except for a piano he now knew he should have sold years ago. He carried the box and books out to the kitchen, where he added a nondescript set of stainless camping cookware. His Dad had composed many a fireside meal in those pans, while teaching the culinary arts that were now Steve's pleasure.

A cardboard carton from the pantry held everything.

After carrying it out to the truck, he came back and got his toolboxes from the porch. A lot of the tools had also been handed down from his father.

The wind continued to rise; the harbinger of yet another dry front. Steve scattered his small pile of firewood from against the house over the yard.

CHAPTER THIRTY-THREE
September 9

Clare entered Steve's kitchen through the back porch. His blond hair was darkened from a shower and he wore fresh jeans and an Old Faithful T-shirt. He turned and smiled at her from the counter where he was dredging chicken breasts in flour flecked with spices. His wooden cutting board was piled with onions, carrots, and a carton of mushrooms.

Two bottles of Chilean Cabernet sat beside the largest copper pot from the rack.

"For cooking." Steve had said that at the Pic and Save when he'd placed them in the cart, but Clare really wanted to have a glass.

"Corkscrew's in that drawer." He pointed with his elbow.

She didn't move.

"As far as I know," he said dryly, "you're not the one who needs to stay off the stuff."

She secured the opener and removed the cork with a satisfying pop.

"I can still name that tune in one note," Steve said with regret.

"You're doing great, though." She poured and tasted the red's balance of grape and oak tannins. "This will go well in the stew."

As she mentally toasted being here with Steve, she nearly blurted out Garrett's offer. What kept her silent was that she didn't know how he would take it. Sleeping with her was one thing, but he'd given no sign he'd be open to anything of a longer term.

Steve rinsed his hands and reached for a hand towel. "I'm sure you heard the North Fork is coming."

"Big time. Can I help you pack?" She looked around his kitchen and wondered what he valued enough to take.

"Already done," he said. "I travel light."

Here she was thinking of moving to Boise to be closer to him. How would a man who traveled light take that?

Deliberately putting the future from her mind, she checked on Devon and found her still sleeping. The spread was thrown back. As Clare re-covered her, she noticed the nightstand was bare.

Of course, Steve would have packed Susan and Christa's pictures.

Clare passed the piano and had a restless impulse to play. For a defiant moment she almost did, to show Steve that his home could have music again. Instead, she went into the kitchen, certain that her technique would be too basic for him.

"Can I help?" she asked from behind his shoulder.

"Just stand back and let the master work." He turned and dropped a light kiss on her cheek. As quickly, he went back to dicing.

She sat at the kitchen table, sipped a long slow glass of wine, and drank in the show. Despite his limp, Steve moved with grace. His hands were sure and exact as he produced clean coins of carrot and slices of mushroom.

When the meal was prepared, she went and asked Devon whether she would prefer a tray or getting up. Dopey from the drug, Devon elected dinner in bed.

An hour later, the aroma of stewed chicken lingered in the kitchen. The delightful blend of spices and the succulent taste had proven that Steve was one primo chef.

"I'll do the dishes," Clare said. He'd done more than his share by cooking when his knees were probably killing him. She located some plastic bags and filled them with ice from the freezer. Wrapped in a kitchen towel, they made credible ice packs. "One for each leg. Off you go."

In Steve's bedroom, she collected Devon's half-eaten dinner and saw that she had fallen back to sleep. She paused and planted a kiss on her daughter's forehead, the kind that would have made her squirm if she were awake.

On her way down the hall, her chest swelled with content. Steve stretched out on the sofa looking so comfortable that she wanted to lie down and put her head against his shoulder.

With a smile that warmed her, he asked, "Would you mind if I looked through your great-grandmother's diary?"

She hadn't had a chance to sit down and really read it yet, but there could be nothing in it she wouldn't trust Steve to see. She knew how he loved history. "I'll get it."

Clare's 'luggage' was on the kitchen windowsill, the paper sack her grizzly T-shirt had come in. It contained the shirt and diary, along with a toothbrush, paste, and comb. She was traveling light, herself.

That felt good. For months she'd lived out of a suitcase, mostly wearing a uniform that bonded her with the brotherhood of firefighting. Black and white, Native American, Hispanic, and Asian, they dressed alike. College student, fire general, soldier and convict, they came together for the season . . . and back apart.

Laura Sutton's leather-bound book felt more fragile, the spine wobbly from all it had been through. Much more handling would see the pages come free from the backing.

A smudge of something rusty like dried blood dulled the burnished gilt on the edge. Clare turned it in her hands and opened it to the last entry before a series of blank pages. Perhaps the ink had once been blue, but it had faded to sepia.

October 15, 1927

It is hard to believe that we are leaving today. The sun shines on the Tetons as though it were any other day, any of the thousands we have passed pleasantly at home over the last twenty-six years.

I sit facing what I have come to regard as my personal and private view of the Grand and wonder what we will do in far away Texas, a flat, baking land that Cord and I have never even visited.

It's all wrapped up here, so nice and neat, the check from the Snake River Land Company folded in Cord's breast pocket for deposit in our new account in Houston. We didn't get as much for our ranch as I thought we should have, but folks all over the valley have been caving in to the tough young men who assured us that we would not see a better offer.

They're waiting for me, Cord already settled in the back of Cordon's noisy automobile. Our son adjusts the lap robe and I am glad he is good at pretending and making it seem as though Cord is not really so ill. It scares me so to see the bluish pallor come and go at his lips, and to watch him massage his chest when he thinks I am not looking.

It was that way with Father, near the end.

Selling the ranch seemed the right decision. We could no longer keep it up and Cordon insisted we move someplace where the climate is not so harsh. I believe that is an excuse, for he knows we have weathered Wyoming winters for many years, as he did growing up. We don't any of us speak of it, but he is the one who wants to make a new life in Texas.

Cord said his good-byes last night. I woke in that darkest hour before dawn and found him gone from our bed. Through the window, I saw him in the autumn meadow before the house, his fine head of silver hair tilted back to look up at the mountains' shadow against the star-studded sky.

This morning Cordon was brusque and businesslike, but I saw his eyes darting this way and that, now to the corner of the hearth where Sophie had her puppies, then scanning the path to the barn. He could usually be found there, communing with the horses, when all his other haunts had been checked.

Everything has been loaded and there is no reason to linger. In just a moment, I will put this journal to rest where it belongs. I do not believe I could bear to read of our joys and sadness here, once we are in Texas. Instead, I will let time soften the edges of memory, in the same way it blurs the lines of our faces and fades the brightness of our hair.

And yet ... the mountains will not let me go, weaving their subtle spell of changing light and shadow. They invite me to stay, to watch the magic of clouds appearing from clear air and day fading to darkness.

Out there in the night, mountains ringed this valley. People would come and go, live and die, and still the heights would endure. The time it took to transform them into the plains of tomorrow rendered meaningless a single lifetime. She was bound to this land, by blood and by a book that reached to her through the years. With her hand on the worn leather, Clare decided. No matter whether she fought fire, no matter what happened between her and Steve, she was coming back.

When she gave the diary to Steve, he was immediately absorbed in turning the pages. She watched him scan rapidly, seeing the scholar in him.

Back in the kitchen, she scraped carrot curls and onion peels into the trash, packaged the leftovers, and washed the copper pot. She didn't like domestic chores, but this evening it gave her a sense of purpose to take care of both Devon and Steve. When she finished wiping the tiled counter, she stepped to the back door.

The chirp of crickets and the chatter of television in a nearby house added to her aching feeling of being at home. Unfortunately, the distant laughter of firefighters swapping stories at the cache reminded her of the threat to this haven. The stately mansions that had once made up Officer's Row were brilliantly lit this evening. It hurt to imagine flame licking at lace curtains and curling the varnish on lacquered wood.

When she returned to the living room, Steve was making up the couch with pillows and a comforter.

Clare took her paper sack to the bathroom. A bathtub on claw feet, small black and white floor tiles, and an almost new pedestal sink spoke of generations of renovation and park people who came and went. A man's razor and a purple handled toothbrush lay on a glass shelf in a house that did not know a woman's touch. All Steve had brought of Susan was a piano, photos . . . and memory.

In the mirror, Clare saw that her color was high. The events of the last two days had dulled her recall of the night with Steve, but now it surged like a flame to the bellows. Earlier he'd offered his bedroom to her and Devon, but the brief intense look he'd given her said he hoped she'd share his sofa.

If Devon had been listening in the hospital, she knew more about her mother and Steve then Clare would have wished. Her cheeks grew brighter pink as she recalled how freely she'd talked about their night in a motel. Yet, spitting toothpaste into the sink, she decided that in this afternoon's talk, Devon had approved of Steve.

Clare wiped her face and borrowed a bit of his hand lotion for moisturizer. It smelled woodsy, like the forest when it wasn't burning, a scent that increased the pull of this land. Her sweet ache intensified, for tomorrow when she and Devon evacuated it would be time to call the airlines.

Dressed in the grizzly T-shirt, she checked on Devon once more and gave her another pain pill. When she paused in the doorway to the living room, Steve indicated that she should close the extra door. "A little advance warning," he suggested softly.

Clare's breath caught in her throat. They couldn't, not with Devon just down the hall.

Yet, as she moved into the room, she imagined wearing something sleek and shining like white silk, or better yet, red and lacy.

Steve waited in the light of a green-shaded reading lamp in gray drawstring sweat pants, barefoot and bare-chested. His knees were still on ice. "Can I get you an Ibuprofen?" the medic in her asked.

He shook his head, bent and shoved the melting packs under the coffee table. His gaze explored her bare legs and upward at leisure. "My very favorite shirt," he chuckled. His voice, pitched low, set her pulse drumming. As though it was the most natural thing in the world, he slid over to make room and threw back the comforter.

She crossed to him, her bare feet whispering softly on the hardwood. The glow of the single bulb turned his hair to gold. When she settled beside him, her head fit against his shoulder and her legs entwined with his.

Steve spoke softly, "Part of me says it's too bad your girl is in the other room, but I wouldn't have it any other way." He stretched to reach the lamp and turned it off. Faint streetlight shone in the barred window in the front door, striping the floor and silvering the gold in his hair.

Profound peace enveloped her. His arms went around her and he drew the comforter over them both. He was so warm and solid, yet that pulse inside whispered of what they'd shared at the Stagecoach.

God help her, she was falling in love with this man. She might be a fool, but there it was.

She listened to the steady beat of his heart and thought about telling him of Garrett's offer. Of asking what he'd feel if she moved West.

Steve kissed her forehead gently. His body against hers bore the heavy lassitude of fatigue and she felt the same. After all the anticipation . . .

"I may have to wake you in the middle of the night," he whispered. "Just so you know I'm holding you."

A smile curved her lips. Comfort and the smooth lethargy of being in his embrace settled over her.

"I promise I'll be here," she murmured.

Without a thought to the nightmares that had been her torture, she settled into the summer's first deep and dreamless sleep.

Steve awakened in darkness and did not know where he was. For a moment, he thought the past four years had been a colossal mistake; that Susan lay nestled against his side. As his eyes became accustomed to the glow from a light outside, he made out the distinct curve of Clare's cheek. Somewhere inside, he'd expected to feel guilt over Susan, but all he knew was joy.

The years with his wife had been vivid, alive with her music and her voice's melody. The Christmas after she died, he'd been at her mother's house for dinner. Washing his hands before carving turkey, Steve had been attracted to a familiar crystal shape on the bathroom counter.

A perfume bottle identical to one Susan had kept on her dressing table.

He lifted the stopper. The marriage of citrus with the earthy scent of iris was the same that Susan had dabbed behind her ears and in the hollow of her elbows, so that it floated behind her like an aura. It nearly brought him to his knees.

He fought it until he folded down onto the rim of the tub. Chill from the porcelain seeped into the backs of his legs. The tile was cold, too, where he leaned his head against the wall and wept.

Lying with Clare, Steve finally said good-bye to Susan.

He marveled that he did it without pain, as if he were suddenly made light. He could no longer summon Susan's music, because Clare's husky voice haunted his dreams, no longer smell Susan's perfume, for the faint spicy smell of Clare's skin excited him beyond belief.

She shifted and burrowed her head more deeply into the hollow of his shoulder. He smoothed her bare thigh where the shirt had ridden up, but she did not awaken.

Tonight was a moment snatched in time, while the clock on his bookshelf ticked toward tomorrow. He wanted Clare with everything in him, to make a new life for himself with her in it. The hell of it was that she did not seem the type of woman to drop her plans and take up with an alcoholic whose job was in jeopardy. He'd bought two bottles of wine today, more than he needed for cooking, only partially because he thought Clare might like some.

He'd managed to stay out of it tonight, but what about another day? And what would happen when he struggled with the depression that was bound to descend after he put Clare on a plane to Houston?

From outside the house came an odd sound, not loud, like the crackling of Rice Krispies, or . . .

Fire!

Steve eased himself out from under Clare, trying not to disturb her and yet move quickly at the same time. When he got up, he found that the pain had settled back into his knees. On the front porch, the crackling was louder and the wind whipped his pant legs. Less than two miles away, the near shoulder of Bunsen Peak was ablaze.

Clare awoke alone on Steve's couch. A current of moving air attracted her attention to the front door standing open. Beyond the checkered lattice, Steve was in the yard.

Down the single step, her bare feet found grass, cool and soft. She said Steve's name softly and slid her arms around him, resting her cheek against his back. He put his hands over hers, pressing her palms against his bare chest.

They stood together for a long moment until he said, "Take a look at this."

She loosed her grip and stepped from behind him. The red glow in the south suffused the sky. "Good God," she breathed.

Her heart set up a tripping as she gauged the wind and the distance between the town and the fire. She was glad that

Garrett was here, for he would know when an evacuation should be called.

"It's beautiful," Steve said. Clare stared at the crimson underbelly of the clouds. "Part of the forest's life, and yet it can be so deadly."

How many times this summer had she both shuddered and thrilled to that splendor? When she and Deering had watched the Mink Creek come down Turret Mountain even the sky had seemed aflame. When the Hellroaring had crowned and chased them to earth in their shelters, she'd felt its elemental fury. Driving away from Old Faithful, they'd passed through the North Fork's undulating scarlet drapery.

Together, she and Steve watched the advance of the North Fork, smelling and tasting its wind-borne tang. It seemed as though they could actually see its progress as it marched down the mountain, now less than a mile and a half from where they stood. Thankfully, the way the wind blew was driving it east rather than directly toward them.

Steve drew Clare back against him. He kissed her and their lips clung with a new intensity she had not imagined possible, something that came from inside both of them. She drew away and studied the clean lines of his face. His eyes met hers and she believed in their unspoken revelation.

"What's done it for us so suddenly?" she wondered.

Steve nodded toward the approaching conflagration. "I suppose it's the shadow of the sword."

There was a battle to fight, but it would not come until sunrise.

CHAPTER THIRTY-FOUR
September 10

"It's time," a man's deep voice called through Steve's front door. Clare realized she'd been half-aware of knocking for some time.

When Steve opened the door in his sweat pants Clare recognized Moru Mzima. She thought he took in the situation, but he didn't look at the rumpled couch or at her until she joined Steve at the door.

"They've called the evacuation," Moru said. The clock on Steve's bookcase read five-forty.

The wind that blew in the door was cooler than it had been earlier, but still lacked the slightest trace of humidity. Through the open weave of the porch lattice, Clare saw that the North Fork had burned down Bunsen Peak to Golden Gate pass. The only remaining natural break between the fire and the town was the jumbled blocks of rock called the Hoodoos, the remains of an old landslide.

Moru looked at her. "I'm sending Nyeri and the kids to Bozeman now. Do you and your daughter want to ride along?"

"You'd better go," Steve told Clare.

There wasn't any doubt that she had to take Devon to safety, but the sight of the crimson fire front had Clare spoiling for a fight. Garrett had convinced her . . . no, she had decided to keep working wildfire.

"I'll go with them, Mom." Devon spoke from the hallway. "You stay."

She turned to find her daughter barefoot and wearing the oversized T-shirt Steve had given her to sleep in. Her hair was mussed, but her blue eyes were clear and steady. "Really, I'll be okay." Her certainty said she understood her mother wanted to fight the fire.

Clare looked at the latest advance of the North Fork with growing certainty. After nearly two months of watching the fires' dark shapes envelop the strategic maps, she wanted to be on the battlefield when the sons-of-bitches were vanquished.

When she and Frank had charged up the apartment house stairs they'd tasted fear, a hot bright edge that could cripple . . . or be forged into a weapon. The challenge was not to live without fear, but to carry on in spite of it.

Fight and fall back!

Clare sweated and struggled as firefighters' lines were leapt, their backfires swallowed on the long retreat into Mammoth Valley. Her hope that the Hoodoos' bare rock would stop the North Fork proved vain, as the fire circumvented the slope on the downhill side. By afternoon, she and the others on the line had been pushed below the last highway curve above town. In the hellish half-light, Jupiter Terrace's glistening surface had taken on the hue of fresh blood.

As the battle was joined, Clare manned a drip torch, side-hilling it below the upper terrace of the hot springs. "This one will do it," she said grimly. She kept moving ahead of the brisk crackle and heat. Burning sage was supposed to be a sacred Native American purifying rite and she hoped Mammoth would emerge unscathed from this day.

When she reached the road, the entire hillside above her was ablaze with only a three hundred yard gap to the main body of the North Fork. "Burn, baby, burn," she entreated the back-fire. The more thoroughly it consumed the vegetation before the main fire arrived, the more effective the firebreak.

Clare turned away and trotted down the shoulder of the highway. A short way down the hill, she saw Steve in his Park Service truck. He waved and pulled into the parking lot above the stables. The horses had been trailered away in early morning.

Steve climbed down stiffly. He wore Nomex fire clothes, along with his badge and the summer straw uniform hat that identified him as a ranger. "Would you believe that even after the park's been closed two days, I'm still rousting campers that haven't heard the news?"

"I'd believe just about anything right now."

Below the parking lot, the team of California hotshots from the Mink Creek rested in the area inside a metal rail fence. As she came closer, Clare realized that it was a cemetery, poorly tended, for the headstones barely cleared the high grass.

"Take a load off," a man called. "If this break doesn't hold, we're to fall back and defend the housing."

Clare looked where he pointed, maybe a quarter mile to the first enclave of park employees' homes. She stepped across the fence and gave a hand to Steve.

He came across awkwardly and sat in the grass beside a headstone. Many were illegible, mainly those of marble. The granite and banded gneiss had held up better, their names and dates a history of the last years of the nineteenth century and the first of the twentieth. Next to Clare's boot was a flat stone, flush with the ground. *Unknown Child*, it read simply.

Sitting down in the grass near Steve, Clare checked her watch and found it midafternoon. She was tired, the good honest fatigue that came from working with a purpose. Around her, sweaty faces showed determination. She removed her hard hat and scratched her head.

"In another ten minutes we should know if this firebreak holds," said the head of the hotshot team. Clare recognized the tough, gray-haired woman who had sounded the alarm at the Mink Creek.

Clare nodded to her and bent to pluck a stem of grass. She bit down and released a sour flood in her mouth.

A deep rumble sounded. Dynamite, someone blasting trees in some firebreak. She wished she had a case of the stuff, to set off a spectacular concussion that would snuff the North Fork like a blown birthday candle. She imagined the long cascade resonating down the valley.

No, it was not her imagination. All around her, firefighters raised their heads. Some looked puzzled, others disbelieving.

"Thunder," Steve said.

The wind's passage could be seen through the trees, tossing and bending their trunks, loud enough to be heard over the crackling roar of flame. The long grass whipped and scrubby sage jerked as though a hand deep in the earth tugged its roots. The advancing wave swept down the hill toward the cemetery, kicking up clouds of grit and raising a miniature tornado in the parking lot.

It hit Clare and gave her a shove as though a damp towel had struck her across the back.

"Goddamn," someone said.

The temperature dropped at least ten degrees within a minute, bringing moist relief to dry, cracked lips. Everyone climbed to their feet, took off their hard hats and looked skyward.

A fat drop stung Clare's cheek. She closed her eyes.

The temperature continued to plummet, cooling her sweaty skin. More raindrops landed, making dark stains on weathered headstones and yellow shirts.

"Here it comes," Steve said.

A long line of silver rain bore down from Sepulcher Mountain above the hot springs. Its shifting curtains replaced the smoke haze as the relentless advance obliterated the view of Jupiter Terrace. The front crossed the highway, drops bouncing high off the pavement.

The North Fork recoiled with an angry hiss. Clouds of steam roiled, an elemental struggle destined to end with the death of the dragon.

SUMMER OF FIRE

🔥🔥🔥

An hour later, Clare kept her arm tight around Steve's chest, to keep from losing him in the crowd of reveling fire-fighters on the Mammoth Hotel lawn. It also didn't hurt that he helped keep her warm after the cold front had swept in. Above, on Sepulcher Mountain and over behind the cemetery, other crews were still fighting to cool the leading edge of the North Fork.

The hotel had closed for the evacuation, but as soon as the danger passed, the bar had been opened to accommodate the celebration. Rows of TV trucks with satellite antennas lined the street, the press mingling with the soot-faced, filthy fire crews.

Carol Leeds of Billings Live Eye clutched her jacket close and passed a bottle of champagne. Clare drank a deep swallow of golden effervescence and the bubbles burned her nose. She didn't know whether to give it to Steve.

He took it and sipped without tipping it far up. A man behind him said, "I heard on TV that there've been sixty-eight thousand wildfires in the U.S. this season."

"Two million acres gone in Alaska," someone else replied.

"Nearly a million just in Yellowstone," Steve said to Clare. "Last month when I said I'd want to stay if a million acres burned, I never thought it could happen." He drank champagne again.

"Damn, it's cold," said a woman whose nose had gone cherry red. She rubbed her hands together and stuck them under her arms.

"You think this is something?" a man in a woolen cap shouted. "Have you heard tomorrow's forecast?" He twisted the dial of a portable radio and the tinny strains of "Let it Snow" encouraged another round of cheering.

Not far from the crowd, a group of elk lay blissfully undisturbed by the revelry.

Steve started to raise the bottle again. Someone took it from his hand. "Moru," he said.

Moru passed the champagne without drinking. "I called Nyeri in Bozeman. They're going to stay the night and drive back with Devon tomorrow."

"Good idea," Clare agreed. The night stretched before her, the time with Steve an impossible luxury.

He pulled her tighter against his side and murmured for her ears only. "This evening, madam, the chef will prepare his special spaghetti sauce, with fennel, basil, and plenty of garlic. Guaranteed to give Technicolor dreams."

Clare didn't plan on dreams anymore, unless they were the good kind. She pressed closer to Steve. "On the other hand, we may not get much sleep."

EPILOGUE
September 11

S teve had always thought the section of the Grand Loop
Road between Canyon and Norris to be the park's most
monotonous corridor of pine.

Today, it was transformed, as broad vistas heretofore
unseen opened before his eyes. At the high point of the Sol-
fatera Plateau, he could see out over the long burned slope to
Nez Perce Creek.

"We need to talk," he told Clare, who rode beside him in
the Park Service truck.

"I know." She spoke so softly that Steve silenced the radio
playing "Frosty the Snowman."

It was chilly in the cab, but although his fingers hovered
close to the lever, Steve did not put on the heat. After suffering
through the summer, he was quite willing to taste the bracing
bite of cooler air. "I'm not sure where to begin," he said.

All at once, he couldn't stand that he had to hold the wheel
and keep his eyes on the road. Not while Clare was beside
him and there were things he desperately needed to tell her.

"I know Moru said Nyeri will be bringing Devon down this afternoon, but they should be a while on the road." He slowed and pulled into an overlook on the left. Here the Wolf Lake arm of the North Fork had wreaked havoc. In an area where a rare tornado-like wind had created a blowdown years ago, fire had swept through the deadwood and left a veritable moonscape.

This was one of the worst looking burns, right beside a major road. The news had featured a reporter on this spot telling the nation in grave tones, "Tonight, this is all that is left of Yellowstone National Park."

What colossal bullshit! Even inside the outlines of the burns, there were broad areas where damage had not been severe.

As Steve drew the truck to a halt, Clare put her hand over his. He killed the engine and turned into her arms. He wanted to drag her into the woods, but only flattened tree trunks surrounded them. With an effort, he broke the embrace and said hoarsely, "We're not talking." He was determined to ask her, against all odds, if she would come and live with him in Yellowstone.

Outside, a huge snowflake drifted down and landed on the windshield. It slid sideways as it melted into a great water drop that sluiced down the glass. Another flake whirled past, and another.

Clare opened the door and jumped down with childlike alacrity. "They weren't kidding about the forecast!"

Steve followed her into what rapidly became a fast-falling whirl. She leaped tree trunks in the downed forest, hurrying to the top of a rise and spreading her arms wide. By the time he caught up with her, her sweetly ragged hair was starred with white.

"This will go a long way toward bringing the dragon to its knees," Steve said.

"Look at that." She pointed.

Embers still smouldered in the heart of a log nearly three feet in diameter, while a sugary dusting frosted the exterior. "It's not over by a long shot," she said. "These fires will burn on and the mopping up will take months."

Steve nodded. "Twenty years from now people will still be questioning whether 'let-burn' was a disaster, or if a hundred years of playing Smoky Bear set the stage for an inferno."

👑👑👑

Clare shivered in the swirling white wind. Steve must have noticed, for he reached his arm around her and drew her under the shelter of his jacket. The way he wordlessly knew what she wanted gave her chest an aching feeling.

They had made love, but neither had spoken of the future.

How many times had she been set in her ways, only to have change upset her delicate balance? For a time Jay Chance had been solid earth. His leaving had produced a pattern of shattered fault lines. Walled alone behind defenses, she'd guarded her heart until the man beside her had broken through.

Clare swallowed her fears and leaned on Steve. "I don't want to leave."

"It gets to you, doesn't it?" He waved his free hand at the slopes and mountains out there somewhere in the driving snow. "Even burned, I wouldn't trade this place for blue water and white sand."

She knew how he felt even as she planned her own return. The barren expanse of ash-covered earth was not without its own ethereal sort of beauty. "It casts a spell. You want to come back, and you haven't left yet, but . . . " she tightened her arm around him, "I wasn't talking about missing a place."

"I was hoping you'd say that." He pulled her to the nearest snow-dusted log and sat down facing her, both her hands in his. "I don't want this to be the end."

She met his eyes and took a steadying breath. "I don't either." The loving look in his eyes made it easy to tell him. "I'm planning on either moving to Boise to work with Garrett, or applying to take over the Fire Cache at Mammoth when Ben Mallory retires this winter."

Her cold hands felt him grip harder. She marveled that his were warm. "God, Clare, I do want you with me. That's what I stopped here to tell you . . . " A shadow crossed his face. "But there's something else. When you leave, I'm afraid I might start drinking again."

Her heart sank as she grappled with his words. His problem was very real, but as she gazed into his gray eyes, she knew she'd love him in bad times, too.

"I've decided to tell Shad Dugan that I'll go for treatment. I never used to drink before Susan and Christa died. I'm serious about staying off the booze. "

They were both getting soaked by the early season snow, but she dared not move for fear of breaking the surreal isolation created by opaque light. In this private world, she could believe that Steve's determination could defeat any adversary.

"You can do it," she told him.

"I will do it . . . for me." He bent and pressed a warm kiss to her chilled cheek. "And for us."

Not since she was young and Jay had declared himself had she known a surge of joy like this one. In the lost and lonely years between, she'd begun to believe that promise was for others.

"I've got a confession to make," Steve went on. "When you asked if there was anyone in my life and I said no, I didn't exactly tell the truth."

She waited.

"Ever since the crash in July when I fought my way through that freezing lake . . . realizing with every stroke that even though I'd been dead inside for years . . . I did want to live . . . ever since I dragged myself onto that shore . . . from the moment I opened my eyes, there's been you."

The snow that was ending the summer of fire blurred through her tears, as Clare permitted herself to imagine. Over the years, the burns would fill in, first with brilliant pink fireweed and later with seedling pine. Colorful aspen that had not had a niche in the mature forest would bring gold to autumn. Elk would browse the burned land and carry on the cycle of life.

Clare had planned to grow old with Jay, but along the way, they'd let the distractions of daily life overshadow their belief in each other. Steve and Susan had charted their future in the stars, but their flight had fallen to earth.

They were no different from all the rest . . . those who

dared to dream as though they didn't realize that only this moment is given. Frank, Billy Jakes, all of them, riding a knife-thin edge of present. Only this instant, when the sun shining through a snowstorm stabbed at Clare's eyes and the cold, cutting wind told her that her tears were real. She blinked to clear the blurred image of a world gone charred black and whirling white.

Letting go her hands, Steve bent and brushed away granules of snow blown into the hollow at the base of a log. "Look," he said softly.

Together, they knelt to discover a single, pale-green shoot, pushing through the layer of ash.

YELLOWSTONE FIRES
September 26, 8:00 a.m.

Here is a list of the fires and approximate perimeter acreages. To date, over 1.1 million acres in Yellowstone National Park (includes NF portions of Clover-Mist and North Fork Fires) and approximately 1.6 million acres in the Greater Yellowstone Area have been affected by fire. However, only about half of the vegetation has burned within many fire perimeters. Throughout the summer, 52 different fires have been started by lightning. Of those 52, eight are still burning inside the park. Fire fighters are working to control them. Any new fires will be suppressed as quickly as possible.

* * * * *

SUMMER OF FIRE

Clover-Mist Fire: 412,550 acres. Mist Fire started July 9. Clover started July 11. They joined on July 22. Shallow Fire started July 31. Fern Fire started August 5. These two fires joined Clover-Mist August 13. Lovely Fire started July 11 and burned into Clover-Mist on August 21. Estimated 83% contained. The fire crossed the Montana border near Kersey Lake. Growth was about 1,050 acres over the weekend. Acreage reduction is due to remapping. 1120 firefighters, 31 engines, 2 bulldozers, and 9 helicopters.

Fan Fire: 23,325 acres. Started June 25. No change. The fire was contained on 9/2. One crew is completing mop-up.

Hellroaring Fire: 83,888 acres. Started August 15. The fire is 100% contained. Mop-up and rehabilitation work continue.

Huck/Mink Complex: 225,500 acres (includes Mink Creek Fire acreage in Bridger-Teton NF). Started August 20. Caused the evacuation of Flagg Ranch. The fire was 100% contained on 9/15. No estimated date of control. Mop-up and rehabilitation work continues.

North Fork: 400,100 acres. Started July 22 by human. Split from Wolf Lake Fire at Gibbon Falls. This fire is about 50% contained with 100% containment expected by mid-October. Some increase in fire activity is expected due to dry, windy weather. Mop-up and structure protection is continuing at Old Faithful and West Yellowstone. 1339 firefighters, 8 bulldozers, and 4 helicopters.

Snake River Complex: 224,000 acres. Red Fire started July 1. Shoshone Fire started June 23. Joined August 10. Falls Fire started July 12. Red-Shoshone joined the Mink Fire on August 31. Acreage includes Continental-Ridge and Mink Creek fires. The fire was declared 100% contained on 9/19 at 1700 hours. Mop-up operations and rehabilitation work continues. Fuel modification in Lake area continues as well. 459 firefighters, 1 engine, 1 helicopter.

Storm Creek Fire: 107,847 acres. Started July 3. This fire was declared 100% contained on 9/17. Mop-up operations continue in the Soda Butte and Pebble Ck. areas.

Wolf Lake Fire (includes Mammoth Complex): 107,460 acres. Fire grew only twenty acres over the weekend despite dry weather and high winds. Most military crews are leaving by 9/28, and they will not be replaced. Estimated date of containment still depends on receiving additional precipitation. 1099 firefighters, 12 engines, 9 helicopters.

Crews on many of the fires continue to demobilize. Unified Area Command operations in West Yellowstone have been shut down. As a result, accurate information on crew sizes and resources for some of the fires was not readily available.

AFTERWORD

Donald Hodel, the real Interior Secretary of the United States under President Ronald Reagan, sent the following letter to newspapers across the country on October 13, 1988. It was also printed in 1989 in *The Fires of '88, Yellowstone Park and Montana in Flames* by Ross Simpson.

To the Editor:

This summer long will be remembered for the forest fires that raged over much of the public lands in the West. Before the season is behind us, I want to extend my heartfelt thanks for the heroic efforts of the over thirty thousand firefighters from across the country who, over the course of the past several months, risked their lives to try and control a natural disaster of unprecedented proportions. Whether called by a personal sense of duty or summoned by obligation, these men and women — working against insurmountable odds — showed exceptional courage and patriotism.

Many firefighters worked twelve to fourteen hour shifts, with days consisting of hot, exhausting work battling fires, and nights spent in sleeping bags. In addition to facing the danger of intense blazes, falling limbs and oppressive smoke, they coped with everything from rockslides to angry yellow jackets. At the end of a workday, many firefighters carrying heavy gear hiked as much as ten miles before being picked up and returned to their camp.

Modern day forest managers and park rangers never have faced the conditions experienced this year in which millions of acres of aged timberlands were parched by four or five years of severe drought. Substantial portions of these great forests were living on borrowed time. Therefore, despite all efforts, it was impossible to control the course of natural events.

We would be remiss if we did not learn from this experience. Now we begin the painstaking study to determine what, if anything, can be done to insure that we will not face devastating fires of this kind in the future. Work must also be done to help the rehabilitation of Yellowstone National Park and other affected areas.

Fortunately, much of Yellowstone escaped the raging fires — and, surprisingly, many acres of lush forestlands within burned areas were left unscathed. We are anticipating a great influx of tourists interested in seeing the extent of the damage and the progress of regrowth. Recreational opportunities will continue to abound.

Yellowstone will not be the same within our generation, but nature recovers from these events by rebirth of the old growth forests and rejuvenation of forage and wildlife. It would be foolish to say that the Yellowstone National Park forest fires were welcomed - but over the course of the next decade, we may witness some beneficial events.

This fact does not offer much solace for the local economies that have been disrupted, people displaced and painful losses suffered. And those of us who love Yellowstone cannot help but view the events as a natural tragedy. But the losses would have been much greater had it not been for the dedication and perseverance of the brave firefighters - and all who supported them in this difficult time. Again, to them, our thanks for doing an outstanding job.

AUTHORS NOTE

As the twentieth anniversary of the 1988 fire season approaches, it remains one of the milestone events in the history of man's summer battles against nature. The firefighting effort was, at the time, the most expensive event in fire suppression, over $120,000,000. Estimates suggest that from 25,000 to 32,000 firefighters fought on the lines, with up to 9000 active at one time: career professional fire experts, smokejumpers, pilots, seasonal groundpounders, college students, convicts, and the armed forces. In 1988 in the United States, 68,396 wildfires burned 3,799,550 acres — almost half that was accounted for by the Greater Yellowstone area.

Fire is a natural part of the forest ecosystem. Many plant species rely on fire for regeneration. Lodgepole pines (nearly 80% of the park's forests,) have cones that are sealed by resin until the fire's heat dries and explodes them, releasing the seeds. Brushy plants such as sage, aspen and willows, along with grasses will burn, but their root systems usually remain, and the years following a fire can be a very productive time. As the natural order proceeded, every few hundred years flames swept over the mountains and valleys. Research in Yellowstone has indicated that large fires occurred during the 1700's.

Once the park was established in 1872, and more people came to Yellowstone, they brought a belief that fire was destructive. Thus, in the latter part of the nineteenth century began the Smokey Bear trend, with the military custodians of the park fighting wildfires. From the 1940s through the 1960s, some began to recognize fire's positive role, and experimentation with controlled burns began. In 1972, it was determined that natural fires caused by lightning in the National Park would not be fought.

Though Yellowstone's forests were "old growth," up to 300 years, with abundant deadfall from the ravages of the pine bark beetle, the years leading up to 1988 did not foreshadow the magnitude of the event. Since 1972, in sixteen years, 235 fires had burned only about 34,000 acres. The years 1982-1987 were wetter than normal, and in the winter of 1987-1988, there was adequate snowfall. April and May rainfalls were abundant, leading to a feeling that the fire season might be a nonevent.

But as summer began, the park experienced a drought along with high daytime temperatures, low humidity, and strong, gusty winds. These conditions caused fires to grow and burn so actively that it was impossible to contain such conflagrations. In the time from late June through July, the driest in recorded history, over twice the acreage burned as had in the previous sixteen years under the "let-burn" policy.

In late July, the National Park Service and the U.S. Forest Service formed the Greater Yellowstone Unified Area

SUMMER OF FIRE

Command, the special fire organization described in this book. Throughout the summer, it tracked 248 fires in Greater Yellowstone. Within Yellowstone, lightning ignited 51 different fires, while one of the largest and most destructive, the North Fork, was reportedly started by a thrown cigarette. The Unified Area Command, in response to the demand for information, began issuing fire maps and statistics that came out on a daily basis.

The following shows the number of acres consumed in the Greater Yellowstone Area along with key events experienced by the characters in *Summer of Fire*.

July 15	8,500 acres	
July 25	75,000 acres	Battle for Grant Village
August 4	150,000 acres	
August 20	350,000 acres	"Black Saturday"
September 7	1,000,000 acres	Siege of Old Faithful
September 9	1,200,000 acres	Defense of Mammoth
September 26	1,600,000 acres	Final report

On July 25, 500 firefighters defended the Grant Village lodge, restaurant and campground. By August 4, large backcountry fires spread in the northwest and northeast quadrants of the park. Fire behavior scientists made a prediction, considered dire at the time, that the 150,000 thousand acres burned might double before season's end.

But August 20, or "Black Saturday" saw a record burning

of another 150,000 acres in a single twenty-four hour period, while firefighters sought shelter and aircraft were grounded. The day hosted a dry front, a wind event that caused the fires to crown and run at unprecedented speeds. The report from fire command at 8:00 a.m. on August 22 revealed that fire trucks and crews were protecting Yellowstone's northeastern gateway towns of Silver Gate and Cooke City.

In early September, the town of West Yellowstone struggled with the decision whether or not to evacuate. By now, Park Service and Forest Service officials were under attack by angry residents who in some cases believed the government would be happy if they were burned out of their homes. Tempers ran high, and one of the local motel marquees invited folks to a "Bar-bee-que," referring to Bob Barbee, the Superintendent of Yellowstone. Locals set up the sprinkler barrier along the abandoned Union Pacific railroad right of way in case the North Fork fire came to town.

The September 7, 8:00 a.m. fire command report told of "fire spotting to within 3/4 mile of Old Faithful Inn," and the evacuation. The sprinklers were moved in from West Yellowstone and installed under power lines at Old Faithful. Then 1608 firefighters, 39 engines, 22 bulldozers, and 6 helicopters defended the complex. All non-essential fire personnel and area residents also evacuated from Silver Gate and Cooke City.

On September 9, resources were reported as being "moved to deal with the anticipated advance of the fires into the area of Mammoth." Residents who had made it back into Silver Gate and Cooke City were forced to evacuate again.

SUMMER OF FIRE

The first snow fell on September 11, easing the powder keg atmosphere and letting a number of personnel stand down. On September 26, the Unified Area Command issued their final report, though the fires smouldered until November.

In the aftermath, park scientists and naturalists are still studying the results of the historic event, while the predicted destruction of the tourist trade did not happen. People came in 1989, and in the twenty-first century, they continue to flock from all over the world to enjoy the wonders of Yellowstone and monitor the forest's rebirth.

Don't Miss The Next Exciting Book From Linda Jacobs In The <u>Yellowstone Series!</u>

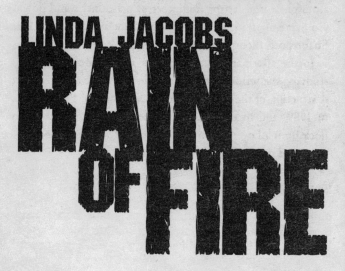

LINDA JACOBS
RAIN OF FIRE

ISBN #1932815279

Gold

$6.99

Fiction

Coming in
June of 2006

LIFE SENTENCES
TEKLA DENNISON MILLER

There are men who take women's lives. There are men who kill their souls. . . .

Celeste Brookstone has the perfect life. On the surface when her daughter takes a job with the Michigan Prison System, she fears for Pilar's safety.

But she's glad she's away from the hell on earth Marcus Brookstone has created within his own home. Pilar Brookstone is an idealist. She thinks she can change things, Make inmates' lives a little better. And never, ever make the mistake her mother made. Chad Wilbanks is a serial killer. He is serving life. Eight young women were his victims.

Is he about to take his ninth?

Men who kill.

The women who love them.

LIFE SENTENCES

ISBN #1932815252
Gold
$6.99
Fiction
Coming 2005

www.teklamiller.com

A
FOREIGN
POLICY

Richard Graham-Yooll

ISBN#193281549X

Gold

$6.99

Political Thriller

September 2005

BLOOD TiES

LORi G. ARMSTRONG

What do they mean?

How far would someone go to sever . . . or protect them?

Julie Collins is stuck in a dead-end secretarial job with the Bear Butte County Sheriff's office, and still grieving over the unsolved murder of her Lakota half-brother. Lack of public interest in finding his murderer, or the killer of several other transient Native American men, has left Julie with a bone-deep cynicism she counters with tequila, cigarettes, and dangerous men. The one bright spot in her mundane life is the time she spends working part-time as a PI with her childhood friend, Kevin Wells.

When the body of a sixteen-year old white girl is discovered in nearby Rapid Creek, Julie believes this victim will receive the attention others were denied. Then she learns Kevin has been hired, mysteriously, to find out where the murdered girl spent her last few days. Julie finds herself drawn into the case against her better judgment, and discovers not only the ugly reality of the young girl's tragic life and brutal death, but ties to her and Kevin's past that she is increasingly reluctant to revisit.

On the surface the situation is eerily familiar. But the parallels end when Julie realizes some family secrets are best kept buried deep. Especially those serious enough to kill for.

ISBN#1932815325
Gold
$6.99
Mystery
Available Now